The Good German Girl
A League of Extraordinary
Women Series:
Book One

Endorsements

With vivid imagery and haunting descriptions, Hogan pulls back the curtain on the fate of those who stood against evil during World War II. Often gritty and heartbreaking, *The Good German Girl* is a tribute to all the victims, casualties, and survivors from Normandy to Birkenau. Fans of Jenna Blum and Tatiana de Rosnay will appreciate this emotional tale of war-torn love as they are reminded of the relentless hope that helps us endure the unimaginable.

—**Janine Rosche**, author of the *Madison River Romance Series*

The Good German Girl is an engaging read about a strong, courageous woman remaining true to herself in the turbulent darkness of World War II. A story of hope, love, and endurance.

—**Lianne Kay**, author of *Tattered*

Erica Marie Hogan pens a sweet romance within a war-torn story that will resonate with readers (and fans) of WW2 stories.

—**Ann Brodeur**, author of *Snowbound in Winterberry Falls*

The Good German Girl is one of the most amazing World War II era books I've ever read in my life! Not only are the characters incredibly well-written and interesting, but the plot keeps you on the edge of your seat and constantly wanting more. There are several instances when my heart was pounding as I flipped the pages to find out what happened next, and there were plenty of tear-jerking scenes that broke my heart. Buy this book immediately! You will not regret this purchase. I can't wait for the rest of this incredible series.

—**Mikaela Miller,** author of the *Tales from Neverland Series*

Hogan weaves a story of intriguing characters and captures the people and the Nazi fever, as well as opponents to it, of the time period well. Very engaging and enjoyable story.

—**Darlene Oakley**, author of *Inner Sanctum* and *Voices of Angels*

I rarely get teared up when I read a book. Mainly because, as a writer myself, my editor cap is always on. But, Erica Marie Hogan's *The Good German Girl* is on the list of one of those rare books that made me cry. This is a beautiful read with a very sweet ending.

—**A.F. Lamonte**, author of the upcoming *Reaper's Apprentice Series*

The Good German Girl

A League of Extraordinary Women Series: Book One

Erica Marie Hogan

ELK LAKE PUBLISHING INC.

PUBLISHING THE POSITIVE
Plymouth, Massachusetts

Cover and Interior Design: Derinda Babcock

Editor(s): Cristel Phelps, Deb Haggerty

PUBLISHED BY: Elk Lake Publishing, Inc., 35 Dogwood Drive, Plymouth, MA 02360, 2021

Library Cataloging Data

Names: Hogan, Erica Marie (Erica Marie Hogan)

The Good German Girl—A League of Extraordinary Women Series: Book One / Erica Marie Hogan

404 p. 23cm × 15cm (9in × 6 in.)

ISBN-13: 978-1-64949-201-2 (paperback) | 978-1-64949-202-9 (trade paperback) | 978-1-64949-203-6(e-book)

Key Words: World War II, Nazis, Romance, Survival, Historical Novel, Concentration Camps, Relationships

Library of Congress Control Number: 2021936777 Fiction

Dedication

For the brother of my heart.
Though time and distance separated us, I never
stopped loving and missing you.
Rest in Heaven's peace, my precious friend.

Chapter One

June 6, 1944
Omaha Beach
Normandy, France

Salt water or blood? Sand? Maybe all three? Bernie Russell didn't know exactly as he dragged his sleeve down his face, drying his skin and clearing his eyes. To the left, the screams of men burning alive as they fell from their transport onto the sand. To the right, the thundering crash of hundreds of bodies dropping like flies into the sea. And all around, the repeated *pop-pop-pop-pop-pop* of machine gunfire tearing up not only the beach but the men attempting to take it. His ears rang with every blast of mortar fire hitting the incoming landing crafts—heart racing frantically as he looked for one familiar face. One pair of eyes still alight with life.

The metal obstacles lining the beach seemed to beckon him forward, urging him to crawl away from the heavy waves pounding his back and legs. Bernie clung to his rifle, the only hope he had for survival now that he was on the beach. Struggling over dead bodies and wet sand, he finally reached a small group of men huddled behind one of the hedgehogs.

"Where's the captain?" he shouted above the pattering gunfire.

"Who knows?" Bruno shouted back, twisting his neck to glare at Bernie. "Probably dead!"

Bernie scooted closer to Bruno, peeking over the edge of the metal rim of the cross.

"What do we do, Bernie?" another voice shrieked above the noise, followed by a heavy hand slapping Bernie's shoulder. "Bernie can you hear me? I said—"

"Give me a minute, Jacobs!" Bernie strained to see past the bodies littering the beach, squinting as he tried to make out the ones that were moving in the hazy air around them. His brow smoothed suddenly, recognition hitting him like a lightning bolt when one soldier raised up enough to shout over his shoulder.

"There's the lieutenant!" he yelled. "We've got to get to the bluffs! That's where he's headed!"

He started to shove off the ground when that same hand gripped his sleeve hard, dragging him back down.

"There's too much gunfire! We'll never make it." Jacobs said, voice stuttering with fear.

"You won't make it if you stay here, kid."

"But I don't think this is where we're supposed to be."

Bernie yanked himself free of the young man's hold. "Jacobs, I don't think anyone is where they're supposed to be."

He got on his feet, head down and shoulders hunched as he leaped over corpses, trying to gain some ground. A strangled shout slipped out when he lost his footing in the wet sand, toppling.

Bruno fell beside him. "You still think this won't be worse than Sicily?"

"Shut up, Bruno," Bernie muttered, catching his friend's grin in the corner of his eye even though the man couldn't possibly have heard him over the chaos all around them.

Regaining his footing, he lunged in the direction he'd seen the lieutenant go. Bullets hissed by, spattering sand and pelting already dead bodies. A heavy *whoosh*, followed by a sharp burn in his shoulder, warned him he'd caught a bullet. Bernie ducked lower, managing to stay on his feet in a crouched position without hindering his pace across the cumbersome ground.

An explosion to his right lifted Bernie right off his feet, slamming him into the sand. There was no mistaking the warm, sticky substance peppering his cheek this time.

Blood. Bernie wiped his face, his hand coming away red before he groped at his body, panic rattling his heart against his ribs.

Bruno fell on his knees in front of him, putting his rifle down to grab hold of Bernie.

"You okay?" he shouted, pulling at Bernie's pants and boots, looking for the wound. "Where's the blood coming from?"

"Bruno!" Bernie grabbed his friend's arm. "Bruno, it's not mine!"

Their eyes shifted, looking to the side. Bernie's neck tightened, a lump forming like a rock in the middle of his throat. The fallen soldier—half of his blood staining Bernie's face and uniform—lay in pieces a few feet away. Bernie swallowed hard.

"Not my blood, Bru," he rasped.

Bernie rolled onto his front, snatching his rifle where it'd fallen before belly crawling toward the gunfire. The enemy had littered the beach with obstacles, crowding the sand to topple their tanks and create more vulnerability for their men. Bernie's head swung from side to side, taking in the cliffs to left and right, steep embankment up ahead and fortified defenses of the Germans' forces. The amount of men dropping to the ground only created more obstacles for those still landing on the beach, putting any reinforcements they received in further jeopardy.

Bernie struggled up to the seawall, gasping for breath as he spun around and fell on the wall, wedging himself between two other guys.

"And you are?" the captain to his left shouted.

Bernie almost laughed at the casual way he asked the question, as if they were meeting for the first time at a social gathering.

"Private Russell, sir!" he answered.

Bruno grunted as he stumbled up beside Bernie, shoving the private on Bernie's right out of his way.

"Agnelli, sir!" Bruno yelled, then pointed his thumb at Bernie. "I'm with him!"

"I see that," the captain replied. "Captain Woodley. Where's your commanding officer?"

Bernie and Bruno exchanged a glance.

"Back there?" Bruno tilted his head sharply toward the beach.

"Seen anyone else from your unit?"

"Where's Jacobs, Bru?" Bernie asked.

"Don't know. Last I saw, still behind the hedgehogs."

"Then I guess you boys are with us." Woodley nodded, as if to finalize the decision. "If we can blast our way over this seawall, we can clear the machine gun taking down most of our guys."

Bruno raised himself on his elbow to get a better look, bullets firing rapidly into the sand the second his helmet appeared.

"I'm thinking if you get one man with a good aim over the ridge you risk less, captain," Bruno announced. "Bernie here's the best sniper in our unit."

"Did I volunteer?" Bernie muttered.

"That so?" Captain Woodley smirked. "Okay, Russell, you're up. We'll provide cover fire to get you and your boy into position."

"Looks like you're coming too, Bru." Bernie grinned.

"Wouldn't miss it," Bruno replied.

"Carter! Morales!" Woodley gestured over his shoulder. The two men he'd called for half-crawled, half-rolled over and around the others until they were crouched beside them. "I want the two of you with Russell and Agnelli. We need to take out that nest before moving the rest of the men over this wall. Keep low until you can clear the trenches and Russell can get a shot at the bunker. We'll be right behind you."

"Yes, sir!" the men replied together.

Bruno snorted. "Well disciplined, aren't they?"

"Nice change," Bernie chuckled.

They dragged themselves closer to the top of the seawall, Bernie cradling his rifle carefully in the crook of his elbow. He nudged Bruno in the side.

"You promised you'd stop offering me up for sniper duty after Sicily."

"I know. So sue me, I tend to lie."

"Good to know."

Woodley slapped Bernie twice on the back when the rain of bullets paused for a moment, indicating the enemy was reloading. "You ready?"

"Ready!"

"Cover fire!" Woodley bellowed, rising up on one knee before firing rapidly over the embankment.

Bernie and Bruno leaped forward at the same time, racing over the top of the ridge before the ground went out from under them. A wealth of curses—including a few in Italian—poured from Bruno's mouth as they tumbled, rolled onto their stomachs, and froze.

Trenches stretched out a few feet in front of them, winding and twisting in the direction of the cement bunkers behind. Bernie squinted into the distance, catching the dark, helmeted figures of two enemy soldiers sitting behind the machine gun causing Woodley's men so much trouble. He slid his rifle back, twisting his arm beneath his stomach as he reached for his belt.

"I need to get closer," he said. "I can't take the shot from here."

His fist came back, curled around a grenade. Bruno nodded, motioning for Carter and Morales to do the same. Shouts echoed from the trenches, followed by a head popping up over the edge of one. Bernie hissed between clenched teeth, grabbing for his pistol. A shot from behind them cut the air, sending the German back into hiding as Woodley provided more cover fire.

Bernie folded his knees beneath him, keeping his forearms pressed to the ground, placing himself in a crouched position. Bruno grumbled as he took a similar stance, also fisting a grenade as they angled themselves more directly in front of the trenches. Bernie felt Carter—or Morales, he hadn't paid much attention to who was who— move a little closer to his side.

"Okay," he whispered, fingers playing with the pin. Sand spat up beside him, swallowing a bullet. Woodley and his men were getting pinned down again by the machine gun. In a few moments they wouldn't be able to provide anymore cover. Bernie's heart thundered—his breath coming shorter. "Okay, okay ... on three?"

Bruno's head jerked in a nod. Bernie hooked his finger through the pin, glancing back and forth between Carter and Morales. Jumping into a trench with two guys he'd never seen before wasn't exactly ideal but considering he hadn't spotted another familiar face on the beach since they landed, two more guns alongside Bruno's was better than nothing.

"One ... two ..." Bernie raised himself slightly onto one knee. "Three!"

He held his breath, the soft click of the pin releasing making his heart race. One swift swing of his arm and the grenade was flying, spinning in a perfect arc into the trench. Bernie fell flat onto his stomach, face down in the sand. Shouts, cut short by the explosions, echoed in his ears as he lifted his head again to look.

"Move!" Bruno shouted, a second before the machine gun fire started up again.

Bernie struggled up, half running, half stumbling into the ditch. He ducked low, the trench offering temporary cover from the gunfire. His gaze swept over the narrow space, taking only a few seconds to observe the damage done by their grenades. The fallen enemy soldiers, nearly torn apart. Blood splattered everywhere, pooling and soaking into the sand and dirt beneath their feet.

Turning, they started making their way along the trench, shoulders hunched and heads down. Carter and Morales at the lead, Bruno at Bernie's back keeping an ever-watchful eye over his shoulder should the enemy come from behind. Bernie peeked over the edge of the trench. The target was situated at the top of the bunker, a near perfect position to keep the shooter safe. But at the right angle and with the right opening, Bernie would have a split-second clear shot to take him out.

Giving Woodley enough time to get his men over the seawall before another guy takes control of the gun.

They stopped near the curve in the trench, Bernie shuffling closer to the man in the lead.

"Which one are you?" he asked.

The man eyed him, irritated. "Carter."

"How many?"

"I counted six. There could be more. Probably are more."

Bernie shifted his rifle in both hands. "Give me some room, Carter."

Carter twisted on his heels, switching places with Bernie.

"Bruno, get ready to move. Fast." Bernie leaned forward carefully, peering around the corner.

They were concentrating their fire on the beach, most keeping their heads down and allowing the more protected men in the bunkers to do most of the work. Bernie leveled his rifle against the wall of the trench, sighting the nearest man while keeping his second target in the corner of his eye. Breathing in, he squeezed the trigger.

Pop! A flash of blood and the soldier toppled. Bernie shifted the rifle in an instant, pulling the trigger again to send another to the ground before the rest of the men had a chance to react.

Bruno was around the corner the next second, followed by Carter and Morales. Bernie pulled his bayonet, jogging around the corner into the scuffle. He lunged for the German soldier coming up behind Bruno, grunting when they collided and slammed to the ground. One upward thrust of his arm and his bayonet penetrated the enemy's chest to the hilt. Bernie rolled away onto his feet, the hiss of his blade sliding from flesh quickly followed by a spurt of blood.

A hand gripped the back of his neck, slamming him into the trench wall. His head spun, temple throbbing from the impact. Bernie twisted, struggling against the pressure on his back. A knee connected with his ribs, doubling him over. He jabbed his elbow up, a resounding *crack* letting him know he'd hit his target. Bernie spun, swinging his

Erica Marie Hogan

arm over the top of the German's head. With one jerk of his
wrists—the crown of the man's head and his jaw grasped
firmly in Bernie's hands—he snapped the enemy soldier's
neck.

"Bruno! Rifle!" Bernie shouted, voice hoarse.

Bruno tossed the weapon from where Bernie had dropped
it, shoulders rising and falling with heavy breaths.

"You got my back?" Bernie asked.

"Always."

He turned, resting the barrel over the edge of the trench
wall. Bernie focused, shutting out the sounds of artillery
shells blasting on the beach—the screams of dying men,
accompanied by thundering bullets filling the air.

High above them, the figures cleared in the bunker.
Bernie's breath halted, his finger tingling where it rested
on the trigger. The distance was still great but getting any
closer wasn't a possibility. He could make the shot.

I have to make this shot ... Bernie exhaled.

The machine gun was firing, twisting to the right and
blocking his target. Bernie rolled his lips, shifting his weight
as he waited for the opening. Waited for them to move in
just the right spot ...

The gun started to shift, swinging to the left. Bernie
inhaled, held his breath, and fired.

The shooter swung away from the gun. Bernie quickly
chambered the rifle, the shell popping from the barrel to
fall at his feet before he aimed again and fired, taking down
the replacement. He repeated the same shot two more times
for every figure that drew near the weapon.

Waiting a few heartbeats, he looked over his shoulder.

"Signal Woodley," he said. "They have an opening."

Bruno nodded, jogging away to get back in Woodley's
sight. Bernie lowered his rifle back to his side, the sound

of a struggle drawing him back around. He froze, the scene before him seeming to slow. Carter, kicking and punching an enemy soldier. The boy had fallen on the ground, barely attempting to fight back as he raised his arms to protect his face. His helmet had fallen off, exposing a mop of blond hair. Bernie started to move forward, opening his mouth to tell Carter to back off when the boy raised his head.

Crystal blue eyes stared straight into Bernie's, glimmering with so much fear and regret it stopped Bernie in his tracks. Every breath, every beat of his heart, halted in that moment. One, maybe two seconds, their eyes held. Then a hard kick from Carter pushed the boy's back to the trench wall.

Bernie's breath returned as Carter pulled his pistol. The German boy raised his hands.

"Wait!" Bernie shouted.

Carter pulled the trigger.

A red haze descended over Bernie's eyes, watching the boy rebound against the trench wall, his hands falling back to his sides as blood poured from the hole in his chest. Bernie's hand shook, rising slowly to point at the boy.

"He was about to surrender," he hissed.

"Sure," Carter grunted.

Bernie lunged, grabbing the man by the scruff of the neck. "His hands were up! He was unarmed!"

He shoved the man against the other side of the trench, Carter grabbing hold of his arms roughly to try to push him away. Another arm circled his chest from behind, dragging him off of Carter.

"Take it easy, Bernie," Bruno muttered in his ear.

Bernie freed himself from Bruno's grasp, walking away. Woodley's men had scaled the seawall, some leaping into the trenches to continue clearing them, while others moved on toward the bunker.

"Carter! Morales! With me!" Woodley shouted, gesturing for the two men. They climbed out of the trenches without hesitation, hurrying to join Woodley as he headed for the bunker.

Bernie slumped against the trench wall, leaning his head back to stare at the sky, clouded by smoke.

"Guess we served our purpose," Bruno commented. "You all right there, brother?"

He tilted his head, rolling his eyes until he caught Bruno in his peripheral. "He shot him point blank. The boy was unarmed and had his hands up, and Carter still shot him."

"Nothing you can do about it now, Bernie. Take a breath, then move on. We've got a bunker to clear." Bruno stepped away, slinging his rifle over his shoulder.

A breath huffed through his lips, the pressure in his chest building to a suffocating ache. Closing his eyes, he pushed away the last few moments. The image of the boy slamming into the trench—the burst of blood from the shooter in the bunker when his bullet hit. Building another wall to tuck them away in a corner of his mind so he could take another step forward in the fight.

Shifting his weight, he pushed away from the trench wall, lifting his feet high over the strewn bodies to follow Bruno. He kept his eyes forward as he stepped over the legs of the boy when suddenly, something gripped the edge of his sleeve. Bernie looked down, finding those frightened blue eyes staring up at him once again.

Chest heaving, blood dripping from the corner of his mouth, the German boy struggled to breathe. Yet, somehow he found the strength to yank Bernie down.

"I-It …" Bernie's heart stuttered to a halt.

He's speaking English?

"It … must … end." The boy pressed something against Bernie's chest with his other hand. "Bitte … meine schwester …"

11

"O-Okay," Bernie rasped. He raised his hand to grasp what the boy was trying to give him. Paper rustled beneath his palm, whatever was underneath stiff and resisted slightly when he tried to curl his fingers around the object.

"*Danke*," the boy whispered on a heavy breath.

Then his hand slipped away, falling to his side in a puddle of blood.

Chapter Two

Bernie slanted his head back, a swirl of smoke lifting from his lips. He watched the curl float delicately upward, starkly white against the grey billows of smoke shadowing the sky from the constant explosions that had torn apart the beach. He dangled his legs over the edge of the trench, kicking his heels on the wooden wall. Keeping his eyes on the sky, he passed the cigarette to Bruno on his right.

Woodley and his men had managed to clear the bunker, the distant sound of peppering gunfire echoing sporadically over the expanse of the beach as each section was slowly opened. Lowering his head, he gazed over the demolished beach. The obstacles had been removed, allowing their tanks to roll onto the sand. Bodies still littered the ground, the water tinted red, rolling and crashing onto the shore.

"We gonna help with the clean up?" Bruno asked, breaking the silence.

Bernie eyed him. "Do you want to?"

Bruno snorted, taking another long draw from the cigarette. "You're asking if I want to scrape men from our unit off the sand? Not really."

"Then why ask?"

Bruno chuckled, lying back on the sandy ground and closing his eyes. "You should at least find someone to look at your shoulder."

Bernie twisted his neck, looking down at the crude bandage he'd wrapped around his arm where a bullet grazed him on his way up the beach.

"Just a scratch. It can wait." He shifted his rifle out of his lap, placing it at his side. The distant rumble of the tanks vibrated across the ground, sending tremors through his muscles and raising the hair on his arms. He looked down into the trench as he peeled off his jacket, staring at the blue-eyed boy still slumped on the ground. The blood had darkened on his clothes—the flow finally having stopped.

Frowning, Bernie tossed his jacket over the rifle and slid down off the edge of the trench wall. He crouched in front of the dead boy. In the chaos, he'd stuck the packet in his jacket pocket without a second thought, knowing that looking inside would probably only cause trouble. He certainly couldn't take a look with Bruno here. His friend would probably grab whatever the contents were right out of Bernie's hands before he had a chance to process whatever the boy had entrusted to him.

It must end ... what does that mean? Bernie reached over, patting the boy's jacket. He didn't seem to have been carrying much on him.

Other than a holster for his absent pistol and his wristwatch, there wasn't much to be found. Bernie sighed, running his hand down the other side of the jacket. He frowned, reaching inside when his finger brushed what felt like the delicate edge of paper. With a small tug, he pulled a photograph loose, the frown smoothing from his face.

A pretty girl stared back at him, the picture slightly wrinkled but otherwise practically new. Her hair was intricately plaited, the grey shadow of the photograph indicating she was in-between being dark-haired and light-haired. Her eyes glimmered, the smile in her full lips brightening them. The combination of bright and dark shades in her irises held his attention—the mix impossible for him to determine if her eyes were blue or brown.

One thing he knew for certain. Her features were far too similar to the boy's for her to be his girl. Turning the photograph over, Bernie found a scratch of writing on the back, his nose wrinkling.

Für meinen bruder. Liebe, Margot.

"Hey, Bru?" Bernie turned, rising from his haunches. "Who was that guy who spoke German in our unit?"

Bruno opened one eye, raising his head enough to catch a glimpse of Bernie. "Gibson? Graham? I don't know. He's probably lying on the beach somewhere. Why?"

"Graham, I think." Bernie grabbed his jacket, thrusting his arms back into the sleeves before bracing his hands on the edge of the trench and lifting himself out with one quick bounce.

"Where're you going?" Bruno mumbled.

"To see if I can find anyone else from our unit."

Grumbling under his breath, Bruno struggled to his feet. "You really think we're gonna find someone? Even if we do, we're probably getting reassigned to another unit. What're the chances one of our officers survived?"

"As long as I can find someone who reads German, I'm okay with that." Bernie waved the picture at his friend.

Bruno snatched it, frowning at the image of the young woman. He whistled softly. "All right, she's pretty. But are you really this desperate, Bernie? Looking into this German girl?"

Bernie shrugged. "So I'm curious. What's wrong with that?"

Bruno rolled his eyes, handing the photograph back.

"I'm just wondering what you're trying to accomplish here. He's not the first boy we've seen die young."

"You got that right."

"Not to mention he wasn't even on our side!"

Bernie raked a hand through his hair. "I just need to know, okay? Once I get my answers, I'll let it go."

"And if you don't like the answers? If they make things harder?"

Bernie ignored the questions, moving between the groups of men making their way up and off the beach. He turned, backing down the path as he scanned as many faces as he could, looking for a familiar one.

"Maybe we should just call him," Bruno suggested. He cleared his throat, cupped his hands around his mouth, then howled, "Graham!"

Bernie chuckled. "Hey, Graham!"

"GRAHAM!"

"Shut up, Agnelli, he's over here."

Bernie spun, spotting the small group of men coming up over the seawall. Grinning, he jogged toward them, reaching out his free hand for the man who'd spoken.

"Good to see you, Paxton," he said when they clasped hands.

"You too, Russell." Paxton smiled, showing off the wide gap between his front teeth. "Where'd you come from anyway?"

"Trenches. You fellas make your objective?"

"Did anyone?" Paxton snorted, pointing his thumb over his shoulder. "These boys here are from the 29th. We met up with them down by the shore."

"You looking for me?" Graham asked, stepping up when Paxton moved passed to shake hands with Bruno.

"Glad to see you made it, Graham," Bernie replied, slapping the man on the shoulder. "I was wondering if you could help me with something."

He reached inside his jacket for the picture, turning Graham back around toward the seawall.

"Take a look at this."

Graham squinted at the photograph, turning it toward the rays of sunlight glimmering through the cloudy sky.

"Beautiful girl. Yours?"

Bernie cleared his throat, turning the picture over. "What's that say?"

Graham's brow winged. "Okay, so not your girl. Uh … says, *For my brother. Love, Margot.*"

"Brother," Bernie repeated, snapping the picture out of Graham's hand. He dug inside his jacket again, returning with the packet and letters. He separated them, holding the envelopes out to Graham. "You think you could translate these for me?"

"Why? You think there might be something useful in them?" Graham asked.

"Maybe. Or maybe I'm just nosy like my mother." Bernie elbowed him. "Do your best, huh? I'll owe you one."

"Sure, Russell."

"Oh, and do me one more favor," Bernie paused, taking a breath. "Don't tell anyone about this, all right? At least not until we know there's nothing important in them."

"You got it." Graham slid one of the letters from the envelope, the soft hiss of the paper sending a shudder of anticipation down Bernie's spine.

He turned away, letting the man peruse the letter. He moved back toward the seawall as the rest of the men continued forward. Finding a commanding officer and getting themselves sorted was the next course of action for all of them. They all knew they wouldn't be on the beach much longer, but if Bernie could prolong the few moments of semi-peace before the next assault, he would.

Lowering himself against the seawall, he turned the brown packet over and over in his hands. The package was nearly an inch thick and squeezing it between his fingers and thumbs, he could tell they were photographs. Bernie frowned, lifting the flap of the packet. He turned it upside down, letting the contents slip out into his palm.

Bernie stilled, his eyes widening as he took in the images staring up at him. Barbed wire fences, surrounding crudely built barracks. Men in striped clothing hard at work—their shoulders well-defined, arms and legs thinner than they should be. The first few photographs reminded him of a prisoner of war camp. Then he turned to the next, nearly adropping the rest when his hand trembled.

A child—a little boy, perhaps seven-years-old—stared back at him. Lying in the dirt on the other side of the barbed wire, he too wore the striped uniform of a prisoner, worn, holey boots on his feet and form so emaciated his cheekbones appeared ready to poke through the thin layer of skin on his face.

But more so, what held Bernie's gaze, were those eyes. Glazed, vacant ... dark. The truth stared at him through the ghostly image of the photograph, chilling him straight through to his soul.

The child was dead.

★★★

Dearest Hans,

Is Hitler God? Do we now live in a world where a man is held so high in the sight of our neighbors as to be equal to God? I sit with my students every day and wonder what to say to them. How do I slip the truth between the lies I am forced to teach? How can I stand before them and tell them their Jewish neighbors are evil when I know the truth? Tell me what to do, brother, for I am more lost now than I have ever been.

I am drowning, Hans. Drowning in the fear of what Germany has become. Berlin is no longer home to me.

Every day, I walk down these streets we wandered together as children, but I do not recognize them. And more than that, dear brother, I fear for the people who once walked beside us. Those of our neighbors who have disappeared, taken away by the gestapo like criminals.

Pray for me, brother. Pray for the souls of those who commit such acts of evil against those we call our friends. And pray for our friend, Horst Stück. I received a letter from our Aunt Adelheid. Horst, like so many others, has vanished. I fear for his life. Too many who disappear are never heard from again. You know what is in the photographs I sent you. You know what it means if Horst was taken to one of those places.

I am trying to fight, Hans. But every day, I feel my strength and courage waning beneath the weight of the Nazis's determination. I do not know how much longer I can bear this silent battle against those who follow Hitler's laws.

I need you, dearest brother. My heart. My twin. Come home.

Love always,

Margot

Chapter Three

Margot Raskopf glimpsed at the watch clipped to the front of her blouse. Her three young students leaned close to their canvases, the soft hiss of their brushes stroking back and forth filling the practically empty schoolroom. Rising from behind her desk, Margot strolled through the room, moving among the children to observe. Five more minutes on the clock and she would send them home, as forty minutes was the time allotted to her for this summer class. She was fortunate she'd been granted permission to use the school in pursuit of giving her three most gifted students some extra credit. In all likelihood, it wouldn't last.

Stopping behind Sigrid, Margot bent slightly at the waist. "Excellent use of color, *schätzchen*."

"*Danke*, Fräulein Raskopf," Sigrid replied with a shy smile.

Margot moved to the next canvas, the corner of her mouth tilting slightly. "Watercolor, Klaus? Interesting choice. Our *Führer* worked in watercolor, did you know?"

Klaus's chest swelled. "*Ja*, this is why I chose it."

She dipped her head in approval, taking two more steps to the left. A frown creased her brow, her heart thundering a little louder against her chest.

"You have a unique style, Brigitte," she murmured. "What was your inspiration for her facial features?"

Brigitte hesitated, her brush hovering over the canvas. Wide blue eyes turned to Margot, a sudden rush of fear tightening her face.

"I ... I ..."

Margot rested her hand on the girl's shoulder, squeezing slightly before she returned to her desk. "Time's up, children. Remember, we will not meet again until next week. Please leave your projects, and I will care for them."

Sigrid and Klaus hastily put their supplies away, Brigitte taking her time—keeping her painting carefully angled so neither of her classmates would see what she was working on. Margot watched from behind her desk, smiling when Klaus and Sigrid approached.

"Do you have your textbooks? I expect you to study over this coming week, as well as practice sketching to improve your techniques."

"*Ja*," Sigrid replied. "May I sketch you, Fräulein Raskopf?"

"You may sketch whatever and whomever you wish, Sigrid. Challenge yourself." Margot gestured to the door. "Now go on, before your parents begin to worry."

Sigrid and Klaus scurried away, whispering between themselves. Margot waited until they were gone before turning to look at Brigitte. She was taking her time gathering her supplies, placing each brush carefully into her box before slipping it in her bag. Then she approached, clutching her sketchbook against her chest. Brigitte leaned close to the desk, raising her worried eyes to Margot.

"*Danke*, Fräulein Raskopf, for my special books," she whispered.

Margot held her breath for an instant, then forced a smile. "*Bitte schön*, Brigitte. Be careful, *mein schatz*."

Brigitte rounded the desk quickly, reaching an arm to encircle Margot in a tight hug. She turned her mouth against Margot's ear.

"I have been studying Modigliani from your book. I find his techniques beautiful, and I think I have done a *gut* copy."

Margot couldn't help the soft smile that touched her lips. "As do I. But for class, you must sketch me something more traditional, *ja*?"

"*Ja*, I will."

Brigitte slipped away, hurrying with her head down out of the classroom. Margot exhaled heavily, pressing her hands into the desk to rise from her chair. She placed a hand against her lips as she came to a stop in front of Brigitte's painting. Incomplete, but the long angles of the face of the woman, narrow eyes and triangular nose was unmistakably reminiscent of paintings she herself had seen years ago as a young student—paintings by Amedeo Modigliani. The girl's instincts to paint in a style she was passionate for was commendable but far too risky.

Taking a breath, her heart heavy with regret, Margot brought her supplies over to the canvas. With a few strategic strokes, she managed to round the face and eyes, adding several layers of blue to the irises and highlights of yellow to the hair. Once satisfied the painting would not cause suspicion, she cleaned the brushes and tucked them away before moving her students' works from the middle of the room, lining the easels along the wall.

"I always believed it was a mistake to hire you," a deep, familiar voice said behind her.

Margot's shoulders tensed, lips pursing tightly as she turned. "Herr Metzger, always a pleasure."

The man smirked, leaning his shoulder against the doorframe as he watched her. His narrow, icy eyes grazed her from head to foot, sending a shudder through her body. Hastening to her desk, she gathered her papers and textbooks, tucking them quickly into her bag.

"You are the youngest teacher in this school—and a woman. Yet even with your talents and unseemly education, I see your students are not advancing in the slightest." Metzger sauntered into the room, squinting at the paintings.

"They are still wet," Margot warned. "And my students are doing fine for their ages. I see true potential in each of them."

"Entrusting you to find the next generation of fine artists for Germany ..." Metzger ended the sentence on a snort, shaking his head.

"Herr Metzger, do explain to me why my education was unseemly." She lifted her bag, turning to him with her free hand on her hip.

"You, Fräulein Raskopf, slipped through the cracks, entering university before our *Führer's* plans could come to fruition. You should be a wife and mother, not an art teacher." Metzger folded his arms across his chest.

Margot grimaced. "I will be a wife and mother when God sees fit to send me a *gut* man. Until then, I will do my best to educate our youth in the beauty of fine art."

She spun on her heels, hurrying for the door.

"I would take care, *Fräulein*," Metzger said, halting her. "Remember, young Sigrid and Brigitte are not meant for university. They *will* be trained to be proper wives and mothers, never to advance beyond these walls to higher education. Remember your place, *Fräulein*, and perhaps you will have a future here."

Margot looked over her shoulder. "I trust you will properly close the school?"

Metzger nodded, the twisted smile on his face burning her blood. Then he straightened, raising his right hand.

24

"*Heil* Hitler!"

Turning, she mimicked him, her voice hoarse as she replied, "*Heil* Hitler."

Margot spun out of the room, putting as much distance between herself and her obnoxious fellow teacher as possible.

★★★

Skipping onto the sidewalk, Margot made room for the group of children marching down the street, waving their flags with their voices raised high in song. Her spine tingled—watching them go by in their little uniforms and hats. The sight made her eyes sting, and she turned away, clutching her portfolio tighter to her chest as she turned the corner for home. After her confrontation with Metzger, and now running into one of the youth marches, her normally optimistic mood was completely shattered.

Turning the corner into her neighborhood, the weight on her shoulders felt a little lighter. Up ahead, she could see the home she'd been raised in since she and Hans were babes in their mother's arms. Many knew the name of Raskopf, her father's wealth and political standing before his death raising their family high in this city. If Margot could go back and wish for anything, it would be for a different life. She would have been far more content if her father had pursued a humbler role.

Knowing her father's name was one of the reasons she'd been granted her own job chafed enough. Being under the watchful eye of the gestapo because of her family was worse. Gustaf Raskopf was a decorated *Obergruppenführer*, but his hasty rise to power under Hitler's rule was cut short by a damaged heart.

Margot trembled, remembering the day her father's heart had simply stopped. How he'd tumbled to the ground, eyes wide with sudden fear and hand clutched to the center of his chest. A few moments and it was over, leaving Margot without the father who'd dedicated himself to protecting her at all costs and with a mother who lived every day since in fear of what the future held.

She quickened her pace, the gate creaking as she lifted the latch, sparing a glance at the black vehicle sitting out front of the house. Her nerves prickled as she told herself the car could belong to anyone. The click of her heels on the stone pathway seemed louder as she approached the door, her hold on her portfolio tightening until her knuckles whitened.

Resting her hand on the doorknob, she took a breath, gathering her wits as well as forming as genuine a smile as possible before pushing the door open.

"Mama?" she called, setting her bag and portfolio on the table beside the door. "Are you home?"

"In here, *tochter*," her mother replied, voice echoing down the hall from the parlor.

Margot smoothed her hands over her braids, making sure every pin holding them in a thick twist at the nape of her neck was in place. She turned for the parlor, a sigh slipping between her lips.

"Mama, is Ilse ...?" Margot bit her tongue, freezing at the edge of the parlor rug.

The young man turned from the window, the sunlight shining through the glass, causing the grey-green uniform he wore to catch her eye. His shiny boot heels clicked, back going straight and head tilted high as he raised his hand.

"Heil Hitler!"

Margot quickly repeated the salute before sidestepping toward her mother.

"Joachim," she murmured. "To what do we owe this honor?"

Her brother's former classmate took a step closer, his stern expression softening into a friendly smile. Chills rushed down her back, a sting of regret passing through her heart that the sight of a friend could cause such fear.

"Joachim was passing," Sofie Raskopf answered, taking Margot's arm to draw her even closer to her side. "He thought to stop in to check on us, wasn't that kind?"

"*Ja*." Margot bobbed her head in a nod. "Very kind."

"We have had disturbing reports of unlawful ... activities ... in this area during the night," Joachim said. "I thought since Franz has been assigned outside the city, I would check on your safety."

"That was *gut* of you, Joachim, but we are fine. Aren't we, Mama?" Margot smiled at her mother, gently patting her knuckles.

Sofie's pale eyes glazed, uncertainty mingling with her nervousness. Margot let her gaze wander for a moment, taking in the new streaks of silver glittering in her mother's hair and the extra lines forming around her mouth and eyes. Margot squeezed her mother's fingers tighter.

"*Ja*, quite fine," Sofie said.

"Mama, perhaps some tea?"

Sofie was out of the parlor before Margot could take another breath. Waiting until her mother's footsteps faded down the hall, Margot faced Joachim again.

"I am not a fool, Joachim," she said, crossing her arms. "There is a man upstairs searching our rooms, isn't there?"

Joachim closed his eyes briefly. "I am trying to protect you, *mein freund*."

"*Gut*, because there is nothing to find in our rooms. At least now, perhaps, the gestapo will leave us in peace."

"Margot—"

"We are Raskopfs!" Margot hissed. "This treatment is unacceptable, Joachim. How could you put my poor *mutter* through this?"

"Margot, I know your father was loyal to our Führer. No one knows this better than I do. But my officers also know your father—before Hitler took power—was a friend to Dominik Baumann, a known Jew."

China rattling on a tray brought Margot hastily around. Ilse stood in the doorway, her dark blue eyes wide as she glanced back and forth between Margot and Joachim.

"Ilse, *schätzchen*, you've brought the tea." Margot hurried over, gently removing the tray from Ilse's trembling hands. "*Danke*, cousin."

"Are you enjoying your stay with your family, Ilse?" Joachim asked.

"*Ja*, very much," Ilse replied, her voice barely above a whisper. "Berlin is very different from Leipzig."

"Until you came, I did not know the Raskopfs had family in Leipzig," Joachim commented, his thick brow arching curiously.

"We were unable to visit with Ilse and her family for many years," Margot said before Ilse could reply, taking the young woman's hand. They sat down together on the settee, Margot keeping Ilse's hand firmly between both her palms. "Since her parents passed, we have been fortunate in her desire to call Berlin home."

Ilse nodded vigorously, twisting her fingers around Margot's hand painfully. The heavy thud of boots drew their eyes to the parlor door. Another soldier appeared, shaking his head slightly at Joachim before he stepped out of sight again.

"Done?" Margot asked, glaring at Joachim.

He cleared his throat, placing his hat on his head. "*Guten Abend*, Margot, Ilse."

She looked away from him, facing Ilse as he strode out of the room. Ilse's shoulders dropped, a soft, strangled sound slipping between her lips.

"Oh, Margot!" she wept as they heard the door close behind Joachim.

"Shh," Margot cooed, drawing Ilse into her arms.

"Every time they come, I fear they know!" Ilse sniffled. Raising her head, she looked into Margot's eyes, her face tight with the strain of the last few moments. "How much longer can we lie, Margot? When he said my father's name ..."

"I know, *schätzchen*, I know." She stroked her friend's hair lightly.

How easily Ilse had fallen into the role of her cousin from Leipzig! With her blonde hair and blue eyes, no one had ever suspected she was anything other than Margot's relative. And with the proper papers provided by friends to remain nameless, she'd slipped perfectly into their lives.

"Is everything all right?" Sofie asked, tiptoeing into the parlor. She wrung her hands, her bottom lip clamped between her teeth. "They are gone?"

"*Ja*, Mama, they are gone. Come hug Ilse." Margot gestured, rising from the sofa so Sofie could take her place. "I will see what mess they left for us upstairs."

She left the room, glancing back briefly to watch her mother gather Ilse in a close embrace, the sound of the girl's soft crying filling the parlor. She rushed up the stairs, rays of the slowly setting sun shining on the steps through the high windows over the turn in the wide-curved staircase.

Her room was the last door at the end of the hall, the window overlooking her mother's flower garden behind the house. For years, she'd sat at her window watching her mother tirelessly at work in the flowerbeds to brighten their backyard with color and freshen the air with the sweet scent of blossoms. The garden was one place her mother had kept for herself, letting Margot help her only a handful of times when she was a child.

Then my mind and heart had turned to art. Margot smiled.

The door was ajar, hinges squealing softly when she nudged it wide. Every drawer was open, clothing hanging over the edges and strewn on the floor. Her wardrobe was open as well, dresses tossed from within onto her bed, leaving the closet completely empty.

Probably looking for a hidden door. She shook her head, gathering her dresses from the mattress to hang them back up. Thankfully, they hadn't ripped apart the bed, or—it would appear—moved the bedframe to search beneath. Perhaps Joachim hadn't ordered a more thorough search. Or perhaps the other officer knew who her father was, keeping his search limited.

After replacing her dresses and closing the wardrobe, she got on her knees beside the bed, lowering herself onto her belly before rolling beneath the frame. Taking a breath— and keeping her head down so she wouldn't bump into the underside of the bed—she ran her hand along the wooden panel beneath the wall. The edge popped up, and she stuck her finger beneath it, lifting the thin block of wood away. Reaching inside, she pulled out her little book, smoothing her hand over the light blue cover of the diary.

The pages crinkled from use, the small book thick with photographs she'd pasted inside. Every entry held a secret. Every page containing a piece of information on the goal she'd been racing toward since Ilse's father was killed and her two brothers left the city to fight for the Führer.

Rap, rap, rap. The soft knock interrupted her thoughts. Margot returned the diary to its hiding place, rolling out from under the bed and onto her feet in practically one motion. She spun as the door opened, finding her mother standing there.

Sofie's eyes flooded with tears. "I want this to stop, Margot."

Her brows drew together. "What do you mean, Mama?"

"You know very well." Sofie stormed into the room, stopping short in front of Margot. Her hands fisted as she restrained herself. "What is under the bed, *tochter*?"

"Nothing, Mama." Margot rounded the bed, turning her back on her mother as she went to stand by the window.

"We both know that is not true."

"*Bitte*," Margot whispered. "Mama, do not pursue this. I want you safe."

"And I want *you* safe!" Sofie slammed the bedroom door, making Margot jump. "I want your students safe too."

Margot stilled. "What do you mean?"

"You know very well what I mean! I saw the sketches Brigitte Schmidt sent home with you when you gave her that private lesson in her home. You are teaching her modern art! Degenerate—"

"Degenerate?" Margot faced her, heart blazing. "I am teaching her to look beyond the small minds polluting this country to the beauty outside these borders! I am teaching her what I knew when I was her age! The world is bigger than our corner, and every piece of art is beautiful no matter how it is depicted."

She took a step across the room, staring into her mother's eyes.

"Do you remember the *Entartete Kunst* Exhibition?" she asked, her voice catching on the horrible words. "I was too young to go, but I begged Franz to get me in so I could see what they were saying about some of my favorite artists. I cried for a week, Mama. What they did to those paintings ... how they degraded such beauty and made our countrymen think they were ugly."

"I remember," Sofie whispered. "But Margot, by teaching Brigitte such things you are putting not only yourself in danger but her as well."

"How can I keep her from what is natural to her? How can I tell her that her passion is wrong? I won't do it, Mama. I cannot. Because it's just not true." Margot returned to the window, hugging her arms tight across her ribs. "If I can help one child to know the truth, then I will. Even if I cannot help any of my other students, at least I will know I helped one child of the next generation to see the truth behind the lies ravaging Germany."

"And when Joachim comes again? When he orders a more thorough search because he has no choice but to do so?" Sofie asked.

Margot stared at her reflection in the window. The way the glass made her golden-brown hair shimmer and caught the glittering flecks of blue and brown peppering her eyes. She'd never forget how Hans used to tease her about her strangely colored eyes. How she wished he was here now to comfort her with brotherly teasing! To put his big arms around her and tell her everything would be all right.

To reassure our mother I am doing the right thing. Margot closed her eyes, plunging herself into darkness. There was no day so horrible as the day her twin felt he had no choice but to put on a uniform and fight for the Führer.

"Go back downstairs, Mama," she said, breaking the deafening silence. "Ilse shouldn't be alone."

"*Bitte*, Margot ..."

"Mama, I beg you, go downstairs." A tear rolled down her cheek. She listened to her mother's breathing, each breath heavier than the last before the soft rap of her shoes on the wooden floor warned she was turning around. The door *clicked* softly when it opened.

"And Mama?"

"*Ja?*"

Margot looked over her shoulder, wiping the dampness from her cheeks. Her eyes collided with Sofie's, holding her gaze steadily.

"We will never speak of this again."

Chapter Four

"Why do you like to sketch me?"

Margot raised her head from her sketchbook, grinning at Horst. A gentle breeze rustled the trees behind her, pressing across her back, moving past her to ripple his curly hair. He shifted his weight, placing his thumbs in his vest pockets. Sitting on the bench, she was eye level with him where he stood on the path. Lowering her gaze again, she lightly brushed her pencil along the paper, defining the roundness in his face before dragging the point down to form his button nose.

"Because you are very handsome," she replied.

Horst snickered. "You are the only one who thinks so, schätzchen."

"I am sure that is not true." Margot closed her book, hugging it against her chest as she rose from the bench.

They strolled down the lane back into the village, Margot looking down at Horst as they approached the first house.

"I return to Berlin in the morning," she commented.

"Ja, I know. We will miss you."

Margot paused, facing him. He tilted his head, looking up at her.

"Promise me," her voice broke, tears rushing to her eyes. "Promise me, mein freund, you will leave if things get worse

for you here. You will get on a train and leave Germany for the safety of other countries."

"It will not come to that, Margot."

"Horst, please." She reached down, snatching his hand. "Promise me."

He sandwiched her fingers between his smaller palms, the crinkles around his eyes well-defined when he smiled.

"Ja, Margot, I promise."

★★★

With a gasp, Margot woke. She rolled over, resting a hand against her forehead. Rays of early morning sunlight peeked through her curtains, warning her if she didn't get up soon she'd be late. Her night had been filled with dreams of the friend she'd left behind last summer. Horst Stück, a man Margot held as high in her heart as her own father. She'd never forget the first time she met him.

She was sitting in her Tante Adelheid's garden in front of an empty canvas when he came strolling up the walk. Instantly, she'd begun to sketch him, fascinated by his figure. Never had she met a grown person who was half her own size, and while so many others had looked away from him—even turned their backs on him—Margot knew the moment she saw him she would never be one of them.

I've never had a more meaningful friendship. Tears burned the corners of her eyes, and she choked on a gasp, attempting to swallow back the lump in her throat.

Twice a month like clockwork she'd received a letter from him. For nearly two months now, there'd been silence. She'd known, that first week when no letter came, that something was wrong. Then, when her Tante Adelheid's letter arrived, saying Horst's home was abandoned, but all

of his belongings still remained—including his luggage—
she'd known her worst fears had been realized. He hadn't
gotten out in time, if he'd even had a chance to try.

Rolling off the bed, she shuffled across the room to retrieve
a fresh dress from her wardrobe. Her plain, cotton burgundy
dress was inconspicuous enough for her meeting this morning
she thought, slipping into it. After brushing and braiding her
hair, then splashing some cold water in her face to banish the
heavy feeling of sleep in her eyes, she slid her feet into her
worn, brown pumps and hurried from her room.

The house was still quiet, a good thing because she was
in no mood to lie about where she was going. Making up
stories to her mother to keep her safe was becoming harder
with each day that passed. But the less involved Sofie was,
the better for all of them. She was terrified enough having
Ilse in the house—she didn't need to know about Margot's
morning meetings every week at the café.

Snatching her hat from the peg beside the door, as well
as her bag containing her identification papers, she slipped
out the front door, closing it gently behind her. The café
was a twenty-minute walk from home, taking her past a few
apartment buildings, giving way to shops. After a brief stop
at the baker to collect a fresh loaf of bread for her mother's
breakfast when she returned, she finally arrived at the café.

There were hardly any customers this early, the outdoor
tables vacant. She quickly seated herself, laying her bag
and bread on the table.

"*Guten Morgen*, Fräulein Raskopf," Ursula murmured,
appearing to her left with a tray. "Here is your *kaffee*."

"*Danke*, Ursula," Margot replied, carefully taking the
shimmering white cup decorated with tiny painted blossoms
in both hands.

The hot liquid steamed, filling her nose with a rich, bitter
scent as she lifted it to her lips for a sip. She'd never cared

too much for *kaffee*, preferring tea. But for these mornings, stepping away from what was normal for her was almost comforting.

The chair at the table behind her squealed, scraping against the stone beneath their feet. Margot deliberately took another sip—slowly. Letting the hot drink swirl over her tongue and burn in a painful gulp down her throat. Then she turned her head slightly, her chin brushing her shoulder.

"What news?" she whispered.

"We've made contact with an undercover in Czechoslovakia," came his gruff reply. "And we have a visitor."

Margot tensed. "Who?"

"Walk with me."

The chair groaned again as he stood, striding away. Margot finished her *kaffee* in one gulp, leaving a few coins on the table before she followed. She moved slowly, watching him walk with his shoulders hunched and cap pulled low. When he stopped at the street corner, she quickened her pace, passing in front of him as he took his time lighting a cigarette. His heavier footfalls soon commenced behind her, keeping a short distance between them.

"Who, Rolf?" she hissed, keeping her eyes forward.

"Polish boy," he replied. "He escaped the Nazis in Warsaw and made his way here when word reached him of our resistance."

"How did he find out about us?"

"They have their own sources," Rolf paused, clearing his throat. "He doesn't know yet."

"What? That we're about to disband?" Margot's upper lip curled, her heart thundering faster against her chest. "That he came all this way, risking his life for nothing?"

"We're not disbanding, Margot. We're trying to keep citizens like you safe. The gestapo are getting close. Too close."

"And your contact in Czechoslovakia?" she asked, quickly changing the subject.

"A British agent. We're trying to establish a safe line of communication."

"Can he help with what we discussed?" Margot stopped at the next corner, looking back and forth down the street.

Rolf came up beside her, his musty scent overwhelming her senses as his shoulder brushed hers. He wasn't tall by most standards, standing only a few inches above her. His pale eyes were shadowed by the edge of the cap, giving her little opportunity to search them in the hopes of discovering what he was thinking.

"Getting one of your students out of Berlin is too risky, Margot. Besides, what about her parents? Do you intend to steal her from her bed during the night?"

"She simply needs the proper papers, Rolf. If you can get me the documents needed, I will do the rest."

"How? Will you walk her to the train in broad daylight? Kiss her goodbye at the station? Send her all alone into the world, of which she'll need to traverse hundreds upon hundreds of miles before she's out of reach of the Nazis?"

Margot's hands curled into fists at her sides.

"I have to try, Rolf."

"Why?"

"Because she deserves a different life. The kind of life that was stolen from you and me. The kind of life she may lose the opportunity of ever having if she doesn't get out now." Margot bowed her head, taking a deep breath to collect herself. "*Bitte*, Rolf. Try. I'll see you next week."

She stepped into the street before he could reply, making her way back toward home. The city was beginning to awaken, people emerging from their homes and more shops opening their doors. Margot kept her eyes down, skirting around a trio of soldiers coming her way and hastily slipping down a back alley toward her street. Most of her days were spent indoors keeping Ilse company when she wasn't at the school or visiting a student.

Hurrying through the gate, she stepped over the pathway and around to the side of the house, stopping at the kitchen door. Her heart skipped a beat in her chest when she heard their cook moving about inside. Taking a moment to breathe, she rolled her shoulders to soothe the tension in her muscles and stretched her neck from side to side. Pasting a smile on her face, she pushed open the kitchen door.

"*Guten Morgen*, Gretl." she greeted.

"*Guten Morgen*, Margot," Gretl replied, looking up from her work at the stove. "Out early again?"

"*Ja*, I enjoy a walk before the city wakes. I brought bread for Mama's breakfast." Margot placed the loaf on the counter before removing her hat. She smoothed a hand over the top of her head, running her fingers over the smooth ridges of her braids.

Gretl smiled, lifting the loaf from the counter to take a long, slow sniff. She sighed, shaking her head, loose wisps of her silvery hair delicately fluttering in the air. Gretl Krüger had been with their family since Margot and Hans were toddlers. She couldn't remember a time when Gretl hadn't been there with freshly baked *pfeffernüsse,* whether it was Christmas or not. Those days of baking had lessened over the past few years, leaving their house absent the warm, comforting scent of fresh dough and sweet pastry.

"*Gut*, it is fresh." The older woman's eyes sparkled.

"Right out of Herr Hoefler's oven." Margot grinned. "Are Mama and Ilse awake yet?"

"I heard stirrings above stairs." Gretl set about slicing the bread, focused now on her task. "Go wash, and I will serve tea and toast in the parlor, *ja*?"

Margot nodded, lightly kissing Gretl's cheek as she passed. Strolling down the narrow hall, she paused at the parlor, resting her shoulder against the doorframe. The worn rug was beginning to lose its bright red color from being tread upon so often, turned now to a near brown and no longer complimenting the cream-colored settees and thick burgundy tapestries. Atop the white marble mantel sat several silver picture frames, safekeeping photographs of her and her brothers.

Throat clogged, her gaze settled on the one containing all three of them. Franz standing behind them, grinning like a fool, while Hans tickled Margot on the settee. How their father had fussed at them to settle down before taking the picture regardless of their antics and capturing what would become their mother's favorite portrait of the three of them.

A tightness suddenly formed in her chest. Margot's eyes went wide, her hand trembling as she reached to clutch her heart. A wave of emptiness swept through her like a raging flood, the room spinning out of control as she felt a piece of herself slip away into oblivion. Her knees buckled, taking her to the ground. Tears rolled down her face when she raised her gaze once more to that picture, a hoarse cry slipping between her lips.

"Hans!"

Chapter Five

NORMANDY, FRANCE

The photographs weighed heavy in his pocket. Bernie took a wide circle around a group of men, wondering if he looked as dirty and tired as they did. Three days and one mission later, he was back on the beach, reassigned to Woodley's unit and now with the added bonus of canvas cover. He grinned, looking around at the camp. Commanding officers beneath their tent roofs consulting their maps and soldiers waiting for orders. They'd cleared a few of the surrounding villages, and it was only a matter of time before they'd be moved off the beach for good.

Leaping over a dune, Bernie plopped down beside Bruno, pulling out the small pieces of paper Graham had translated the girl's letters onto. The bridge of his nose pinched with a frown as he tried to make out Graham's messy scrawl, unable to help comparing his friend's rough pencil strokes to the delicate swirls of the girl's script. He squinted at the paper, reading and rereading.

> Horst, like so many others, has vanished ... Too many who disappear are never heard from again.

> I am trying to fight, Hans. But every day, I feel my strength and courage waning beneath the weight of the Nazis determination.

I am drowning ... drowning in the fear of what Germany has become.

You know what it means if Horst was taken to one of those places.

My twin ... come home.

Bernie raked a hand through his hair before reaching for his canteen. Bending his neck back, he took a long swallow, the liquid cooling his belly. Maybe there would be more in the next letter Graham was still working on for him.

Even if there isn't, I know what I want to do. He tugged two blank sheets of paper out of his pocket, along with a pencil. Sand scraped against his back, irritating his skin even through his uniform. Somehow the little golden grains had found their way into his boots and socks as well, tempting him to take them off.

Bruno looked up from cleaning his Colt, frowning at the paper. "Where'd you get that?"

"Press box. They'll never miss them," Bernie answered.

"What do you need paper for? Last I remember, you don't gotta girl waiting for you back home, and your father hasn't spoken to you since you were eighteen." Bruno lifted his sidearm, the magazine sliding out into his palm.

"Remember that Brit we met when we were training in England?" He tapped the point of the pencil on the paper. "The one who got drunk and bragged about being connected with British Intelligence and Secret Service?"

Bruno's eyebrow twitched. "Yeah. What about him?"

Bernie grinned slyly. "He owes me a favor. I'm cashing in."

His friend shook his head, chuckling. Paxton appeared, lifting his feet high over their legs before falling to the ground on Bruno's other side. He took off his helmet, resting the crown of his head back in the sand as if it were a pillow.

"I was wondering where you two got to," Paxton mumbled. "What do you think of Woodley?"

"In comparison to Evans?" Bruno pressed his lips tight, chambering the Colt. A shell popped and he caught it in his palm before it hit the ground. "Not bad."

"Do we even know what happened to Evans?" Bernie wondered, raising his gaze from the paper.

Paxton cleared his throat, shifting awkwardly on the sand. "Washed up on the shore. They say he never made it off the craft."

Bernie's fingers tightened around his pencil, trembling for a moment before he steadied again. He crossed himself, Bruno mimicking him.

"Rest in peace, captain," they murmured together.

Bruno returned his attention to his gun, reloading the magazine.

"The guy made it through Africa and Italy just to take one in the head in France," Paxton growled, scratching the dark stubble on his cheek. "Real shame."

"Hey, Paxton!"

Their heads turned in unison, watching a young man come jogging over, rifle clutched in both hands as if ready to use it. He stumbled slightly over the dune, forcing Bernie to swallow a chuckle before he sat down across from them. His green eyes sparkled, freckles scattered across his nose and cheeks like paint splatter and a toothy, bright white grin Bernie already found annoying gleaming at all of them.

"Bruno Agnelli, Bernie Russell, this is Joey O'Donnell, one of Woodley's boys," Paxton introduced him.

"Hi," Joey said, waving his hand in greeting.

Bruno grunted. Bernie returned to his letter. Joey cradled his rifle on his lap, wiggling like an excited little boy.

"I've really been wanting to meet you guys. Morales told me what you two did when we landed on the beach."

Bruno smirked. "You ever seen combat before, kid?"

"Look at him, Bru," Bernie muttered. "He's as green as they come."

"Bruno and Bernie landed with me in Sicily," Paxton announced. "Never saw anything like what they did there. Inseparable, those two."

Bernie half-grinned, losing his concentration when he glanced up at the wide-eyed boy sitting in front of them.

"What was that like, Agnelli?" Joey asked.

Bruno frowned. "What?"

"You know ... fighting in Sicily. You are Italian right?"

Bruno thrust the magazine into place before resting his elbows on his knees.

"What was it like killing your own countrymen?" Joey's head tilted in what appeared to be genuine curiosity.

Bernie's pencil froze. He looked up, eyes darting back and forth between his friend and the kid.

"It was a lot like growing up in the Bronx," Bruno answered, voice dripping in sarcasm. "We lived next door to the mob. I saw at least one dead body every other week."

Bernie pinched the bridge of his nose, swallowing a laugh. Then Bruno leaned forward, still holding the Colt in both hands.

"Let me tell you something, *ragazzo*," Bruno growled. "First, I might've been born in Italy, but I was raised in the USA since I was five—not to mention my family originates from Naples, not Sicily. Believe it or not, that's important. Second, I signed up to shed blood for America, because it is the home my father taught me to love and take pride in. Not once in my life did my father let me stray from a path of courage, against all enemies of our new homeland. And three ... hey, Bernie you wanna take three?"

Bernie sat up straighter, lifting his head to glare at Joey. "Three, you're talking to a man who didn't just take Italian blood. Before that, he was in Africa and before that, I trained with him under the toughest, meanest son of a mother you never had the good fortune to know or would've survived if you had. They don't make guys like Bruno Agnelli very often, boy, so shut your mouth and show him some respect. Because when the bullets start flying, you're gonna want a guy like Bruno watching your back."

"Got all that, kid?" Paxton asked.

Joey bobbed his head nervously, shifting his rifle out of his lap onto the ground. Bernie rested against the sand once more, planting his feet firmly so his knees were raised. A breeze threatened to take the papers out of his hands, forcing him to grip the edges firmly. He stared at what he'd written so far.

Her brother spoke English, so perhaps she did too. If not, then all of this effort would be for nothing.

But I'll know I did something. Bernie exhaled, placing the pencil to paper once more.

Graham slid down the dune, bumping into Bernie's shoulder. The pencil slipped, scraping a silver line across the page.

"Ugh!" Bernie snarled. "Watch it!"

"Sorry." Graham elbowed him, holding out a few more sheets from his small notepad. "Translated some more for you."

Bernie's eyes went wide. Quickly, he folded his unfinished letter, tucking it safely away inside his jacket before reaching for the pages.

"Thanks," he mumbled.

Graham pulled back, moving the translation out of his reach. "Bernie ... this one ... I'm not sure I can believe it."

The hair on his arms prickled and ice slithered down his spine. Once again, the contents of his pocket felt heavier, calling to him—making his fingers itch.

He held out his hand. "Let me see."

Graham hesitated a moment more before gently laying the paper on Bernie's palm along with the original letter. Bernie inhaled, holding the breath as he began to read.

Dear Brother,

I am enclosing a precious package to your care. I know this is dangerous for you to carry, but you must see what is going on. A few weeks ago, Rolf received these photographs from an unknown sender and entrusted them to my care. With Ilse in the house, I cannot risk them being found. If you choose to burn them, I understand, but I could think of no one else I trusted to send them to.

You will see in these photos the proof of Hitler's intention to wipe out the Jews. These camps, they go beyond anything we ever imagined. This is where our neighbors vanished to. These places are where thousands across Europe are being taken to work and die.

To be murdered.

I cannot unsee these photographs, Hans. I cannot banish these horrible images from my mind. All I can do now is try to find a way to put a stop to it. To all of it.

I am afraid, brother. But more than that, I am angry. Angry for what one man is doing to—

"Hey!" Bruno hissed, stabbing Bernie in the ribs with his elbow. "Woodley's coming."

Bernie stuffed the letter out of sight, squinting up in the sunlight as their new commanding officer approached. The corners of his mouth were turned down, helmet tilted low to shadow his eyes. Every step he took seemed heavy, his strides long as he headed their way.

"He doesn't look happy," Paxton commented under his breath.

Woodley stopped once he reached them, eyes moving between each of them quickly before he shrugged.

"Get your gear, men," he said. "We're moving out."

He was gone before they could ask him any questions. Bernie grabbed his rifle, slinging the strap over his shoulder before pushing to his feet. Graham hurried to join him, staying close to his side.

"Bernie," he murmured, glancing over his shoulder at the others. "Do you know what she's talking about? Did ... did you take anything else off the boy?"

Bernie kept his head down, patting his colt at his hip before grabbing his helmet off the ground.

"We need to go, Graham."

"Hey." Graham gripped his sleeve, stopping him from walking away. "Come on, man. We've known each other since training. Tell me what's going on with you."

Bernie shook him off. "Nothing's going on with me, Graham. We've got a job to do, so let's do it."

"You brought me into this, Bernie. I can't just put it out of my mind now."

"I know. But give me some time, okay?"

Bernie circled around him, hurrying after Woodley. A shuffle to his right drew his gaze, eyebrow arching when Joey came up alongside him. He was lanky—nearly as tall as Bernie, and if his long legs and arms were any indication, he might even have a bit more growing to do. A wide grin spread his mouth.

"Where do you think we're going?" he asked.

Bernie rolled his eyes. "Don't look so excited. It won't be Paris."

Joey shrugged, unfazed. "I'd just like to see you in action that's all."

"You didn't land until most of the shooting was over, did you?"

Joey averted his gaze sheepishly, kicking at a clump of sand without losing pace.

"Kinda. I sorta ... got knocked out." He rapped his knuckles on his helmet. "Hit my head and another guy fell on me."

Bernie grunted. "Lucky you. How old are you, anyway?"

"Eighteen."

"Figures," Bruno said, coming up on Bernie's left. "Who knew we'd be babysitting, huh, Bernie?"

"I don't need a babysitter." Joey scowled.

"Of course you don't."

Bernie tilted his head up, looking over the heads of the men beginning to gather. There were only a few familiar faces among them—Carter and Morales included—but most were new faces. New names he'd probably hear, but never get the chance to commit to memory. He'd been lucky. Bruno tended to stay alive. He didn't think anything could kill his friend at this point.

Looking Joey's way, the constant knot in his stomach tightened. Despite the irritating goofy grin and misplaced sparkle of excitement in his eyes, Bernie sensed his heart was in the right place.

Eighteen ... He shook his head.

He supposed he could take the boy under his wing. Could try to help him stay alive and make it to the end of the war—whatever or whenever that end would be.

Has that plan ever worked for you in the past? Bernie shook his head again. Bruno was right. They weren't babysitters. He'd watch the kid's back, just like he'd watch the back of any man beside him. But he wouldn't be his friend.

Without thought, he moved his hand to his jacket pocket, the crinkle of the papers hiding away reassuring.

"You good, Bernie?" Bruno asked, nodding slightly at Bernie's hand over his heart.

"Yeah," Bernie answered. He cleared his throat. "I'm good."

Bernie quickened his pace, hoping to avoid any more conversation as they joined the rest of their new unit up ahead.

***

To William Newitt,

My name is Bernie Russell. I'm hoping you'll remember me since I have a favor to ask. We met a couple years ago where you were kind enough to share a few of your secrets. Including your connection with the Secret Service. It's my understanding that you have connections all across Europe, which is why I'm reaching out to you. I have a favor to ask, and you owe me one for keeping my mouth shut.

Enclosed with this letter, you'll find another. I'd like you to send this letter along through your agents into Berlin. And if you have any doubts, then let me tell you I will find a way to get back to England and storm right into your headquarters on Baker Street just to prove I remember *everything* you told me that night.

If you want to read the letter, feel free. It's in English. I have my reasons for contacting this woman, laid out on the first page. If anyone can get it to her, I figured you could.

Sincerely,

Bernard G. Russell

Chapter Six

The Reich Chancellery stood tall across the street, the sun peeking over its roof and casting the building in a golden glow. Pillars rising high, stone horses with manes frozen in twists and waves, heads down with feet stomping. Margot hugged her ribs, watching people pass the chancellery without a second glance at the formidable building. How many times a day did they have to pass it? In their daily route to work or home, how often had they passed one of the places Margot despised most?

Moving to the left, she kept her gaze fixed on the building. Nearby, the *Führerbunker* stood, the shelter a constant reminder—at least for her—that Adolf Hitler would always be protected. Rolf had been trying for years now to find a way into these secret places where Hitler would hide with little success, foiling every plan they ever made. Now, word had reached them that the Americans successfully landed in Normandy, fueling Rolf's determination to get to the *Führer* before they had a chance to.

Margot rubbed the center of her chest, the pain in her heart having remained constant since that awful moment. She'd always known when Hans was in trouble, from the time they were tots. Never could she explain her twin intuition to anyone, but there was no denying this ongoing feeling of emptiness.

Hans is dead. The corners of her eyes stung, the sudden rush of tears blurring her vision.

Turning away from the chancellery, she made her way back toward home. Her shopping bag swung on her arm, the few items her mother asked her to pick up barely weighing her down. Every step these past weeks felt heavier than ever before. With her certainty of Hans's fate and news trickling slowly in from the American front causing Rolf to constantly change his plans, holding onto hope for the future was becoming increasingly difficult.

She'd gone out of her way for the shopping today. Unable to resist walking by the Reich Chancellery. Watching uniformed men enter and vacate the premises. Wondering how many times her father had entered that building before he died, playing his part so they'd never suspect he was harboring a Jewish girl under his own roof.

Margot paused at the corner, closing her eyes for a brief moment. She could still remember the look on her father's face when Ilse had arrived at their door in the dead of night to announce the only reason she escaped was because her father had stepped between her and the Nazis. She could still remember the tears glimmering in his eyes when they realized Dominik Baumann was dead. The next morning, he'd left the house at dawn. When he returned that night—nearly midnight—he had with him fresh identification cards for Ilse, declaring her to be Ilse Raskopf, his deceased brother's daughter from Leipzig.

Margot had never asked him how he'd procured the papers in such a short time. It was enough that he had, offering Ilse a sense of security. Then, two weeks later, he was dead. She knew her mother continued to keep Ilse close in honor of her husband—if it had been up to Sofie, she might've tried to get Ilse out of Germany long ago, forcing her to risk a dangerous journey through occupied Europe.

Turning right, Margot chose the long way home. Her heart sunk as she passed Herr Kauffmann's former bookstore. The windows were still broken—any remnants of the books he'd once sold completely cleaned out. And the man himself ... gone. Continuing on, she came to Frau Morgenstern's café and pastry shop. It, too, was boarded up, put out of business when Margot was still in university. Frau Morgenstern, along with her husband and three children, were also gone. Memories of sitting at one of her tables eating pastry and sketching the plump, raven-haired woman behind the counter flooded her mind.

Moving on, she crossed the street at the next junction, keeping her eyes down to avoid looking at yet another abandoned building. Herr Nussbaum's music shop. Where beautiful instruments had sent strands of music into the streets as he taught a lesson in the upstairs apartment while his son operated the shop below. She kept moving, the sight of so many successful businesses now closed too heartbreaking to bear any longer. Their names booming through her head like a gong.

Kauffmann. Morgenstern. Nussbaum. Baumann.

All gentle souls. All wonderful, generous people who never hurt anyone in their lives. All Jewish.

All gone.

Herr Morgenstern had been killed resisting the gestapo who came to take his family away more than three years ago now. Margot never saw his wife or children again. Herr and Frau Kauffmann—according to one of Rolf's men—attempted to leave Berlin, hoping to make their way out of Germany into neutral territory until they could procure passage on a ship. If her friend's source was correct, they never made it across the German border.

And Herr Nussbaum. Sweet, musical, talented Herr Nussbaum walked calmly out of his shop, hat on, suitcase in hand and a proud tilt to his head.

"Do not worry, *meine freunde,*" he'd said to the people watching as the gestapo pushed him from his doorstep. "I will return home soon."

Of course, he never returned. His son's whereabouts remained a mystery—no one saw him leave the shop, and he hadn't been spotted in Berlin since. Perhaps the gestapo snatched him off the street in the night. Or perhaps, by some miracle, he'd made it out of Berlin.

We'll probably never know. Margot quickened her pace.

She was never more relieved to see home. A few more blocks, and she'd be safe within the walls of her house. Once again separated from the memories a walk in the city provoked. Circling around the side of the house, she entered through the kitchen to drop off her mother's shopping.

Gretl twisted around from the counter, her eyes big when Margot stepped through the door, warning her instantly something was wrong.

"Gretl ..." she said slowly, setting her bag carefully on the counter. "Are you all right?"

"Parlor," Gretl replied, her voice nearer a croak. "Now, *kleiner.*"

Margot nodded, her hand brushing Gretl's arm as she passed. She hurried to the parlor, coming to a stop at the door. Ilse and Sofie leaped from the settee at the same time, eyes round with worry.

"Margot," Sofie hissed. "Did you tell him it was all right to come here?"

"Who, Mama?" Margot held up her hands, confused.

"Margot."

She spun, her heart swelling in her chest. He was disheveled, to be sure. His brown hair tousled from his cap, holes in the elbows of his coat and boots splattered with dried mud. But his hazel eyes gleamed with relief at the sight of her.

"Gerhard!" she exclaimed, rushing to throw her arms around him. "I thought you were in Poland!"

Gerhard Engel held her tight, his big shoulders trembling. "I was, *mein freund*."

"Did Rolf get you back into Berlin?" Margot grabbed hold of his arms, stepping back to look into his eyes.

Her childhood friend averted his gaze, holding onto her arms the way she held onto his. Her stomach clenched, watching how his eyes pinched and feeling his muscles tense beneath her palms.

"How I got back into the city isn't important," he replied. Raising his head, he looked straight into her eyes, his own glistening with unshed tears. "I've come from Auschwitz, Margot."

Auschwitz. The word froze her blood. Turning, her gaze collided with Ilse's. Through Rolf's connections, they had heard of this place of death for years now. But none of their sources had been able to get close enough for an elaborate description.

Until now.

"Mama, take Ilse from the room," she said.

"Margot, this is dangerous. Gerhard should not—"

"Mama," Margot interrupted, firmly. "Gerhard is our friend, and he has news from our Polish neighbors. News I will share with you later if you wish. But for now, Ilse need not hear. *Bitte*, Mama, take Ilse upstairs."

"I am strong, Margot," Ilse said, though her voice trembled. "I can hear what Gerhard has to say."

"*Nein*, Ilse." Gerhard strode across the room, taking her hand. "Go now, *bitte*. I will come to you afterward."

Ilse hesitated, her fingers tightening around Gerhard's hand for a brief moment. Then, she held her head high, nodding subtly before taking Sofie's arm. Ilse urged Sofie from the room quickly, both glancing over their shoulders at them briefly before they disappeared into the hall.

"Come, Gerhard, sit," Margot said, tugging on his sleeve to encourage him as she settled herself on the settee.

He shook his head, turning his back on her to stand by the window instead. Margot waited, clasping her hands tightly in her lap as she watched him.

"I got as close as I could," Gerhard whispered. "What I saw and what I heard was beyond anything we could've imagined, Margot. Last year, new arrivals were sorted between those who could work and those who could not. Children, pregnant women and the elderly they were … they were sent immediately to …"

"To their deaths," Margot finished for him.

Gerhard nodded, turning his back to the windows. "I have been making my way across Poland for the past year, staking out as many of these camps as I could. Treblinka was … I cannot even describe it. I was near there last month when we received word the Soviets were moving in. The Nazis began burning villages all around the Treblinka camps, and I could do nothing for the prisoners who remained or the villagers. I barely made it out, Margot."

She held out her hand, beckoning him to her side once more. Gerhard accepted this time, gripping her fingers so tight she lost feeling in moments. He sat down beside her, trembling without control.

"Margot, the reason I have come to you first is because … because Ilse …"

A soft smile touched her lips. "I know how you feel about her, Gerhard."

"*Nein*, I mean, *ja*, but that is not why I am here." Gerhard bowed his head, hiding his eyes. "You remember, Ilse told us her father helped her to escape by getting in the Nazis way."

"*Ja*," Margot said, heart sinking.

"They did not kill him," Gerhard continued, his voice getting lower and lower the more he spoke. "He was transported ... to Auschwitz."

"Oh, God ..." Margot stood now, suddenly unable to sit. She pressed her hands against her mouth to muffle the sob rising in her throat as she walked across the room. "Are you certain, Gerhard?"

"*Ja*," he replied. "I had a source inside the gates. He named Dominik as one killed after only a few weeks of labor."

"Shot?"

"*Nein* ... the chambers."

A dismayed moan shuddered her chest, legs shaking so hard she pressed her hand on the wall for support. Margot took a breath, shoulders hunching as she hugged herself.

"I will tell Ilse," she announced. "She should know."

"Margot, *nein*." Gerhard stood, coming up behind her to grip her shoulders. "*I* will tell Ilse. It is I who brings this news. So I will be the one to tell her."

His hands slid from her shoulders, the sound of his heavy footfalls vibrating across the floor as he left the parlor.

Margot remained where she was, staring at the dizzying pattern of the wallpaper as she listened. Listened to the sound of his footsteps moving up the stairs—the muffled thud of his boots, taking slow steps down the hall to the bedrooms overhead.

The seconds ticked by on the clock. Every nerve in her body trembled. Every beat of her heart louder than the last.

Then, finally, Ilse's cry filled the house.

Margot's heart shattered.

★★★

Sleep was impossible.

Lying in bed, staring at the ceiling, Margot listened to the tomblike silence of the house. Ilse wept for hours after Gerhard left, finally crying herself to sleep a few minutes ago. The moon was high in the sky now, surrounded by thousands of stars brightening the black canvas of night. As glad as she was that Gerhard made it out of Poland alive, the news he'd brought had only served to further dampen her spirits. He carried with him such hopelessness that Margot did not think she could ever crawl out from under the weight.

Rolling over, she curled her arm beneath her pillow, using her other hand to pull her braid over her shoulder. The day had commenced in silence after Gerhard's visit. Ilse wouldn't come down, Sofie would barely look at Margot, and Gretl threw herself into her work—the mantel shining brighter than ever and the floors never so clean.

Margot herself had sat in front of an empty canvas, dry paintbrush in hand and colors spread out before her on her table. She had stared at that canvas for hours, her heart wanting to paint, but unable to place the brush in a beginning stroke. When the sun began to set outside, she'd finally packed up her supplies, tucking them away in the bottom of her wardrobe once more.

Clack. Margot's head jerked off the pillow, brow trembling over the sound. *Clack. Clack. Clack.*

Shoving her blankets away, she slipped out of bed, hurrying over to her window. Peeking through the curtains, her heart lurched into her throat. Rolf stood in her mother's garden half hidden in shadow. He raised his arm, waving it in a wide arc before he backed away completely in the darkness.

Margot grabbed her shawl from the desk chair, tiptoeing out of her room and down the hall. She'd reached the top of the stairs when another door creaking open caught her attention.

"Margot?" Ilse said, lazily. "Is everything all right?"

"*Ja, meine liebe*," Margot answered. "Go back to bed."

She waited until Ilse closed the door again, holding still a few moments more to be sure the rest of the house remained quiet before making her way down the stairs. Wincing with every groan and creak of the staircase, she finally made it to the bottom, running down the hall, through the kitchen, and out the back door.

"Rolf?" she hissed, tiptoeing down the rough path. "Rolf? Where are you?"

"Here, *kleiner*," he responded.

She caught his silhouette in the darkness, followed the sound of his nervous feet shuffling near her mother's rose bushes. Then, his hand was on her arm, tugging her into the deeper shadows with him. Margot squinted, making out his features—the worry crinkles surrounding his eyes and the pinched, flat line of his mouth.

"What are you doing here?" She gave him a small shove. "Do you know what danger you are putting my family in?"

"*Ja*, I know. But I did not think this could wait. I have something for you." Rolf stuffed his hand inside his jacket, returning with an envelope.

The page crackled when she took it between her fingers to hold it up to the moonlight. Margot squinted harder, making out her name on the front of the envelope. She didn't recognize the handwriting, but there was certainly something masculine about the script. Her blood warmed as she looked up at Rolf again.

"Why are you giving this to me? Why am I not receiving this letter through regular post?" she asked.

Rolf thrust his hands in his pants pockets. "Because the letter is not from a German."

The delicate hair on the back of her neck rose.

"And ... how did you come to have it?"

"One of my sources," he answered, vaguely. "This letter has come a long way to reach you, Margot. Be careful."

Margot bowed her head over the envelope again, the handwriting catching in the light. When she looked up again, Rolf was gone, disappearing into the night as silently as he came.

Returning to the house, she turned into the parlor, deciding not to risk waking her mother or Ilse by passing by their rooms again. She settled at her father's old desk in the corner, making sure the heavy tapestries were closed completely before switching on the small lamp for only enough light to read by.

Rolf was right. The letter had been through a lot. The paper was wrinkled and worn a bit thin from passing from one hand to the next. How long had it taken to get to her? Who passed it into Rolf's keeping to be delivered to her? She supposed she'd never know.

But who is it from? That is what is important now. Holding her breath, she lifted the flap of the envelope, every rustle of the paper making her cringe. How loud such a small sound was in a quiet room.

The letter slipped from its hiding place easily enough, writing on both sides of the page catching her eye. She unfolded the paper carefully, anxious to read but frightened at the same time. English words sprang up at her from the page, setting her skin to tingling. Her father had taught her and Hans to speak English in preparation for a trip to

America that was never to be. Years had passed since she'd used the language, but she remembered well enough.

> Dear Miss Raskopf,
>
> My name is Bernie Russell. I'm an American soldier, and I recently landed in Normandy. I don't really know how to say this, and I'm sure you're wondering why a stranger is writing to you. The truth is, I have come into possession of some photographs as well as some letters written by you.

Margot's heart nearly burst through her chest, tears flooding her eyes and overflowing down her cheeks. She put the letter down, far away from the danger of her tears ruining the handwriting. Wiping her cheeks, she sniffled, exhaled to relieve the pressure in her chest, and started reading again.

> I want to express my deepest condolences, miss. Your brother, Hans, gave me your letters and the photographs right before he passed. That is the main reason I am writing to you. I felt you deserved to know what happened to your twin. He was killed on June 6th during our landing on Omaha Beach. I truly believe your brother intended to surrender to us, but that chance was stolen from him, as was his life. I am very sorry.

She gasped, unable to hold back her tears any longer. Everything she already knew in her heart was now on paper, right in front of her. The evidence was clutched in her hands, undeniable.

> In his last moments, he entrusted me with a packet of photographs. I think you know which ones. As I write, I know you may never receive this letter. But I had to try. I know what it's like to lose someone and never know exactly what happened. When I saw the trust you put

in your brother by giving him those photos and read the things you wrote to him, I couldn't help the need to write.

Until your letters came into my possession like a gift, I didn't know there were people like you in Germany. On this side of the war, we sometimes forget there can be a difference between a German and a Nazi. When it comes to life and death, a gray veil falls across our view of the world. Even our view of people. You reminded me that no matter what country may have fallen under tyranny, there are a courageous few who will fight back if they must.

I can feel the pain in your letters. I can sense your despair. So I need to know more. More about these photographs. If you are able to tell me, with no further risk to yourself, then please try. Maybe your reply will never reach me. Maybe, if our forces make it into Germany, I will find the answers for myself.

Until that time, please know your photographs are safe. Your words are safe. *You* are safe. I will do my best to guard these photos and your letters with my life, as your brother did.

Do not lose hope, Margot Raskopf. We're coming.

Most Sincerely,

Bernie G. Russell

Laying the letter flat, she smoothed her fingertips over the signature, still trying to fully process everything he'd written. A soldier—an American soldier from the front— wrote her a letter and found a way to get it to her. Every question she could think of raced through her mind.

Her imagination instantly took hold, picturing a tall, handsome man wearing an American uniform and sitting on French soil scribbling these words on a piece of paper. Taking time out of his life in the middle of a war to write to her. Blinking rapidly to dry her tears, she yanked open the desk drawer, pulling out a crisp piece of paper and retrieving her father's fountain pen.

Because of the many questions that circled through her thoughts, the question of whether or not she would respond to Bernie Russell's letter was not among them.

Chapter Seven

Once upon a time, there was a good little soldier …
Bernie closed his right eye, peeking through his scope with his left. Over the rubble and ruins he could make out a few buildings up ahead still standing. Including the bell tower. His heart lurched.

If holding this town was his objective, that's where he'd be.

Up high. Perfect vantage point to pick off incoming enemy troops. Inhaling, then exhaling, he scooted back, turning his rifle in a slow semi-circle to the right. No movement. Turning back, he searched the left. Still, nothing. No sign of hidden troops—no indication any had remained after their planes had flown over, bombing Marigny practically to dust.

He was a strong little soldier with the biggest heart in the whole wide world … His mother's voice chimed in his ears. She'd been haunting him since he'd sent those letters off to William Newitt weeks ago.

Every story Laura Russell ever told him as a boy had featured a soldier. Her respect for men in uniform had made joining up an ambition of his, despite his father's desire for him to follow in his footsteps by attending medical school. When he'd announced to his parents he was planning to join the army as soon as he was through with college, his father stopped speaking to him, forbidding him to come home until 'he saw sense'. He supposed his decision was simply the tipping point for both of them.

We never did get along, even when I was a boy. Bernie shifted, planting his elbows more firmly in the ground to steady his rifle.

As bad as their relationship had been, and despite how little they had in common, Bernie never anticipated his father's cruelty. The day before he was going to ship out to Africa, he received a small, single-page note from his father to tell him his mother had died two years previously. No explanation as to how—no reason given why he wasn't told before. Why a healthy, strong woman like Laura Russell died at the age of forty-nine would remain a mystery.

Didn't even tell me how. The man's a doctor and wouldn't even write a few more lines to explain how she died. Bernie mumbled under his breath, pushing thoughts of his parents aside as he adjusted the scope to take another look at the bell tower.

"Is he *sleeping*?" Joey asked, suddenly.

Bernie peeked over his shoulder at the gaping kid before twisting further to glance at Bruno. He smirked, staring at Bruno sitting cross-legged among the rubble with arms wrapped around his gun and head down. His chest was rising and falling with deep breaths, every exhale releasing a gentle wheeze.

"Nah," Bernie replied. "He's praying."

Joey eyed him, doubtfully. "Does he always snore when he prays?"

"He's not snoring, he's grunting. It's an Italian thing."

Joey rolled his eyes, scooting up a little closer to Bernie.

His cheeks were sprinkled with dirt and ash. Uniform covered with patches of dust and dark circles framed his eyes. They were all exhausted—very little time for sleep over the past weeks. But somehow the kid still had the same sparkle in his eyes.

"You're messing with me," he mumbled.

Bernie grinned. "Just give him a nudge. He'll wake up quick enough."

"How does he do that?"

"What? Drop off?" Bernie shrugged. "Don't know. Guess it's a gift. Seriously, kid, give him a kick."

Joey chuckled. "No way. Not me. He'd probably shoot me."

"Yeah, you're right." Bernie rolled onto his side, kicking Bruno's knee.

His friend snorted, head snapping up and finger on the trigger the next second. "What? What is it?"

"You fell asleep." Bernie returned his attention to the town.

Grumbling and sniffling, Bruno crawled over to Bernie's right side, supporting himself on his elbows.

"Remind me again what we're waiting for? Woodley sent us to make sure this area was clear. Looks clear. So why aren't we moving in?" Bruno asked.

"I don't like the look of the tower," Bernie replied. "Too far away. Too high. We'll be exposed on the way in."

"Have you spotted anything?"

"Not yet."

"Then there's probably nothing there."

Bernie arched a brow, staring at Bruno pointedly. "If I was defending a town and by some miracle the bell tower managed to escape the bombing, that's where I'd be, waiting on the enemy to move in."

Bruno's eyes narrowed. "But only if you survived the bombing. You've got nothing that says anyone did."

"I've got my gut. In the past, that was good enough for you." Bernie turned back, peeking through the scope.

"Yeah, still is."

A scrambling shuffle came up from behind, followed by the heavy breaths of Paxton and Morales.

"What's the hold up?" Paxton asked. "Sergeant Ellis wants to know."

"You can tell Ellis to go—"

"Bru!" Bernie snapped.

Bruno scowled. "Fine, I'll be nice."

"Bernie doesn't like the tower," Joey said.

"The tower," Paxton repeated. "What don't you like about it, Russell, the color? The shape?"

"You're hilarious, my friend." Bernie slid away, turning around to face Paxton and cradle his weapon. "I've got a feeling, that's all."

"Well, Ellis isn't going to go with your *feeling*, Berns. As long as we can't see any movement from here, then we've got to move in."

"I know. But you know my opinion. So keep your eyes open."

"Can I take lead?" Joey asked, fidgeting anxiously.

Bruno barked a laugh. "Yeah. No."

"I'll take lead," Paxton said. "Bruno, I want you up front with me. Morales, you're in the rear. We go in slow. All we need to do is establish this section is cleared before we call in Ellis and his men. In and out, real easy."

Let's hope so, Bernie thought, following close on Morales and Paxton's heels.

They moved together, spreading out on the street, Joey to his left and Morales right behind. The eerie silence prickled every bad feeling in his gut, stirring every instinct that told him something was very wrong. Curling his fingers tighter around his rifle, he raised it to his shoulder, staying prepared as they approached the buildings still standing.

A few houses had managed to stay upright, some of the windows broken. Debris lay scattered throughout the streets, forcing them to step carefully over the rubble as they started to pass. The street took them around the first building in full view of the bell tower.

Paxton turned, raising his arm to signal their next move.

Hiss. Pop!

"Down!" Bernie shouted, watching Paxton jerk back, slamming onto the broken ground. He shoved Joey aside, dropping hard to the street himself. He rolled away, slamming his feet firmly on the ground to rise and fall back against the side of a house.

Looking back where they'd been, he found Joey was huddled behind the less than adequate cover of a pile of wreckage. Bruno and Paxton were out of his line of sight, making him tremble.

"Pax!" he shouted.

Silence.

"Morales?"

"Here!" Morales's gruff shout replied, wherever he was hiding out of Bernie's range of sight. "I'm okay!"

Another echoing gunshot filled his ears.

"*Bruno!*"

"I'm good!" Bruno's reply came. Bernie breathed a sigh of relief. "Paxton's alive! Shoulder wound! I've got him!"

"Russell?" Joey's uncertain call drew his gaze. He had the same wide-eyed look as usual. Only this time, the sparkle was gone, and his mouth was turned down—grim with fear. "I-I think I can make it to you!"

"No!" Bernie yelled. "Stay there, Joey! Don't you move!"

"I can make it ... I know I can!"

"Joey, don't move! You stay where you are!"

"If I stay low, I can reach you. I'm a fast runner!" Joey rose slightly on his haunches, rifle clutched so tight his knuckles were white.

"I said no! Joey! NO!"

The kid lunged.

Bernie went cold as ice—the shot he knew would come thundering through the air. Joey's head snapped back, a stream of blood spurting from the center of his forehead as his feet stumbled. Lanky arms flailing, knees buckling, he toppled to the street. His helmet rolled off his head, revealing a mass of red hair beneath.

Funny. Bernie never realized Joey was a redhead until this moment. A dribble of blood rolled down the boy's face, seeming to follow the pattern of his freckles over the round curve of his cheek to his ear. Bernie stared into his green eyes, slowly glossing over lifelessly.

Breath quickening, he turned his head, inching slowly toward the corner of the wall. He peeked around, catching sight of the bell tower.

"Bruno!" he shouted. "Joey's dead!"

Silence answered him.

"Bru, can you see the window to my right?"

"Yeah!"

"Take out what's left of it, okay?"

Bruno's rifle pattered rapidly seconds later, the sound of shattering glass following quickly. Once the gunfire faded, along with the glass crashing to the floor of the house, Bernie pulled a grenade from his belt.

"I'm gonna need some cover, Bruno," he called, eyeing the house across the street behind Joey. "Can you see the bell tower?"

"Yup."

"I'm gonna blast a hole through the house behind you to draw his gaze away and get up on the roof through the gable up top. Once I'm up there I'll need some cover fire."

"Think it'll work?"

Bernie shrugged, even though Bruno couldn't see him. "We'll know in a minute."

"You're sure he's in the tower?" Bruno asked.

Bernie looked at Joey again. Remembering the downward trajectory of the bullet, the sound of its journey from high to low in the air. The rush of wind that accompanied it, coming from above.

"I'm sure," he answered.

He took a wide step away from the wall, swung his arm, and sent the grenade flying. The following *boom!* got his feet moving, spinning around the corner of the house before diving through the broken window. He grunted when he fell on the broken glass, a shard nicking his cheek as he rolled away, keeping low to the ground.

"Bernie! You make it?"

"Yeah!"

He strapped his rifle across his back, pulling out his Colt instead. Keeping his back to the wall, sidearm raised, he made his way upstairs. The staircase felt confined, the narrow steps and close walls offering little room for an advantageous fight should the enemy appear. Steadying his breath, he reached the top, every heavy step he took shaking the weak floorboards and quickening his heart.

Finding the bedroom he was looking for, he could tell the enemy had taken up a post here at some point. The placement of the furniture, along with the curtains removed, told a story all their own. The bombings wouldn't have caused such precise rearrangement. Sliding his Colt back into its holster, he shoved open the windows, jumping back quickly. He pressed his shoulder against the edge of the window frame, trying to stay out of sight.

"Bruno!" His voice echoed across the street.

"Still here!"

"I need that cover now!"

"You got it!"

Bernie waited one … two … three seconds and then Bruno's gun started firing. He hesitated only a moment, closing his eyes briefly to gather his courage and wits before climbing out the window.

He lost his footing, grumbling and cursing when he slid down the slope of the roof a few feet before catching on the shingles. Dragging himself back up, he started climbing for the minimal cover of the gable, cringing when a bullet blasted through a shingle mere inches from his hand. He moved faster, scrambling until he was behind the gable.

"I'm good, Bru!" He raised his voice above the shots splitting the air.

He turned onto his belly, getting his rifle into position over the top of the gable. Bernie adjusted the range of his scope before bending his head to look through. The top of the bell tower cleared, light bouncing off the enemy sniper's scope. His breath caught, every muscle in his body quivering.

The sloping helmet of the German soldier came into view. Bernie breathed in and out, waiting for his opening. Taking a moment to observe what he could. The sniper was steady, taking slow, deliberate movements left to right as he searched the street below. The golden gleam of an expensive watch caught Bernie's eyes. He squinted, trying to discern the make—something very familiar about the piece sending a tingle down his spine.

Then, he froze.

The man who killed Joey stepped away from his rifle, pulling down another soldier to take his place. Bernie blinked a few times, trying to figure out what was happening as the sniper he was after moved completely out of his line of sight and left another man—clearly shorter, perhaps even a bit younger—behind the scope.

He's switching off? Bernie shook his head. Nothing about this made sense.

Taking a breath, he waited, watching the new sniper take position. He let off a shot and Bernie winced, trying to stay focused. Then, the shooter turned, exposing the left side of his face.

Bernie fired. The sniper fell.

Keeping his position, he waited for the first shooter to reappear. Three … four … five seconds ticked by and nothing. No sign of the original sniper. Satisfied there wasn't going to be anymore shooting, Bernie slid down the roof, spun, and leaped back through the window. He slung his rifle over his shoulder, marching down the stairs. Glass crunched beneath his boots when he crossed the front room and stepped out the door.

"Clear!" he shouted, drawing Morales out of hiding.

Bernie strode across the street, going to one knee beside Joey. He stared into the dead boy's face, placing his palm gently on the center of Joey's chest. Blood had pooled beneath his head, darkening his strawberry red hair to another shade. Bernie rubbed his thumb against Joey's icy cheek, the blood smearing.

"I'm sorry, kid," he whispered. "This was my fault."

Turning on his heels, he straightened, staring up at the bell tower. He moved down the street, stopping when he found Bruno and Paxton, crouched between a wall of debris and a shop.

"How's he doing?" he asked.

"He'll be fine," Bruno answered, keeping his hands pressed firmly to Paxton's shoulder. "You get the shooter?"

"Yeah. Stay here."

Bruno looked up. "Where're you going?"

Bernie walked away hearing Bruno curse then call for Morales. A second later, he heard the sound of running feet.

"Bernie, what're you doing?" Bruno asked, slightly breathless.

"Nothing."

"Hey!" Bruno grabbed his sleeve, yanking hard. "What's going on?"

"Back off, Bru!" Bernie hissed, shoving him away. "Leave me be."

He jogged away, ignoring Bruno's presence close behind. Climbing over a mound of stone and plaster piled against the side of the church, he crawled through a broken window. The building looked less than stable, definitely shaken to its foundation from the bombing. Every pew was toppled, dust and dirt covering the floor and the crucifix behind the pulpit askew.

Heart too ablaze to bear looking at the crucifix, Bernie moved quickly, searching for the stairs. A small, narrow door in the far right corner of the church a few feet from the pulpit seemed a good bet. Shoving it open with his shoulder, he smirked, taking the winding stairs two at a time. Bruno was still following, his curiosity itching the back of Bernie's neck. Another door came in view at the top. Pulling his Colt, he took a breath, then kicked the door in.

A gentle breeze swept across his face, cooling his skin as he stood a moment in the doorway, sidearm raised. The circular room was abandoned, save for the dead man slumped beside the window. Bernie took a slow step across the room, his heart thumping uneasily in his chest. He crouched beside the Nazi to press his fingers against the side of the man's throat.

"What are we doing here, Bernie?" Bruno wondered, voice rough with caution.

"I want his rifle," Bernie muttered.

Taking the strap from his shoulder, he tossed his own weapon at Bruno. His friend caught it midair, a dark frown creasing his brow.

"Joey wasn't your fault, Bernie," he said.

Bernie ignored him, picking up the German's rifle. He weighed it in his palms, chambering it to release the shell before raising the butt to his shoulder, staring through the scope.

"Why do you want his rifle? You've got a rifle."

"This isn't the man who killed Joey," he announced. "Or the one who shot Paxton."

Bruno took a step closer. "What're you talking about?"

"They switched off. I saw them while I was on the roof. The guy who killed Joey switched with another shooter and took off."

"Bernie ... no one left this tower."

He looked up at his friend, the worry lines around Bruno's eyes tightening his chest.

"I know what I saw, Bru."

"Look, Berns, you're tired. We're all tired. Your eyes played a trick on you that's all. He probably just stepped away for ammo and you thought—"

Bernie shot up from the floor. "I know what I saw!"

Bruno sighed, shoulders slouching. "Fine, Bernie. Let's say you're right. You still haven't told me why you want the rifle when you have a perfectly good one, army issued."

Bernie clutched the German rifle in both hands, staring down at the dark, gleaming weapon. His blood heated to boiling. Closing his eyes, his fingers curled so tight around the barrel of the gun they started to numb.

Once upon a time ... there was a good little soldier ... with the biggest heart in the whole wide world ... A flash of bright green eyes, an irritating grin, and dozens of freckles covering round, milky cheeks, crossed his vision.

Then he whispered, "I'm gonna kill him with his own gun."

"What?"

Bernie raised his head, looking straight into Bruno's eyes.

"I'm gonna find the coward who killed our boy and ran. I'm gonna find him ... and I'm gonna kill him with his own gun."

Chapter Eight

Rubber, smoke, and sweat. The combination of scents irritated Bernie's nose as he leaned back against the large tire of the truck. Bowing his head, he stared at the picture clutched in his hand. The moonlight caught on her smile, making the whole photograph shine. Every time he looked at her, he saw something he hadn't seen before. Like the few strands of hair fallen loose from her braids, curling delicately against the sides of her neck. Or the realization she was standing outside when the picture was taken—the blurry rose bushes in the background and gleam of sunlight glinting off the top of her hair giving subtle evidence to that fact.

Margot. He shifted his gaze from the picture to one of her letters, grazing his thumb across her name.

Over a month had passed since he sent his letters. For all he knew, she'd received it and if not, he could only pray it hadn't fallen into enemy hands.

I knew the risks when I sent them. Bernie sighed, tucking the letter out of sight. He continued to stare at her picture, trying not to think about Joey. Trying not to think about Paxton being shipped off to a hospital to recover. They said he was going to be fine, but whether he'd be joining them again after his recovery was still in question.

A body falling down beside him shifted Bernie's attention. His eyes widened and he started to jerk up.

"Captain Woodley—"

"Relax, soldier," Woodley murmured, waving off Bernie's sudden rush to attention. "I'm catching my breath, that's all."

Bernie nodded, settling back against the tire again. Woodley removed his helmet, scrubbing a hand through his dark hair. Silver glistened at his temples in the moonlight, and a soft smile touched his lips when he rested the crown of his head against the side of the truck.

"I'm sorry we lost O'Donnell," he commented.

Bernie winced, the thought of Joey sending a shot of pain through his chest. "Yeah, me too."

"Your friends are worried about you. Especially Bruno." Woodley planted his feet and rested his forearms on his knees. "You wanna talk about what happened in the tower?"

Bernie cleared his throat. "Not really, Cap."

Woodley waited a few seconds more, his eyes boring into Bernie. Then he shrugged.

"Okay, then." He grunted, shifted and crossed his arms. "So, where're you from?"

The corner of Bernie's mouth tugged. "Manhattan. Born and bred."

"Oh yeah? You know your pal, Bruno, takes a lot of pride in growin' up in the Bronx."

"That he does." Bernie tilted his head back. "I haven't seen home in a long time, though. Even before all this started, I hadn't been back."

"Where were you?"

"School in Boston. My dad wasn't too thrilled about my choices. Told me not to come home until I saw things his way." Bernie's brow puckered. "Kept me from my mom."

"I'm sorry to hear that, son." Woodley raised a canteen to his lips, taking a long swig before offering it to Bernie.

He accepted, the water inside slightly warm but good enough to quench his thirst. Woodley pointed to the picture still pinched between Bernie's fingers.

"Pretty," he said.

Bernie quickly tucked Margot's image inside his jacket. "Yeah. She is."

Woodley chuckled. "So, you're the possessive type."

He didn't comment. Better the captain thought he was hiding a picture of his girl than learn the truth. Not many people would understand why he kept a picture of a girl he'd never met over his heart ... much less keeping a picture of a German girl beside his heart. *I'm not sure I fully understand myself.* Bernie's cheeks rounded with a heavy breath. Interlocking his fingers, arms over his knees, he bowed his head.

"I know you're having a tough time, Russell," Woodley said, his voice surprisingly soft. "First O'Donnell gets it, then Paxton—who, I hear, you've been with since Africa—gets sent off to a hospital for recovery and probably won't be back. You've got an enemy sniper in the wind and a Kraut rifle on your shoulder."

"No disrespect, sir." Bernie paused, rubbing his moist palms together. "But what's your point? We're in a war. We're all having a tough time."

"True. But my point is I have boys in this unit who didn't see combat until the second they set foot on that godforsaken beach. Then I've got you and Agnelli and Graham. To the boys in my unit—boys like Joey—you're already heroes. You three managed to survive Africa and Italy *and* Omaha." Woodley angled himself in Bernie's direction without quite looking at him. "I'm saying they need you. I need you. You're the best sniper I've got, Russell, and I need to know your head's in the right place."

Bernie started to grin. "Trying to make me feel special, Captain?"

Woodley laughed. Then, as quickly as he'd smiled, he sobered, reaching over to grip Bernie's shoulder tight.

"He's not the last kid who's going to fall, Russell."

"I know, sir. Like you said. I've been in this for a long time now."

"Then what was different about this?" Woodley asked.

Bernie hesitated, letting the question fully settle in his mind. He rubbed his eyes, bringing his fingers together to pinch the bridge of his nose. All he could see when he closed his eyes, were those two snipers. The moment replayed in his mind over and over again, how the first shooter pulled the second one down into his place and then simply vanished.

Raising his head, he looked at his captain.

"I can't stand for it, sir. I would never switch off with another man so I could get away. No matter how much you, or anyone else in this unit needs or wants me alive, I would not put another man behind *my* rifle to be shot so I could slink off to continue the fight elsewhere." Bernie breathed deeply, letting his words hang between them for a moment.

Then he continued, "That's what's different about this, Cap. For a few seconds, I looked right at the man who killed Joey, and I know he saw me too. And when he did … he ran. Because he knew."

"Knew what, son?"

Bernie rested the crown of his head back against the side of the truck, staring up at the moonlit sky. "He knew I was better than him."

He felt Woodley staring at him but didn't lower his gaze from the sky. Then, the captain stood, huffing a deep exhale.

"Get some rest, soldier," he said, starting to walk away.

Bernie lowered his head. "Hey, Captain?"

Woodley stopped, looking over his shoulder. "Yeah?"

"Where are you from?"

The captain smiled, shifting his rifle from one shoulder to the other.

"Virginia. Little place called Bedford." Woodley closed his eyes for a moment, his warm smile easing the tension from his features. "Miss it every day."

"You'll see it again, Cap," Bernie whispered.

Woodley's smile faded, hand tightening around the strap of his rifle. He walked away without another word, disappearing among the rest of the trucks and the hustle of the men preparing to move out. Bernie looked up at the sky again, the clouds shrouding a blanket of twinkling stars.

"I'm not losing another captain," Bernie whispered. "You hear me up there? You get that man back home to Bedford."

The rumble of engines and stomping feet was his only reply. Bernie crossed himself, shoved to his feet, and marched away from the truck to find Bruno. Weaving through the hustle and bustle, he searched every face, tuning in to their voices trying to find his friend in the dark. The line of trucks was starting to move, men walking alongside or ahead with tanks rumbling not far behind.

Bernie reached a truck near the end of the line, catching sight of Bruno perched on the tailgate with his jacket tied around his waist, baring arms and shoulders in his sleeveless white undershirt. His rifle was crossed over his lap, arms threaded tight over his ribs and head down. Bernie jumped up beside him, startling him into raising his head.

They eyed each other for a moment, Bruno's concern glistening in his eyes even in the darkness of the night. The truck thundered to life, making them both shift with the sudden movements as the wheels turned. Bernie reached out his hand. Bruno grasped it, gripping so tight he thought his knuckles might give beneath the pressure.

"You good, Berns?"

Bernie nodded. "I'm good, Bru."

He swung the German rifle around, resting the weapon across his lap. Grazing his fingers along the barrel, up over the scope, across the bolt and down the stock. Feeling Bruno's eyes on the gun, he turned, placing it behind them on the floor of the truck.

"I can't let this go. I know what I saw," he said. "But I've got your back. Always."

Bruno's mouth lifted in a half-smile. "That's all I needed to know, Bernie."

Placing his arms behind him, he leaned his weight into the heels of his hands, staring up at the stars moving slowly by as the trucks began making their journey deeper into France. Bernie closed his eyes, the rustle of the photographs hidden on the inside of his jacket pumping his heart faster.

"So." Bruno cleared his throat. "You gonna tell me how you plan to find the Kraut sniper who killed Joey?"

Bernie opened one eye to look at Bruno and grinned.

Chapter Nine

"Do you think I will be able to paint the way I wish in America?"

Margot looked up from her sketchbook, smiling at Brigitte where she sat by the rose bushes. The young girl's brush *hissed* softly, forming the delicate petals—the bright red paint brightening the plain canvas. She'd appeared at Margot's front door that morning looking for acceptable inspiration, easel and canvas filling her arms. The roses seemed a good choice for a school project.

"My hope, Brigitte, is you will one day be able to paint however you wish wherever you wish." Margot skimmed the edge of her pencil across the page, leaving light, delicate lines forming the contours of Ilse's face.

A warm breeze tickled the back of her neck, sweeping over her in gentle waves. The envelopes tucked safely in her apron pocket rustled softly when she shifted her position on her stool—keeping her eventual meeting with Rolf today ever present in her mind. Shaking those thoughts away, she returned to her drawing.

Her book was filled with pencil-sketched portraits—some vibrant with color before she'd run her colored pencils down to stubs, the purchase of them no longer economical if she wished to continue supplying herself with paints. Choosing paint over pencils had been easy in the end, as sketching wasn't her favorite activity.

And I can share my supplies with Brigitte. Margot smiled, glancing up at her young student once again as she dipped her brush lightly in Margot's red paint.

The back door opened, and Gretl appeared a moment later, carrying a tray.

"I was able to procure fresh biscuits from the baker," the housekeeper announced, head raised proudly. "I thought you might like some."

Brigitte's eyes brightened as she hastily set her paintbrush aside, rubbing the smudges of paint on her fingertips away on her apron. She reached for one of the golden squares when Gretl placed the tray on the small table between them, lifting the biscuit slowly to her lips for a nibble as Margot poured them each a cup of tea.

"*Danke*, Gretl," Margot said, watching Brigitte's enjoyment over their little treat.

"Are they all right, *schätzchen*?" Gretl wondered, resting her hand on Brigitte's shoulder.

"Mmm-hmm," Brigitte hummed in response. "Delicious. *Danke*, Frau Krüger."

Gretl bent over to kiss Brigitte's forehead, winked at Margot, then strolled back into the house. The woman's humming whispered in the air through the open windows, the warm sound comforting in the quiet of the afternoon. Margot closed her eyes, listening as she slipped her hand into her apron pocket. Her fingertips grazed the edges of the envelope, the precious words it contained weaving through her mind, the same way they had since she first read Bernie Russell's letter.

How in the world did he get it to me? Her hand brushed the second envelope beneath Bernie's, her heart skipping a beat. Tugging her hand out of her pocket she returned to her sketchbook.

"Fräulein Raskopf?" Brigitte sighed, shoulders slouching as she set her paintbrush aside.

"*Ja*, Brigitte?"

"Do you really think you can get me papers so I can leave Berlin?" Brigitte bowed her head, plucking at her paint-stained apron.

Margot turned in her seat, watching the girl warily. "I am going to try, Brigitte, if you truly want me to."

"I think my *mutter* would like to see me leave Berlin," Brigitte replied with a slight shrug. "She is worried. Yesterday, she found my private sketchbook. She is afraid of what I draw and knows I will be safer away from Germany."

"Perhaps," Margot hesitated, rolling her lips to moisten them. "Perhaps, *schätzchen*, you should not draw in your secret sketchbook so much. Taking a break from such dangerous things may be in order."

"But you always say I should follow my heart. I cannot help drawing the way I do, Fräulein Raskopf."

Margot reached over, gripping the girl's hand. "I know it is hard, Brigitte. But for your safety, and your *mutter's*, perhaps you should stop. Just for a little while."

Brigitte sighed heavily, her shoulders falling in defeat. Her head bobbed, a blonde curl falling loose to bounce against her temple. Margot tucked it away for her, bending forward to lightly kiss the girl's cheek.

"Finish up the roses, *mein schatz*, then be off. We do not want to worry your *mutter*."

"*Ja*, Fräulein Raskopf." Brigitte picked up her brush, swirling it a few times in the jar of water beside her canvas before dipping the tip in fresh, red paint.

Margot watched her for a moment—catching the slight tremor in her hand when she started to fill the outlined petals, deepening and richening the color. Rising slowly, she hugged her sketchbook to her chest, sidestepping away from her student toward the back door. There was something calming about watching another person paint, but despite the momentary peace Brigitte's visit brought, Margot had run out of time to enjoy it.

Turning on her heels, she entered the kitchen, tugging at the ties of her apron with one hand while slipping the letters out of the apron pocket and into her dress pocket with the other.

"Gretl," she murmured, tossing the apron onto the counter. "Please give Brigitte my apologies, but I have an appointment."

"Oh? With whom?" Gretl wondered, looking up from her work with a slight frown.

"A friend, Gretl," Margot replied simply. "I may be late, so please tell Mama not to worry."

She hurried out of the kitchen before Gretl could say anything more. Rolf had agreed to meet with her this afternoon, despite her reluctance to tell him why. Perhaps his curiosity about the letter she received had gotten the better of him, urging him to agree to the tête-à-tête she'd requested.

With very little news reaching them from their new contact in Czechoslovakia, and the Polish boy safely on his way out of Germany, there'd been mostly silence from her friends in the resistance. Rolf's good intentions to keep her out of their dealings for her own safety didn't go unnoticed. But the more he tried to push her out, the more information she desired.

Especially with the arrival of Bernie Russell's letter. Margot's hand automatically moved to her pocket. Stroking her fingertips along the delicate edge of the envelopes, her heart beat a little faster. Rolf might not even agree to her request and even if he did, he might not succeed in fulfilling it. But she had to try all the same.

Pinning her hat on her head and snatching the bag containing her identification cards, she stepped out the front door. The sky was beginning to overcast, clouds billowing and rolling across the sun to dim the light. If the sunlight continued to fade, Brigitte wouldn't stay much longer to paint.

The lake glimmered when she reached the park, the surface of the water rippling with each gentle stroke of wind as Margot sat down on a bench. The park wasn't a far walk from home, which Rolf wouldn't like. As bold as he'd been delivering Bernie's letter right to her back door, it annoyed her to no end that her choice for meeting places always met with his disapproval.

She rested her hand possessively over her pocket, her heart racing with each second that ticked by. He was late, which wasn't good. Her eyes strayed to two officers walking by the lake, chatting and laughing. The rule was if Rolf was more than five minutes late, she was to go home. Which meant her next meeting with him wouldn't be for another week if he didn't show.

Margot took a few calming breaths, the clouds overhead turning ominously dark along with her mood. Then a heavy hand pressed down on her shoulder.

"You're trembling, *mein schatz*," Rolf said, his voice never more a comfort than now. "We must be quick today."

Margot dug in her pocket. "I have a letter. I need you to get it out of Berlin."

She lifted the envelope over her shoulder without looking back at him. Rolf slipped it out of her hand. She could almost feel his frown as the letter rustled between his fingers.

"Tell me something, Margot," his deep, raspy voice whispered near her ear. "Have you lost your mind?"

Margot spun around on the bench, glaring at him. "He found a way to get a letter to me. I am responding."

"Do you have any idea how dangerous this is? How do you expect me to get this to an American soldier?" Rolf hissed.

"I expect the same man who delivered his letter into your hands can deliver mine into his. What is the difference?"

Rolf came around the bench, sitting down beside her. "The difference is you are not a soldier who is constantly on the move. How do you expect anyone to find him? If he landed in Normandy, then his division has been on the move ever since!"

"*Bitte,* Rolf, try! He wrote to me. Do you understand that?" Margot grabbed his hand, squeezing as hard as she could. "This man—this incredible, American man—had a heart so big, he wrote to a woman who should be his enemy to tell her how her brother died. That woman happened to be me. I have never felt, and never will feel again, the way I did when I read his words. How can I not try to respond?"

"Do you know what will happen to you if this letter falls into the wrong hands? Do you know what could happen to him?"

"He took that chance, why shouldn't I?"

Rolf huffed softly, mouth pursing tight in anger. He stood up, taking a few steps away from the bench.

"Rolf ... *bitte* ..." her voice broke, tears flooding her eyes so fast they burned. "I *must* write to this man. He needs me."

"Needs you?" He turned to face her. "Margot, have you ever stopped to think that ... that I ..."

Rolf took a breath, closing his eyes briefly before sitting down beside her again.

"Haven't you ever wondered why I have worked so hard to keep *you* safe, Margot? Why, more than anyone else, I have pushed you away from what we're doing?"

Margot stared at him, her lips parting as every single thing she could think to say froze in her mind and on her tongue. Staring now into his big, sad blue eyes, nothing she could think of seemed adequate enough. She'd known him nearly from the start of the war, almost five years now. In the beginning, they'd met twice a week in secret places, along with other members of their group who wanted to fight back. Some were dead now, others simply didn't come out during the day anymore—too risky.

November 1940. That's when we met. Margot bowed her head, unable to look him in the eye anymore.

Rolf sighed, placing his hand over hers where it rested on the bench.

"I'll pass your letter on," he said. "You understand, *kleiner*, it may never reach him."

"*Ja*, I understand." Margot tilted her head high. "But at least I will know I tried."

Rolf nodded. He stood, tucking her letter on the inside of his jacket as he started to walk away. Margot's shoulders dropped, breathing a little easier now that he'd stopped arguing with her.

"Rolf!" she called softly, rising from the bench.

He stopped, turning his head slightly so she'd know he was listening.

"The papers ... for Brigitte ..."

"Tomorrow," he replied.

Margot watched him go as the first drops of rain fell on her cheeks. She brushed them away as she walked out of the park. Searching deep inside, she supposed there was a part of her that suspected Rolf's unspoken feelings. How she'd missed it until now, she didn't know, considering she'd racked her brain for weeks for the reason behind his pushing her out of the resistance.

It was strange, thinking of Rolf having feelings for her. She'd looked at him the way she'd always looked at Hans or her older brother, Franz. A figure in her life she could respect and hold dear. But one she could not feel for the way she now realized he'd like her to.

Feet suddenly heavy, she barely noticed the rain pattering her hair and soaking her dress before she was even halfway home.

★★★

"Were you trying to make yourself sick?" Ilse scolded, tugging hard on Margot's hair.

She winced, tightening her shawl around her shoulders. They sat cross-legged on her bed, Ilse tightly braiding Margot's still-damp hair in preparation for bed. Her mother had had plenty to say as well when she'd returned home, soaked through and with no explanation as to where she'd run off to.

Ilse gave another sharp tug to Margot's hair. "You should not worry your *mutter* so, Margot. Every time you walk out that door ... well ... we all worry, *meine liebe*."

"I know." Margot closed her eyes with a sigh. "Did you see Gerhard today?"

Ilse's touch softened, giving Margot hope her question would change the subject.

"*Ja*," Ilse whispered. "He came to see me. Gretl let him in through the kitchen. You know, Margot, when he is not here, I fear him coming. I fear what could happen to him—to us—if he were seen. But when he's here ... I feel so safe."

"And you're glad he came."

"*Ja*, very glad." Ilse tied off Margot's braid then tapped her shoulder.

Margot scooted around to face her, threading her arms across her ribcage as she leaned forward, staring into her friend's eyes.

"Ilse, *mein schatz* ... would you like to leave Berlin?" she asked.

Ilse's shoulders straightened, a sparkle lighting in her eyes. Not of a surprise, but of hope.

"Would you and Gerhard like to get on a train and leave this city to be together? Forever?"

Ilse took her hands, twining their fingers together. "More than anything, Margot. You know that. But so many have tried already. Even Gerhard believes it is safer for us to stay here for now."

Margot shook her head. "I don't. I want you safe, Ilse. I want you and Mama safe. *Really* safe."

"What about you, Margot? What about you being safe?" Ilse wondered.

Margot shrugged, reaching up to tuck loose strands of Ilse's hair behind her ears, tracing a fingertip down the girl's forehead before tapping her on the tip of her nose to make her giggle.

"Do you remember," Ilse said, a wide smile stretching her mouth, "the summer when we were thirteen?"

Margot bit her bottom lip. "Our families went to the country when we were let out of school."

"And Franz gave me my first kiss." Ilse's cheeks bloomed with color.

"You were his first kiss too, remember?"

Ilse went quiet, bowing her head to stare at her hands. Margot tilted her head, gently massaging her friend's arm to comfort her.

"What made you think of that summer, Ilse? Why now?" she wondered.

"Because you have been my sister long before that summer. Because when I look back at my life, there was never a time you weren't in it." Ilse sniffled, raising her gaze to look into Margot's. "If you want me safe, Margot, then you must be safe too."

"What do you mean?" Margot asked, deep in her heart already knowing the answer.

"I won't go without you." Ilse cupped Margot's cheek in her palm. "Gerhard and I already spoke of the possibility of escape. We agreed. We will only leave if you leave with us."

Raising her arms, she drew Ilse into a tight embrace, crossing her arms over her friend's back to hold her firmly. Ilse leaned heavily into her, resting her cheek on the curve of Margot's shoulder. Then she started to tremble.

"I-I know y-you don't want to l-leave Berlin because of Franz," Ilse stuttered. Moisture sinking through the thin sleeve of her nightgown let her know the girl was crying. "I know you want to be here, as close to him as possible since we've lost Hans. B-But Margot ... I cannot go without you. Y-you are m-my rock!"

"Hush," Margot breathed the word, lightly kissing Ilse's hair. "Hush, *mein schatz*. Do not cry."

"I've lost too much!"

"*Ja*, Ilse, I know." Margot sat back, taking the girl's face between her hands. "You will not lose me."

Her friend clung to her arms, fingernails digging through the material into her skin. Margot smoothed her thumbs in light circles over Ilse's cheeks, wiping the dampness of her tears away.

"Do you promise?" Ilse whispered.

A rock clogged her throat, every beat of her heart telling her she shouldn't make such a promise. But looking into her poor, lost friend's eyes, how could she not?

"I promise, Ilse. No matter what happens, I will always be with you. And if you want to leave Berlin ... I will go with you."

Chapter Ten

Rays of sunlight bathing her in gentle warmth woke Margot the next morning. She sighed, glancing at the clock on her wall to see how late she'd slept. Ilse breathed deeply beside her, a soft whistle whispering through her parted lips every time she exhaled. Rolling off the bed, she tiptoed across the floor to the window, gently pulling back the curtain to peer down at the garden below.

Her skin prickled when she saw Brigitte sitting by the rose bushes, her hair falling loosely around her shoulders, as if she'd run a brush hastily through her tresses before she dressed. Why had she come so early?

Gretl must have let her in. Margot turned away. Moving as quietly as possible so as not to wake Ilse, she put on her old brown dress, not bothering to slip into stockings in her hurry to get downstairs.

Reaching the kitchen, she spared Gretl a quick smile before stepping out the back door, smoothing a hand over the top of her head in a weak attempt to tame her hair. She approached Brigitte from behind, the girl giving no indication she heard her approach. Observing the painting, Margot felt a swell of pride. Even knowing Brigitte would rather paint anything else but flowers, the girl's talent for bringing any kind of scene to life on canvas was undeniable. Even things she hated to paint, she painted well.

Raising her hand, she lightly tapped Brigitte on the shoulder. The young girl turned slowly, eyes red with tears, alarm bells instantly clanging in Margot's head. She went to her knees, taking Brigitte's hands.

"Oh, *schätzchen*, what's wrong?"

Brigitte whimpered, her chest convulsing with repressed sobs. "I-I am so s-scared, Fräulein Raskopf!"

"Why, Brigitte? What's happened?" Margot stroked the girl's cheek, letting her fingers drift gently through her hair.

"I went home last night and ... and my *mutter* wasn't there." Brigitte bowed her head. "We ... we've been ... helping people. That was the real reason why she was so frightened when she found my sketchbook! We were already trying to be careful."

Margot's eyes fluttered closed. Fifteen-years-old and trying to help people ... she couldn't even imagine the kind of fear swirling through her student.

Or can you? Margot swallowed, hard.

"What order was the house in?" Margot asked, every muscle telling her she should get Brigitte inside the safety of the house but unable to move at the same time.

"A mess." Brigitte raised her eyes, looking directly into Margot's. "My secret sketchbook and textbooks were gone."

If Margot was unable to move before, she was completely frozen now.

Rolf. I need to get her to Rolf. Tightening her grip on Brigitte's hand, she yanked her to her feet.

"Come, *mein schatz*, we're leaving."

"Where?" Brigitte's eyes rounded.

"Somewhere safe."

She turned for the back door, mind racing with any and every place she could hide Brigitte until they were able to get out of the city when the back door burst open.

Margot's thoughts came to a grinding halt. The uniformed officer standing in the door glared at her, his eyes raking her from head to foot before his attention shifted to the young girl beside her. Margot tucked Brigitte behind her, the girl's arms wrapping tight around her waist as she buried her face between Margot's shoulder blades.

"Brigitte Schmidt," the officer said, approaching. "You will come with us."

"Why?" Margot replied.

"This does not concern you, *Fräulein*."

"You have come into my home and are standing on my property. I think it is my concern."

"*Nein*, Fräulein Raskopf," Brigitte whispered. "Don't."

"Get out of the way, Margot."

Her heart halted. Staring up at Joachim's face, she wondered where the sweet schoolboy he once was had gone. Where was her brother's friend in that stony expression?

"Joachim, *bitte* ..."

He averted his gaze.

"Enough! Move out of the way!" the officer demanded.

"*Danke*, Fräulein Raskopf. For everything!" Brigitte sobbed.

The officer grabbed her arm tearing her away from Margot.

"*Nein*!" Margot shouted trying to shove her way between them again.

The back of his hand struck her cheek, followed swiftly by the sharp, metallic taste of blood as she stumbled and fell on the pebbled path. Brigitte screamed—Margot's head spun. She watched from where she lay on the ground, their figures blurring and spinning as they dragged Brigitte away around the side of the house.

Then the officer bent over her and hissed, "You are fortunate you're a Raskopf. If you were anyone else, I'd kill you."

Margot's fingers sunk into the rough dirt and pebbles, fisting tight against her palm.

"Leave her, Boehler," Joachim ordered. "Remember what we discussed."

The officer hesitated a moment, his hot breath beating down on the back of her neck. Then he stood up, striding away after the others.

"Margot!" Gretl cried, appearing at her side. "Oh, Margot! I am sorry, *mein schatz*! I tried to stop them."

Margot couldn't move, the thunder rumbling in her head overwhelming all her senses. Gretl gripped her arm in an attempt to pull her into a sitting position.

"I do not understand how they knew where she was!" her housekeeper exclaimed. "And why did they not arrest you?"

"Joachim," Margot rasped. "He must've done something to protect me."

The echo of car doors slamming, followed by the low roar of engines brought Margot out of her stupor. Pressing her palms into the ground, she rose on shaking knees.

"Stay here, Gretl," she whispered.

"Margot ... *nein* ..."

Ignoring the woman's quiet plea, she followed the path around the side of the house. Her steps quickened the further she went, tossing open the gate to the picket fence and leaping out into the street. The vehicles were hastening away, the figures inside barely visible the further they went.

Margot started running, ignoring the curious stares of her neighbors watching from their windows. Ignoring the knowledge that the gestapo could see her following in their mirrors. She chased the cars, her heart and soul screaming inside her.

This could not be happening. Not to sweet Brigitte. Not to the student she'd encouraged down this dangerous path. It should not be her in that car.

It should be me! Arms pumping, legs burning, she ran faster. But the cars only seemed to be getting farther and farther away.

The breath was sucked from her lungs when another body rammed into her. Margot's scream cut short when a large palm slammed over her mouth as she was dragged off the street and between two buildings.

"Margot! It's Gerhard!" his voice whispered hoarsely in her ear.

Margot went limp, clinging to his arm as the tears began to course down her cheeks. Softly, he turned her around, tucking her warmly in his embrace. She burrowed against his chest, her tears quickly soaking into the front of his shirt.

"This is all my fault!" she wept.

"*Nein*, Margot."

"*Ja*, it is! You know it is!" Margot stepped back, wiping the tears from her cheeks. Inhaling deeply to calm her rattling heart.

"You're bleeding," Gerhard said, rubbing his thumb against the corner of her mouth.

Margot shook him off, wiping away the drop of blood herself before looking up at him, brow furrowed. "Why are you out here in broad daylight?"

Gerhard's eyes darkened as his hand moved toward his jacket pocket. "I was ... bringing you ..."

Margot couldn't look away from his pocket, her fingers trembling when she brushed them against his knuckles.

"*Nein*," she rasped. Then her voice rose, "*Nein*, Gerhard. Do not tell me you have Brigitte's papers. Do not tell me that is why you were on your way to my house!"

He yanked her back into his arms. Whether to muffle her cries or offer her sincere comfort she wasn't sure, but she latched onto him all the same. He stroked her hair, whispering well-meaning comforts in her ear that, in the end, simply didn't help at all.

"I am so sorry, Margot," Gerhard said.

Margot clasped her arms around his waist as tight as she could, trying desperately to expel the feeling of being all alone.

"Listen, *mein freund*." Taking hold of her shoulders he pushed her away enough to look into her eyes. "I did not just come here to bring Brigitte her papers. I came to tell you and Ilse—"

"You have papers for us too," Margot finished for him.

He nodded slowly. "*Ja*. And for your *mutter* and your Gretl. Rolf has been planning for weeks to get all of you out and I think, now more than ever, it is time for you to go."

She shook her head, touching her forehead to the center of his chest to fully catch her breath before she looked up at him again.

"Oh Gerhard ... I fear you couldn't be more wrong." Margot hugged herself, buffing her arms for much needed warmth.

"What do you mean?" He frowned.

"I cannot leave! They will be watching me now, more than they ever did before. If I were to vanish, they will chase us. They will be on our heels and we'd never make it out of the city, much less out of Germany." Margot wiped her cheeks completely dry this time, shoulders rising and falling with another breath. "But bring the papers."

Gerhard went still. "Margot ..."

"Bring the papers for Ilse, Mama, and Gretl. I will talk to them when I get home."

"*Nein!*" He took hold of her, his fingers sinking into the soft flesh of her upper arms. "I will not let you, Margot!"

"Gerhard." She raised her hands, taking soft hold of his face. Smoothing her thumbs over the prickly brown stubble on his cheeks, looking deeply into his gentle sea blue eyes. "*Bitte, mein freund*, do as I ask. They have a chance, even if I do not. As long as I am seen, our enemies will not suspect they have gone. At least not right away."

His eyes closed, grip loosening then tightening. "I ... I cannot ..."

"You can." Margot let her hands drop, removing his from her arms before she put more space between them. "Gerhard, you must."

They stood together, staring at each other in silence as the truth settled on their shoulders. The fear shining in his eyes nearly destroyed her, but they both knew there was little more to say after what she'd done today. Gerhard bowed his head.

"All right, Margot. I will do what you've asked."

★★★

Keeping her head high the whole walk home was difficult. But as she started to pass her neighbors's houses, Margot forced herself to walk as straight and tall as possible. They were all watching, even if she could not see them. She could feel their eyes on her so deeply she thought she might break into pieces in the street.

Somehow she managed to walk calmly up to her home, closing the gate behind her slowly and deliberately. Every muscle in her body wanted to launch her into a race to the door. Instead, she took each step slowly, as if she were simply taking a morning stroll.

Ilse appeared in the hall the moment she opened the door. Margot's chin trembled, but she pulled back, keeping herself from crumbling as she closed and locked the front door behind her. She walked past her friend without a word, ignoring Ilse's tears—ignoring the worry creating lines around her friend's eyes.

Sofie was sitting on the settee in the parlor, sniffling and drying her eyes with a handkerchief. Margot walked up to her, lowering herself gingerly to her knees in front of her mother.

"*Tochter*," Sofie cooed, leaning forward to rest her forehead against Margot's. "I am sorry about your student. She was such a sweet girl."

Margot took her mother's hands, sandwiching them between her palms. "Mama, I have something to tell you."

"What, *meine liebe*?" Sofie tilted her head curiously.

"Tonight, a man is going to come to the door. He will bring with him papers for you, Gretl, and Ilse. You will be ready for him with your bags and you will get in the car and let him drive you away from here."

Sofie's chest began to rise and fall rapidly, her eyes reddening as she listened.

"W-What are you s-saying?" Sofie asked, her voice a low squeak.

"I am getting you out of Berlin, Mama. Tonight."

"But ... but *tochter*, what about you?" Sofie's bottom lip trembled and she tried to pull her hands away. Margot held her firmly, forcing her to stay still. Forcing her to look at her.

"I cannot go yet, Mama," Margot whispered. "I have to stay."

"*Nein! Nein!*" Sofie shook her head fiercely. "I will not! You cannot!"

Margot pulled her forward, wrapping her in a warm hug. "It's all right, Mama. I will be right behind you, I promise. I need only stay until the gestapo stop watching! After a few days, things will settle again and then I will come find you."

Sofie took a few gasping breaths. "Really?"

Margot leaned back, forcing a smile she hoped would calm her mother.

"Of course, Mama." She took the handkerchief, wiping her mother's cheeks. "Now go tell Gretl and begin packing. Take only what is needed, Mama. You must travel light."

Sofie nodded, standing up. She started to walk away, then turned, hurrying back to embrace Margot again.

"I love you, my beautiful girl. You are the treasure of my heart, and I am so proud." Sofie stepped back, stroking Margot's cheeks with her fingertips. "Your father would be so proud too."

Margot's eyes welled. Before she could respond, Sofie left the parlor, brushing a hand against Ilse's arm as she passed. Silence stretched on after her footsteps faded toward the kitchen. Ilse stood frozen in the door to the parlor, mouth pursed and eyes narrowed.

"I am not going," she announced, breaking the silence.

"Ilse, *bitte*, do not argue." Margot turned her back, stepping across the room to the windows. "You must go."

"*Nein*. You promised, Margot. Last night you promised if I went, you would go too."

"Then the morning came, and Brigitte was taken." Margot closed her eyes, plunging herself into darkness. "I stepped between a girl and the gestapo, and I will pay for it, Ilse. If you do not go now, you may never leave Berlin."

"You promised you would not leave me. You promised you would always be with me. Is your heart bigger than mine? Is your love for me greater than my love for you?"

Margot's eyes fluttered, her lashes moist as she turned around to face Ilse again. A tear rolled down her friend's cheek, clinging to her chin about to drop off.

"If you stay, I stay. I will not argue about this, Margot. Last night, you made me a promise. This morning, I make you one." Ilse took a small step forward. "I will always be with you, as you promised you would always be with me. Tonight, your *mutter* and Gretl will leave ... and I will stay. For as long as it takes."

A small smile began to spread on her friend's face. "And one day, we will cross the border out of Germany. Together."

Margot covered her mouth, muffling a sob. She closed the distance between them, threw her arms around the only sister she'd ever known, and melted in a burst of tears.

Chapter Eleven

THE FRENCH COUNTRYSIDE
LATE-AUGUST, 1944

Bernie wasn't a big fan of Cole Porter. But he had to admit, as Bruno whistled "You're the Top" over and over on their trek across the open field, the man's style was beginning to grow on him. His mother had done her best over the years to transform him into as big a fan of Porter as she was—one of their last conversations had been about their different tastes in music.

A gust of wind rustled the tall grass, tugging at their uniforms as they moved slowly across the field, rifles clutched in their hands and eyes narrowed, keeping watch. Moving across France toward the German border had been accomplished through a series of skirmishes, accompanied by the news their unit would not be going to Paris with most of the others.

I told Joey so. Bernie shook his head, wishing for the hundredth time the kid was here to take his teasing.

"Does anyone actually know where we are?" Morales asked over Bruno's whistling.

Sergeant Ellis glanced over his shoulder, hazel eyes twinkling and a goofy grin on his mouth. "Right where Patton wants us."

Bernie snorted. "Speaking of, has anyone actually ever laid eyes on the general? I've been hearing orders from him since Africa. Never actually saw him, though."

"Really?" Sergeant Ellis grunted. "You've been busy, eh Russell?"

"Putting things mildly, yeah." Bernie shifted the weight of his rifle to his left arm. "You see him, sarge?"

"Couple times before I was transferred outta the 2nd." Ellis glanced over his shoulder. "Bet cap's heard the general's voice a lot these past weeks."

Bruno moved on from whistling to singing, voice no higher than a whisper. Bernie cringed, rolling his eyes to look at Graham's scowling face.

"Guy can't carry a tune in a bucket," Graham mumbled.

"Hey, Bru," Bernie said over his shoulder. "You do know you whistle better than you sing, right?"

Bruno chuckled in response.

"Go back to whistling before we all go deaf."

"Come on, Berns, I've gotta be better than the silence."

"You'd think so, wouldn't yah?"

Ellis held up his fist, silently calling for a halt. Every man came to attention, Bernie raising the stock of his rifle to his shoulder. Then Ellis motioned them to drop, each taking a knee in slow movements. Bernie scooted up a bit closer.

"What's up, Sarge?" he asked.

"Not sure. Thought I saw something." Ellis eyed him. "Hunker down a bit more, private."

Bernie nodded dropping slowly to his belly so the tall grass rose above his helmet. Ellis signaled for the others to stay put and get low, joining Bernie flat on the ground before they started to crawl. They moved up a few feet before stopping again, Bernie adjusting his scope and Ellis reaching for his binoculars.

"Those trees are perfect cover," Ellis grumbled. "Why can't we have perfect cover, just once?"

Bernie grinned, peering through the scope. "What did you see, anyway?"

"Don't know. A flash? You know, like sunlight glinting off glass, maybe."

"Or sunlight glinting off a scope?"

Bernie and Ellis stole a glance at each other. The crease of his sergeant's brow did nothing to encourage good thoughts as Bernie returned to his observations.

The cluster of trees up ahead seemed a bit out of place on the field. Just a small group before giving way to another field behind. To his right, the woods thickened—to the left more open ground. A couple of clicks and he'd adjusted the range on his scope a bit more, searching the general area Ellis had indicated.

His finger brushed the trigger, his racing heart battling every ounce of restraint and concentration. Every small rustle of the grass in the wind, every soft creak of tree branches urged him to start blindly firing in case Ellis's instincts were right.

Tilting his rifle back, he started to search the trees. A prickle stung the back of his neck, raising gooseflesh on his arms. A white flash, like the sun glaring off metal, brought him swiftly back to the left.

"Gotcha," he muttered.

"What?" Ellis edged closer to him.

"I've got one. Don't see any others." Bernie squeezed his right eye closed, focusing with his left through the scope.

"You think he's alone? Out here in the middle of nowhere?" Ellis asked, doubtfully.

"I didn't say that exactly, sarge. I meant I only ... see ..." Bernie's voice faded as his heartbeat loudened.

He couldn't see the man's face behind the shelter of the branches. But what he could make out clearly was the shape of the rifle, the glistening scope above the barrel, the large hands gripping the weapon tight ... the gold watch shining on his wrist.

Bernie's breath quickened, every inch of his skin burning. He'd seen this before. Through the window of a bell tower.

"Russell, what is it?" Ellis hissed near his ear.

Bernie's finger tightened on the trigger. "He's alone."

"What? Come on, Berns, he can't be alone!"

"He is."

Bernie fired, the crash of the bullet echoing through the air. A branch snapped—the sniper jerked back, tumbling from his hiding place before catching on a lower branch. Bernie fired again, but the shot was off, giving the sniper enough time to hit the ground and vanish behind the trunk.

"Russell!" Ellis grabbed him by the sleeve. "What do you think you're doing?"

Bernie shook him off, pushing up onto his knees as he leveled his weapon to look again. Zero movement among the trees.

"Answer my question, private," Ellis snapped, still lying flat on the ground.

"He's alone, Sarge. I'm going in."

"Berns!"

Can't let him get away. Not again. Bernie started to stand.

"Private Russell!" Woodley bellowed from behind.

Bernie's eyes closed, fingers tightening around his weapon so hard his knuckles cracked. He turned, boldly presenting his back to the trees.

"Captain," he said hoarsely as Woodley came to a stop in front of him.

"Did your sergeant give you the order to move in, private?" Woodley asked.

"No, sir."

"Then what the devil do you think you're doing?"

Ellis struggled to his feet, turning to face Woodley. "Russell made a call, sir. There was a sniper in the trees, and Russell believes he took him down."

"Did you?"

Bernie shrugged. "Only one way to find out, Cap."

Woodley hesitated, narrowed eyes moving back and forth between Bernie and Ellis before he nodded.

"Okay, let's go find out."

Bernie started to turn.

"But Russell."

"Yes, sir?"

"Next time, wait for your sergeant's command."

Woodley didn't give him a chance to answer before striding around him, shouting orders over his shoulder for the rest of the unit to stay put before motioning for him and Ellis to follow. They started after him a few steps behind.

"What got into you, Berns?" Ellis mumbled.

Bernie didn't answer, lengthening his strides after Woodley toward the tree line. All three slowed, weapons raised as they moved among the trees. Broken branches and freshly fallen leaves told him he'd found the right one, spinning quickly around the trunk with rifle raised.

Nothing.

"He's gone," Bernie announced before cursing softly under his breath.

Just like the bell tower. Vanished. He rested the rifle against his shoulder, knowing there was no need for it any longer.

"Russell!" Ellis called.

Following the sound of the sergeant's voice, he weaved between the trees, coming to a stop beside one of them. Ellis was crouched in front of the tree, Woodley standing beside him. The sergeant looked over his shoulder, standing. Bernie's gaze lowered, staring at the dead soldier sitting up against the tree. Eyes rolled back, mouth agape and skin a sickening green indicating he'd been here for a while. His rifle lay across his chest and shoulder, the bayonet securely in place. Ellis pointed to the knife.

"That's what I saw," he said. "Sun hits that just right, would set off a glare."

"Don't know what you saw, Russell, but looks like the Germans moved on from this area a while ago." Woodley walked away from the boy, signaling the area was clear so the rest of the men would move in.

"It was the sniper."

Woodley's head turned sharply, his hand still raised. "What?"

Bernie looked back at him. "The sniper from the bell tower in Marigny. He's the one I saw."

"Russell." Woodley returned to his side, gripping his shoulder tight. "There's no way he could've gotten away without someone else seeing. You saw something all right, but not a man."

"He was wearing the same gold watch," Bernie insisted. "Captain, I swear it was the same man."

Woodley exchanged a swift look with Ellis, then leaned back slightly on his heels, crossing his arms.

"All right, private ... then where did he go? And how did he get away?"

Bernie's mouth pressed into a thin line, staring unblinking at the captain. Every weak explanation he could think of popping into his head but not coming out his mouth.

Because as much as he wanted to convince Woodley he'd actually seen what he knew he saw, he had no answer for the captain.

***

"You're convinced? Same guy?"

Bernie nodded as he and Bruno walked down the street of the small French village. He picked at a loaf of bread, generously provided by the local baker when they passed his shop. The shadows of night were pulling back from the sky, sending fresh rays of sunlight down on the rooftops of the town as their trucks rumbled through.

"It was weird, Bruno," Bernie muttered. "This feeling came over me when I got him in my sights. Don't even know how to describe it."

"That why you went off shooting before we knew for sure we were in the clear?" Bruno's eyes narrowed.

Bernie cringed. "Yeah. Sorry about that."

Bruno shrugged and grunted in response, stuffing a large piece of the bread in his mouth. They continued in silence, moving around the mix of civilians and soldiers on the streets. Up ahead, he could see Woodley and Ellis talking with the new lieutenant. Norris? Norbert? Bernie wasn't even sure he cared. New officers were never a walk in the park—though he had to admit, Woodley was the exception.

Not like having the same commanding officer since training, like Evans, but a good leader all the same. As far as he was concerned, Ellis should've been promoted before a new face was brought in. But he didn't make the rules, only followed them.

"If he was the same sniper," Bruno said, reclaiming Bernie's attention, "seems like you won't have to worry about finding him. It's starting to feel like he's looking for you."

Bernie's brow pinched. "I doubt that, Bru. I think he's on the run, looking to catch up to whatever unit he was with before they got separated at Marigny. Only explanation as to why he was all alone out there."

"Yeah, I s'pose." Bruno handed him the last piece of bread.

A shoulder slammed into Bernie's, knocking the food out of his hand. A scramble of hands and a flash of brown eyes made Bernie spin, watching the woman take a few backward steps as she broke away from their brief entanglement. She stared at him, a scarf covering her dark hair and the sun gleaming on her delicate, porcelain skin before she ran away, vanishing around the corner.

"What was that all about?" Bruno mumbled. "There was plenty of room on the street. Besides, if she wanted to get her hands on an American soldier, why not me?"

Bernie chuckled, elbowing his friend in the side. "Be respectful."

He took hold of the edges of his jacket, straightening his clothing. The rough rustle of paper made him frown, looking down at one of his lower pockets. The letters from Margot were safely tucked inside his jacket, along with the photographs.

A shudder rushed down his spine as he slid his hand into his pocket and came back with a crisp, white envelope.

"Uh ..." Bruno stared, looking back and forth between the letter and where the girl had disappeared. "Where ... what?"

Bernie focused on his name, the delicate swirl of the handwriting across the front of the envelope shockingly familiar. His hand started to shake, the impossibility of it all rushing through him so fiercely he thought his knees would buckle.

"Give me a minute, Bru," Bernie whispered, stepping away from his friend. "I'll catch up."

Bruno nodded without question, watching him briefly before he continued down the street. Bernie perched himself on the edge of the sidewalk, forearms resting against his knees as he took a moment to breathe, studying the gentle, feminine handwriting. There was no mistaking that hand— no mistaking the large curves of her script.

Margot. He turned the envelope over, gently tearing open the back flap to release the pages within.

His heart thundered faster, wondering if all of this was a dream as he began to read.

Dear Bernie Russell,

Upon receiving your letter, I had only one question.

How?

How, in the middle of this war stretching across country after country, mile after mile, did you manage to get a letter to a German girl? Then my question changed. Why? Why would you take the time out of your life, when life is so precarious right now, to write to a girl who should be your enemy? To have a heart so large as to write to a German girl and tell her how her brother died ... are you even real? Have I imagined you so I might have some comfort in these troubled times?

But as I wonder if I imagined you, I hold your letter in my hand and know you are real. Even as I write, I can hear your words—imagine your voice. You have brought me such peace in this time of grief and war that I can barely breathe.

You asked me for more information regarding the photographs my brother gave you. I can share what I know, though even my knowledge is limited. In Berlin, we do not see firsthand what is happening in Poland, we only hear from our sources.

I have heard the names Auschwitz, Treblinka, Dachau, all whispered in dark corners. These camps are not meant for prisoners or simply for forced labor. They are meant for death in the most horrible of ways. Do I believe those who go through the gates are never meant to come out? Yes, I am terrified to say I do.

In my home, there is a girl whose father went to such a place. I received word only yesterday that he is dead, killed in a gas chamber along with hundreds of others. A wonderful friend of mine has also disappeared, who I can only now assume is dead too. Innocent men, women, and children have been herded into these places, each for separate reasons.

They are Jewish. They are Romani. They were born different. They are considered criminals for standing against Nazi rule. I am living in a nightmare, Bernie Russell. But then I received your letter, and in that moment, you were a bright light in my darkness.

As you weren't certain your letter would ever reach me, I am uncertain if mine will ever reach you. If it does, I hope it finds you well and strong. I hope you feel as keenly as I do, the miracle of our words spanning these many miles to find each other. I hope this letter has given you the answers you so desperately sought.

You told me in your letter not to lose hope, that you were coming. Well, Bernie, I did lose hope. I was drifting so far away from the hope I had when the war first broke out I thought I would disappear.

Then there was you. All I can say now, is thank you. Thank you for not only restoring my hope, but my faith in humankind. Thank you for being the last face my brother ever saw and for being the kind of person—in the brief moments before his death—he knew he could trust with his deepest secrets.

I pray my words give you the same comfort yours gave to me and that, perhaps, you will find a way to write to me again. And if you do, please, call me Margot.

God be with you,

Margot Raskopf

Bernie rubbed his eyes, then turned the page back, starting over. Seeing his name alone, written in her hand, lifted the weight directly off his shoulders. He couldn't even describe the feelings the rest of her letter provoked.

A shadow fell across the page and he looked up, squinting when a ray of sunlight impaired his vision.

"You wanna tell me what you're doing sitting around when we're getting ready to move out?" Woodley asked, eyes blazing.

Bernie quickly put the letter away, scrambling to his feet. "Sorry, captain. I, uh, was reading a letter."

"Yeah, I saw that."

They started walking, Bernie surprised the captain was keeping stride with him instead of rushing ahead to the front of the line. They continued side by side, Bernie's fingers itching to reach for Margot's letter.

"Let me ask you something, Russell," Woodley said, coming to a stop.

Bernie faced him, noticing the lines around his eyes— the salt and pepper stubble beginning to shadow his face. He couldn't help wondering how many more lines would be added to the man's face by the time this war came to an end. How many more strands of gray would highlight his hair?

How many more shadows will cloud his eyes? Bernie swallowed the lump in his throat.

"Are you positive you saw the sniper from Marigny in the woods?"

His mouth went dry. "Yes, sir. Absolutely."

"How?" Woodley shrugged, mouth turned down. "If I've learned one thing about you over the past couple months, it's you don't mess around. You're not the sort to just ... you know ... lose it." He twirled his finger in a circle beside his temple. "I also don't think you're one of those guys who would fake it to get discharged on a Section Eight. So tell me, how are you sure?"

"I told you before, Captain. The watch," Bernie answered, tapping his own, bare wrist. "His stance. His movements. I knew it was him."

"But you still can't tell me how he got away with no one else seeing him?"

Bernie grimaced. "No, sir. That I can't explain."

Woodley squinted, staring at Bernie intently for a few heart thundering moments. Then, Woodley removed his helmet, raking a hand through his hair with a deep sigh.

"Twice now, you've seen a man no one else has seen. You do know I talked to Bruno and Morales. They're convinced the sniper who killed O'Donnell was killed in that tower. By you."

Bernie's brow trembled in a near frown. "Bruno said that?"

"Bruno's your friend. He'd never directly say anything against you, Bernie. But you have to admit your story is pretty hard to believe."

Bernie took a moment, the German rifle weighing heavier across his back. Then he slipped his hand into his pocket, the rough scrape of the paper against his fingertips sending a tingle up his arm.

I hope you feel as keenly as I do, the miracle of our words spanning these many miles to find each other. He closed his eyes, thinking about her smile, immortalized in the photograph tucked in his pocket.

"You know, Cap," he murmured. "I'm starting to believe in the unbelievable."

Woodley smirked. He raised his hand, slapping his palm down on Bernie's shoulder. He sunk his fingers in, giving him a gentle shake.

"Okay, Russell. Sure." He inhaled, pausing a moment. "I want you and Bruno to hang back a bit. I don't want you in the heat for a while, okay? I'll let Norton and Ellis know."

"You don't have to do that, sir."

"Yeah, I do. I'm gonna need the two of you to pull your weight when we reach Germany. So this is, quite literally, the least I can do for you now."

Bernie opened his mouth to respond, but Woodley was already walking away to rejoin his lieutenant and sergeant. Taking a breath, he called out.

"Hey, Cap!"

Woodley looked back.

"I'm not crazy. I swear to God I'm not crazy."

The captain's face softened with compassion. The look reminded Bernie of the way his mother used to look at him when she was trying to be patient. That longsuffering, gentle look only a parent can give to a child.

"I know, Bernie," Woodley replied. "You'll be fine, son."

Bernie's stomach dropped. He bowed his head, taking Margot's letter back out of his pocket.

I pray my words give you the same comfort yours gave to me, and perhaps you will find a way to write to me again. Bernie raised his eyes, catching sight of the soldier he sought before jogging forward.

"Graham!" he gasped, breathless as he came to a stop beside his friend. "You got any paper left?"

Graham's brow arched. "A couple of small pieces from my notepad."

"I need to borrow some if you can spare them. It's important."

Chapter Twelve

BERLIN, GERMANY

How many weeks had passed? Three? Four? Margot had stopped counting after the first five days—the emptiness of the house in the aftermath of Gretl and Sofie's departure creating a hole in her heart she hadn't been prepared for. When she closed her eyes, she could feel her mother's arms around her and the soft press of her lips on Margot's temple in a goodbye kiss. She could feel still feel the cool dampness on her cheeks when Sofie had pressed close to whisper in her ear.

Soon we will be safe, tochter, and we will start a new life. Come after me soon. Her mother's words rang in her ears, overwhelming her nearly to tears.

Feet dragging, she walked away from the school, her soul as heavy as her heart. The empty seat in her class today had distracted her to no end, as well as catching the attention of her other students. They'd stared at Brigitte's vacant chair and easel, whispered amongst themselves when they thought she wasn't looking, and stole telling glances at Margot herself throughout the day.

How fast had her prying neighbors spread the word of her chasing the gestapo? How far across the city had word reached that Brigitte was arrested in the Raskopf home?

Fast and far enough that my students knew. Margot stopped at the corner, clutching her portfolio to her chest.

A heady musk filled her senses, alerting her instantly to a man's presence near her shoulder. Margot kept her eyes forward, his body heat tingling through her when he took another step closer. Then his hot palm pressed into the small of her back.

"Take a walk with me," Rolf breathed near her ear. "I have some news for you."

"Too dangerous." Margot's eyes darted, watching every person walking down the street. Feeling their gazes when they passed. "They're watching me."

"This won't take long. I am simply a friend walking you home." Taking her wrist, he tucked her hand through the crook of his elbow and guided her across the street.

Margot dug her fingers into his sleeve, her blood warming as she attempted to stay calm. He was being bold today, which was of little comfort to her. Perhaps after what she'd done, he thought being seen together during the day wouldn't make much difference anymore.

Or maybe what he has to say cannot wait. Margot's stomach twisted. Good news was not likely to come from Rolf if he was willing to show his face in such a public place.

Their pace quickened as he turned her down another street, reaching into his coat pocket.

"Your *mutter* was forced to change course at the checkpoint," he murmured, setting her heart on fire. "It may take them longer to get across the border now."

"But she is safe?" Margot asked, breathless.

"*Ja*, she is safe." He covered her hand with his, pressing on her knuckles firmly. "You need to leave the city, Margot. Everything is in order. Your papers, your course … it is simply a matter of when."

"Soon, Rolf. I promise." Margot glanced over her shoulder at the sound of a truck passing on the street behind them.

"I have something for you." He dug in his pocket, coming back with an envelope. "He's getting closer to our borders, so this one came faster."

Fingers shaking, she took the envelope, hastily hiding the missive in her pocket.

"One day, you will have to explain to me how this was possible," she commented with a smile.

"It's complicated. But I have friends in France." Rolf gave her hand a gentle pat. "Keep your head down, *kleiner*. As soon as you're ready, I will get you out of here."

He slipped away, disappearing down an alley. Margot didn't slow her pace, continuing along her usual route toward home. Every corner she turned, every grumble of a car engine, she was certain it was the gestapo. Watching her—stalking her. Her neighbors had never been so quiet in the early hours of evening. Quieter since the gestapo came to take Brigitte away.

They're afraid to associate. Margot winced, hurrying up the path and through her front door.

"Margot?" Ilse called from the direction of the kitchen.

"*Ja*, Ilse, it's me."

Margot slipped the pin from her hat, hanging it on the peg beside the door before making her way to the parlor. Ilse announced there would be tea and biscuits in five minutes. Hoping this would give her enough time, she sat down at her father's desk, taking the new letter from her pocket. She smiled, tracing the handwriting with her fingertips, hardly believing he'd been able to get the note to her so quickly. The flap of the envelope snapped softly when she opened it, removing the wrinkled pages from within.

The paper was smaller than his first letter, edges jagged as if ripped from a diary. Margot rested her forearms on the desk, leaning forward as she began to read.

Dear Margot,

I can't even begin to describe what it meant to me to receive your letter. Thank you for your explanation about the photographs. There are no words to express what I am thinking in light of what you've told me is going on in Poland. But the truth stares at me every day in the photographs, and I find myself overwhelmed with more questions. The most prominent being ... who took the pictures.

Margot paused, smiling. If he only knew she asked herself the same question every day. The photographs had arrived into the hands of Rolf by an anonymous source. She always wondered if perhaps they'd been taken by someone within the camps. Perhaps a guard trying to fight back from the inside? Like so many other questions in these times, this one would probably go unanswered.

As I write this, your questions flood my mind. How did I get my letter to you? Not easily. That first letter took a journey from Normandy to London and—somehow—into Berlin. I had little hope the man I entrusted my letter to would be able to fulfill my request. Imagine my surprise and elation when your response arrived, informing me my efforts had not been in vain.

You also asked me why I wrote to you. When I read your letters the first time, something changed. I was compelled to know you better. I was drawn to you in a way I have never been drawn to anyone before. Your words spoke to something deep inside me. Perhaps you think I am strange, feeling the need to reach out to you. I suppose you sensed there was more to my reaching out than simply wanting to tell you what happened to your brother. I can't really explain it.

All I know, is you gave me something without even knowing. Before you even knew I existed, you were giving me a reason to put one foot in front of the other. After

Africa, Italy, and Omaha, I was in desperate need. What I didn't tell you in my first letter, was that *you* gave *me* hope. In letters you wrote that weren't even meant for me, you unknowingly gave me hope.

I wrote to tell you what happened to your brother, because I never knew what happened to my mother. My own father didn't tell me how she died nor did he give me a chance to say goodbye and be at peace. I knew I needed to give you that gift—of knowing. Of saying goodbye. Who you were, where you were from, simply didn't matter. I couldn't let you live the rest of your life without answers.

You said in your letter you hoped I felt as keenly as you did regarding the miracle of our correspondence. I want you to know I do. In a war, I think a lot of people lose faith in miracles. I was one of those people. Until the moment your letter came into my possession. Believing the unbelievable has never been my strongpoint. You've made me believe in the impossible. You've made me believe in miracles.

Forgive the awful sheets of paper. I had to borrow them from a friend. I hope this letter finds you well and safe. Perhaps this will be our last correspondence as I am now continuously on the move, but I certainly hope not.

I do not know how many of our forces may travel into Poland. But I hope we do so we can find these places. I hope some of us are able to help—to put an end to the horrors I see in your photographs. To show the world what's been happening there. Crimes far beyond anything anyone ever imagined.

Please, Margot, keep yourself safe.

Your friend,

Bernie

The pages crackled as she gathered them together, folding them gently back into the envelope. The rattle of teacups behind her brought her around in the chair, smiling at Ilse while hiding the letter away.

"How was school?" Ilse asked, setting the tray down.

"Uneventful." Margot gripped the back of the chair, pushing herself onto her feet. "Why don't you pour yourself some tea? I think I'd like to change my dress and freshen up a bit. I won't be long."

Ilse's eyes glittered with concern as she settled herself on the settee, hands folded neatly in her lap. She didn't reply, her silence almost worse than her searching gaze following Margot all the way out of the parlor.

Once in the privacy of her room, she kicked off her shoes and crawled beneath her bed. The loose wedge lifted away easily before she stuffed her hand beneath the board, returning with her diary. Replacing the board, she crawled back out, settling herself on the edge of her mattress as she opened the little book.

The entries dated back nearly to the beginning of the war. Every private thought she'd had about the way Germany was changing. Every hint of rebellion that raged through her heart even now, caressed these pages in her harsh, sometimes frantic, script. And to accompany them, were the sketches.

Page after page, sketches of Horst, Ilse, her mother and brothers. A few of her father, though those had become painful to draw. Closing her eyes, she wondered what Bernie Russell looked like. In her mind, she could picture a strong man. Fierce but gentle. With sparkling eyes, a handsome grin. Perhaps blond ... no. No, dark haired, brown or black curls. Maybe with a mustache as well.

Margot grinned, shaking the multitude of images from her mind. She stepped across the room holding the diary against her heart as she reached into her desk draw for a sheet of brown paper and a string. Pressing a kiss to the cover of the diary, she laid it flat on top of the paper then opened it, tearing out a blank page.

Using one of the pencils, she scribbled a quick note, her heart aching to say so much more but knowing there was truly no time to waste. This could very well be the last letter she ever sent, and she needed it to be on its way as quickly as possible. Folding the page, she rested it on top of the diary, then proceeded to wrap the book in the brown paper, carefully folding every edge before sliding the string beneath it. She twisted the string multiple times, making sure the package was completely secure before tying it off tight.

In the corner of the rectangle, she wrote his name. The name of one of the only people left in the world she trusted. The name of a man she'd never laid eyes on.

Bernie Russell.

A tear splashed on the package before she even realized she'd started to cry.

★★★

Lying shoulder to shoulder with Ilse, Margot stared up at the stars shining down on them. They'd turned out all the lights before tiptoeing outside in their nightgowns. The neighbors were quiet, making her heart settle in the warmth of the summer evening. Moments like these, when the city was quiet and the sky was glittering with millions of stars, she could almost forget the dark cloud hanging over them.

"What made you think of doing this?" Ilse wondered. "We were children the last time we snuck out to lie under the stars."

Margot took Ilse's hand, interlocking their fingers. "*Ja*, I remember. I've missed this. The peace of simply lying under the dark sky, in the quiet of the evening. When was the last time we were so at peace, *mein schatz*?"

"Hmm," Ilse hummed. "Not for a long time, *mein freund*."

Breathing in the fresh, crisp air, Margot closed her eyes. Their fingers tightened together, the soft blades of grass tickling their palms.

"Your student, Sigrid, stopped by today," Ilse announced. "She was disappointed you were still out."

Margot frowned. "Did she come to paint?"

"*Ja*, I think so. I let her borrow some of your supplies. I hope you don't mind."

"*Nein*, that's all right."

Ilse inhaled, her breath shaky. "How much longer, do you think, until we can leave?"

Margot's lashes fluttered, her cheek brushing on the grass when she looked at her friend. The shadows and starlight emphasized every contour of her delicate features— making her porcelain skin glow. For days now she'd been racking her brain, trying to find a way to convince Ilse to go on without her. Perhaps she could convince her that had to be the plan—for Ilse to go on ahead. Perhaps she could convince her it was safer if they didn't leave together but met up somewhere once out of Berlin.

She'll never believe me. Not the way Mama did. She'll know. Margot inhaled deeply, forcing a smile.

"Soon." Her weak answer whispered between them. She'd tell Ilse anything she wanted to hear—anything other than the bitter truth.

I can never leave Berlin. Not without the gestapo on my heels. Margot looked away when she heard a twig snap. Squinting in the dark, two of the shadows took form and she smiled.

"Someone's here to see you, Ilse."

Ilse sat up, fingers slipping out of Margot's grip. A relieved sigh slipped passed her lips as she scrambled to her feet, rushing across the garden into Gerhard's arms.

The spot she'd vacated was filled a few moments later by Rolf. A rough exhale deflated his chest as he settled on his back beside her.

"You have something for me?" he asked.

Margot nodded, reaching inside her robe for the small, square package. Her hand shook slightly when she handed it over.

"This is the last one," she whispered.

Her heart sank, tears rushing to her eyes when her package vanished within the inside pocket of his jacket.

"You do know it will be harder now, don't you? The last I heard, his unit was approaching our borders. My resources can only infiltrate American forces so much ..."

"*Ja*, I know. That is why I will not put you, or them, at risk beyond this last package." Margot propped herself on her elbow, looking down at him. "You have been such a good friend to me in this difficult time, Rolf. I want you to know I am grateful."

Rolf's brow furrowed. "If you start talking to me like you are saying goodbye, Margot, I will leave."

"There's only a matter of time before they begin to question where my *mutter* is. Gretl will soon be missed as well." Margot stole a glance at Ilse, standing near the rose bushes with Gerhard. "I need you and Gerhard to convince Ilse to go. Before it's too late."

"How? She will not leave without you, Margot. Not unless we carry her out of the house screaming and bringing the gestapo straight to your door."

"She is in love with Gerhard. He can persuade her."

"*Ja*, she loves him, and he loves her. But you have been her family far longer than she's loved him. You know her greatest desire is for the two of you to leave together. She is living in a dream we all know will never come true."

Margot sighed, hand sliding across the ground to pluck gently at his sleeve. "And you? Will you also leave Berlin now the gestapo are breathing down your neck?"

"I will leave Berlin when every person I love is safe. Not before." He sat up, resting his forearms on his raised knees. "We shouldn't have come tonight. But I had—"

"A feeling?" Margot finished. "*Ja*, me too."

The pages crinkled as she revealed the remaining letters in her pocket. Eyes welling, she looked up at him again.

"I have to burn these," she said hoarsely. "I cannot risk keeping them anymore. I cannot risk his name falling into their hands. They will think I have been sending information to him."

Rolf shrugged. "Do you really think it matters? He is a soldier. How could they possibly find him?"

Margot shook her head. "You found him."

"My connections found him ... and just barely."

"All the same, I must keep him safe."

Rolf pulled off his cap, scrubbing a hand through his hair, agitated. "I still do not understand why he means so much to you. What did he say to you?"

Margot rubbed her thumb across his handwriting, smiling. Today, Bernie Russell had been a redhead with eyes greener than fresh grass. Today, his hands were large and rough but gentle. Today, he smelled like the woods. That crisp, earthy scent that rejuvenated her whenever she went for a walk in the park. He was six feet tall, a bit lanky but still reassuringly strong.

"I do not expect you to understand, Rolf. I am not even sure how to explain this connection I feel to a man I've never even seen," she whispered. "Can it be enough he does mean something to me?"

Rolf brushed his knuckles softly against her cheek.

"*Ja*, it can." He stood up. "Gerhard! Time to go."

"Be safe, *mein freund*," she said, head tilted back to stare at his face, shadowed in the dark.

"You too, Margot."

She watched them go, blending into the darkness as if they'd never even been there. Ilse stood for a moment, staring into the darkness where Gerhard had disappeared. She rubbed her arms, even though it was a warm night, before turning to bend over Margot. Smiling, she held out her hand.

"We should get some sleep," she said.

Margot accepted her hand, letting Ilse pull her back onto her feet.

"You go up." She tugged her forward in a warm hug. "There's something I have to do."

After they went inside and she'd waited for Ilse to disappear at the top of the stairs, Margot made her way into the parlor. The small lamp on the desk was shining, creating a dim glow in the room to guide her steps to the fireplace. Eyes welling, overflowing with tears, she slipped a match from the box atop the mantel. The letters shook in her hand, every fiber of her being fighting against what she knew she had to do.

Because if the gestapo were to come for her tomorrow, Bernie's letters would make things ten times worse.

Not only for me, but for Ilse as well. They will not believe she wasn't involved. Margot inhaled, her lungs inflating painfully.

The match hissed, a small flame blooming on the tip as she crouched in front of the fireplace. Hand trembling harder, she laid Bernie's letters down, the flame on the match flickering wildly. Her throat shuddered with a sob, the thought of his words being turned into ashes tightening her chest.

She'd read and reread them a hundred times today in preparation for this moment. Memorizing everything he'd said—tucking deep in her heart the words that had connected her to a stranger across thousands of miles. Clinging to the hope he'd given her. Those things wouldn't go up in flames just because his letters did.

With a gasp, she released the match, dropping it on top of the paper. They smoked and crackled, the pages curling as the fire licked at them hungrily. Margot closed her eyes, pressing her hand over her heart as she listened to some of the last treasures she possessed reduced to ash.

Chapter Thirteen

"Ach!" Margot growled when the tip of her pencil broke, leaving a black dot with a spray of gray dust across her sketchbook. The half-finished sketch of her mother effectively ruined, she tore the page from the book and collected a new pencil from her desk drawer to begin again.

Sigrid had been the last student to leave the classroom. There was something strange in her expression today. A mix of worry and fear—even a little sadness—glistening in her sky-blue eyes that set Margot on edge throughout the day. The lingering unease had made her itch for the calm sketching brought to her heart, fueling her decision to sit awhile longer in the quiet of her classroom.

She could hear the other teachers leaving, the sound almost strange after a summer spent with the building nearly all to herself. Bending over her sketchbook, she tried to drown the echo of their footsteps vibrating down the halls. She rested her temple on the heel of her left hand, fingers sinking into her loose hair as she began to outline the shape of her mother's cheeks. Attempting to immortalize the woman's face on paper, the way she'd been the last time Margot had seen her.

Smiling, despite her tears. Eyes filled with hope. The pencil moved swiftly, forming her mother's delicate brow, softly curved nose and full lips.

Just as she'd begun on the eyes, the soft rap of knuckles on her door brought her head up. Holding back a grimace, she forced a tight smile.

"Herr Metzger," she said, then raised her hand. "*Heil Hitler.*"

The man's upper lip curled, surprise pulsing through her when he didn't return the salute. Sauntering across the room, he settled comfortably on one of her student's stools, crossing his arms and hunching his shoulders.

"I am surprised to find you still here, *Fräulein*," he commented.

"Oh? Why?" Margot returned to her drawing, wishing she could ignore the roach-like man.

"I thought you might hurry home. Particularly today."

"*Ja?*" Her pencil moved faster, stroking and forming the irises of her mother's eyes.

"*Ja.* Do you not wish to know why?"

Margot sighed. "Will you tell me, even if I do not wish to know?"

His chuckle sent a thousand spiders crawling down her spine. "Do you know, Margot, I think I will."

"Then do proceed, Herr Metzger."

The stool creaked when he shifted his weight, the soles of his boots clicking softly on the floor when he planted his feet.

"You know, *Fräulein*, I was always curious about your cousin. I could not remember her ever having been mentioned in the many years I've known your family."

Margot went still, staring unseeing at her sketchbook. Herr Metzger stepped down off the stool, moving closer to her desk. The heavy sound of his steps echoed in her suddenly ringing ears.

"Then I remembered ... your *onkel* never married."

Margot took a breath. "That does not mean he didn't have a child. I never said Ilse was born in wedlock."

"True. But then I remembered the photograph you used to keep on your mantel. The one of your family with Dominik Baumann and his *tochter* ... Ilse."

Her heart was about to burst right out of her chest, swelling and thundering into her ribcage so hard she began to ache.

"You see, I had to be sure," Metzger continued. "I could not accuse a Raskopf without proof, of course. Then, I thought, what better way to get what I needed than through one of your students."

Margot's eyes closed.

"Were you not curious why Sigrid came to see you that day?"

Her fingers tightened around her pencil. "I was not home. Ilse let her in."

"Ah ... so you would have stayed with her the entire time, *ja*? You would not have given her the opportunity to tiptoe up to your room and remove the photograph from your dresser drawer, so carelessly overlooked by the gestapo."

"The gestapo did not know what Dominik looked like."

"Convincing Sigrid to betray you was not difficult in the end. A few well-placed threats against her poor little family and she was practically begging to be sent into your home to find the evidence."

Slowly, Margot raised her head, looking up into the man's cold, gleefully glistening eyes.

"Do not worry, Fräulein Raskopf. If the gestapo did not know what Dominik Baumann looked like before, they certainly do now."

Abandoning her sketchbook, she launched out of the chair, feet sliding on the slick floor in her haste to get out of the classroom.

"That's right, *Fräulein!*" his shout echoed after her. "Run home! Run home to your little Jew! They will be waiting there for you!"

The ringing in her ears rose to a high-pitched whistle. She couldn't breathe. Each gasp of air was painful as she raced out of the school and down the street toward home. Pushing people aside, leaping off and on the sidewalk to quicken her pace, lengthening her strides. She ignored every insulted shout—every pair of eyes that turned in confusion to watch her. She could barely hear them, her head spinning wildly, nearly stealing her sense of balance.

Margot stumbled to a halt at the end of her street, her eyes widening and burning when she caught sight of her house. Three vehicles were parked in a straight line in front of her fence, the gate hanging crookedly on its hinges, as if kicked in. The windows had been thrown open, torn mattresses in the yard—one hanging from an upstairs window—and feathers still settling in the air. Clothes, furniture, photographs, all scattered across the grass.

The shouting traveled down the street, the sounds of more glass breaking and feet stomping mixed in her ears. Two men emerged from the front door, pulling out cigarettes and chuckling among the ruins that was her life.

"*Psst!*" a hiss to the left made her jump. "Margot!"

Looking, she found Rolf crouched beside the house at the end of the street, keeping low to the ground as he used the building to hide. He gestured to her wildly, eyes large with fear.

"Come on, *kleiner!*" he ordered. "I can get you out of here!"

Margot almost took a step toward him—almost reached out for him so he could rescue her. Take her far away from this place.

Then the front door to her home opened again. Ilse came out, bare feet stumbling on the path. Weeping when one of the men gave her a firm shove, sending her violently onto the sidewalk. The sleeve of her dress was torn—a bruise blooming on her jaw where one of them had shown no mercy. She curled into a ball on the ground, hiding her eyes against the top of her knees with her arms wrapped tight around her shins.

No matter what happens, I will always be with you. Margot's words screamed in her mind, sending her heart rocketing into her chest.

Rolf's face blurred behind a rush of tears. They spilled over, moistening her cheeks. Slowly, she shook her head and clenched her hands into fists at her sides so they wouldn't shake. Taking one step, then another, she started walking toward her house. Keeping her eyes fastened on Ilse.

Suddenly, all she could think about was Herr Nussbaum. A kind old man who'd packed his suitcase and walked proudly out of his shop into the gestapo's custody. He had not fought. Had not shouted or even wept when they'd thrown his instruments to their destruction on the street. When they'd destroyed everything he'd ever touched. If they could have burned his shop to the ground without risking the other buildings surrounding it, they would have.

And he bore it like no one else. Margot tilted her head up, wiping the tears from her face as she came closer.

The gestapo looked surprised by her approach, as if they couldn't quite believe what they were seeing. None of them stomped over to grab her. None of them even said a word as she came to a stop beside Ilse. Gently, she went to her knees, gathering Ilse in her arms. Tucking the crown of her head beneath her chin to stroke her back soothingly.

"I am here, *mein schatz*," Margot whispered. "You are not alone."

A pair of glistening boots appeared in front of them. Margot lifted her head, bending her neck sharply to stare up at Joachim.

"I tried to keep you safe," he hissed. "I've done everything in my power, Margot. But this ... I could not make any excuses for this."

Margot pursed her lips, anger quickly replacing the fear tightening her chest.

"Joachim," she rasped, another hot tear falling. "You. Did. Nothing."

The corners of his mouth turned down, thunderclouds coiling in his eyes. Then, he snapped his fingers.

"Load them into the truck. We're finished here."

Chapter Fourteen

NEAR THE GERMAN BORDER

Crouching with his back up against a tree, Bernie watched the invisible line between their division and enemy forces. The kid to his left kept checking his rifle—loading, chambering, reloading—maybe he thought the bolt was going to jam. Or maybe he was trying to distract himself from the impending fight. Either way, all his fussing didn't drown out Bruno's soft snores coming from the ditch in which the rest of the guys had taken cover.

Bernie swung his rifle around, resting the stock against his shoulder to peek through the scope. Supposedly, they'd reach their objective by tomorrow if they could push through this small cluster of Nazis at the top of the ridge.

I'm not worried about what's at the top of the ridge, more worried about what's on the other side *of the ridge.* Bernie exhaled heavily, zoning in on every shadow that moved passed the tree line.

The kid chambered again, the sound so loud in the night Bernie cringed.

"You wanna quiet down over there?" he snapped.

"I'm just trying to be prepared."

Bernie lowered his rifle slightly, eyeing the boy. "What's your name?"

"Jensen. Danny Jensen."

"Well, Jensen, Danny Jensen, I can assure you, your rifle isn't going to jam. So quit playing with it like it's a toy." Bernie leaned his head back, the back of his helmet thumping on the tree trunk. "You land on Omaha with the rest of us?"

"Yeah."

"Did your rifle jam then?"

"No."

"I think my point is made."

Jensen went quiet, only the soft rustle of his clothes briefly filling the air when he shifted his position.

"You're Russell, right?" Jensen asked, the question barely reaching Bernie's ears.

"Yup, that's my name."

"You're a sniper."

Bernie let his head lull toward his left shoulder, squinting at the young man in the dark.

"I heard about what happened in Marigny. How you got up on a roof and took out that sniper in the bell tower."

"Yeah, that's part of my job. So?"

Jensen cleared his throat. "I was just wondering, how'd you get to be such a good shot?"

Bernie smirked. "Practice. My uncle taught me—used to take me shooting all the time in the country when I was a kid. It's just years and years of practice."

"I heard you don't think you got the guy who killed Joey O'Donnell," Jensen continued, readjusting his helmet on his head to reveal another inch of forehead—the moonlight brightening his eyes. "Is that true?"

Bernie hesitated. Woodley and Ellis already thought he was crazy. Bruno even had his doubts about whether or not Bernie's eyes were playing tricks on him.

Is it a good idea to add another person into the equation? He exhaled, choosing to go with it.

"Yeah. And I don't think. I know."

Jensen stared at him a moment longer, the grim expression on his face igniting Bernie's curiosity. "Do you think you'll get a chance to kill him?"

"That's my intention if I see him again, yes." Bernie nodded.

Jensen hesitated, as if thinking about that for a moment. Then he murmured, "Good. O'Donnell was a friend of mine."

Bernie shook his head, returning his attention to the line. His mind drifted to the letter in his pocket. The edges worn, the crease thinning, close to tearing from having been read so many times. Closing his eyes briefly, he thought back to that little French town. How he'd quickly scribbled his response on the small pages from Graham's notebook. How he'd jogged down the streets, ignoring the curious stares of the other soldiers, slowly making the march out of the village while he searched every street.

Every street until he saw that scarf. That brightly colored scarf, resting over an abundance of dark, curly hair. Those compelling brown eyes that seemed to look straight through him to his heart. It was as if she'd been waiting for him to find her, standing on the corner by the baker's shop. She wasn't surprised to see him, that was clear as he handed her the letter.

"I don't have an envelope," he'd said the only thing he could think of at that moment.

"Do not worry," she'd answered, her English surprisingly good and her warm French accent not as thick as he would've expected. "I will take care of that."

The next questions burning on his tongue burst out. "Who are you? How did you find me?"

She'd merely smiled. "Good luck, Bernie Russell."

Then she'd turned, walking calmly away as she tucked his message to Margot in her pocket. His mother would've said the mystery of it all made the circumstances more romantic. Bernie would've preferred a few straight answers. He never had cared much for mysteries.

Opening his eyes again, he lifted his rifle to peer at the shadows moving across the ridge. If he let his thoughts run away with him, he could imagine a dozen Panzers. Thousands upon thousands of Nazis. Mortars and machine guns. All hiding on the other side of that ridge, waiting for them.

After another hour or two, the sun began to peek up over the ridge. Shuffling and snapping twigs brought Bernie's attention around, watching Ellis approach with Lieutenant Norton. Following close on their heels was a man Bernie had made a point of avoiding since Omaha. A face he'd never forget—burned into his memory during one of the worst moments of his life.

Carter. Bernie scowled.

Norton whispered something to Ellis before he walked away, heading for the group of men a few paces down the line. Ellis watched him go, shaking his head slightly before he approached, crouching beside the edge of the ditch. Bernie signaled for Jensen to join him, keeping their heads down as they jogged over to listen.

"So," Ellis paused, clearing his throat roughly. "We got our orders."

"We taking the ridge, sarge?" Bruno asked.

Ellis nodded. "This is going to be a rough one, boys, I'm not gonna lie. The enemy has the high ground, and we have no idea what's on the other side waiting for us."

"I can get up top," Bernie suggested, gesturing over their heads at the trees. "Pick off any machine gunners as you start the climb."

"Ordinarily I'd say yes," Ellis replied. "But Woodley wants you and Agnelli at the front this time, not the rear."

Bernie shrugged, the decision making little difference to him. As Ellis proceeded with orders and formations, Bernie found himself staring at the man crouching near the sergeant's right shoulder. The question of how Carter lived with himself teetered on the tip of his tongue, threatening to interrupt Ellis's orders. Hearing the sergeant, or not, didn't really matter—he'd just follow Bruno's lead. Besides, taking a ridge across nearly three miles of open ground seemed pretty straightforward.

"Hey, Russell?" Ellis reached over, nudging him. "You with us?"

"Yup. Right here."

"Okay. Let's get it done."

The sergeant stood up, leaping over the ditch. Carter started to follow when Bernie rose from his haunches, grabbing the private by the shoulder before he could get past him.

"We take prisoners this time," he hissed, looking into the man's dark eyes. "I swear, Carter, if I see you take out another unarmed man who's about to surrender, I'll report you to Woodley. Understood?"

Carter shoved his hand away, lip lifting in a snarl and muttering as he walked away. "Whose side are you on anyway?"

Bernie joined Bruno at the tree line, looking right then left. The thundering roar of their tanks making their way toward the front of the line was encouraging—perhaps the most beautiful sound Bernie had heard in a while. Hunching close to the ground, his shoulder brushed Bruno's. Ears ringing when one of their tanks let off a blast, eating at the ridge.

Bernie's heart raced. No matter how many times he did this, the moment the fighting began, his body always competed in a race between his heart and his lungs. Either his pulse was going to speed until giving out, or his lungs were going to explode with a held breath. But the minute they started the charge, he would calm. Because there was only one way to go from here.

Forward.

The tanks were tearing apart the ridge—the cut-off sounds of shouting from the other side making him cringe with each thundering explosion as their guys attempted to make the climb to the ridge safer for their units on foot.

To his far left, he caught sight of Woodley, standing at the front of the line. They'd be moving in on the ridge from the south, southeast and southwest. From his left and right, the mortar crews were beginning to set up right within the tree line, prepared to fire on the ridge should their men need the aid.

The tanks suddenly ceased fire, the ringing tremors of silence filling his ears. Jensen appeared on his right, sidestepping close to his shoulder.

"Mind if I stick with you?" he asked, fingers clenching tighter around the barrel of his rifle.

Bernie gave a single nod, turning back to the left to look at Bruno. His friend was rolling his shoulders, stretching his neck from side to side as he prepared for the impending charge up the hill. Bruno looked at him, not even sparing a glance to his weapon as he loaded up, every movement memorized after these years of fighting.

They didn't have to say anything. At this point, they knew if they were going down, they'd be going down together.

But we won't go down. Bernie squared his shoulders, bending slightly forward to get a glimpse of Woodley.

Breath held until his lungs began to throb, he waited for the signal to charge.

★★★

Thinking back to when he was a boy, Bernie couldn't help recalling one of the only times he and his father got along. Visiting his uncle's ranch in Montauk when he was eight years old, Bernie had decided he was going to learn how to ride a horse. His mother had been wary—his father had, surprisingly, agreed. He'd spent weeks on top of the gentlest horse in his uncle's stable with his father right at his side to make sure he didn't fall off. And the man who never seemed to smile, smiled at him that whole summer.

Even more surprising to him in this moment as he lay flat on the ground while the Nazis pelted their men with bullets, wasn't simply the memory coming to him, but the realization he would have liked the reassuring presence of his father right now. Despite their differences and the man's vindictiveness over the past few years, Bernie would never forget how comforting it was having his father at his side when he was a vulnerable eight-year-old sitting a full grown horse for the first time.

Rolling a few feet to the left, his shoulder rammed into Bruno's. Jensen appeared again on his right, breathing heavily—with nerves or exertion, he wasn't sure. He wiped the drops of sweat from his eyelashes, trying to clear his vision before lifting himself on his elbows to check the progress of the others.

Ellis was moving in from the left. Bullets spattering into the top of the ridge, followed by return fire from the Nazis. Bernie lifted himself onto his feet, taking a few stumbling steps up the ridge before crouching on his knees again. The blast of bullets slicing through the air attempting to deafen him as they inched closer toward their objective.

"Keep moving!" Woodley's voice bellowed, the sound seeming to come from every direction at once. "Go! Keep moving forward!"

Huffing and grunting, Bernie pushed himself further up the ridge. In the corners of his eyes, to both left and right, he could see Bruno and Jensen following close on his heels. The soil gave beneath the heavy fall of his boots, shifting underneath the pressure of his palm. Every scent, from the choking gunpowder to the moist earth, registered in his nose. And the unrelenting feeling that something wasn't quite right made each step harder.

They'd nearly reached the edge of the ridge, every muscle in his body tensing when he heard the soft *click* of Bruno's grenade releasing the pin.

"Everybody down!" Bruno shouted before swinging his arm.

Bernie watched for a split second, the explosive spinning through the air before disappearing on the other side of the ridge. He shoved his face down into the dirt, curling his legs up close to his ribs. The following *boom* made him shudder, then he was moving again, flipping himself up and over to the other side of the ridge.

"Argh!" Bernie grunted when he landed on the limp body of the machine gunner, rolling and sliding against the other side of the hill.

He was up the next second, slamming into the nearest body. One quick thrust of the stock of his rifle, the man's nose was broken. The squeeze of the trigger, and his enemy felt no more pain. Bernie jerked back at the spurt of blood before moving forward, tugging his bayonet loose from his belt.

When he'd landed in Africa, he would count how many bodies had piled in his wake. Now, he knew better. Keeping track didn't do anything other than make the next kill harder. Not thinking about it—simply pulling the trigger, thrusting the blade, or snapping a neck without pausing to contemplate his actions—did everything to keep him putting one foot in front of the other. When there was no choice but to kill ... there simply was no other way to get the job done.

His feet went out from under him, the pressure of the Nazi tackling him to the ground stealing the air from his lungs and threatening to crack a few of his ribs. Bernie brought his knee up, doubling the man over in pain before tossing him off and burying the bayonet in his chest. He didn't look at his face, pulling the knife loose before he started to rise.

"Get down!" Jensen's voice shouted.

Bernie's head swung, looking over his shoulder. His eyes widened. The boy had turned the machine gun around, the barrel pointed directly at him.

"Get down, Russell!" he repeated.

Looking back, Bernie dropped to his stomach, clearing Jensen's view for the oncoming group of enemy soldiers thundering toward him. The continuous *pop-pop-pop-pop-pop-pop* of the bullets whizzing over his head made him shiver. When the firing ceased, he raised his head, staring at the pile of bodies lying a few feet away.

Bernie lifted himself on his forearms, getting his feet back underneath him before rising. Shoulders tensed, bayonet still firmly gripped in his fist, he turned a slow circle, sparing a brief glance at Jensen who was gasping softly behind the smoking machine gun. Distant explosions rocked the ground, the fading sounds of men shouting and sporadic gunshots filling his ears.

Blood dripped from the blade in his hand, red smeared across his fingers and knuckles—staining the cuff of his sleeve. He wiped the bayonet clean on his pants before tucking it away on his belt again.

"Bruno?" he called, his voice a low croak.

"Here," Bruno answered to the left. He appeared at his shoulder a moment later, looking out over the terrain where the Nazis were beginning to pull back.

"You all right, Jensen?" Bernie bent, retrieving his rifle from the ground.

"Yeah." Jensen came toward him, lifting his feet high over the bodies in his path.

The three of them stood for a moment in silence staring at the carnage—watching some of their guys gather together those enemy soldiers who'd surrendered, while any who'd slipped their grasp were disappearing into the woods. Bernie frowned, squinting at the distant buildings rising high over the treetops to the south. He started to raise his rifle to get a better look through his scope when the heavy thud of feet behind him brought him around.

"What are you three standing around for?" Ellis mumbled, striding around them. "We're not done here yet."

"Everyone all right?" Woodley asked, following close behind the sergeant.

"All good, captain," Bruno answered.

"Glad to hear it." Woodley paused beside Bernie, his shoulders rising and falling with a deep breath. "Next stop, Aachen."

Bernie's brow creased.

"Aachen?"

Woodley eyed him, nodding slowly.

"That's right." He took a few steps forward then spun, backing away from them with his arms spread. "Welcome to Germany, boys."

Chapter Fifteen

Today, Bernie Russell had blue eyes. Hair as black as a midnight sky void of stars and skin a glimmering olive color. And a beard. Yes, today, Bernie Russell had a beard.

Margot's mouth trembled in a smile as her body swayed with the constant movement of the train. Her whole body ached—empty stomach rumbling angrily at her, demanding food. After their arrest, Margot had spent days wallowing in a dark cell, waiting for them to come with a final decision about what to do with her. Separated from Ilse and wondering if her dear friend had been processed to a camp already … wondering if her father's name would be her ultimate escape.

Now, sitting on the floor of a cattle car with Ilse sleeping against her shoulder, she'd give anything to whisper in Joachim's ear. To beg him, just once, to tell her to what fate they were being sent. But the last face she'd seen before getting on the train hadn't been Joachim's but Boehler's. What she didn't understand was why it had taken so long for them to decide? They didn't know about her connection to Rolf and his resistance. They only knew she'd harbored a Jew in her home.

So why so many days withering away in a prison cell? Margot let her head lull against the rough wood of the train compartment.

She tightened her arm around Ilse's shoulders, keeping her close. Listening to the heavy *whoosh* of the train flying down the tracks, the rattle of the wood with every shift and tremble of the cars. Margot could nearly lose herself in daydreams. She could pretend this train wasn't taking her to whatever punishment the Nazis had chosen for her but to freedom. She could pretend Joachim had reached out to every influence in his control, to every person who remembered her father's name, and had instead put her on a train to a new life far away from danger.

But when the train dipped with a turn in the tracks, unsettling the other prisoners in their car, every hopeful thought slipped away. Looking around the car, there was no escaping the truth. Those doors would not open and reveal a new, safe future for her. Wherever they were going would test her to her limits, she was certain.

Ilse moaned, her head falling slightly forward before she pushed away from Margot's shoulder. She rubbed her eyes before gently sliding her fingers through her loose hair.

"Where do you think we're going?" Ilse asked, drawing her knees up against her chest.

Margot curled her legs tighter beneath her, rubbing her arms to bring some warmth into her blood as another cold October breeze swept through the cracks in the walls of the car. The thin material of her dress wasn't enough to shield her from the dropping temperatures of autumn.

"I wish I knew, *schätzchen*," Margot replied.

There was one thing she knew for certain. Joachim had to have arranged for her and Ilse to be on the same train. There was no logical reason why they wouldn't have been separated by now. He must have altered some paperwork somewhere to have them sent to the same fate. She watched Ilse look around the car at the others. Mostly women, each keeping quiet and to themselves. Some with bruises and cuts, as if they'd sat for weeks in a prison cell as well being tortured for information while others looked as if they'd simply been snatched off the street. One woman even still wore a burgundy velvet hat atop a bundle of dark hair.

Margot shook her head. She'd allowed her braids to fall loose days ago, every strand lying light against her shoulders and down her back. Sitting here on the dirty floor of the train car with torn stockings, dust and dirt soiling her dress, she wondered how this woman managed to look as if she'd stepped out her front door for a social outing only moments ago.

"Margot." Ilse tugged on her sleeve. "I think we're stopping."

Margot's heart plummeted. She pushed up onto her knees, bending slightly to try to peek through one of the cracks. Her throat clogged when she caught a glimpse of barbed wire fencing and watchtowers before a building blocked her view.

The train came to a trembling halt and she spun away, pressing herself against the wall of the car as shouts could be heard on the other side of the door. Ilse scooted closer to her, the fear filling the car nearly suffocating her as the heavy door slid open.

"Out!" An officer shouted, the sunlight gleaming off his helmet. "*Schnell!* Out!"

Margot stumbled to her feet, holding tight to Ilse's arm as they hurried for the door, leaping out onto the platform. A hard hand shoved her shoulder, pushing them into a line with the other prisoners. Her head swung back and forth, taking in the filthy platform, the barracks in the distance, the barbed wire fencing and walls that seemed to stretch mile upon mile before her. The SS officers shouting rough orders at them as they were pushed further in.

She held onto Ilse tighter, knowing exactly where she was but too terrified to allow the word to formulate in her mind. Then Ilse stopped dead. Margot bumped into her, gasping as she tried to regain her balance.

"Oh, Lord ..." Ilse rasped.

"What? What Ilse?" Margot shook her arm.

Ilse looked at her, tears flooding her eyes. "Margot ... perhaps it was not a mistake we were sent *here*."

Margot's brow pinched and then she turned, looking where Ilse pointed. If there had been anything in her stomach, she would have been rid of it in an instant. The first thing she saw was his broad back—the SS uniform framing his perfectly square shoulders and his black belt and boots gleaming in the sunlight. A hint of his dark golden hair peeked from beneath his hat, snipped across the nape of his neck in a perfect line.

Then he turned and she saw a flash of gorgeous blue eyes—eyes she knew so well. Eyes that had once held love and compassion. That glittered with happiness whenever she would walk into the room. Eyes that glowed with protectiveness whenever she came to him crying.

Eyes she never wanted to see so tainted with darkness, as they were now.

"Franz?"

***

Margot had never cared for short hairstyles. Instead of following the latest fashion, she had preferred to let her hair grow. Allowing her tresses to fall down her back, nearly to her waist. Preferring the braided styles her mother had always pinned them up in instead of the shorter, curled styles many ladies her age had chosen.

She supposed, when forced to have one's hair cut nearly to the scalp, most women would cry. But looking at the female officer who'd taken the shears to her tresses, she'd refused. Hair could grow back—she was not concerned about that. And she would not give them the satisfaction of her tears over something so frivolous. They might take many things from her here, but she would hold her head high.

At least, that was what she told herself as she was forced to strip down to her skin. Forced to bathe herself in a room full of other women with no privacy. Attempting to ignore the intrusive gazes and lewd comments of the male guards. Forced to sit at a table while a number was harshly etched into her arm forever with ink. Forced to don a rough, striped dress and worn, old brown boots before being shoved out a door to be inspected by the SS guards.

All of those things, she could bear. Until the moment they pulled her from the inspection, separating her from Ilse. Dragging her away, past block after block, out of sight of the one person she'd been determined to cling to for what little remained of her life. Now, she stood in the middle of a room surrounded by Nazi propaganda and facing a large desk neatly organized with stacks of files, stationery, and books.

But why? Margot inhaled deeply, her chest inflating painfully.

Her mind was still attempting to fully process everything she'd been through in the last hour. A heavy haze had fallen over her, filling her head with smoke. Numbing her entire body as she replayed their arrival over and over in her mind.

Franz. Oh, Franz! Why did you never tell me you were stationed here? Margot swallowed the tears clogging her throat.

"Fräulein Raskopf," a gruff male voice said, followed by the thud of heavy boots. "Welcome to Auschwitz."

Margot raised her gaze from the floor, watching the uniformed man stride behind the desk, tossing his gloves on top of the files before clasping his hands behind his back to observe her.

"Commandant Höss," she whispered, the rasp of her voice foreign to her own ears.

"This is highly irregular, as I'm sure you're aware," the commandant said, as if she'd not spoken. "I do not usually … meet … with the prisoners."

Margot lifted her head a bit higher, clenching her teeth. What could she possibly say to this man? What did he want? She stared at him, his hair neatly combed back from his broad forehead, his triangular nose twitching as if it itched and his round cheeks puffing out slightly with a breath. She had seen Höss once before, several years ago near the outbreak of the war. They had attended an event with her father where several highly regarded SS officers were present.

The truth was, she'd barely thought about this man since that day. She'd heard his name once when word first reached them about Auschwitz, but her thoughts had been preoccupied at the time. Now, facing the man in command over the camp in which she was now imprisoned, she wished she'd paid more attention. She wished she knew more about him.

"However, when I heard you were to be transferred here as an inmate, I thought it best I speak with you in person." Höss shifted slightly, tilting his head.

"Forgive me, commandant, but … why?" Margot asked.

The guard at the door started to move toward her, a breath hissing through his teeth as he prepared to say something. But Höss raised his hand, waving off whatever reprimand the man was going to give.

"You can go," he told the guard.

Margot's heart nearly stopped, the thought of being alone with the commandant unsettling. Even the guard looked a bit wary as he took a backward step then turned, slipping quietly out the door.

"Your *bruder* has been a loyal soldier to our *Führer*. He has repeatedly shown his faith in our cause here at Auschwitz. So when I heard you were to come here under arrest, you can imagine I was ... concerned. For Franz."

Margot winced, her fingers slowly curling into fists at her sides.

"I do not doubt his loyalty, so you may rest assured he will not suffer any consequences for what you have done."

She swallowed the lump in her throat. "*Danke*, commandant."

"However," he continued. "For his sake alone as a trusted guard in this camp, I wanted to offer you some ... help."

"Help?" Margot's brow pinched.

"*Ja*, help." Höss leaned forward. "There are ways of making this go away, Margot. Ways ... of making *you* go away. I could, with the stroke of my pen, declare you dead and have you sent away to a new life. You could never return to Germany, of course, but to avoid trouble for your *bruder*, and in memory of your father, this I could do."

Margot's lips pressed tight. She could hardly believe what she was hearing. Was he actually offering her a way of escape? Was he actually suggesting a way out of all of this? Simply because he was fond of her brother?

I don't believe it. Margot shook her head slowly.

"Why would you do this? Forgive me, commandant, but I cannot believe you would do such a thing for a *guard* in your camp."

"Not any guard, Margot. A Raskopf."

Margot's eyes narrowed, her fingernails digging deep into her palms. "I came here with a girl. A Jewish girl called Ilse Baumann. Would she too be released?"

Höss's lips pursed tight. "*Nein*, of course not. This offer is for you alone."

Margot started to shake her head, opening her mouth to refuse his offer when he sighed, pressing his palms into the desk.

"Come now, *Fräulein*. You have always been a *gut* little German girl. You have always been true to your country. You are an artist! Already you have wasted your talent, your life, by consorting with a Jew. This is your chance to be a *gut* German girl again. Show me now you are still that girl. Be true to your *bruder*."

Margot stared at him, the urge to giggle bubbling so fiercely in her chest she wasn't sure she would be able to contain herself. Then she took a breath, releasing her fingers from their fists so they lay limply at her sides.

"You are right, commandant. I have always been a *gut* German girl. But, I think, you and I have very different definitions of what being a *gut* German girl is." She tilted her head higher. "If Ilse stays, I stay. I reject your offer."

The commandant's eyes darkened. "Very well."

He barked the guard's name, calling him back into the room. Margot didn't even feel the man take her by the arm, dragging her toward the door.

"Oh, and *Fräulein*?" Höss said as they reached the door.

She looked over her shoulder with a questioning frown. He wasn't even looking at her, instead rearranging the files on his desk carefully.

"I thought perhaps you'd like to know. Your *mutter* was stopped at the border."

Ice engulfed her, swallowing first her bones then traveling through her blood before surrounding her heart.

"Gretl Krüger was a fool. Stupid woman thought to give your *mutter* a chance by stepping in front of a rifle. She died instantly." Höss sighed, as if the story was tedious to tell. "As for Sofie Raskopf ... well, what a true shame it was. Shot three times in the back, running for the border. They say she took a while to fade away. But she did die, eventually."

Margot's legs trembled, her chest convulsing with short, painful breaths. Höss waved a dismissive hand.

"Take her away now," he ordered.

Her feet stumbled over each other as the guard yanked her out of the building into the cold October air. They had taken only a few steps before her stomach heaved, what little food was inside her splattering on the damp path. The guard let out a shout of disgust, shoving her to the ground. Margot curled up tight, covering her head with her arms.

"You little—!" He raised his rifle, as if to strike her with it.

"Stop!"

Margot pulled her arms down, eyes opening wide to stare as Franz came striding across the path. He bent over, hauling her back to her feet. The desire to fall into his arms— to cling to him the way she did when she was in trouble as a child—nearly overwhelmed her. But instead, she stood at arm's-length from him, allowing him to hold her firmly by the wrist.

"I will take her from here," Franz said sternly.

The other guard hesitated, looking back and forth between the two of them briefly. Then he nodded slightly, turning to march away.

Leaving Margot standing in the middle of the path staring at the stranger who was her brother.

Chapter Sixteen

*M*y name is Ilse Baumann. I am a German. I am a Jew. I will survive this.

Ilse's shoulders shook. Her feet nearly slipped out of her boots as she walked across the compound, following the SS guard away from the last place she'd seen Margot. The chill of mid-October prickled her practically bald scalp, reminding her of everything they'd stripped from her. Her dignity, her beauty, her friends and family.

Papa. Papa died here. Ilse's breath froze in her lungs.

She never dreamed when she left Leipzig that she would end up in a place like this. The journey she had taken, the path she'd traveled to the Raskopf's front door ... it was not supposed to lead here. She was supposed to escape! Her father fought for her to escape, to survive the war and live her dreams.

So, what will happen now? Ilse couldn't breathe, unable to stop herself from looking over her shoulder—back in the direction where her hand had been pulled out of Margot's. Where they'd cruelly separated them for reasons they did not care to explain.

Jagged nails dug into her arm harshly, and Ilse hissed through her teeth, head jerking harshly to the right where she found another inmate at her side. The woman was a bit taller than she, her thin frame covered in the baggy, striped uniform of the rest of the prisoners and—like Ilse's own—a yellow star alongside a row of numbers glared at her on the woman's left shoulder.

"Do not look back," the woman hissed, her sunken cheeks tightening as the Yiddish words flew off her tongue. "The Beast will see and if you look at her, you will be gone."

The Beast? She did not ask which guard the woman meant—she did not want to know.

"Gone?" Ilse whispered.

One of the woman's thin brows arched, eyes darting toward the smoke billowing into the sky from one of the larger buildings in the distance. A lump blocked Ilse's throat, heart rocketing faster against her chest. The sudden desire to reach out for the woman beside her nearly overwhelmed her. So long since she'd spoken Yiddish! Not since she'd left Leipzig—not since she'd spoken her last words to her father had she uttered a word in Yiddish.

The guard glared over her shoulder at them, freezing her into silence. Ilse breathed slowly, clenching her toes to drag her boots out of the mud with each step she took. Her knees ached with every strained step, the urge to look over her shoulder stronger since the woman told her not to. Subtly, she leaned toward her fellow prisoner.

"Where are we going?" she asked, voice barely above a whisper.

The woman frowned at her. "Did Raskopf say nothing?"

Ilse shook her head slowly, the thought of Franz twisting a new knot in the pit of her stomach. Seeing him standing there—knowing all this time since he'd left Berlin this was where he'd been assigned—had shattered her. In that moment, all she could think about was the summer she was thirteen when the Raskopf family had made the trip from Berlin to Leipzig to spend their vacation with her family.

Franz had seemed so dashing to her back then—so handsome and sweet compared to the other fifteen year old boys she knew. What's more, he'd noticed her. She'd received more compliments from him that summer than she had in her entire life, and when he'd smiled at her in that way ... well ... she couldn't help but kiss him. No one except Margot had ever known she'd given her first kiss to Franz Raskopf. Their infatuation was forbidden, of course, considering Franz wasn't Jewish.

Gerhard is not Jewish either. Ilse sighed heavily, knowing the man she'd picked to be with for the rest of her life would have disappointed her father.

"You do have medical experience, don't you?" the woman continued, taking no notice of Ilse's silent contemplation. "The guard, Raskopf, said you did."

Ilse blinked slowly, wondering why Franz would say such a thing. Certainly, she'd volunteered a few times at the hospital and yes, her father had been a doctor, but she herself had never had any interest in the field or ever paid particular attention to her father's work.

"They are assigning you to the infirmary."

The sickly sweet, smoky scent permeating the air made her head spin. Ilse attempted to process what this woman was saying as they passed through another block—the guard taking her farther and farther away from Margot. The sense they were being separated—that she was purposely being disoriented so she couldn't find Margot again—overwhelmed her with every single step. The smaller the gates grew in the distance behind her, the greater her surety she'd never see her best friend again became.

Panic tightened her chest—bile burned her throat. The woman's hand tightened.

"If the guard lied," she hissed in Ilse's ear. "Do not let them know. Do as I do. Your only job now is to stay alive and keep out of their way."

Ilse nodded slowly. "W-What is your name?"

The woman's eyes flickered with uncertainty, the corner of her mouth tugging as if resisting a slight smile.

"Rivka," she finally answered.

"I am Ilse," she replied.

Rivka dipped her head in a single nod, gentle warmth pooling in her bloodshot eyes. Staring into the woman's shadowed gaze, Ilse couldn't help but wonder where she'd come from. Who she'd been before she too was callously taken from her home and placed behind these treacherous walls.

The fences hummed whenever Ilse came close enough to hear. The distant, heart-stopping sounds of people screaming in agony followed shortly by a deafening silence that nearly brought her to her knees, all worked together to shatter her soul.

Ilse kept moving, forcing herself not to lose pace as the guard approached one of the many looming buildings. Constructed much like one of the barracks they'd passed, it seemed to stand alone on this side of the camp. There was something halting about the place—as if one could sense they should not enter without warning.

Her gaze darted to Rivka who would not look at her. In fact, she seemed reluctant to even look up from her own feet in the mud, keeping close on the guard's heels. Ilse did the same, biting her lip to resist speaking. Perhaps if she simply followed Rivka's example, everything would be all right after all.

The guard shoved the door to the building open, motioning harshly for Ilse and Rivka to enter. Their shoulders brushed as they stepped through the door at the same time, Ilse coming to an immediate halt as she raised her gaze from the floor.

First, she was struck with how large the room was, and yet how small. People crowded on the floor—every thin, wiry cot occupied by a body. Some moved ... some didn't. Others groaned, coughed, vomited ... the rest lay in silence.

Some walked among them, seeming to make attempts to help ease their suffering. At the back of the room, she saw one woman, also wearing the same drab work dress she'd been forced into upon her arrival, wrapping another woman's head in a soiled bandage. Her elbows stuck out beneath her skin—the grey pallor of her face almost as sickening as the stench of excrement and urine confined to the unfiltered air of the building. But she was standing and helping, and she did not waver.

Ilse followed Rivka further into the room, blood like ice in her veins as she passed the cots—the ringing in her ears overwhelming their pitiful pleas for help.

They stopped in front of the woman with the bandages, Ilse's body unmovable when her marble black eyes fell upon her.

"You have come to help?" she asked, hoarse voice booming in the room.

Ilse's tongue turned dry as dust, unable to form an adequate answer.

How can I help when I do not even know where to begin? Oh Margot, where are you?

★★★

Franz spun Margot off the path, tugging her between two of the blocks. He turned her around, her back bumping into the wall before he released her. Franz took a few steps away, resting his hands on his hips with his head bowed. Margot watched him cautiously, holding fistfuls of her skirt in her hands. Her head spun with anything and everything she could say to him at this moment. But, after a few unbearable moments of silence, she said the words most prominent in her mind.

"Did you know?"

Her brother faced her again, his eyes darkening with thunderclouds.

"About what?"

"Mama and Gretl. Did you know?" Margot wrapped her arms around her ribs.

As if summoned, an icy breeze swept over her, raising gooseflesh on her arms and legs, even her scalp—reminding her how closely her head had been shaved. She didn't want to touch her head, knowing there would be nothing there but prickly stubble.

Hair will grow back, she reminded herself again, putting aside what vanity she had left.

The delicate skin around her brother's eyes tightened, his mouth thinning into a straight line. Then his head jerked in a quick nod.

"*Ja*, I received word," Franz replied, shrugging his shoulder indifferently. "I commended the soldiers for their actions against two enemies of the *Führer*."

Margot could resist no longer, her eyes welling and overflowing. "How could you say such a thing, *mein bruder*?"

"Our *mutter* was attempting to cross the border with false papers acquired by traitors." Franz's face never changed—mouth tight, eyes narrowed nearly to slits. "And you, Margot, hid a Jew in our home."

"Ilse, Franz! This is Ilse we speak of!" Margot reached out, grabbing him by the sleeve. "Ilse, who picked wildflowers with me when we were ten. Ilse, who sang songs with you and Hans around a campfire. Ilse … who was your first kiss." She shook his sleeve fiercely.

Franz brushed her off, taking a step away. Margot's heart began to harden once more, a fire rising in her belly to engulf her chest.

"Ilse, who you knew our father was trying to protect." She moved closer, not allowing him to put distance between them. "Does your precious Commandant Höss know that, Franz? What would he say if he knew Papa had taken Ilse under our roof before you left Berlin? That you *knew* she was living with us before you received your orders?"

Franz stared at her, the sudden drop of color in his face and his hands trembling into fists at his sides telling her all she needed to know. Margot shook her head.

"So, you live a lie within these fences. Do you truly believe in what is happening here, Franz? Have I lost you too?"

Still he didn't answer. Instead, he took her arm, turning her roughly around back toward the path. She stumbled in the muck alongside him, the sting of his large fingers sinking into the soft flesh of her arm making her cringe.

"You will be working in the kitchens," he announced. "If you are pulled from duty in the kitchen, you will sort clothing or help in the children's camp."

"Why? Why have I been chosen for such duties?" Margot pressed him.

Franz didn't spare her a glance, continuing to drag her across the compound. Her stomach churned when a group of inmates went by. Some of the women wore scarves over their heads, their bodies thin as rails and cheekbones prominent in their faces. Their skin, a horrid shade of gray. Margot shuddered, searching every face they passed for Ilse. Hoping beyond hope that in the vast expanse of the camp, she'd be able to find her again.

"Do as you're told, Margot," Franz hissed. "Follow instructions, do not fight back. Survive. That is all I have to say to you."

He yanked on her arm, bringing her to a sudden halt as he raised his opposite hand to signal one of the female guards. Then he turned to her, his mouth brushing against the soft skin above her ear.

"Horst is here."

Her eyes went wide, the pit in her stomach transforming into a million butterflies.

"W-What? How?"

"Do not ask me how. He has survived, where others in his ... *position* ... did not. I do not know how much longer he will last but he is here. I thought you'd want to know."

He started to turn to leave her in the hands of the other guard who was fast approaching. Margot took hold of his arm again, clinging tight.

"Tell me you are doing what you must to survive," she gasped. "Tell me you live a lie here. That *mein bruder* is still in there."

Margot placed her hand over the center of his chest. Subtly he raised his own, grazing his fingertips against her knuckles before he twisted away on his heels, striding across the camp without a backward glance. She watched him go, the turmoil roiling inside of her almost more than she could bear. Another breeze threatened to take Franz's hat from his head. She watched him reach up hastily, pressing his hand down on top of it to keep the article in place. He moved across the camp with such familiar ease.

Bile burned the back of her throat—the thought her brother was comfortable here shredded her heart.

"You are the Raskopf girl," the female guard hissed behind her.

Margot turned slowly, peering into the woman's fiery eyes. A smirk twisted her lip as she looked Margot over from head to toe. Then she nodded sharply over her shoulder.

"Follow me."

Margot obeyed, folding her arms tight across her ribs with shoulders hunched against the wind. Her shoes squished softly in the mud, the distant sound of the inmates at work, the stench of the smoke billowing from the crematorium chimneys, and the roar of the train departing from the platform flooded her ears.

"If you steal food, you will be shot," the guard announced, stopping in front of one of the buildings. She turned to face Margot, looking her over a second time. "There will be no exceptions."

"Of course," Margot whispered.

The woman hesitated a moment more before pushing the door open. She yanked Margot inside by the sleeve, the dimly lit room and rush of heat from the ovens making her squint her eyes tight. She was pulled across a rough wood floor and stopped in front of a crooked table, covered with potatoes.

"Peel," the guard ordered, slapping a small, dull knife in her hand.

Margot grazed her thumb along the blade, leaving not a nick in her skin. How was she to peel with this? Inhaling deeply, she picked up one of the potatoes, her stomach dropping when her fingers pressed in—the vegetable too soft. Realizing they were all on the verge of being rotten, her empty stomach tightened in a painful clutch.

She could feel the guard's gaze on her as she began to peel, her hand trembling slightly as she set to work. The soft shuffle of light feet across the floor brought her eyes up, watching a young girl come to the other side of the table. She was an inch or two shorter than Margot—in all likelihood, no older than eighteen—and patched to the right shoulder of her dress was a yellow star. Wrapped tight across the top of her head was a dirty gray scarf and when she reached for a potato, her fingers were red—calloused.

"You will get used to Geisler," she whispered, looking up at the guard through her lashes subtly.

Margot took a moment to register the Polish words slipping between the girl's lips, her mind racing with the translation. It had been so long since she'd practiced the language, she had to think for a moment before responding.

"What is your name?" she asked, keeping her voice just as low.

"Hanna," the girl answered. "Hanna Krakowski. You?"

"Margot Raskopf. I am glad to meet you, Hanna."

"No talking!" Geisler snapped, scowling at them. "Work!"

Hanna bent over her potato, slapping a similar knife to the one Margot held against the vegetable in a feeble attempt to remove the skin. They worked for a few moments in silence, the brownish color of the potato beneath the skin churning her insides.

"Your friend," Hanna whispered suddenly, keeping her head low. "Ilse?"

Margot's heart skipped a beat. "*Ja*. Is she all right?"

Hanna bobbed her head. "She is still alive. Selected for outdoor labor, I think. I do not know where she will bunk, but I saw her pulled from the line. For now, you are both as safe as any of us who were not selected for extermination."

Margot's breath came easier, the thumping of her heart lighter against her chest.

She is still alive. These words repeated over and over in her mind, whispering sweetly in her ear.

They were both alive. They'd survived the platform selection, the indignities, the brutalities. She'd survived the commandant's cruelty and her brother's indifference. Ilse had survived whatever the guards had put her through thus far.

We can survive the rest. Margot glanced over her shoulder at Geisler, watching the woman's stony face as she silently observed them at their work.

We will survive. We must.

Chapter Seventeen

AACHEN, GERMANY
MID-OCTOBER, 1944

"How many today, Graham?"

Bernie raised his head, blinking the crust of sleep from his eyes when Bruno asked the question. He cleared his throat, smacking his lips and working the kink out of his jaw. Every day he'd been waking up with teeth tightly clenched, as if even in his sleep he was expecting the worst.

"Three dead, ten wounded," Graham replied. He clamped the stub of his pencil between his teeth. "Better than yesterday."

"How many yesterday?" Jensen wondered, sitting against the opposite wall.

Bernie rested his rifle against the wall beside him, pulling out his colt next. With one quick tug and *click*, he put a bullet in the chamber while Graham checked his notepad for the numbers Jensen was asking for. Their howitzer had blasted hole after hole through the buildings of Aachen to keep as many of their men as possible off the streets and out of direct line of Nazi fire.

Now, sitting in the rubble up against a wall barely standing, he tried not to take stock of the destruction their guns had brought to one of the most beloved cities in Germany. Morales was behind the machine gun, Graham close to his shoulder with additional ammo, waiting for the Nazis to make the next move as well as on orders from their officers for their next move further into the city.

Shifting his colt from his right hand to his left, Bernie reached inside his jacket, tugging Margot's photograph loose. He brushed his thumb gently over the curve of her cheek, tracing the point of her chin and the full curve of her smile. He had her smile memorized now—such joy brightening her face. But he still couldn't determine what color her eyes were. Sometimes, holding it up so the light caught her image, he was certain her eyes were blue. Other times, staring at the darker rim around her pupil, he was sure they were brown.

Bernie shook his head, skimming his fingertips over the photograph again from her hair to her chin. It felt like such a long time had passed since he received her letter. There'd been no word—not from her or anyone else for that matter. No stranger to stuff a message in his pocket. Not one letter delivered for him when the other men received theirs. He could only pray the joy he saw in her picture hadn't faded. That her hope was still there.

He'd read her letter so many times the page was worn to nearly transparent. The crease where it was folded beginning to separate. He kept it tucked with her picture inside his jacket, along with the letters she'd written to her brother—both the originals and the copies Graham had written for him.

Sometimes, he stared at the letters she'd written to Hans. Despite not being able to understand the language, he still studied every page. Letting his fingers drift over the paper, tracing the very tip of his finger along the words. He supposed it was comforting enough that she'd written them.

"Twenty-two," Graham finally answered, breaking Bernie from his thoughts. "Twenty-two yesterday. All dead."

Jensen's helmet thumped against the wall when he let his neck bend back. "Yesterday was my birthday."

Bernie shared a glance with Bruno.

"No kidding," Bruno muttered. "Happy Birthday, Jensen. Hopefully you won't have too many more like this last one."

"How old are you?" Bernie wondered.

Jensen continued to stare at the ceiling, feet planted firmly, knees apart, and rifle clutched in both hands, standing upright between his legs. Then slowly, he lowered his gaze, looking Bernie in the eye.

"Twenty-two."

Every head turned, Graham lowering his notepad and Morales scowling over his shoulder.

"That's not funny, private," Bruno said.

"Wasn't a joke, Agnelli." Jensen shrugged his shoulders. His eyes glossed, still staring into Bernie's. "I turned twenty-two yesterday. Same day we lost twenty-two men. You ... you think maybe ... maybe I'm cursed or something, Russell?"

Before he could tell him how ridiculous that was, Bruno snorted.

"Yeah, maybe you're a jinx or something, Jensen."

"Bru," Bernie growled, nudging him hard in the ribs. Then he leaned forward. "Now you listen to me, Jensen. You are not—"

The crash of a bullet hitting the wall behind his head cut him off.

"Here we go again!" Bruno cursed, tripping over the rubble as he turned around and scrambled over to Morales's side.

Bernie thrust Margot's photograph back inside his jacket. Sliding up against the wall beside the window, he peeked out carefully, holding his pistol in both hands. The

M1919 suddenly went off—Morales pounding bullets across the street. Bernie watched the rounds hit, powder and pebbles spattering into the air.

Leveling the colt, he squeezed his right eye closed, aiming at the source of the enemy fire. He squeezed the trigger, the rebound jerking his wrists up. The bullet shattered the window across the street, followed quickly by the rapid patter of distant gunfire joining Morales's as the rest of the city came alive again. The blast of a howitzer rattled his ears as their men got to work clearing another path deeper into the city.

The glass right beside his cheek shattered and Bernie grunted, jerking away from the shards grazing his face. He slid back down, falling hard on the debris on the floor as he clutched the cut in his cheek.

"Berns!" Graham grabbed him by the shoulders. "You okay?"

"Yeah," Bernie huffed, every breath a wheeze as he raised his hand, staring at the spots of blood staining his palm. He shook his head, ignoring the hot sting of the insignificant wound.

"Ammo!" Morales shouted over his shoulder. "I need more ammo!"

Jensen fell beside him with a fresh supply, reloading the gun so Morales could continue returning fire.

Bruno was flat on his belly, his rifle poking through a hole about a foot wide in the wall. He peeked over briefly, waiting for Bernie to give him a reassuring nod before returning to his watch, firing off a shot every few seconds.

Ellis leaped through the opening in the wall, bracing his hand on the ground as he observed them.

"We're pulling back, boys," he announced.

Bernie's brow rose. "We're retreating from the city?"

"Not exactly. Just making room for a larger division to come through. We've lost too many guys and don't have the numbers anymore. Our relief is on the way."

"And if we don't feel like leaving?" Bruno asked, glaring over his shoulder. "We've held this position for hours, sarge. Why should we pull back now?"

Ellis took a deep breath. "Come on, boys. We gotta take what relief we can get. You've worked hard. You've done your duty, and our captain would like to see what's left of this division survive to the end of this mess."

"Come on, Bru," Bernie murmured. "I think we earned the break."

Bruno looked back and forth between him and Ellis. Then he nodded, dragging his rifle away from the hole. Morales carefully dismantled the M1919, making it easier to carry as he moved backward, further away from the opening to the street.

Bernie swiped his sleeve on his cheek, leaving a streak of red on the cloth from the cuts. Keeping his shoulders hunched, he stepped to the rear of their group, following close behind. He stole a glance over his shoulder, taking a deep breath when the wall he vacated was peppered with gunfire, making the stones shake.

They kept close on the sergeant's heels, moving back toward a street that had been cleared. Progress through the city had been sluggish—days had turned into weeks. Two weeks to be exact. Two weeks of pressing further and further into the city, losing men every step of the way.

At this rate, if we continue suffering such heavy losses, we'll run out of men before we even get a glimpse of Berlin. Bernie ducked through another opening, broken bricks and glass crunching beneath his boots as they moved cautiously through each building.

He reached inside his jacket, reassuring himself Margot's picture was still there. The fresh cuts in his face still burned, beginning to throb softly as a fresh drop of blood dripped down his face and neck. He could feel the bruise growing from the deeper nicks, his eye already feeling a bit swollen. Graham came alongside him, wincing when he glanced at the cuts.

"You should have that looked at," he suggested.

"It's nothing, just a few scratches," Bernie replied. "I've been hurt worse and kept going without much help."

Graham shook his head, opening his mouth to say something else when the wall to Bernie's right exploded.

He flew backward, the force of the blast carrying him a few feet in the air before slamming him down on the rubble. Bernie groaned, his back arching over a small pile of bricks and legs flailing, trying to get a firm hold on the ground again. He rolled off the pile as the bullets started flying, every muscle aching as he searched for some form of cover.

"Everyone all right?" Bruno's shout echoed in his ears, the vibration of the explosion still muffling his hearing.

A pain-filled cry brought his head up, catching sight of Morales dragging himself across the ground. He spun around, clutching his thigh in both hands—a heavy spurt of blood slipping between his fingers. Bernie crawled toward him, getting his legs back under him as he slid to a halt in front of the man.

"You're okay," he said, fingers trembling as he undid his belt. "I got you."

Morales nodded, his gaze fixed on the mix of shredded material and skin covered with blood pouring from the wound. Bernie wrenched his belt off, shoving the thin leather beneath the man's upper leg before tying it off tight, trying to stop the blood flow.

"Bernie!" Bruno bellowed.

"Yeah, I'm here!" Bernie answered without looking up from his task, pressing his palms down hard on Morales's leg. The man moaned, pressing the crown of his head back into the wall. "Morales is wounded!"

"How bad?" Ellis shouted.

"Bad!" Morales shrieked, saliva spattering his chin.

"Can he walk?"

Bernie shook his head. "I don't think so, sarge!"

"Think you can carry him, Bernie?" Graham asked.

"I'm gonna try! Jensen, you still with us?"

"Yup!"

"I'm gonna need some cover, kid!"

"You got it!"

A shuffle, the crash of rubble and Jensen was at his side, rifle firmly held near his shoulder.

"We'll give you a head start, Berns!" Bruno yelled. "You get him somewhere safe! Behind the tanks!"

"On our way!" Bernie grabbed his helmet from where it had fallen, placing it back atop his head. Grabbing Morales by the wrist, he yanked him forward, ignoring the man's shout of pain while pulling him across his shoulders. Bernie planted his feet firmly, rising a few inches off the ground before twisting his neck to look at Jensen.

"You ready?" he panted.

Jensen's helmet wagged when he nodded, jaw set with determination.

"Okay," Bernie paused, taking a few deep, slow breaths. "Let's go!"

He straightened his legs, the weight of Morales pressing down on his shoulders making him grunt before he sprinted toward the edge of the city where the tanks were waiting for them. Bruno, Ellis, and Graham's rifles all thundered behind him, giving him and Jensen some cover as they moved quickly down the street. Each stride was longer than the last, every breath labored as Morales bounced on his shoulders.

Wet warmth was soaking through his jacket where the man's leg was pressed into his side. He hoisted him more securely on his shoulders, holding onto him tight. Jensen kept close to his side, rifle raised. A bullet snapped away a rock near Bernie's foot but he kept his pace, letting Jensen fire into the wind at anything that moved.

"R-Russell," Morales stuttered, his cheek lulling on Bernie's shoulder. "I ... I can't ... feel ..."

"Hang in there, Morales," Bernie huffed. "We're almost there!"

Another bullet *cracked* through the air just as he caught sight of one of their tanks near the edge of the city. As if someone shoved him in the back with their hands, Bernie's body thrust forward, his feet twisting beneath him as both he and Morales went tumbling to the ground. Bernie shook his head, his helmet rolling away as the cuts in his face pounded in rhythm with the beat of his heart.

He looked up, watching Morales roll onto his back with a moan, the bloom of fresh blood spreading across his side where a new bullet had found a home. Bernie growled a curse, slamming his fist into the ground before scrambling forward, resting the flat of his palm on the wound.

"Not today," Bernie muttered. Then he hollered over his shoulder, "Jensen! Get me some help here!"

Jensen rushed ahead, his shouts booming in the air. "Medic! We need a medic over here!"

"Come on, Morales." Bernie pushed his other hand down on his knuckles, pressing in on the gushing wound in his side. "Hang in there, buddy."

"Hey, Bernie?" Morales said hoarsely.

"Yeah?"

"M-My name ... is ... Antonio." He took a few short, quick breaths. "Don't ... think I ... told you that before."

"No, don't think you did." Bernie grimaced, the rush of his blood soaking his hands, squeezing between his fingers and over his knuckles. "Now keep still, Antonio. Medic's on the way."

Morales coughed, blood bubbling between and staining his lips. "I-I need my w-wife to know—"

Bernie shook his head fiercely. "Anything she needs to know, you'll tell her yourself, you hear?"

"Her name ... is Isabela ..." His eyes rolled back, head falling to the side.

"Hey! Antonio, don't you do that!" Bernie grabbed him by the chin, the blood on his hand smearing his cheek as he rattled him. "Open your eyes, boy!"

He shook him, slapping his cheeks in the hopes of getting a response. The sound of pounding feet behind him, made him turn.

"Give me some room, soldier," the medic said, falling to his knees beside Morales.

Bernie shuffled out of the way, falling onto his backside with hands limp in his lap. He watched the medic work, wrapping Morales's wounds in bandages and administering a small dose of morphine. He wiped his hands on his pants, staring in silence as Jensen joined him, collapsing at his side.

"Is he gonna be all right?" Jensen gasped, sweat dripping down his temples from the run.

"Can't tell yet," the medic answered as another soldier joined them, going down to one knee on Morales's other side. "We'll do what we can, boys."

Bernie nodded, unable to form words on his tongue. He watched the two men lift Antonio from the ground—watched his friend's hand fall completely limp, swaying back and forth as he was carried off out of sight.

"He's gonna be okay, right Bernie?" Jensen asked. "I mean … it couldn't have been an artery. He would've bled out by now and—"

"He caught another bullet," Bernie interrupted, sharply. "In the side. Coughing blood."

Jensen bowed his head. "Dear God …"

"He could still make it." Bernie gripped Jensen's shoulder, squeezing. "There's always a chance, kid."

Tilting his head back, he stared into the sky. The distant sound of a howitzer blasting followed by the clatter of rifles and machine guns firing filled the silence between the two men. He didn't know how long they sat like that. Both simply staring at … nothing.

A shadow fell over them. Bernie tilted his head, feeling absolutely nothing when he met the grim gaze of the medic wiping Antonio Morales's blood off his hands.

★★★

Bernie dragged his feet toward the huddled circle of men, hunched up against the wall beside the street. Jensen's footsteps echoed his, his wary gaze burning Bernie with every step they took closer to their friends. They hadn't spoken since the medic returned with the news. The silence wasn't so bad. Actually, it was a welcome change from all the noise.

His clothes and hands were still stained—the red of the blood fading to brown as it dried. The cold rectangle of metal between his fingers sent a chill rushing up his arms. He rubbed his thumb across it, the rough, raised lettering scraping his calloused finger. They came to a stop in front of the men, Bruno rising slowly from where he was crouched.

"How is he?" he asked.

Bernie bowed his head, taking off his helmet. Then he leaned forward, holding the dog tag out to Ellis.

"Can you give that to the captain for me?" he murmured.

Ellis hesitated, staring at the tag as if Bernie was offering him a rotten apple. Then he snatched it, stuffing it quickly in his pocket before rising to walk away. Bernie turned back, staring at the dark shadows in Bruno's eyes.

"On the way in," he whispered. "Morales took another bullet in the side. He didn't make it."

Bruno's hands curled, his shoulders beginning to shake. Then he turned, walking a few paces away before stopping. Bernie started to follow, stopping short when Graham spoke.

"It's a real shame." Graham pulled his notepad out of his pocket. "I didn't want to put his name on my list."

"You and that blasted list," Bruno growled. "Why are you making it? Does it make all of this better? Does it bring Morales back to life for you?"

"Bruno, I didn't mean to—"

"Yeah, yeah." Bruno waved a dismissive hand. "No one means to do anything over here. We all have our own ways of coping, right? I make jokes, you make lists of dead men, and Bernie sees Kraut snipers who wear fancy gold watches!"

"Bru," Bernie mumbled in warning.

"No!" Bruno spun around, throwing his helmet across the street. Then he shouted, "Where does it end, Bernie? Where does the madness stop? When Graham runs out of paper and you're sent home on a Section Eight?"

Bernie tilted his head higher. "Bruno, you're upset. Calm. Down."

"How many more, Berns? How many more have to die before we're done here?" Bruno took a step forward. "We have been through every step of this war from Africa and Italy to Normandy. Now, we're in Germany. How much more do we have to give before they let us go home? Who has to die next, you?"

"That won't happen, Bru."

Bruno chuckled, thrusting a hand through his hair. "How could you possibly know that? You can't."

"I know because you just said it." Bernie took two cautious steps toward him, hands steady as he reached out to grip him by the shoulders. "We have survived practically every step of this war for nearly four years. That's what we do, brother. We *survive*. I've come this far, and there's no way I'll let them get me now."

"Amen to that," Woodley's voice boomed behind them.

Bernie looked back at him, a half-smile tugging at the corner of his mouth. Woodley approached, propping his rifle against his shoulder as he stopped near the edge of their circle, Ellis close on his heels.

"I'm pulling you fellas out of the city. They're gonna want us at the front lines in the Hürtgen, and I want you boys rested." Woodley paused for a moment, regarding each of them in turn. Then he caught Bernie's eye, a glimmer of sadness flashing in them. "I'm sorry about Morales. You did good, Russell, trying to get him back. Medic said if it had only been the leg wound, he might've made it."

Bernie cringed. Captain might mean well, but it didn't make him feel better to know if he'd ducked—if he'd anticipated the shot—Morales would still be with them.

"Do we got a shot at Berlin, Cap?" Bruno asked, retrieving his rifle from the ground.

"Could be." Woodley shrugged. "We gotta push through this next stage first. Gather your gear together and get some food. Gonna be dark soon, and I want you boys safe at the back of the line by then. The 26th has got it from here."

Bernie stared at his back as he marched away to spread the word of what remained of their unit.

"Where'd my helmet go?" Bruno grumbled, hoisting his rifle on his shoulder.

Bernie stepped away, distracted now by how heavy Woodley's steps seemed. How his shoulders hung, spine curved with exhaustion, pain ...

Defeat. A lump blocked his throat.

"Let's get moving," he murmured, watching until Woodley disappeared. "The sooner we're out of the city, the sooner Woodley is too."

Chapter Eighteen

AUSCHWITZ II – BIRKENAU
LATE-OCTOBER, 1944

If Margot could wish for anything, she would wish for a sketchbook and pencil. To feel the smooth, yet coarse, sensation of drawing paper beneath her fingers. To smell a freshly sharpened pencil and hold it between her fingers.

To sketch the many faces of Bernie Russell.

Standing in the yard shivering and trying to keep her hands steady holding the metal plate swirling with what they told her was food, she tried to picture him again. Tried to create another new face in her mind. A smile to warm her heart and banish the icy chill of early winter sweeping over Poland. A voice so deep and strong to hold her up—keep her on her feet. Keep her moving forward.

Do not lose hope, Margot Raskopf. We're coming. She squeezed her eyes closed, trying to form the sound of his voice saying those words as she lifted the plate to her lips.

She tasted nothing of the cold soup sliding over her tongue and she was thankful. If she had registered the taste, she worried the broth would come right back up. The thought she'd helped cook what was being served only made her stomach twist more. But she downed every last drop before nibbling on the stale crust of bread she'd been rationed.

Hanna was crouched beside the kitchen wall, keeping a close watch on the guards milling nearby while she ate quickly. Her gaze seemed fixed on one of the men who kept strolling circles around the inmates huddled together to eat. She watched him with such caution and fear, raising a thousand questions in Margot's mind. How long had the girl been here? What horrors had she witnessed? What horrors had she suffered herself?

Ilse appeared in her mind, causing her eyes to well. The many days she'd been here she hadn't caught sight of her again. Not since they'd separated them the day they arrived. Wherever she'd been placed, whichever block they were keeping her in, Margot had the distinct feeling they were being kept apart on purpose. Franz hadn't come forward to speak to her again, but she could only hope he wasn't the one behind Ilse's apparent disappearance.

What has she been through so far? What work is she being forced to do?

"*Psst!*"

Margot gasped, nearly choking on the dry bite of bread she'd put in her mouth. Frowning, she turned in the direction of the sound, searching the ground briefly for a snake.

"*Psst!*"

Her eyes went wide, catching a quick glimpse of a small hand gripping the edge of the wall—the spikes of slowly growing light brown hair and the shine of smoky gray eyes. Margot glanced back at Geisler, sidestepping carefully toward the corner of the building. The woman was distracted, studying the prisoner who was serving the soup, making sure she gave no more than was allowed. Margot put her plate on the ground before slipping away.

She squinted, catching another flash of the small figure hurrying between the buildings. Margot followed, her heart beating a little faster. The remaining pangs of hunger from the inadequate meal rolling her stomach into a tight ball.

Margot gasped, pulling back to duck beside one of the buildings when the heavy squish of boots in the mud approached. She waited, watching the two guards take their time walking together past the barracks before vanishing behind another. Margot kept her shoulders down, gripping handfuls of her skirt as she continued on. She was approaching the crematoriums now—the rumble of the ovens sending a shiver down her spine.

Suddenly, a hand reached out, dragging her down between two of the blocks. Gasping as she fell on her knees in the mud, she wrapped her arms around Horst Stück, the threat of a sob rising in her throat until her lungs ached. He was dirty, frail, stunk to the very heavens, and she could feel his bones when she tightened her grip.

But he was alive.

"There, there," Horst whispered against her ear. "Collect yourself now, *mein schatz*."

Margot sniffled, leaning back to swipe her sleeve along her cheeks and nose. "H-How?"

Horst managed a smile, his button nose twitching. A scar marred the corner of his right eye and his lower lip was swollen with a fresh scratch. His eyes were sunken— the hair on his head beginning to grow back in fuzzy tufts.

"I am clever," he replied. "And I am small."

Margot couldn't help a small laugh, the irony of his statement hitting her like a crate of bricks.

"I have been taken on by a doctor," Horst continued, his eyes darting nervously. "He thinks of me as a ... well ... never mind. I believe as long as I continue to assist him, I will survive."

"Where? How can I find you?" Margot took his hands, squeezing until she could no longer feel her own fingers.

"*Nein*, too dangerous. I will find you."

"But—"

"You must hurry back now, Margot. I promise, I will find you." Horst started to turn away, but she gripped his sleeve.

"What doctor has helped you? What did you mean when you said you assisted him?"

Horst bowed his head, his shoulders trembling. Behind her, she could hear the other prisoners gathering for turns at the washroom and toilets. They had only an hour or two now before the final gong of the evening, ordering their return to barracks for sleep. If she didn't hurry back, she might lose her chance to wash before returning to her crowded bunk.

Yet, staring at his small form. Catching note of fresh scarring on his face, as well as rough, calloused scars to either side of his neck, Margot couldn't bring herself to move from this spot. What had Horst done to survive so long in a place where he was so different? Where he was regarded as less than human?

How did Hanna survive? How do any of us? Margot breathed, the questions burning her mind.

"I cannot say now. I must return before I am missed." Horst glanced back, his glossy eyes piercing her. "I will find you again and tell you everything, Margot, I promise."

He walked away before she could stop him, the familiar limp in his step seeming more pronounced now than she remembered. He got smaller and smaller as he walked away, hurrying back to wherever he'd come from. Margot swiped the tears from her cheeks, breathing deeply through her mouth to avoid the smells filling the camp.

Bracing a hand on the wall beside her she pushed back to her feet, slapping at the muck clinging to the hem of her dress and shins. She headed back the way she'd come, keeping her head down in the hopes she wouldn't be stopped and questioned. Horst's need for secrecy could mean only one thing. Even in this time between their last meal of the day and sleep, when there was little for them to do but gather for the washroom or briefly see the people they knew from other blocks, he'd made it clear being seen with him would not bode well for her.

Margot made her way back to the yard where they'd had their dinner. Stopping short, her eyes went wide, keeping herself halfway back behind the corner of the building. She stared at the guard who'd been circling them, her heart thumping faster and head spinning. He had Hanna by the arm, dragging her across the yard and out of sight behind one of the blocks.

Margot sprinted forward, glancing briefly to see Geisler was nowhere to be found before she followed. Fear wrapped around her like a rope, tightening until she could barely breathe when she caught sight of them again. He was pulling her further and further away from any sign of other people. Hanna didn't fight him, her head bowed deeply—feet stumbling in the thick mud of the path.

She didn't know how long or far she'd followed him before they reached a spot Margot had never seen before. Buildings, still in the process of being constructed—a new expansion to a camp that was already so large she couldn't even comprehend how the place was managed.

Hanna finally made a sound. A soft cry as the guard shoved her around one of the buildings, out of Margot's sight. Her heart was beating so loudly now she couldn't hear her own footsteps as she approached, keeping herself hidden on the other side of the wall. Every breath came faster when she heard the soft rip of material, the clink of a belt buckle. The sound of Hanna's body being thrown against the wall again.

"Hold still!" the guard snapped.

Margot couldn't move. Her hand slapped over her mouth, tears burning her eyes so hotly she thought she'd go blind. Hanna's quiet cries filled her ears, followed suddenly by an odd scraping noise.

Her eyes rounded, watching the rifle drop from where the guard had propped it on the wall. Glittering up at her in the setting sunlight was the bayonet where he'd attached it to the weapon. The question of why he'd placed the freshly sharpened knife to his rifle passed swiftly through her mind before she found herself reaching for it.

The bayonet disengaged easily with a soft *click*, her hand quivering as she curled her fingers firmly around the handle. Then, moving before thinking, she stepped around the corner.

The guard looked up, mouth gaping in surprise. She took only a moment to take in Hanna, the side of her face pressed firmly against the wall and her skirt torn up the side, nearly to her hip. The guard standing behind her with his pants open. The tears staining and reddening Hanna's usually porcelain white cheeks.

Before either could make a sound, Margot leaped forward, thrusting the bayonet up into the side of his ribs. A gurgled cry slipped through his mouth as he fell backward. Margot's hand still clutched the handle, the guard's blood spilling over her knuckles and wrist as the blade released from his flesh before he stumbled all the way to the ground, splashing in the mud.

Margot stared in stunned silence as he writhed on the ground, groaning as he clutched the deep wound. Then he looked up at her, the fiery rage in his eyes making her scuttle back.

"I will kill you," he rasped, pushing himself back to his feet with one hand still over his side. "I will—"

Hanna shrieked, yanking the bayonet out of Margot's hand.

"Hanna ... wait!" Margot cried, but she was too late.

Hanna slashed, the blade carving a crooked line across the guard's face. She tackled him back to the ground, stabbing him over and over in the chest and throat. Blood splattered and spouted onto her, staining her dress as well as the scarf covering her head.

Margot grabbed her around the waist, pulling her off the dead man before shoving her hand over the girl's mouth to muffle her wails. The bayonet slid out of Hanna's hand as she went limp, shaking and weeping in Margot's arms.

They stood like this for a moment, both staring at what they'd done. The guard's body sprawled, eyes wide open and mouth still gaping in a silenced shout of pain. Hanna's breaths became erratic, her small hands scratching at Margot's wrist to release her mouth.

"What have we done?" she gasped when Margot removed her hand. "Oh, Margot, what have we done?"

Margot spun her around, gripping her by the arms.

"We have to go now, Hanna."

"B-But ..." Hanna gestured to their clothes.

Margot looked down, face blanching when she focused on the blood covering both their work dresses and hands. The blood spotting Hanna's neck and face—smeared over her scarf.

"Mud," she said, dropping to her knees. "Cover the blood with mud."

Hanna joined her, both of them burying their hands in the thick, wet soil. They smeared every spot they could find. Margot tugged the scarf off the girl's head, scrubbing the blood from her cheeks and neck before using her hands to dig a small hole, burying the scarf as deeply as she could. No one would question why Hanna's head was suddenly bare—they would assume another inmate had stolen the scarf from her.

"What about him?" Hanna asked, her upper lip twisting when she looked at the Nazi.

"I don't know." Margot turned away, not wanting to look at the man again. "But we have to go."

"They will not give us new dresses. How are we ever going to—?"

"I don't know, Hanna!" Margot sunk her hands into the ground, forcing herself to look into the girl's eyes. "But we have to try."

Taking her by the hand, she pulled Hanna back to her feet, spinning around to head for the washrooms. Margot froze, Hanna bumping into her back. The figure was shrouded in the quickening shadows of twilight, his cap pulled low to shade his eyes, but the buttons of his uniform clearly glittered in the rising light of the moon.

Then he stepped out of shadow and her blood rushed. He looked between her and Hanna to the dead guard, fists clenched tight around his rifle.

"Franz," she whispered hoarsely. "*Bitte* ... help us."

Her brother stood still for a moment, letting his gaze continue to drift between the three of them. Then he spun the rifle around, strapping it across his back before marching toward the guard.

"Margot, take his ankles," he ordered.

She hesitated only a moment before she realized trusting him was her only option. Bending over, she gripped the guard by his boots, grunting softly when she helped Franz lift him out of the mud, struggling to carry him over to one of the half-built barracks. Franz dropped his front end into a hole beneath the building and Margot shrieked softly, losing her grip to allow his legs and feet to follow.

Erica Marie Hogan

"Come." Franz took hold of her upper arm, pulling her back over to Hanna. "Keep your heads down and stay behind me."

Margot bobbed her head, gripping Hanna's fingers tight. They started walking, Hanna pressed close to her side.

"I knew he would protect us," Hanna whispered suddenly.

Margot frowned. "How?"

Hanna bit her bottom lip, a shadow falling over her eyes before she answered softly, "Because he helped me once before."

Margot's brow smoothed, gazing at her brother's back as he marched stiffly through the camp. The gong could ring at any moment, forcing them to their barracks and to bed before they had a chance to wash the mud off. The prospect of not making it before the gong was terrifying. The thought they might've missed some smears of blood—that any moment someone could stop them and question why they were covered in fresh mud—overwhelmed her.

Then, she noticed the camp was strangely quiet. Margot lifted her gaze slightly from the ground, tightening her grip on Hanna's fingers.

"Franz?" she whispered.

He ignored her, striding across the yard toward the washrooms.

"Franz did the gong already ring?" she asked.

As distracted as they'd both been, she supposed they could've missed the sound of the gong. Could've missed the call for the inmates to immediately return to their barracks. For herself, she hadn't been able to hear anything but Hanna's cries and the guard's groans. Her brother kept moving, never once looking back at her when she spoke.

Then he stopped at the washroom, turning to face them. There was no line—no sign of anyone. Margot's heart dropped like a stone into her belly.

"Go inside," Franz said. "Leave your clothes at the door. Clean yourselves as best you can."

"Franz—"

"Do as you're told, Margot," he snapped. "You must trust me as you used to."

Hanna hurried inside without question, glancing back only briefly before she disappeared on the other side of the door. Margot stood for a few heartbeats, staring into her brother's face. The same question raced through her mind over and over despite what he was doing for her and Hanna. Even as she stepped into the washroom, the question plagued her.

Can I trust him? Can I really, truly trust him as I used to?

★★★

The cold water left in the trough did very little to clean them, but by the time they were through, any trace of mud and blood had been thoroughly scrubbed from their bodies. Margot had rubbed the water on her body until her skin felt raw, determined to be rid of the entire incident. When they'd scuffled back to the door, shivering and damp, they'd discovered two work dresses waiting for them. They'd been used before—dirty but they fit.

Knowing it was best not to ponder the dresses' previous owners, Margot and Hanna had slipped them on in silence, surprised to discover two fresh scarves beneath the garments for their heads as well. Margot wrapped hers tight across her head, thankful for the little bit of warmth it offered in the continuing dropping temperatures of the night.

The sun had completely set by the time they stepped out of the washroom, Franz waiting for them right outside.

Without a word, he turned for the barracks, guiding them in the darkness across the yard.

"We do not sleep in the same barracks," Hanna whispered, worry lacing her voice.

Margot simply squeezed her hand. Every shadow made her jump. Any small movement or sound sending her heart racing out of control. Franz halted, gesturing for them to stay back as he approached the guard standing close outside the barrack's door. They exchanged a few words before the guard walked away, leaving Franz in his place. Once he'd vanished in the darkness, Margot hurried forward, bringing Hanna with her.

"Go inside," he mumbled.

"But I do not have a bunk in these barracks," Hanna replied.

"I will make room for you." Margot put her arm around the girl's slight shoulders. "Even if you have to sleep atop me."

Hanna's laugh faded into quiet weeping. She burrowed against Margot's side, pressing her face into her shoulder. Margot turned her for the doors, pausing before going in. Looking over her shoulder, her gaze collided with her brother's.

"*Danke*, Franz," she breathed.

Franz kept his lips pressed tight, the shadows of night playing softly across the hard lines of his features. He didn't respond, instead he presented his back to her, facing out toward the rest of the camp. Margot stared at him a moment longer, wanting to ask him again. Wanting more than anything to get an answer to the question she'd asked him on the day she arrived here.

Are you doing this to survive? Tell me you are doing this to survive! The words screamed in her head, begging to be released on her tongue.

Instead, Margot followed Hanna into the barracks, letting the door drift closed behind her.

Chapter Nineteen

The bunk quaked beneath her. Margot blinked rapidly, the darkness of the barracks difficult to adjust to. Hanna was pressed close to her body, both of them curled near the very edge of the bunk, the two other women sharing the space with them pushed tight against Margot's back. She shook her head, shifting to readjust her arms around Hanna. The feeling must've been a dream of some sort, or perhaps a noise from one of the other women in the barracks, startling her.

She started to drift away again, seeking sleep in the darkness, when the distant rumble of thunder shook the barracks. Frowning, she started to sit up, Hanna stirring beside her. Another crack of thunder, closer this time, made her stumble out of the bunk, moving between the beds to the center aisle of the barracks.

"Margot?" Hanna whispered, groggily. "What's happening?"

"I am not sure," Margot replied, breathless.

Another blast rent the air, shaking the bunks harder. The rest of the women in their barracks began to stir, soft murmurs filling the air. Margot stood still, staring at the ceiling when Hanna came to her side, taking her tightly by the arm with both hands. When the barracks shook again, she knew for certain.

Not thunder. Explosions. Margot lunged for the doors, dragging Hanna with her close behind.

She shoved the doors open, not caring if the guard was outside. They all stumbled out, staring into the sky. A Luftwaffe plane shot through the air across the stars, followed swiftly by another fighter plane. Her heart leaped, hope flooding her so quickly she thought she'd burst from the feeling.

Americans!

"Come!" Margot gripped Hanna's hand, pulling her across the yard.

If they could get to the gatehouse, perhaps they could signal the Americans. Perhaps this nightmare could finally come to an end. Margot stumbled when one of the buildings to her left went up in flames, smoke and dust clogging her lungs. She coughed, wrapping a firm arm around Hanna's shoulders as they continued on, struggling through the thick muck.

"Margot!" a familiar voice shouted. "Margot!"

Her neck twisted around. "Ilse!"

The girl fell into her arms, shivering and sobbing. A sudden rush of heat from one of the burning buildings wafted over them, banishing the coolness in the air.

"Are you hurt?" Margot asked, gently taking Ilse's face between her palms.

"*Nein*," Ilse replied, shaking her head. "What's happening?"

Margot's response was swallowed by another explosion. Taking both girls' hands, she raced across the yard, her boots catching and sticking in the mud—her muscles ablaze as she pushed herself to move faster.

Then suddenly, Hanna and Ilse's hands fell out of hers. Margot gasped, spinning around as a billow of smoke encompassed her, blocking her vision.

"Ilse!" she shouted, her voice echoing back to her. "Hanna!"

The sounds of the blasting and planes whizzing overhead began to fade. Swallowed now by the heavy sound of boots on the ground. Margot faced the gatehouse, her eyes rounding slowly. The gates had been thrown open, soldiers marching through with rifles ready. Their silhouettes moved in and out of the clouds of smoke, the pepper of their gunfire raising gooseflesh on her arms.

Then one man started toward her. His head was bowed, face covered in shadow. She couldn't make out his features at all. Only, he was tall—taller than any man she'd ever seen. His arms were long and strong, feet taking each long stride with determination as he came toward her.

Before she could react, he pulled her into his arms, burying her face in the warmth of his chest. Margot burrowed into him, wishing she'd had a chance to see his face.

"Bernie," she whispered.

His large palm covered the back of her head. Then his voice—deep, soft, strong—answered quietly, "I told you we were coming ..."

★★★

Margot gasped, her whole body convulsing as she woke abruptly from the dream. Her arms were wrapped tight around Hanna, keeping her from falling off the bunk where they were squeezed in on the thin mattress. She shuddered, the sweat coating her skin from the dream hastily cooling in the late autumn air filling the barracks.

Gently so as not to wake Hanna, she slipped her arms from around the girl and slid toward the end of the bunk.

Her boots silently met the floor and she crouched, slipping out so she could stretch her legs. Coughing and wheezing echoed through the barracks every few seconds followed by the shuffle and moans of those trying to find some semblance of comfort in the cramped space allotted to them.

She tiptoed toward the door, wondering if Franz was still standing guard over them. Her heart still cried for an answer from him. Every beat telling her to trust him since he'd saved their lives earlier. But the way he'd turned his back on her after delivering them safely to their barracks—the strange, empty look he'd given her—she couldn't be sure.

I knew he would protect us ... because he helped me once before. Hanna's words echoed in her ears.

Pressing her fingertips lightly to the door, she pushed it open, cringing when the hinges creaked. Franz turned around, his eyes brightening in a glare when he saw her.

"You should be sleeping," he growled, turning away from her again.

Margot stepped out cautiously, glancing around to be sure there were no other guards marching about.

"I had a dream." She leaned back against the wall of the barracks, tucking her hands behind her. "*Danke*, again, Franz. For what you did for Hanna."

His eyebrow arched when he looked back at her again. "And for you, Margot. Am I wrong in assuming you stabbed him first?"

"*Nein.*" Margot grimaced. "You are not wrong. He was going to violate Hanna. I had to do something. I reacted."

"In here, reacting will get you killed." Franz faced her now, taking a step toward her. "Do you understand? If you were to even stumble—fall down—during the morning roll call, you would be killed. Can you imagine what they would do to you if they discovered you murdered one of the guards?"

Margot lifted her head, jaw clenched tight. "Would you have walked away if you'd come upon them? Would you have let him do such a terrible thing?"

"I would have found another way to stop him."

"Well, I could not!" Margot closed the space between them until their noses nearly touched. "I am a prisoner, Franz! There was no other way for me to stop him."

Franz sighed, his shoulders drooping slightly. The wind whistled between them, reminding her painfully of how thin her work dress was—how inadequate her boots were to fend off the cold. She tightened the scarf around her head and then cleared her throat.

"Hanna said you helped her once before," she said. "Is that true?"

Franz's eyes darkened. "*Ja*, it is true."

"How? How did you help her?"

He hesitated, his hand clenching into a fist at his side before he flexed his fingers, stretching them.

"You should ask Hanna," he replied, the edge of warning in his voice unsettling her heart. "There are things that happen here—secrets that are not mine to share, even with you, Margot. If you truly want to know, then ask Hanna."

Margot's lips parted in preparation for another question, but he turned away again.

"Go back inside now, Margot," his hoarse whisper reached her in the quiet. "Get some rest. The morning gong will sound soon."

Margot bent her neck back, resting the crown of her head on the wall as she watched him now in silence. The sky was beginning to lighten—the stars twinkling one moment then vanishing the next in preparation for the dawn. She supposed he was right. Best to be back inside the barracks when the gong rang, instead of caught outside where she was not supposed to be. Carefully, she slipped her hand between the small opening of the door, sidestepping away from the wall.

Then she glanced back, letting the words on her tongue spill out.

"I love you, Franz."

She didn't wait to see if he heard her before tiptoeing silently back into the barracks.

★★★

After the morning gong rang, stirring each of them from their bunks, Geisler stopped Margot right outside the door of the barracks, announcing she would not be working the kitchens today. Sparing a parting glance over her shoulder at Hanna, she followed the stern guard across the yard, her head ducked and her stomach rumbling louder when she realized Geisler was not going to let her have her morning cup of coffee.

Or tea. I still have not determined exactly what it is supposed to be. She shuddered thinking about the liquid she forced herself to drink every morning.

She didn't realize where she was being put to work until the piles upon piles of clothes came into view. Remembering Franz had warned her she might be transferred to sort clothes, Margot went to work without question, moving numbly through the task of sorting the belongings of people most likely dead.

The other women cast strange glances her way, which she ignored. Many others had looked at her in a similar fashion, and she preferred not to contemplate why. Whether because they knew she was German or because they knew she was a Raskopf or because they knew her brother was a guard, she honestly didn't care.

She only cared that among their faces, she still didn't see Ilse's. Of all the many faces she'd seen over the time she'd been here, how had she not been able to find Ilse's? She couldn't believe Franz didn't know where Ilse was being kept, but she hadn't had the courage to ask him. Ilse had felt so real in her dream last night, she imagined if she closed her eyes, she could reach out and touch her even now.

As she began her task of sorting through a stack of shoes, a small figure caught her eye. Margot's stomach fluttered. Stealing a glance over her shoulder, she made sure the guards weren't watching before she stepped around the pile and crouched low, coming to Horst's side where he sat in the dirt, keeping himself hidden from the guards and prisoners alike.

"Is there anywhere in this camp you cannot sneak into?" Margot whispered, hunching her shoulders to keep as close to the ground as possible.

Horst smirked. "A few. I saw that woman, Geisler, bring you here. I thought perhaps this would be an opportunity for us to speak."

"*Ja.*" Margot nodded. "You still have to tell me who this doctor is who keeps you alive."

Horst bowed his head, running a hand up and down over his scalp. She waited quietly, feeling the tension bounce off his body.

"He does not so much keep me alive," Horst said, voice barely audible. "As he will use me for his purposes until he grows weary of me."

Margot reached out, brushing her fingertips against the side of his neck.

"How did this happen?" she asked, the scars marring his throat akin to burn marks.

Horst grabbed her hand, squeezing her fingers as he drew them away from his flesh. Gently, he raised her fingers to his lips, kissing them the way he did when he'd greet her at his front door on one of her summer visits to his home. Staring into the clouded gaze of the man she revered in her heart as high as her own father, her breath stopped short. The pain intensifying the wrinkles around his eyes—the lines around his mouth—could not be missed. The horrid pallor of his skin, the sharp bones of his shoulders, all served to tell their own story.

"Who is the doctor who keeps you alive?" she asked again. "Did he give you those scars?"

Horst cringed. "He, among others. Must you know?"

Margot sandwiched his hand between her palms. "*Bitte*, Horst. Tell me."

Her friend hesitated a moment longer, staring deeply into her eyes before sighing heavily. He hunkered down on the ground, glancing over his shoulder to be certain no one was watching. Margot did the same, every shuffle of the other inmates milling about at their work making her jump.

"They tried to kill me, Margot," Horst said quickly, as if anxious to have the story told and done with. He skimmed a hand along one of the scars across the side of his throat. "I was hanging, the ropes so tight around my throat they scraped and burned by skin. Then, as if someone took a knife to the noose, the rope broke. That was when Me—" he stopped short, looking away from her as he changed what he was about to say, "—the doctor, took me to his workroom. He tells me every day he will kill me one day soon, but until then I am his dog. The dog that narrowly escaped death but will not do so again."

"Oh, Horst," Margot wept, her throat tightening. "What does he make you do?"

He shook his head, his round fingers tangling around her bony knuckles.

"I cannot say. I have told you enough."

"*Nein*, you have not. Not nearly enough." Margot forced a breath into her lungs, trying to ease the horrible pressure in her chest.

"*Bitte*, Margot, is there not enough pain here for you already? Must you force me to give more?" Horst grabbed her face in his palms, pulling her forward to press a rough kiss to her forehead. "I love you, *schätzchen*. I am furious you are here with me in this awful place. But here you are, and I want you to live. Do you understand? The less you know—the more you keep yourself quiet and invisible—the better off you will be."

Margot clung to him, gripping fistfuls of the front of his work shirt. The garment was far too large for him, hanging over the baggy striped pants nearly to the ankles. The material was just as thin as her work dress, the sleeves torn near the wrists to give his hands freer movement.

"The longer you are here, the more you will understand. There are no exceptions here, Margot ... even if your *bruder* is one of the guards."

Margot closed her eyes. His mouth pushed deeply on the center of her forehead again before slipping away, leaving the cool air in his place. When she opened her eyes, he was gone. Swallowing a cry, she rose unsteadily to her feet, the tremors rushing over her body having nothing to do with the cold. She returned to her work, trying to put the images Horst's story created out of her mind.

For the most part, she followed the lead of the other women sorting the clothing. Moving articles from one pile to another. Arranging some shoes by size, others by color. Gathering an armload, she stepped across the yard, her heart nearly leaping out of her chest when the large shadow of a man fell over her.

"Margot Raskopf?" his hoarse whisper breathed heavily beside her ear.

She looked up, the soft, light eyes watching her strikingly familiar.

"I am Ludwig Volk. I was a school friend of Hans'." He continued to walk beside her as she dropped the pile she was carrying.

Margot passed her gaze over the SS uniform he wore, nearly identical to her brother's. She didn't answer him, continuing her work in the hopes of not drawing any unwanted attention. He stood near her without directly facing her, looking out over the yard.

"I want to help, if I can," he said. "Do you remember me?"

Margot stilled, her hand gripped around the soft material of a shawl. More than anything, she wanted to wrap that shawl around her. Wanted to sneak it back to the barracks to drape over herself and Hanna in the hopes of staying warm tonight. Instead, she let the delicate garment drop again, moving to walk away.

Then, subtly, she turned back, taking a few backward steps.

"*Ja*," she answered. "I remember you."

She watched him only long enough to see a sparkle brighten his eyes before hurrying back to her task.

Chapter Twenty

To some, Dominik Baumann was a miracle worker—a healer unlike any other.

To Ilse, he was simply her dear Papa.

Eyes burning, Ilse held her breath as she wrapped a woman's blistered arm with a grey strip of cloth. The rotten aroma lifting off her fellow inmate's body was doing its best to bring up the putrid liquid she'd been forced to gulp down that morning for breakfast. But she swallowed back the bile and took another deep breath.

The scratch of rats scurrying across the room made Ilse gasp, jerking quickly to the side when a brush of coarse fur tickled her ankle. The dimly lit room gave her only a glimpse of the small bodies racing to and fro in the corners of the building. They kept to the shadows, waiting for their opportunity to pounce if they thought food was near.

Like many of these poor souls. Ilse shuddered, tying the bandage in a tight knot before taking a step back.

"Go," she whispered. "Before they decide to keep you here."

The woman padded away before Ilse finished speaking, slipping out the door to get as far from the infirmary as possible. Gathering what was left of the bandages, Ilse started back down the center of the room, now immune to the soft cries and groans of pain attempting to flood her ears.

Rivka wasn't here today—at least, she hadn't come in from the barracks so far. Whether pulled to perform other duties or perhaps one of the many who disappeared during the night, Ilse wasn't certain, and she wasn't sure she wanted to know. They'd barely spoken since the day they met.

Because what is there to say?

A sharp shriek rent the air and Ilse spun, eyes expanding. The woman lying in the corner of the room writhed, leg shaking furiously in an attempt to dislodge the rat that had sunk its teeth into her calf. Another was crawling over her chest, nibbling her collarbone before she knocked it away with one of her flailing arms.

Ilse stood in stunned silence, fingers clenching tighter around the dirty bandages and heart pumping out of control.

What would Margot do?

The strips of cloth dropped to the floor and she was moving, picking up her pace until she was running. With a small shriek of her own, she kicked the rat biting the unfortunate woman's leg, sending it flying into the wall before reaching down to grab the other by the tail to fling it away. Gasping and clutching her bloated stomach, the woman strained back on the thin blanket lying between her and the cold floor.

Ilse winced, fingers shaking as she took care to observe the oozing bites. There was a green tinge to the woman's skin, blending with the dark streams of blood flowing over her legs. She'd lost so much weight, the rat bite had broken her skin straight through, the stark white of her bone glistening up at Ilse. Her breaths became labored as Ilse attempted to wrap the wound, a gruff cough trembling her chest.

She needs water. Ilse pressed her lips tight. There was hardly any water for the infirmary and what buckets there were to collect it were polluted from being used for inmates to relieve themselves.

After securing the bandages, she leaned over, finding the woman lying deathly still with her eyes closed. Thready breaths slipped between her cracked lips, warning Ilse she might not have much time.

"I will try to find water," she whispered, unsure if the woman could even hear her. "I'll come back, I promise."

Turning on her heels, Ilse rushed back toward the door. She was just reaching for the handle when the sliding door swung open. Ilse leaped to the side, instantly bowing her head as the SS guard pulled a stumbling inmate alongside her. Rivka was close on her heels, eyes round when she saw Ilse before she continued on. She watched as she deposited the woman like a rag doll in between two cots.

"You!" the guard shouted, drawing the eyes of the woman across the room.

Ilse glanced up, staring at the same woman she'd first seen upon her arrival in the infirmary make her way across the room. It had become abundantly clear after the first day that this woman had once been a doctor herself before coming here and—considering the type of examinations Ilse had seen her perform—she could only assume she'd specialized in the female body. Since she and Rivka had started their work with her, she had come to think of her simply as 'the doctor'. She'd never offered her name, and Ilse never even thought to ask.

Hearing the low moan of the woman who'd fallen prey to the rats, Ilse remembered her mission. She slipped out the door before the guard could notice her, an immediate late-autumn breeze sweeping coolly against her bare head.

Water. Where can I find water?

Ilse started walking without really knowing where she was going. Perhaps if she could get into one of the bathhouses she might be able to find a way to bring back some close to fresh water. There wasn't a well nearby, and she wasn't absolutely certain the guards would allow her to collect a bucket if she tried to draw some.

Mind racing in circles, she didn't notice when the SS guard stepped in her path. Ilse gasped, bumping into the man's chest. She leaped back, a terrified apology on the tip of her tongue when she looked up into a set of familiar blue eyes.

Franz stared at her for a few unbearable seconds before he sidestepped around her to walk away. Ilse frowned, looking over her shoulder to watch him. He stopped beside one of the buildings, glancing back at her with brow curved expectantly. She stumbled slightly, realizing he wanted her to follow. Ilse trailed quickly after him, clutching fistfuls of her skirt. He stopped at the back of the building, turning to face her.

She waited, the silence between them as thick as the air before a steady rain. Ilse wrung her hands, stomach trembling as every possibility of what could happen to her if she was caught with him thundered through her mind. And yet, as she faced him for the first time since her arrival, only one question continued to replay itself in her mind. He started to open his mouth, chest swelling with a breath as if prepared to finally speak when her own tongue finally loosened.

"Did you tell Gerhard about my Papa?"

Franz's teeth clicked, lips tightening together in a thin line.

"Tell me," Ilse whispered, taking a small step closer. "Tell me you are the man inside the fences who tells the resistance all he can when he can. Gerhard would not give me a name but when I saw you here … *bitte,* Franz, tell me you are still the boy I once loved."

A sharp inhale hissed through his clenched teeth, eyes going wide in surprise for the briefest of moments before he reached out. His hand grazed hers, moving up slowly until his fingertips brushed her elbow. Still, he didn't say anything to her, merely drew her closer. Ilse pulled back when he seemed to be bringing her close, as if to take her in. She shook her head, eyes watering.

"I … I smell."

Franz's hand fell back to his side. Ilse hugged her ribs, shoulders tensing tight until they nearly touched her earlobes.

"I need water. A woman in the infirmary …" Ilse clenched her lips firmly, swallowing the words as the image of the rats chewing the dying woman's leg overwhelmed her mind.

"I will do what I can," he replied raspingly.

The sound of his voice alone was enough to steal the breath from her lungs. He was everything familiar. He was everything of home and family and love she could remember.

And his smile is exactly like Margot's. Ilse's chest strained as she attempted to regain her breath.

But before she could say anything further, he turned on his heels and marched away. Ilse stepped back around the corner, pausing only for a moment when she briefly caught the edge of one of the women's guard's skirts brush the door as she entered the infirmary. Ilse shuffled forward, slipping in before the door had a chance to shut. On the tips of her toes, she sidestepped with her back to the wall in the shadows of the room.

She recognized both the SS doctor and the guard walking through the room. They had come before, passing through the rooms and making their … selections. Ilse cringed, moving further into the corner, keeping herself in as much shadow as possible so they would not see her. Rivka was standing beside the inmate Ilse had seen one of the guards bringing in a few moments before, keeping her head bowed deeply, hands trembling at her sides when the doctor moved past.

Ilse watched in cold silence as they picked from the inmates in the room, forcing them up from where they lay— the female guard giving some a heavy strike with the riding crop she carried. She waited, pressing her hands against the wall, biting back a screech when she felt one of the rats raced over the top of her boot.

Then they turned, the SS doctor barking harsh orders as the guard filed the swaying inmates out of the infirmary. Ilse's gaze settled on the doctor, watching the unyielding smirk twisting his ugly mouth, the way a strand of his shiny, dark hair slipped from the rim of his hat against the center of his forehead. Those eyes, so bright with a rejuvenation she only now understood.

He finds this thrilling. He enjoys it. Ilse's nails scraped and broke against the wall when she bent her fingers into fists.

Once the doors closed after them, Ilse launched herself away from the wall, hurrying across the room to join Rivka. She went down on her knees on the other side of the sick young woman they'd brought in. Rivka joined her, pressing her hand softly on the girl's forehead.

"We live another day, Ilse Baumann," Rivka murmured without looking at her.

Ilse nodded slowly. "What is wrong with the girl?"

Rivka hesitated, glancing over her shoulder at the woman doctor who was tending to another inmate.

"Doctor says s—syph ..." Rivka bit down on her lip, choking on the word she didn't want to say.

Ilse sat back, shaking her head. She stared, now noticing the rash that was spreading on the girl's body.

"But ... how?"

Rivka looked up at her, brow pinched tight together at the bridge of her nose. "Because all of us do what we must here."

"She's ... she's so young and ... and cannot be more than eighteen! I do not understand. If they hate us so much why would they—?"

"Because she was pretty and young, and she wanted more ... more bread!" Rivka's upper lip lifted in a scowl, and she slammed her fist on the ground. Then her eyes lifted, piercing through Ilse darkly. "And we do not know it was a guard, Ilse. The men's camp is not far, and they are willing to trade."

Ilse gasped, pressing her hand to her mouth. She turned, knees scraping on the rough floor as she forced herself to her feet again. She shuffled away between the cots, heart sinking into the pit of her stomach as she rubbed the tears off her cheeks.

Where is Franz? Where's the water? She stomped for the door, gulping back the rest of her tears.

But when she peeked outside, there was no sign of Franz.

★★★

Ilse had never been a deep sleeper. From the time she was a little baby, the slightest noise would rouse her from slumber, even if only the soft footfall of her mother passing her cradle. Though Amalie Baumann had always taken great care to never wake her only child, she always claimed Ilse's inability to sleep peacefully in her cradle was from a deeper desire to be held. She always seemed able to drift right off as soon as she was in her mother's arms.

But her inability to sleep in peace had increased once more over the years. Ever since Amalie had passed away when Ilse was fourteen. A cough, a sigh, a whisper ... anything could wake her at any moment, so for her the question became—why sleep at all?

Staring at the ceiling, Ilse kept her body as still as possible. As she was on the top bunk, one wrong move and she'd plummet to the floor, most likely breaking an arm or leg upon landing. The sounds of the other women in pain was almost as frequent in the barracks as it was in the infirmary. Every time her eyes grew heavy, a quiet cough resounded or the moan of the bunks as someone turned over or the soft tears of someone who was simply too overwhelmed to hold them back any longer had Ilse awake once more.

Breathing in and out slowly, she tried to think of something else. Something other than her empty stomach screaming in agony or the pressure building in her chest as she resisted the cough that had tickled her throat all day.

A sharp cry followed by the hasty hiss of whispers brought her head up. Ilse frowned, squinting in the dark at the group of shadows moving near the back of the barracks. Careful not to disturb the three women bunking with her, she slipped off the thin mattress, landing with a thud on the soles of her feet.

Biting back a grimace when pain shot up her calves from dropping to the floor so hard, Ilse tiptoed around the edge of the bunk, frowning at the shadows. She started toward the figures, her heart beginning to pound harder when the noise rose then faded, as if someone had placed their hand over the mouth of whoever was weeping. The thought alone set her stomach to roiling—the scuffling, as if someone were struggling, the small, stifled gasps ... the sudden silence.

Ilse stopped in her tracks. Slowly, one of the women turned, her palms cupped as if holding something and with dark liquid dripping from her dirty hands. Ilse's breaths quickened, shoulders shaking so hard now her vision began to blur. Then Rivka appeared—her eyes shrouded in an agony Ilse could not begin to express, and the weathered lines on her face more defined than they were before.

When she saw Ilse, her lips parted in surprise, one bloodied hand reaching out gently.

"Ilse ... let me explain ..."

Ilse shook her head, spinning on her heels as she stumbled back toward her bunk.

"Wait!" Rivka followed, her softer footsteps padding along quickly on her heels.

Ilse fell to her knees near the door, stomach heaving. Only there was nothing to come up, causing tears to burn her eyes and her throat to swell. She retched and choked, the realization of what she'd just seen twisting her stomach into a thousand knots.

"Ilse ... please ..."

She glared over her shoulder at the woman, forcing herself not to focus on the blood still staining her hands. Her empty stomach turned over for the tenth time in the last minute, knowing she had to face this here and now.

"How could you?" she hissed, shaking too hard to get back on her feet. "I don't understand you!"

"I think you understand more than you care to admit," Rivka answered, stony eyes returning her heated glare. "Like I told you before, we do what we must to survive."

"Survive? You call that surviving?" Ilse struggled, forcing herself back onto her feet. "You murdered a child!"

Rivka shoved her and Ilse landed hard on the ground with a gasp, the heels of her hands scraping on the rough flooring. The woman crouched in front of her, grabbing her by the shoulders and staining her dress with blood.

"The doctor does what she must so the women in these barracks will have a chance! Would you rather the SS find out she was pregnant? Would you rather they take two lives? That girl has the chance to be a mother again someday!"

Horror like none she ever felt before rushed over her like a bucket of ice water. Rivka sat back, shoulders slumping in defeat.

"Do you think I wanted to help? Don't you know I will never look at myself the same way again? That is if, by chance, I am one who makes it out of this camp alive, I will live with this until the day I die." Rivka brushed harshly at her damp cheeks, now doing everything she could not to look at Ilse. "If the SS had discovered she was with child, they would have taken her away and two lives would have been lost. If we have helped her live another day, then perhaps she will leave this place when the war is over and have another baby one day."

Cool drops coursed Ilse's cheeks, her fingers digging against her palms. "But ... but that poor child ..."

"Would have died anyway." Rivka rose from the ground, her face covered in shadow as she stared down at Ilse. "Do you really think the Nazis would have let that child breathe? If the mother had managed to come to term and birth the babe, the moment it let out its first cry it would have been condemned."

Before Ilse could respond, Rivka turned, dragging her feet back to where she'd come from. Wrapping her arms around her legs, Ilse rocked back and forth on the ground, listening to the gentle weeping of the mother as the last piece of her heart shattered like glass in her chest.

Chapter Twenty-One

Every warm breath slipping between his lips steamed on the cold air. Bernie lay nearly flat on his back in the foxhole, the kraut rifle digging painfully into his back and his own weapon clutched tight in both hands. He turned his head, his helmet crunching the snow and icy dirt beneath him. November had brought a drop in temperatures, along with a light snowfall, coating the forest in a glistening blanket of white. Yet while the landscape strived for beauty, it was anything but in his eyes.

Looking up at the nearest tree, he flinched. Shredded bark, the trunk completely torn apart from the recent shelling. The pitter-patter of gunfire still filled the air even as he tried to block the sounds. Threading his arms across his ribs, he held himself tighter, even though he knew it would do little to hold the warmth inside him.

Bernie never thought Aachen would look good compared to the Hürtgen. But after making the attempt to push their way to the Ruhr River, he'd give anything to hunker down among the wreckage of the city once more. After so many days fighting more to survive than anything else in this godforsaken forest, he'd stopped asking Graham about the death count.

Turning over, he crawled up toward the edge of the hole alongside Jensen manning the M1919. The boy squinted, rubbing his bloodshot eyes as he changed his focus from the line to Bernie.

"You got a cigarette?" he mumbled groggily.

Bernie reached into his pocket, the nearly empty packet light between his fingers as he drew one of the thin white roll-ups out and placed it between Jensen's lips. The match hissed softly when he struck it, the tiny flame letting off a quick puff of black smoke.

"Thanks." Jensen puffed a couple of times before taking it out of his mouth, fingers trembling where he gripped it. "Can I ask you a question?"

"Sure." Bernie rested his rifle at his side and folded his arms in front of him, placing his chin on top of his knuckles.

"Who's the girl? The one whose picture you're always taking a peek at whenever the shooting stops?"

Bernie frowned, reaching instinctively for his jacket pocket. "Why do you want to know?"

Jensen shrugged. "Because Bruno said you don't have a girl. He says you don't have anyone, really, not since your mother died. You hate your daddy—"

"I don't hate him," Bernie interjected. "We just … disagree. About everything, come to think of it."

"Such as?" Jensen took hold of the machine gun, squinting down the sights.

"Career. Life. Love. Religion. You name it." Bernie chuckled softly. "I remember the day I told him I was switching over to a new church. Can't even begin to describe the look he gave me when he realized it was a Catholic church."

"You're avoiding the original question, Bernie," Jensen commented.

Bernie took the cigarette back, pressing it tight between his lips for a long draw before handing it back to Jensen.

"Bruno's wrong. Not about me not having a girl, but about me having no one." Bernie patted him lightly on the shoulder. "I've got you boys."

Jensen smirked. "Still not an answer."

Bernie sighed, letting his forehead drop heavily on his wrists. Reaching inside his jacket, he tugged her picture out, rubbing his thumb gently across her face. Clearing his throat, he turned to Jensen.

"She's not really my girl," he muttered. "I mean she feels like my girl. In here," he paused, thumping his fist lightly over his heart. "But officially, she's ... well, she's ..."

Jensen raised his brows, waiting for the answer that couldn't seem to form on Bernie's tongue.

"She's not your girl ... but she's something. She means something to you. Is that what you're trying very badly to say?"

Bernie nodded. "Yeah, I guess."

"How'd you meet her?" Jensen put the cigarette out on the ground, crushing what was left of the roll-up in the snow.

"I haven't," Bernie muttered.

His friend turned slightly, eyeing him with a thick brow arched. "You haven't what?"

Coughing to clear his throat, Bernie focused on Margot's picture.

"I haven't actually ... met her. In person, that is."

Jensen rolled slightly onto his side, the corner of his mouth lifting in a grin.

"How'd you get her picture then?" he wondered. "What? Some random girl just sent a guy she's never met before her picture?"

Bernie closed his eyes, wishing he'd kept his mouth shut in the first place. He hadn't told anyone the details surrounding the photograph he kept in his pocket. Bruno and Graham, of course, knew where he'd gotten it, but they never questioned him. Woodley thought what most of the other men did. She was his girl back home, and he was possessive of her image. Whatever prompted him to tell Jensen more, he didn't know.

Maybe being unable to talk about her is simply catching up with me. Bernie pinched the bridge of his nose.

"It wasn't like that," he replied.

Jensen checked the ammo, the gunfire getting louder in the distance. "Okay, Russell. You don't have to tell me about her if you don't want to."

Bernie opened his mouth to explain it wasn't that he didn't want to, more that he didn't know how to, but Jensen continued before he had a chance.

"My girl and I grew up together. Little town in Georgia. We're gonna get married as soon as I get back," Jensen said, all without looking up from his task. "Her name's Rachel. We've been together since we were fourteen."

He dug in his pocket, producing a worn, creased photograph of his own. Passing it across the gun, Bernie took a look, grinning at the picture of Jensen in civilian clothes, hair longer and curlier than it was now and his arm wrapped around the shoulders of a petite brunette. Her eyes were shining, looking up at him. Thin lips spread wide in an adoring smile and a light spatter of freckles across her nose and cheeks.

"She's cute," Bernie answered, handing the picture back for Jensen to tuck away again. "Together since you were fourteen, huh?"

"Yeah. I think our parents always hoped and planned for us to get together. Luckily, we fell in love." Jensen hugged the machine gun to his shoulder, gently resting his finger on the trigger. "I hated leaving her."

"She'll be there when you get back."

"I sure hope so."

Bernie reached over, slapping Jensen on the shoulder. "You've been together for eight years, kid. Trust me, that girl's not going anywhere."

The shuffle of running feet, followed by the grunt and thud of Bruno landing in the foxhole turned both their attention back to the line. Bullets spattered the dirt, following close on the heels of Sergeant Ellis joining them.

"I hate trees," Ellis growled, sinking low in the foxhole.

"Didn't you grow up in the Blue Ridge?" Bruno asked with a teasing grin. "Lots of trees up there."

"Shut up, Bruno."

"Where's Graham?" Bernie asked, brow creasing.

Bruno's head swung side to side looking around, fingers tightening around the barrel of his rifle when he, too, noticed they were missing a man.

"He was right behind us," he grumbled.

Ellis cursed, throwing himself clumsily across the small space of the foxhole to look out where they'd come from. Another spatter of gunfire pelted the edge of the hole, bringing Jensen to full attention as he returned fire. Bernie squinted into the dense mid-evening air, looking for a shadow—listening for the snap of a twig. Anything to tell him Graham had simply fallen behind and not fallen down dead.

"Graham!" Bernie shouted.

His voice echoed back to him, hastily followed by the clatter of gunfire. Bernie ducked, eardrums throbbing when Jensen fired again, the shells falling to the ground beside him. Cheeks rounding, every breath a low puff between his lips, Bernie forced himself to peek over the edge of the foxhole again.

"Graham!" he bellowed, louder.

A grunt and scuffle nearby made his heart leap. Then Graham's voice called out roughly, "Bernie!"

"Graham! Where are you? You close?"

"Yeah, I think so!"

"Can you move?" Bruno asked.

"No!" Graham's shout was laced with frustration. "They've got me pinned down good, Bru!"

Bernie and Bruno locked gazes, Bernie huffing every breath in rhythm with his heartbeat. Then Bruno's jaw firmed—lips pressed tight.

"We going?" he asked.

Bernie closed his eyes briefly before nodding. "Yeah, we're going."

"Now hold on a minute." Ellis held up his hand, giving them a moment of pause. "I can't risk all three of you. If Graham stays put, maybe we can find a way to get him out of the line of fire without risk to the two of you."

"Sarge," Bruno said quietly. "You can order us to stay if you want. We respect you, you know that. But Graham has been with us since Africa. No way we're leaving him out there a second longer than we have to."

Ellis narrowed his eyes, letting his stare drift between the two of them before he nodded sharply. Jensen stopped firing, twisting his neck to look over his shoulder.

"I've got you two covered. If you're going, go now."

Bernie leaned his weight into his heels, inching himself up toward the edge of the foxhole. He and Bruno moved as one, leaping out of the shelter of the trench and among the trees. Bullets ate at the trees and ground as they scuffled through the forest, backs hunched and heads down to keep as low as possible.

Another shot sprayed splinters of bark into Bernie's face. He dropped, spinning to press his back into the nearest trunk. Bruno was a few feet across from him, knees bent to the ground and rifle raised as he searched for the enemy.

"I see him," Bruno announced.

Bernie turned his head, watching his friend.

"Krauts are dug in," he continued. "Graham's about ten feet to your left, Berns, pinned behind a fallen log."

"You got the krauts in your sights?" Bernie asked, breathing heavily.

"Yeah."

"Let 'em have it."

Bernie twisted back to his feet, briefly catching sight of the log Bruno mentioned before making a run for it. Bruno's rifle blasted behind him, accompanied by a symphony of German machine gun fire. Bullets ate up the ground at Bernie's feet as he raced between the trees and leaped over the log, falling on the hard ground with a grunt.

"Berns!" Graham's eyes widened in surprise.

Bernie scrambled up to his side, helmet thumping on the log as he took a moment to catch his breath. The log cracked and spit with every bullet it took, leaving splinters dusting their jackets.

"You wounded?" Bernie rasped.

Graham shook his head. "You?"

"Nah." Bernie took a breath, pressing his shoulders into the log in an attempt to see over the top.

The shots had suddenly stopped—deafening silence filling the woods all around them. Graham shifted, grunting and grumbling as he rolled awkwardly onto his belly and dragged his rifle up alongside him.

"You shouldn't have come after me, Bernie," he whispered.

"We couldn't leave you."

"We?"

Bernie shrugged slightly, then shouted, "Bruno!"

"Still here!" Bruno answered.

"Only one way to do this, Bru." Bernie chambered his rifle. The shell popped, spinning in midair before making its swift journey to the ground beside his elbow. "We gotta make a run for it!"

"Krauts are dug in ten yards dead ahead of you," Bruno replied. "Come back the same way you went in, Berns! I'll do my best to cover both of you."

Bernie looked back at Graham.

"You ready?"

Graham nodded.

"Okay ... now Bruno!"

Bernie stood up.

Suddenly, he could hear nothing. Not the sound of the gunfire, or the stomp of their feet as they ran. He could see Bruno, crouched behind one of the trees—shells popping one after another from his rifle as he fired into the wind, attempting to cover them. Bernie's head swung, looking in the direction of enemy fire.

Something gold glinting in the sunlight caught his eye. His feet stumbled, catching on a tree root. He fell forward, landing hard on his side and rolling into the nearest tree trunk.

"Berns!"

Head spinning, he raised half-lidded eyes. Graham had made it to Bruno, crouching low behind him in the cover of the tree. Bernie shifted onto his back, his head propped against the tree trunk and fingers wrapped tightly around the barrel of his gun.

I'm not crazy. His breaths came harder—rougher. *I'm not crazy.*

"I'm not," he grumbled out loud, staring up through the tree branches overhead. "I'm not crazy." Rolling, he raised his rifle, looking quickly through the scope toward the Nazi's foxhole.

Nothing. No sign of a glistening gold watch. Not even the glimmer of sunlight on a sniper's scope. Just trees and brush and the flash of flying bullets whistling through the air. His heart dropped as he realized he'd wanted to see the gold band around the faceless man's wrist. Anything to make his own growing doubts about what he'd seen all those weeks ago disappear.

"Bernie!" Bruno hissed. "Let's go!"

Bernie stared a moment longer, his finger slick on the icy trigger. A rush of wind swept over him, chilling the beads of sweat on the back of his neck. The sharp crack of gunfire ceased, either because they couldn't see him or because they were reloading ... Bernie didn't care.

Taking his chance, he loped across the ground, falling beside Bruno and Graham.

"What was that?" Bruno growled over his shoulder. "Why'd you hesitate? Did you see something?"

Bernie closed his eyes, trying to recreate in his mind exactly what he had seen. The glint of sun on the thin layer of snow? The flash of a stray bullet? The shimmering wristband of an expensive watch?

Slowly, he shook his head.

"Nothing, Bru," he muttered, preparing to make another run back for their foxhole. "Absolutely nothing."

Chapter Twenty-Two

AUSCHWITZ II – BIRKENAU

Once, the sight of a child brought joy. Perhaps, one day, it would again. But right now, standing near the edge of the children's block, a profound wave of sorrow swept through Margot so swiftly she wondered if she would die of this feeling instead of starvation and disease. Her skin burned beneath her dress, the stench rising in the air reminding her of her visit to the latrines. Reminding her it was only a matter of time before she succumbed to one of the many diseases dashing through the camp.

For now, though, she watched the children. Watched the small group being led away from the block. One little girl with her hand clasped firmly in the large palm of one of the SS guards, as if they were going for an innocent evening walk after dinner instead of her being taken to her death.

A soft tug at her sleeve pulled her back into the line, following her group back toward the barracks. Margot kept her head down, rubbing her fingers along her dry, cracked lips. She didn't dare glance back, preferring to walk away rather than watching the children disappear in the distance. Raising her head slightly, her shoulders stiffened—lifting nearly to her ears with stress at the sight of the guard marching their way.

Ludwig Volk barely glanced at her when he passed her . Their shoulders brushed, something rough passing into her palm. She curled her fingers around the material, neither she nor Ludwig breaking stride as he passed the secret present into her possession. Margot kept her fingers tight, completely concealing the gift against her palm. Quickening her pace, she barely breathed until they stepped through the barracks door.

"Hanna?" she called, squinting in the dim light of the room. She made her way between the bunks, finally coming to the one Hanna had been sharing with her since that horrible night she'd been attacked.

The girl was already there, curled near the edge of the mattress and holding Margot's spot for her. She sat up, crossing her legs beneath her as she scooted in, making room for Margot to join her.

"I have something for you," Margot announced, opening her fingers.

Hanna looked down, staring unblinking at the twist of string in her palm. She reached out, her bony fingers trembling as she brushed them against the rough twine.

"H-How?" she asked quietly.

"An old friend." Margot grabbed Hanna by the ankle, bringing her foot into her lap.

The sole of the boot was hanging by a thread, revealing the girl's bare, bleeding foot within. Wincing, she pressed the shoe back together, forcing herself to ignore Hanna's painful whimpers as she wrapped the string three times around the shoe before tying it off as tightly as she could.

"It is not much, but it should help a little." Margot gently tapped the side of the boot before moving Hanna's foot off her lap.

The barracks were almost as cold as outside. If anything, the walls seemed to create even more icy air rather than hold it at bay. They sat up together for a moment, the other women scuffling about, squeezing into their bunks and curling up together in the hopes of finding some semblance of warmth. After so long, no one really cared about the smells emanating from each other's bodies. Trying to keep warm was more important.

"Is this the same old friend who assists in the selections?" Hanna asked quietly, head bowed.

Margot's lip twisted. "Do not dwell on what he is forced to do, Hanna, *bitte*. Dwell instead on what he tries to do to help."

Hanna stroked the string holding her shoe together. "How do you pay for what he does?"

"What do you mean, *schätzchen*?" Margot tilted her head.

"He must ask for something in return. The ones who risk giving us things we are not allowed to have always do."

"He has asked me for nothing. He has asked only for the opportunity to help us survive."

Hanna reached up, slowly sliding the scarf from her head. Her hair was beginning to grow back, rich black hair grown nearly an inch long from her scalp. She ran a hand over them, twisting the short strands in different directions. Scratching the uncomfortable bits growing near the nape of her neck before tying the scarf around her head tighter.

"Did my brother ask for something in return?" Margot asked, unable to hold her tongue.

Hanna went still, her hands still raised behind her. She tugged on the ends of the scarf, tightening the knot before letting her arms drop heavily to her sides.

"*Nie*," Hanna replied. "He did not. Others have. But not him."

Her dark eyes softened, dry lips shaking into a gentle smile.

"You said ..." Margot hesitated, plucking at the hem of her dress. "You said ... that terrible night ... that he helped you once before. That was why you knew he'd protect us. Can I ask you how?"

Hanna's eyes grew large in her head, making Margot take note of her sallow cheeks and sunken sockets. Then she lowered herself onto her side, curling her arm beneath her head. Margot joined her, lying down so they faced each other on the bunk.

"When first I came here," Hanna whispered, a tear rolling from the inner corner of her eye and over the bridge of her nose. "I'd been married only eight months. When I stepped off the train, I was already beginning to ... show."

Margot's insides trembled.

"Your brother was there, assisting in the selections. He ... he saw. Saw I was with child. Knew what it would mean for me. But he passed me through for labor anyway." Hanna took a breath, closing her eyes to release more tears. "I'd heard some pregnant women in the camp were treated better than others. But I did not trust these SS to keep their word. Something in my heart warned me their promises were lies."

Margot slipped her hand into Hanna's and she clasped on, twining their fingers together.

"Your brother helped me hide my belly. He snuck me an extra bread ration when he could and when my time came, he stood guard outside the barracks to be certain no other guards would hear my labor, even though I made not a sound. My fear was greater than my pain."

Hanna sniffled, squeezing Margot's hand tighter. "I had a boy, Margot. He was perfect but ..."

"But?" Margot encouraged gently.

"But he was too small. He was not breathing when he was finally delivered." Hanna wiped the back of her hand on her cheeks to be rid of her tears. "Your brother took him for me, and the next day, I went on as if he'd never been born."

"Oh, Hanna," Margot choked on the words, drawing the girl into her arms. She tucked her against her chest, resting her chin atop Hanna's head. "I am so sorry."

"Later," Hanna whispered, "your brother told me he hid my baby boy in his coat and buried him for me beneath the tallest tree he could find in the forest. It was then I knew your brother—no matter what else he might do—was not hollow inside. His heart was still beating, even if only for an innocent babe."

"Hush." Margot stroked the top of her head. "Hush now, Hanna. Sleep."

Hanna wrapped her arm around Margot's waist, the warmth of her tears soaking through the front of Margot's dress.

"Sometimes," Hanna said, her voice getting smaller, softer as she began to drift off into sleep. "I think I can hear him crying. Even though it was never a sound I was to hear, I will wake in the middle of the night and think I hear a child weeping, and I ... I know it is him."

Margot squeezed her eyes closed, holding onto Hanna tighter until her breaths deepened in sleep. She replayed the story in her mind—what Hanna said about Franz ringing in her ears late into the night before she too finally fell asleep.

***

Margot woke with a start, her eyes slowly adjusting to the darkness of the barracks. Horst's form appeared slowly, his hand sliding away from her arm where he'd shaken her from her sleep.

"I need your help," he whispered.

Deciding to put aside her question of how he got into the women's barracks without being seen, she slipped out of her bunk with a hesitant glance back at Hanna before tiptoeing after him. Her feet sunk into the mud when they left the block, threatening to take her worn boots right off. Passing block after block, her heart beat faster, wondering where he was taking her.

They came to a small structure, shrouded in darkness. From within she could hear the soft cries of children—one of the voices rising to a piercing shriek. Margot froze, her skin as icy as a winter morning. Hanna's voice whispered in her ear, twisting her insides into a tight knot.

Sometimes ... I will wake in the middle of the night and think I hear a child weeping, and I ... I know it is him.

"What is this place?" she rasped.

Horst didn't answer. He opened the door, the hinges creaking softly. Every beat of her heart crashing in her ears warned her to run away. Every instinct told her to close her eyes. Instead, she walked across the threshold, eyes wide open. Margot covered her mouth, the stench threatening to bring up what little food she'd eaten that day.

If she'd been able to look around, she would've. But her gaze only briefly caught the crude instruments, the flash of metal, and her nose barely caught the sharp scent of a variety of medicines. Her focus, instead, was on the children, lying back to back on the table. A boy and a girl, same height, same features. Clearly twins.

Margot nearly fell in her rush to get to them, her feet sliding on the bloodied floor. They were bare from shoulders to waist. Blood and muck smeared on their pale, greying skin. Her hands trembled, reaching for their shaking forms.

"Oh, my poor darlings," she wept, stroking their hair.

Her eyes clasped on the source of their pain. The crude stitches, tying their backs together. The sickly green infection spreading toward their stomachs. The blood and pus oozing from the wound. They could be no older than four.

Margot looked up at Horst, his own eyes glistening.

"Do their parents live?" she asked, forcing the words passed her lips.

"The *mutter* still lives," he answered, head bobbing. "I saw her when she was once permitted to visit the children."

Margot nodded. "I need Franz."

Horst turned without a word, vanished back through the door. Margot grabbed the cloth rumpled near their feet, dragging it up to cover the horrid wound. She leaned over them, whispering softly to comfort them, pressing kisses to their sweaty foreheads. They couldn't open their eyes, the pain too severe for them to even try.

The door opened again, her brother appearing with Horst close behind. He went still, eyes widening and lip twisting.

"Mengele," he spat.

"Help me," she begged. "Help me move them."

Franz shook his head. "I cannot! Too risky! He will know."

Margot slammed her fist on the table. "I know that! I do not care! Listen to me, *mein bruder*, I know there is very little you can do for me in this place. Perhaps you think you have already done too much. But by God, you *will* help me with this!"

He hesitated a moment more, then tore at his buttons.

"They cleared another block today. We can take them there, but we must be quiet."

Margot nodded, watching him remove his jacket.

"Can you lift them?"

"I can try." Margot yanked off the cloth, bending over their little bodies. "*Schätzchen*, *bitte*, be as still as possible."

Franz waited, coat fisted in his hand. Margot took a breath, preparing to slide her arm beneath their bodies.

"Wait," Franz said, snatching the cloth from the table. He tore a few strips then looked into her eyes. "Put pieces in their mouths."

Margot's eyes rounded.

"Margot, they will scream. They are in too much pain not to. This will help keep them quiet."

She nodded, taking one of the strips and rolling it into a ball. Franz did the same, leaning over the little boy to stuff the piece between the child's teeth. Margot bent close to the girl, stroking the soft, shorn hairs on her head.

"I am sorry, *schätzchen*," she whispered, gently wedging the cloth between the girl's lips.

Squeezing her eyes closed, she nudged her arm beneath their bodies. The girl moaned, the boy shrieked, the cloths in their mouths muffling the sounds. Then she raised them and they both screamed. Margot threw her other arm around them, holding onto them as tight and still as possible.

"*Schnell*, Franz!"

Her brother tossed his coat across the table and she lowered the children onto it. Together, they tucked the jacket around them, tying the sleeves together to nestle them within its warmth. Margot folded their legs gently in the confines of the coat before looking up at her brother.

"How far is the block?" she asked, hardly able to speak at all.

Franz stared back, mouth pressed into a thin line. Choosing not to push for an answer, she rounded the corner of the table, taking a firm hold of the collar of the jacket beneath their little heads. Franz took the other end.

"Ready?"

He nodded.

"One ... two ... three!"

They lifted together, the combined weight of the children no heavier than a puppy. Their lack of nourishment alone would've been enough to bring tears to her eyes. But this ... this was shattering her soul like a stone through glass.

Horst held the door for them, peeking out before nodding they were clear. They moved quickly, Margot keeping her head down and her eyes on the whimpering twins. Allowing Franz to guide her through the dark camp to the emptied block.

They stepped into the abandoned barracks, the toe of Margot's shoe nearly catching and sending her tumbling with the twins. She regained herself quickly, moving to the nearest bunk to lay them down. Franz stepped back as she untied the sleeves of the coat, releasing some of the little ones' restriction.

"What now, Margot?" Franz asked through heavy breaths. "You cannot hide them here for long."

Margot perched herself on the edge of the bunk, stroking the little boy's head. "They have a *mutter*."

"I will find her," Horst's voice said from the door.

She hadn't even realized he'd been following until he spoke. Looking over her shoulder, she was in time to catch a glimpse of him slipping back out the door, into the night.

"I don't know how he gets around the way he does," Franz mumbled.

"He is clever, and he is small." Margot repeated some of the first words Horst said to her when she arrived here. Then she arched a brow, glancing over her shoulder at her brother. "Is that not why he's here?"

Franz bowed his head, staring at the floor beneath his feet. "I'll need my coat back."

Margot narrowed her eyes. "You will get it. But there is something else you must do for me."

She stood up, moving to his side. After whispering her instructions in his ear, she stepped away, staring straight into his eyes. Franz's gaze shifted between her and the twins.

"Can you do it?" she asked.

He hesitated, large hands curling into fists at his sides. Then he sighed.

"Stay quiet. I'll be back."

He sidestepped around her, boots thumping on the weak boards as he strode out of the barracks.

Margot sat down on the edge of the bunk again, cooing softly as she brushed her hands against their fiercely hot skin. They shook with the fever. Margot gently tugged her brother's coat tighter around them in an attempt to keep them warm.

"Mama ..." the little boy called, his tiny voice rough. "Mama?"

A tear slipped from her lashes, catching on her cheek. Margot wiped it away, bending until her forehead touched his temple.

"She is coming, *mein schatz*." She kissed his cheek, his skin boiling hot beneath her lips. "Try to sleep now. Try to rest."

She stepped around to the other side of the bunk, kneeling beside the little girl. The cloth was still stuffed in her mouth, her little chest convulsing with uneven breaths and her lids fluttering, revealing only the whites of her rolled eyes. Margot reached her finger between the girl's lips, tugging the cloth gently out.

Every breath was a gasp once the cloth was released. Her little hands moved, tiny fingers swollen from the infection rapidly spreading through her blood. She reached out her arms blindly, seeking comfort. Wanting to be held. Margot lightly took the girl's hands, kissing every fingertip before sliding closer on her knees, letting the child grip the collar of her dress in as comfortable a hug as she could manage. She lifted her arm over the girl, placing her hand soothingly on the boy's chest so he'd know she was still there.

She didn't know how long they were alone. Thirty minutes? An hour? After a while listening to their soft cries, their struggling breaths, she didn't care. When the door opened, her head jerked up, heart racing out of control until the moment Horst appeared.

"I found her," he said, the utter awe in his own voice resonating through her.

Margot rose, giving the girl one more kiss before she circled away from the bunk. The woman before her stood several inches shorter than Margot—so thin, the prison gown she wore looked more like a tent hanging on her bony shoulders. Her head was wrapped in a dirty gray scarf and her dark, round eyes stared curiously at Margot.

"Why am I here?" she asked, her thick accent making the Polish words flow like a song off her tongue.

Once again, Margot thanked God her father insisted she be educated. Her Polish wasn't perfect but good enough.

"I have your children here," Margot replied, gesturing behind her. "They … they need you now."

The woman's legs shook so hard, she nearly buckled to the ground. Without a word, she ran past Margot, falling to her knees beside the bunk with a cry. Margot closed her eyes, more tears caressing her cheeks as she listened to the woman sob over her dying children. She hugged herself, forcing one foot in front of the other toward the door.

The moment she reached it, the hinges creaked, revealing Franz standing on the other side. They said nothing, simply clasped eyes, holding steady. Margot wanted nothing more than to throw her arms around him. To seek his comfort, the way she used to when she was a child.

But we will never be children again.

"Did you find some?" she asked.

Franz nodded, holding out his fisted hand. "Are you sure, Margot?"

Bowing her head, she watched him unfurl his fingers to reveal the glistening vials on his palm. She wouldn't ask him how he'd gotten to the morphine—she wouldn't ask him how much he'd risked. She only cared that he'd done what she asked.

"*Ja*," she murmured. "I'm sure."

Returning to the mother's side, she knelt on the ground, her knees scraping the rough wood flooring. Softly, she took the woman's hand, pressing the cool vials in her palm. Looking between the medicine and Margot, the mother of the twins began to tremble.

"W-what is this?" she stuttered, the vials clicking together in her unsteady hand.

Margot looked deeply into her eyes, closing the woman's fingers over the morphine.

Then she whispered, "Mercy."

Understanding lit on the woman's face. She turned away, returning her attention to her children. Margot rose, turning to leave her alone with them. She walked to the door, standing between Franz and Horst as she looked out over the dark shadows of night covering the camp's buildings.

"I was supposed to find him when they woke," Horst said over the sounds of the mother's tears joining her children's. "Mengele ordered me to get him, whether he slept or not."

"But you came to me instead." Margot looked down at him. "Is this what he makes you assist him with? Is Mengele the *doctor* who keeps you like a dog?"

Horst bowed his head, hiding his eyes. His silence was all the answer she needed.

"I will tell him the children died and were sent to the crematorium by mistake," Franz announced, drawing both their gazes. "I will take full responsibility, Horst. You don't have to worry."

"*Danke*," Horst murmured.

They fell into silence, listening only to the sounds of the night and the soft weeping behind them. Hours they stood there, Margot hugging her arms tight across her ribs with feet planted firmly together on the ground. Only as the sun began to rise over Auschwitz did she notice.

The twins had stopped crying.

Chapter Twenty-Three

Franz hadn't shown himself in days. Not since Ilse asked him for water. The days seemed to grow longer since he'd said he'd try to help, just like the distance between her and the people she loved. With every minute that passed, Ilse felt them slipping away from her forever—as her father had after she fled Leipzig so long ago now.

Looking back, she wondered how she could have ever thought hiding out with the Raskopfs would last. Every path she'd gone down since running to them seemed to have ultimately led her here. No matter how Margot had fought for her, no matter how her own fear had kept her sequestered within the walls of their home—out of sight of everyone else in Berlin for the most part—she knew now she would have still come to this place, or another like it, eventually.

A harsh cough shook her chest. Ilse pressed her palm flat on her breastbone, taking a few deep, wheezing breaths. She'd avoided acknowledging the cough along with the aches and shivers that had been attempting to overwhelm her since she woke that morning. She knew what they meant, but as long as she was strong enough to stand on her own two feet, she would not recognize their presence in her body.

Pushing forward with that thought, Ilse dropped the bundle of bandages on the table and began to sort through them. Rivka was standing on the other side, watching her from beneath her long lashes. She hadn't spoken to the woman since that awful night in the barracks—avoiding eye contact at all costs. There was nothing to say. Nothing Rivka could say would change what she'd seen or make her feel differently about it.

No matter how true what she said might be. Ilse cringed, tossing aside one of the dirtier bandages.

Whether Rivka was right, that the child and mother did not have a chance, Ilse didn't want to contemplate. She only knew what she'd seen. She only knew how watching it had made her feel.

The door to the barracks burst open and Ilse spun, feet in motion the moment she saw the guard callously dragging the limp woman behind him. He tossed her toward one of the cots, recently vacated when the doctor had made his rounds again, selecting. Ilse and Rivka moved as one to the bloodied woman's side.

Ilse's face twisted in disgust, watching the way the woman's jaw flopped, blood pouring between her lips and both eyes swelling so rapidly she couldn't open them anymore. Looking at her frail state, Ilse knew several bones had to be broken from the beating she'd taken. Running her hand down the woman's leg, she could feel where her knee had been crushed beneath the strike of a club.

"Is she dead?" the guard asked, deep voice a low rumble.

Ilse frowned but forced herself not to look at him.

"Almost," Rivka replied for her.

The guard sniffed, shrugged, and strode out of the infirmary, leaving the door open behind him. Ilse tugged the scarf off the woman's head, shaking her own.

"What could she have done to deserve this?" she wondered.

"What did any of us do, Ilse?"

Ignoring Rivka, Ilse began to remove the woman's clothing. Hands shaking, she found her heart racing nearly out of control—the breath catching in her lungs and causing her to cough again. The thought this pitiful creature lying on the filthy ground could one day soon be her was too much. The horrible realization that one day she might do something deemed wrong, which would then warrant such a severe beating making her head spin.

"I ... I cannot ..." Ilse bent over, the nausea stirring her stomach making her dizzy. "I cannot ... do ... this ... anymore!"

"Ilse!" Rivka hissed, snagging her by the sleeve. "Control yourself!"

"I can't!"

Ilse spun away on her knees, crawling a few feet before getting her feet under her again. She started for the door and stopped short, a chill enveloping her body until she couldn't help but tremble. Franz was standing in the door, staring steadily back into her eyes. Then he turned, disappearing around the corner of the building the same way he had during their first meeting.

Swallowing back the sick feeling, Ilse marched, ignoring Rivka's warning whisper for her to come back. She followed him, her boots sinking in the mud the moment she stepped outside—the harsh sting of Winter air making her hiss through her teeth.

He was waiting for her beside the building, head down and arms tucked behind his back. Ilse hugged herself, leaning back on the wall.

"Where were you?" she asked.

"I'm sorry Ilse, but something ... happened."

Her fingers sunk into her palms. "Margot?"

Franz cringed. "*Ja*. She is all right, though."

"Why are you here, Franz?" Ilse sighed, pressing her head back into the wall. She watched him through the heavy shadow of her eyelids. The way his brow furrowed in confusion, the curious tilt of his head as he tried to understand what she was asking and why she was asking it.

"I was assigned—"

"*Nein*," Ilse interrupted, holding up her hand to stop him. "Why are you *here*? If you have no intention of helping me when you said you would, then why are you here?"

"Ilse, I tried—"

"Did you?" Ilse lurched forward, the top of her head barely reaching his chest. She tilted her neck back to glare furiously into his eyes. "Why did you have them put me here? Why did you tell them I have medical experience? I don't know what I'm doing here, Franz! I can barely breathe in there, and ..."

Her voice trailed followed by the coughs she'd been suppressing—each one harder, louder than the last, swallowing her words.

"Ilse?" Franz placed his hand on her shoulder.

She shrugged him off, stepping away to put distance between them once more.

"Why, Franz? Why did you let them take me away from Margot? I need her! I cannot do this without—!"

"They wanted to send you to the left!" He grabbed her by the arms, yanking her close until she could smell him.

Ilse's head spun, the scent of male sweat mixed with a spice she couldn't name overcoming her senses. Her knees knocked together as she began to process what he'd said.

"To ... the left?" she repeated.

Franz closed his eyes, bowing his head until his forehead touched hers.

"When Mengele was making his selections on the platform, he … he wanted to send you to the left line which … which would have meant …"

"Immediate termination?" she choked, the sob tightening her chest making her cough worse.

He nodded, his forehead rubbing hers roughly. "I told them you had medical experience in the hopes he would spare you, and he did."

Ilse burst into tears, wrapping her arms around his neck and burying her face in his shoulder. She didn't care if someone saw them—she didn't care what her fellow prisoners would think or what the SS guards might do if they caught them. She needed him. And as his arms went around her, she realized he didn't care, either.

"I am so sorry, *mein freund*." Franz's warm breath tickled the side of her throat.

Ilse lowered herself from her tiptoes, her heels sinking into the soft mud. Breathing deeper, she looked up at him.

"I am sick, Franz," she whispered.

His eyes fluttered closed, hands tightening on her upper arms until she thought her bones might break.

"I know you did this to save me, but now—"

"I had to try! Would you rather I had let them send you to your death?"

"Franz—"

He pulled her forward before she could finish. Ilse gasped when his mouth touched hers, kissing her deeply. She stumbled back and he came with her, falling back against the infirmary wall. Her lips tingled beneath the pressure of his, the desperation in his kiss so deep she could feel it to the tips of her toes.

Gently, Ilse pressed her hands flat on his chest and broke away from him.

"I have always loved you, Ilse," he gasped, breathless.

A tear rolled over the curve of her cheek. "I know, *mein freund*. I know."

Softly, she ran her fingertips down his cheek. Even with her mouth still warm from his kiss, all she could think of was how he'd put himself at risk by such contact. She did not know what illness she had. She did not know how soon he himself might now begin to show symptoms.

Why would he do that? Ilse bent her head, reaching to remove his grip from her arms.

The door to the infirmary opened and Ilse gasped, nearly falling when Franz yanked her further away out of sight. Boots splashed in the mud, the soft cries of people being removed from the building filling her ears.

"Move! *Schnell!*" one of the guard's gruff voices shouted.

Ilse frowned, leaning forward slightly until she could see around the corner. Her eyes went wide when she saw Rivka marching in line, supporting one of the weaker inmates with a steady hand. Despite being weighed down by the body of the other woman, she held her head high, eyes shining with courage and only a slight tremor in her bottom lip giving away her hidden fear.

She looked over her shoulder, as if sensing she was being watched. Ilse opened her mouth to call out, but Rivka's lips firmed, her head wagging slightly in a silent order for her to keep her silence. Only then, did Ilse know for sure—did she understand.

I will never see her again.

"*Schnell!*" the guard yelled again, giving Rivka a hard shove.

Ilse backed away, fresh tears flaming in her eyes. Turning back, she gripped Franz's sleeves, taking a few deep breaths.

"Franz," she paused, licking her lips before forcing herself to look into his eyes. "If you truly still love me ... then you must do something for me."

His eyes narrowed, uncertainty glimmering in his gaze.

"I need you to make me a promise and keep it, no matter what. Can you do that?" Ilse held her breath, his silence nearly stopping her heart.

Then, he nodded.

"*Ja*, Ilse. I will do anything you ask without question."

Ilse smiled.

★★★

Margot stared down into the thin, sickly brown soup rippling on her plate. Her hollow stomach rumbled painfully. Stealing a glance at Geisler, she slipped the potato peels she'd snuck out of the kitchen from the folds in her scarf. Keeping close watch on the guard, she nibbled one of the peels along with her bread ration before passing the rest subtly into Hanna's hand. Her friend smiled, also pressing a peel against her piece of bread to eat them together before handing some off to the person beside her.

They ate quietly, their small rations gone within moments. Winter's furious bite clamped over her entire body, reminding her of the night before. The sight of the children had made her completely forget her own frozen skin, stiff bones, and aching muscles. A shivering breath tapered her lungs as she pushed the memory away from her. Her eyelids hung heavily in exhaustion.

Margot hadn't slept at all after walking the mother quietly back to her barracks. They hadn't spoken a word. Merely walked together in total silence, leaving Franz to carry the bodies of the dead twins away in the glow of the rising sun. She'd looked at Margot for a few breath-halting moments before disappearing inside her barracks. Horst had seen her safely back to her own. It hadn't been long before the morning gong had rung, rousing all of them from their bunks.

She'd moved throughout her day as if asleep on her feet. Doing her work, keeping quiet, and obeying any commands given by the guards. Her one act of defiance in the wake of the horror of the night before had been to steal the potato peels. They tasted better than the soup and stale bread they were rationed every day.

Hanna pressed a hand to Margot's arm, smiling softly before following the other women toward the washrooms. Margot took her time finishing, knowing she might miss her chance at a turn in the washroom if she didn't go now. But free time in this place was precious, and after last night, she wasn't going to miss her chance to see Horst again.

He hadn't spoken to her when they left the mother at her barracks. He, too, had guided her in silence, both of them narrowly evading the guards beginning to patrol the camp grounds, preparing to sound the morning gong. Only when they'd reached her barracks had he whispered for her to meet him after their evening meal.

Margot hurried away from the rest of the inmates, keeping her head bowed and hands folded steadily in front of her. If she did not meet their eyes, then perhaps they would not see she was not where she was supposed to be. She took the same path she'd followed the first time she'd caught sight of Horst here, scurrying quickly between the two buildings where he'd pulled her in for their long-awaited reunion.

He was waiting for her, leaning with his back to the wall and his head tilted up to stare at the sky. Margot joined him, standing at his right side. She kept her eyes on the ground. Nothing but their breaths and the distant sound of the people marching about filling her ears. Then, inhaling deeply, she finally found words.

"Tell me everything," she whispered. "I want to know what he makes you do. I want to know why he makes you do it. And most of all, I want to know you do not do it by choice."

"Of course not!" Horst hissed, hands clenching. "I do what I must to survive, like everyone else in this place."

"Very well. Then tell me what you have been forced to do." Margot placed her hands over her heart, trying to prepare herself for what Horst was about to tell her.

Her friend covered his eyes with his hand, small shoulders rising and falling with a shaking exhale.

"His name is Josef Mengele," Horst whispered. "When I survived my intended execution, he decided to allow me a reprieve from death on the condition I work for him. I was forced to stand by while he executed and dissected people born like me. I was forced to help prepare syringes so he might inject children with medicine to kill them."

Tears rolled down Margot's cheeks, and she dug her jagged fingernails deep into her arms. Horst paused briefly, turning his face away from her.

"The children last night were one of his many experiments. To see, if joined outside the womb, twins could survive—could share blood and body. He was furious to discover they were gone today," Horst murmured. "My time here is coming to an end, Margot, I can feel it."

"*Nein*," Margot gasped, taking hold of his shoulders. Forcing him to look up at her. "*Nein*, you have survived this long. You must continue to go on, Horst. You must!"

"How?" Horst shoved her hands off, taking a step back. "How, when I know any day he could wake up and decide today is the day he will put me to death and send my corpse back to Berlin to be studied like all the others?"

"You will survive the same way we all do! Any day my block could be cleared and marched to the gas chambers with every woman in my barracks. But I do not give up!"

"You have not seen what I've seen!"

"*Ja* I did! Last night! Or have you so soon forgotten I was there when those poor babies died?"

Silence dropped around them like a dense cloud, thickening in the air until she could barely breathe.

"I will never forget, Margot," Horst whispered. "I think you will never forget, either."

She shook her head fiercely. "*Nein*. Never."

Horst reached out between them, taking her hand once more. "Forgive me. In my heart, I think of you as being the innocent child I once knew. But you, like so many others, have been completely stripped of such innocence within these gates."

Margot scrubbed her sleeve on her cheeks, the material burning her skin.

"For so long I have heard of these places, Horst. I have tried to cling to the belief that God will trample these camps beneath his feet and save us all. From a distance, I could believe he was at work somehow. But being here … how could God do this?"

Horst's broad brow wrinkled with a frown. He reached for her hand, squeezing her fingers softly.

"This is not the work of God, Margot. This is the work of men. Men who have given themselves to an evil we cannot comprehend. But do not look at this place and think this is what God has done."

Margot shook her head, sniffling quietly as she blinked away the remainder of her tears.

"Promise me you will protect yourself, Horst. As best you can."

He smiled gently, patting her knuckles. "Return to your barracks now, Margot. The gong will ring soon."

She nodded, reaching down to grip him in a tight hug before spinning away. His footsteps squishing in the mud, the sound reaching her from behind, but she did not look back to watch. The gong rang as she reached the washrooms, stealing her chance to attempt scrubbing her soiled body. Margot could feel the guards watching as she joined the group heading for her barracks, subtly searching their faces.

Franz hadn't shown himself all day. Neither had Ludwig. Where they were and what duties they were performing, she did not know and was not certain she wanted to. If given the opportunity, she would've asked Franz more about what he'd done for Hanna. Would've asked him how he managed to get away long enough to bury the child without anyone knowing.

Would have hugged him, as I have wanted to for so long now. Margot wrapped her arms around herself. The night air swirled around her, wrapping her in its frozen embrace.

She dragged her feet into the barracks, letting most of the women pass her by. How could she sleep after all of this? Even as her eyes continued to weigh, she couldn't imagine sleeping. Her mind spun with images of the twins. Her ears still filled with their cries of pain, their gasping breaths. Her fingertips still tingling with the feel of their hot skin.

"*Bitte*, are you Hanna?"

Margot froze, the familiar voice shattering her thoughts.

"I am looking for Hanna. *Bitte*, she knows *mein freund*."

Heart thundering, a lump rising in the center of her throat, she pushed her way between some of the women still standing.

"*Bitte*, are you Hanna?"

"*Tak*," Hanna's voice answered. "I am called Hanna. Do you speak Polish? My German is not so good."

Margot came to a skidding halt before Hanna's question could be answered. Slowly, the girl turned, her blue eyes striking Margot so hard her legs nearly collapsed beneath her. Golden hair was beginning to grow back on her head, her dress stained with mud and her form slighter than Margot remembered. But there was no mistaking those eyes, or that smile.

"Ilse!" Margot lunged, throwing her arms around the girl.

They nearly toppled, clinging to each other—their cries echoing against the barracks walls.

"Where have you been?" Margot gasped, taking Ilse's face between her palms. "What happened to you, *schätzchen*?"

Ilse shook her head, her throat convulsing with repressed sobs. "*Bitte*, Margot, I … I cannot speak of it. Franz brought me here. He told me if I could not find you to ask for Hanna, because you would be with her."

Margot kissed her cheek before dragging her back into her arms. A rough cough shook Ilse's body, and she turned away, covering her mouth to muffle the awful sound. Margot massaged her back, drawing her toward the bunk so they could squeeze in. Hanna looked at Ilse warily, tugging on Margot's sleeve.

"Is she sick?" Hanna hissed. "We cannot have her here if she's sick."

"She is fine," Margot muttered, even as she felt the heat generating from Ilse's skin and felt her tremble.

She trembles because it is cold. Nothing more. Margot laid down, pulling Ilse with her as Hanna curled close on her other side.

"You said Franz brought you," Margot whispered near Ilse's ear. "Did he know where you were this whole time?"

"*Ja*," Ilse replied, resting her cheek on Margot's shoulder. "But he could do little for me until today."

Margot held her friend tighter, stroking the rough hairs on top of her head. Then Ilse sighed, falling heavily into her side.

"Promise me something, Margot," she said.

"Anything, *schätzchen*."

"Promise me you will not be angry with Franz. He has brought me to you, and that is what matters. He is still the *großer bruder* you remember."

Margot closed her eyes and squeezed Ilse tighter.

"I think, *mein schatz*, I am beginning to believe he is again."

Chapter Twenty-Four

Every muscle in Bernie's body ached. His body weighed down with the heaviness of exhaustion and the impossibility of sleep. After nearly a month of fighting in the Hürtgen, they'd finally been moved to a rear area for some much-needed rest. But despite them telling him these days were for rest, he'd gotten very little. His mind racing with the beating they'd taken in the woods, the numbers they'd lost ... the gold shine of a watch he was almost sure he'd seen.

He sat up, leaning forward to rest his head in his palms and elbows on his knees. Bruno groaned a few feet away, rolling over on the sofa. He crossed his arms, mumbled something, then resumed snoring. Bernie shook his head, pushing himself off the floor. The abandoned farmhouse was somewhat of a comfort for their unit. Four walls, an intact roof, and shuttered windows gave a small sense of security for some of them.

For Bernie, the emptiness of the place seemed to mirror the growing hollowness in his heart. He moved quietly through the house, passing the room occupied by Ellis and Graham—listening to the distant murmurs of Woodley meeting with the other commanding officers. Coming to the front door, he found Jensen standing there, leaning on the doorjamb and staring at the trucks and tanks bordering the property.

Bernie stopped beside him, leaning on the other side of the doorway. Jensen looked at him from the corner of his eye, threading his arms across his chest when a chill breeze swept over them. The yard was covered in fresh, white powder. The recent mist of snow left behind not only the cold, but an icy blanket from the meadow to the forest. Jensen's shoulders trembled when he fixed his gaze on the distant trees.

"We lost this one," he muttered, breaking the silence. "Didn't we, Russell?"

Bernie cringed, roughly scrubbing his palm against the back of his neck. He didn't want to answer, the truth in his words ringing in his heart. There was no denying they'd been thoroughly and viciously beaten in the Hürtgen, but he wasn't quite ready to admit it out loud. He shuffled, boots scraping on the wood floor.

"You hear anything about where we're going next?" Bernie asked, rubbing his eyes and bringing his fingers together to pinch the bridge of his nose.

"Not yet."

"You sleep at all?"

Jensen shrugged. "A little. Couldn't seem to settle."

"Yeah, I get that."

Heavy footfalls from behind made them both twist to look over their shoulders. Woodley appeared, his brow pulled together in a deep frown. He stood for a moment in the hall, massaging his palms together to warm them. Then he made a sharp gesture with his hand.

"Russell, Jensen, come with me."

They hesitated a couple of seconds before turning in unison, following quietly in the captain's footsteps. He stopped briefly to call Graham and Ellis out of the dining room before heading into the parlor where Bruno was stirring.

"Captain," Bruno mumbled, sitting up.

"At ease, Agnelli," Woodley answered without breaking stride over to the windows.

He stood for a moment in silence, staring through the cracks in the shutters before spinning on his heels to face them again.

"Boys," he began, voice low. "I wanted to tell you this first. You've all been real assets to this unit. And I know you were all hoping we'd get a chance at Berlin."

Woodley stopped, inhaling sharply.

"Why does this sound like bad news, Cap?" Bruno asked, pushing slowly to his feet.

"We're needed elsewhere. We're moving out first thing in the morning to the Ardennes … in Belgium."

His words fell like a boulder in the middle of the room. Bernie's gaze shifted between each of the men, watching Bruno's face slowly redden, Ellis bow his head low, and Graham stare glossily at Woodley, as if he wasn't fully comprehending what had been said.

"Are you telling me we're going backward, sir?" Bruno growled.

"I'm telling you we've received our orders. Our men on the Ardennes front need reinforcements and we're it." Woodley hooked his hands low on his hips, scuffing the toe of his boot on the floor.

"So you're telling me, we've spent the last two months taking a German city, getting our butts kicked in that hell they call a forest, losing over half of our division," Bruno paused, his broad chest rising with a deep inhale. "And we don't even get a shot at Berlin? We get pulled out to fight in another godforsaken wood *outside* Germany?"

"Agnelli," Woodley rumbled, his voice edged with warning. "Like I said, we have our orders. It doesn't mean I like it any better than you do."

The captain stomped across the room, brushing past Bernie. He watched him go, noting how every time he saw him his steps seemed heavier. His shoulders more deeply hunched and the circles beneath his eyes darker. If he wanted to, Bernie could stop asking Graham how many men they'd lost. Woodley had to live with the numbers every day.

Now he's taking us to another unknown future. Bernie turned back, catching Bruno's eye.

"This is not right, Berns," Bruno hissed. "It's not fair."

"No, it's not," Ellis answered before Bernie could. "But don't take it out on Woodley, Bruno. He's doing his job, just like the rest of us. And right now, our job is to move out for the Ardennes."

Bernie turned away from the room, following in Woodley's steps toward the door. He charged through the doorway, ignoring the wind whipping like shards of ice into his face. Taking long strides, he covered the distance between the house and the line of trucks, finally coming to a stop. Resting his palm flat on the side of the truck, he hung his head heavily, quick exhales steaming on the air.

Then he turned, slamming his fist into the truck. Pain shot up his forearm, his knuckles cracking against the hard side of the vehicle. With a shout he kicked the tire, fists flying as he punched the truck over and over, releasing his wrath on tire and metal instead of on his officers. When his knuckles were raw and his throat hoarse, he dropped to the ground in the slush, slamming his back into the tire.

He closed his eyes, resting his head back. A soft shuffle, then the brush of a shoulder against his warned him someone had joined him, but he kept his eyes closed.

"Get it out of your system, private?" Woodley asked.

"I think so," Bernie replied.

"Good." The icy ground crunched beneath the captain's boots when he shifted.

Bernie kept his eyes closed, listening to the soft whistle of the wind, the rustle of Woodley's clothes as he shifted his weight side to side. Breathing in the crisp, cold air and nearly choking on the scent of smoke and rubber that came with the chill.

Then Woodley's voice murmured, "Are you ready for what's next?"

Bernie opened his eyes and turned his head to look at him. The captain looked him square in the eye, the glimmer of a secret shining back at him. He'd told them only that they were needed, he hadn't told them how bad things were going to be. He hadn't told them exactly what to expect in this next step of their journey.

But it didn't matter. Bernie was used to the unknown.

"Yes, sir," he answered. "Ready as I'll ever be."

Chapter Twenty-Five

AUSCHWITZ II – BIRKENAU

"I dreamed about Bernie again last night." Margot looked up at Hanna and Ilse through her lashes. They stared back placidly, hands moving automatically as they sorted through the pile of clothing.

After waking from a nightmare three nights ago, Margot had finally confided her deepest secret to her friends. How his letter had reached across three countries to get to her—how somehow her reply managed to fall into his possession. How, right before the gestapo came, she'd sent off her diary to the American man who'd given her hope and would probably never know if he received the little book filled with all of her inner secrets and thoughts.

They'd listened to her go on with gentle patience and held her when she was finished. Reassuring her everything was going to be all right. Being able to talk about him lifted a persistent weight off her chest, filling some of the emptiness inside.

"Do you really believe the Americans could make it this far?" Hanna wondered with a sniffle, her nose turning red with the cold.

"Bernie Russell believes so," Margot replied. "His faith gives me hope."

"It would be amazing," Ilse commented on a raspy whisper. "To have the Americans march in here to free us all."

"*Ja.*" Margot reached over, squeezing Ilse's fingers. "It certainly would."

"I was able to speak to another prisoner from the men's camp yesterday," Hanna said, leaning forward to speak in confidence. "I traded him some bread for more string for my shoes. He believes the Russians will reach us before the Americans do."

Ilse let out a wheezing cough, turning her head to muffle the sound against her shoulder. Margot stared at her, twisting a sweater around in her hands. Deep down, she felt Hanna suspected what Margot already knew, she simply didn't say anything. Not since that first night. There was no denying Ilse's fever grew with every passing day. No denying there was only so much time left before Geisler or one of the other guards noticed she was sick and sent her to the camp infirmary.

But we will hide it as long as we can. Margot pressed her lips firmly in determination before continuing the sorting.

The heavy crunch of boots marching closer drew her gaze. A frown creased her brow when she saw Ludwig heading their way, worry glistening in his eyes. His pace slowed as he came closer, glancing over his shoulder at the other guards. Margot took a small step to the side, bringing herself near him as he came to a hesitant stop.

"Something's wrong," Ludwig said, voice low. "They're gathering all the women for—"

"Volk!" the sharp shout of another male guard behind him made him cringe. "Bring those three!"

"*Ja!*" Ludwig answered, his face hardening to stone. "*Schnell!* Come!"

He yanked on her arm, pulling her away from her work before doing the same to Hanna and Ilse. Margot grabbed both their hands, keeping them close as Ludwig hurried them away. They stumbled when Ludwig pushed them faster, the rockier ground near the tracks giving way to slush and mud as they marched. Up ahead, Margot caught sight of all the women being lined up, as if for roll call. Her heart beat faster. It wasn't time for the evening roll call, so what was happening?

Three SS were heading their way, speaking quietly between each other. Margot caught herself staring at them, something about the one in the middle tickling her warning instincts. She tried to breathe through the feeling, even as she was unable to look away. He was smiling about something, his uniform cap shadowing his forehead. Then he turned his head and their eyes met. Margot's lungs filled, the air halting—making her head spin.

She'd never seen him before, but she couldn't look away. Something deep inside her told her she knew him. Knew him only for the danger gleaming in his eyes. He too couldn't seem to avert his gaze, both of them staring into each other's eyes as they walked directly past one another, Margot's neck twisting to hold his stare for a few moments longer.

Finally, she turned away, quickening her pace as Ludwig hustled them into the line. One of the guards grabbed Ilse by the arm. Margot bit back a sound of protest as her friend's hand was pulled out of hers. She frowned, watching Ilse be brought between two other women at the very front of their formation. Ilse's bony shoulders hunched, her entire body shaking as the cold wind drifted between their bodies.

Her heart lifted when Franz appeared, marching toward them alongside a superior officer. They stopped in front of the line, the superior officer pacing back and forth in front of them. Margot's hands tightened into fists at her sides every time he passed by Ilse. Then, Franz's voice rose on the air.

"One of you is a murderer," he announced. "The body of a guard, Dietrich Fürst, was found beneath the platform of one of our new buildings."

Margot nearly buckled to the ground.

"He'd been dead for some time," Franz continued, beginning to pace with his superior.

"And near his body," the superior officer said, reaching into his pocket. "We found this."

Hanna grabbed her hand when he pulled out the muddied scarf, dry and stiff now. Margot twisted her fingers around Hanna's.

Franz will protect us ... he will protect us ... Margot's mind spun with these silent reassurances, watching the two of them study each of the women.

"Someone must pay for this," the superior officer growled. "One of you killed your guard. One of you stabbed him to death right here in this camp."

Margot felt the tension rise among the women. Felt every time one of them shifted nervously or whimpered in fear.

Franz will protect us ... he will ... he ... will ... Margot's thoughts came to a stuttering end in her head when her brother stopped pacing, coming to a halt.

Right in front of Ilse.

Her throat burned, watching her brother lean close until his nose nearly touched Ilse's. She started to shake her head, the rock in her stomach growing larger until she thought she would split apart.

"Did you not used to wear a scarf?" Franz hissed.

Ilse's head tilted, meeting his eyes. "I ... I ..."

"This one."

Franz pulled Ilse out of the line, dragging her a few feet away from the other women. The other officer watched calmly, bunching the scarf into his fist and a small smirk tilting the corner of his mouth.

This isn't happening! Margot's inner voice screamed. *It cannot be happening!*

She watched as her brother spun Ilse around to face him. Watched as he easily slipped his luger from the holster at his belt. Ilse's head was down, the sunlight catching on the short blonde hairs on her head and the dirt smearing her pale skin.

Nein ... nein ... Margot shook her head as Franz leveled the pistol at Ilse's head.

The girl looked up, her gaze colliding with Margot's. A soft smile touched her lips, the peace glistening in her bloodshot eyes piercing her as sharply as a bullet.

The gunshot stabbed her ears.

Ilse's head flew back, a stream of blood flashing through the air. Her body toppled, arms falling limp and legs collapsing beneath her as she crashed to the ground. A swirl of smoke rose from the barrel of her brother's luger, his arm slowly lowering back to his side.

Suddenly, Margot could hear nothing but the beating of her own heart. Staring at Ilse's body, twisted and lifeless on the ground, her chest began to tremble. Hanna's grip tightened, but not enough to hold her back.

A scream rose in the air and it took her a moment to realize it was coming from her. Hot tears streamed her cheeks as she shoved through the crowd of women, knocking some to the ground as she charged directly for her brother. Franz turned, eyes wide and lips parting when he saw her breaking formation.

She lunged for him, hands reaching to claw his face— heart filled with murderous intent. But the strong arm of the superior officer slammed into her chest. A breath caught in her throat as she was thrown backward, his fist curling around a handful of her dress. Before she could even glimpse his face, balled knuckles smashed into her nose and mouth. Margot grunted, legs twisting as she fell in a heap to the ground, her hands sinking in the thick mud along with the side of her face.

Blood gushed from her nostrils, pouring over her lips and chin like a river. Margot wailed, her eyes burning as tears poured down her cheeks. Then she heard the click of a pistol and went still. Her fingers curled, feet scrambling in the mud.

Then, she pushed herself up, spinning around on her knees ... and stared up the barrel of the officer's pistol.

Margot's shoulders rose and fell with short gasps, ignoring the taste of blood and mud slipping between her lips. She stared at the weapon poised to kill her, wondering why his finger hadn't pulled the trigger yet. Feeling her brother's eyes staring at her in silence. Making no move to save her.

The officer leaned forward slightly, the pistol pressing against the center of her forehead. Margot closed her eyes, waiting for him to have done with it so all of this would end.

"Wait! Stop!" a voice bellowed across the camp.

Margot whimpered, falling back when the officer pulled the gun away. Her hand splashed in the mud as she reached back for support to keep herself from collapsing. Her eyes closed, the soreness in her nose and face growing to a fiery throb. A hand grabbed her chin, rough fingers digging into her cheeks as her head was forced back. Margot's eyes squinted open, a bolt of surprise rushing through her when she saw the same man she'd passed only moments ago. The one who looked her square in the eye.

His thumb gripped her upper eyelid, forcing her eyes wider as he looked into them.

"Hmm," he purred. "Look! Look, do you see? The blues and greens on the outside of the iris and the brown on the inner rim circling the pupil. Do you see?"

Margot's chest convulsed as he did the same to her other eye, the painful press of his thumb on her eyelid nearly matching the pressure in her nose. Then, as suddenly as he'd grabbed her, he let go, rising to his full height.

"Bring her," he ordered.

Margot let her feet drag when two guards grabbed her by the arms, pulling her off the ground as they followed the man. She remained limp, her eyes only partially open as they brought her along through the camp.

The further they went, the more her feeling the first moment she'd seen him made sense. The more she knew in her heart who he was.

Mengele.

They dragged her across the threshold of a dimly lit room, dropping her on a chair against the wall. Margot's hands fell in her lap, fresh drops of blood rolling from her nose, creating new trails down her chin.

"*Hund!*" Mengele shouted.

Dog ... Margot's eyes fluttered, squinting in the shadowy room. Horst appeared from the corner, taking small, hesitant steps toward her.

"Clean her face," Mengele ordered, the clink of medical instruments ringing in her ears.

Her eyes darted, looking back and forth between the two men. Horst disappeared, returning moments later with a bucket and a cloth. Mengele still stood with his back to her, preparing his instruments. Her gaze settled on the table in the center of the room, bringing her back to that night not so long ago. Two trembling little forms lying on a bloody table, left to die.

Horst started wiping her face, the freezing water sending shivers rushing across her arms and down her back. Then, one of his hands settled over hers. Margot raised her head, staring into his eyes.

"He's going to kill me, isn't he?" she whispered.

Horst's fingers tightened on her hand, the other one holding the damp cloth going still against her cheek. He quickly finished wiping the blood from her face, tossing the cloth into the bucket of water with a splash. Margot closed her eyes, settling herself in the darkness and simply listening to Mengele's movements.

When her eyes opened again, Horst was gone. Her head was still spinning from the punch, the water Horst had used to wash her face slowly drying, leaving her skin stiff. Mengele moved about the room, speaking quietly to himself.

"*Hund*!" he shouted again.

No response came. His head swung back and forth, searching the corners of the room before he mumbled something. Then he turned, walking toward her. Margot groaned when he forced her head back so he could look into her eyes again. She stared back into his, heart thundering so hard in her chest she thought her ribs would snap.

"I am surprised you were not brought to me sooner," Mengele commented, forcing her eyelids open. "You are German, *ja*?"

"*Ja*," Margot whispered.

"Hmm." His hand curled around her upper arm, forcing her out of the chair.

Margot didn't fight, allowing him to force her onto the table. Allowing him to shove her down on her back and ignoring the sting of her head slamming into the hard boards of the table. The next moment, he appeared with a syringe, hovering over her for a moment. His eyes lit as he began to bend toward her, the glitter of the needle lowering slowly toward her eye.

"Do not move," he ordered.

Margot's heart stopped. Then she gasped, "*Nein*!"

Her hand flew up, shoving at his arm. The syringe fell to the floor and Mengele roared, slapping her across the cheek. Margot barely felt the sting of the hit, legs scrambling as she let out a piercing scream while he worked to hold her down.

Suddenly, the door burst open, rebounding on the wall. Margot's breaths came fast and short, staring in stunned silence when she saw Franz standing there. A small movement behind him caught her attention and tears rushed to her eyes when she saw Horst.

"Commandant Höss wants to see her," Franz announced.

Margot's brow shot up.

"What?" Mengele growled, releasing his hold on her to face Franz fully. "What are you talking about?"

Franz arched a brow. "Need I explain? She is a … favorite."

Margot slid onto her back slowly their voices growing softer as she blocked out whatever excuse Franz was making for her escape. A hand came around her fingers and her head rolled to the side, watching Horst where he stood by the table. He gave her hand a squeeze of encouragement before he stepped back, vanishing in the shadows.

"If you wish to speak to the commandant, you may. For now, she is not to be touched." Franz brushed passed Mengele, taking hold of Margot.

He pulled her to her feet and out of the building. His hands gripped her, supporting her every time her legs shook. Keeping her moving across the block, as far away from Mengele's lab as possible.

Hands with Ilse's blood on them. Margot trembled.

Franz stopped beside one of the blocks, turning to face her. Before he could speak, she raised her hand and struck him across the face. Her brother didn't react, simply closed his eyes, worked his jaw and looked at her again.

Margot slapped him a second time, every ounce of fear transforming into rage bubbling inside her like boiling water. She hit his face, punched his chest, kicked his shins and he took all of it in silence until she finally collapsed, her cheek smashed against the breast of his jacket and the fight completely drained from her.

"Why?" she sobbed. "I do not understand."

"We all do what we must here, Margot, you know that."

She raised her head to look into his eyes.

"And you *had* to kill Ilse? There was no other choice?" Margot shook her head, waiting for him to respond. Waiting for him to explain why he'd pulled a girl they'd both loved out of the line and killed her.

"*Nein*," he whispered hoarsely. "There was no other choice."

Margot pressed her lips tight, her tears stinging the swelling cuts on her face from the beatings she'd taken. Then she leaned in.

"I am so ashamed of you, Franz," she hissed. "And Papa would be ashamed too."

She didn't wait for him to answer, stumbling around him back toward her barracks. The sun was setting slowly on the horizon, casting the sky in a multitude of colors as the chill of winter grew with the fading sunlight. She started to pass through the yard, then came to a halt.

Margot stared down at the puddle of blood. Stared at the imprint Ilse's body had left in the soft ground. Stared at the last place she'd seen—or ever would see again—the dearest friend she'd ever had.

A pair of feet appeared on the other side of the puddle, the string wrapped tightly around the boots giving away they belonged to Hanna. The girl's soft breaths matched her own, followed by her gentle whisper.

"She is with God now, Margot."

Slowly, Margot raised her head. Hanna stared back at her, the streaks through the dirt on her face evidence of recent tears.

"Hanna," Margot rasped. "God was never here."

She lowered her gaze again, staring at the red slowly blending into the dark brown of the mud. Hanna's feet disappeared a moment later, her footsteps fading slowly as she walked away.

Margot stood there, frozen, until the evening gong rang.

Chapter Twenty-Six

THE ARDENNES FOREST
MID-DECEMBER, 1944

When the shelling had finally stopped, Bernie thought for a moment he'd never be able to hear again. Perhaps the explosions had made him permanently deaf. Perhaps his own fear, slithering through him like a snake, had caused him to shut out every blast along with every scream that accompanied them. Sliding down another inch in the foxhole, Bernie tried to remember what peace felt like. Tried to remember what it was like to sit in a quiet place or walk in a calm forest without fear the tree beside him was going to explode or the ground beneath him was going to rise to swallow him whole.

Bruno, Ellis, and Graham had all gone out on patrol that morning. There hadn't been any word from them since. In all likelihood, they'd dug themselves in until the bombings stopped.

Or were captured by the enemy. Or are lying dead in the middle of the woods. Bernie closed his eyes, taking a deep breath. He never did like waiting.

There'd been about a half hour of quiet now, giving each of them a much-needed respite from the enemy fire eating up the Ardennes. Jensen sat curled up on the other side of the foxhole, his head down and arms wrapped around his rifle. The morning after Woodley told them they'd be falling back from the Hürtgen to the Ardennes, they'd each climbed into the back of the truck in silence. Each settled themselves for the drive out, shivering in the light snowfall veiling the air with glittering white flakes.

There hadn't been anything to say as they left behind their failure in the Hürtgen. The word retreat hadn't crossed anyone's lips, though he couldn't help feeling every man sitting there with him was thinking it as the trucks rolled away from their objective. Even Bruno hadn't let loose with even one snide remark as they passed out of Germany into Belgium.

A true miracle. Bernie swallowed a chuckle.

In the distance, he could hear someone moving from foxhole to foxhole. Boots crunching in the snow, followed by a quick whisper before continuing on. Bernie strained to see who was bold enough to be walking about when any moment they could be hit again by another round of shelling. He frowned, the figure shrouded in the mist of a light snowfall and thin layer of smoke still settling on the air.

A fellow soldier, helmet almost seeming too large for his head as it shadowed his face by falling far over his forehead. A light poncho hung from his shoulders to block out the cold, and in his hand he carried a beat up package. Small and rectangular, it looked like it'd come a long way.

Bernie's heart thundered in his chest, the surety of who'd sent it rushing over him in waves as the soldier approached. Jensen raised his head, eyes bleary when the soldier crouched beside their foxhole.

"I'm lookin' for Bernie Russell?" he said, then coughed into his sleeve.

"That's me," Bernie answered.

"This is for you. Came from the aid station." He tossed the package, Bernie catching it in both hands. Before he could respond, the man was jogging away for cover.

Jensen snorted. "How is it you get mail in the middle of all of this while I haven't heard from home in weeks?"

Bernie smoothed his hand over the rough brown paper enclosed around the object, Margot's faded script staring back at him—practically screaming his name in his ears.

"This isn't from home," he replied.

He snapped the string with his finger, hands trembling from nerves or anticipation he wasn't certain as he removed the paper. His brow creased as he turned over the little diary, rubbing his palm over the cover before slipping the letter that accompanied it loose.

Dear Bernie,

I wish I could write and tell you everything I am feeling right now. But I fear there is little time left for me here in Berlin. Our mutual enemy is getting closer to me with each passing moment. I know now, I will not leave this city unless by the will of the gestapo. So, I enclose this diary to you. Inside are not only sketches of the most precious people in my life but stories about our resistance. Secret thoughts and hopes I have written and hidden for years now as well as the truth about the camps spread across Poland. I send them to you because I know you will keep them safe.

Goodbye, Bernie Russell. And thank you. For everything.

Margot

Bernie blinked a few times, taking in her words before he opened the diary. Every entry was written in German, but he scanned the pages anyway, pausing to stare at the sketches. A girl with long, yellow hair and sparkling blue eyes. A man, shorter than average, with a little nose and broad forehead. A woman with delicate wrinkles around her eyes and a smile that glistened as only a mother's could.

Some were in color, but the closer he came to the back of the book, the more she'd begun to use regular black pencil. But the facial expressions were still there—her talent so profound he felt each sketch was about to come alive and talk to him. Her certainty she was in trouble rocked him, and he knew it must be true or she wouldn't have sent the diary. Whatever else the pages contained had been too precious for her to burn them. Clearly, she was willing to take the risk of the book falling into the gestapo's hands rather than destroy years of thoughts and feelings.

"What'd you get?" Jensen wondered, gesturing to the diary.

Bernie closed the little book hastily, stuffing it on the inside of his jacket. "Nothing."

Jensen frowned, shrugged, then curled up again to try to get some sleep. Bernie tilted his head back, looking up through the broken trees at the sky overhead. He rested his hand over his left shoulder, feeling the press of the book beneath his palm.

Let her be all right. He closed his eyes. *Please. Let her be alive and well somewhere.*

Only when a hand shook his shoulder did he realize he'd fallen asleep. Jerking up he glared at Ellis.

"'Bout time you got back," he muttered, blinking rapidly.

"Berns ..."

"Where's Bruno?" Bernie looked around, catching sight of Graham leaping into another foxhole nearby.

"Bernie ... we lost Bruno."

Bernie went still, staring into the glum eyes of the sergeant. He looked worn to the bone, his rifle lying on the ground beside him where he crouched and the circles beneath his eyes so dark he looked bruised.

"What do you mean you lost him?" Bernie growled. "Is he dead?"

Ellis cringed. "They started shelling and we got separated. When Graham and I were sure the round was over, we called out. Bruno didn't answer. There was blood."

"So, you just left? You didn't go looking for him?"

"Bernie … listen." Ellis gripped his shoulder tight, digging his fingers in. "If Graham and I had gone looking, we would never have made it back. If Bruno's lucky, he was wounded and taken captive by the Germans."

"You call that lucky?" Bernie shrugged his hand off.

"Better than him being dead, Berns."

Bernie hesitated, thinking about that for a few heart-stopping moments. Then he shook his head.

"Not to me."

He stood up, launching himself out of the foxhole. Ellis rose quickly.

"Where're you going?"

"To find Bruno." Bernie checked his rifle and ammo before looking down at the sergeant. "I'm bringing him back."

"I can't let you do that, private."

Bernie glared at him. "Try to stop me, Sarge."

"I'm coming with you," Jensen announced, beginning to pull himself out of the foxhole.

"No," Bernie snapped. "You're needed here. I go alone."

"*You're* needed here, Bernie," Ellis said. "How am I going to explain to Woodley if both you and Bruno end up dead?"

"I think Woodley knows that was a likely outcome either way." Bernie stared into the dense forest, fingers curling tighter around his rifle. "You giving me a direct order to stay, Sarge?"

Ellis's lips thinned into a straight line. Bernie waited about five seconds before he turned, stomping through the snow.

"Bernie!" Ellis called.

His head swung, looking over his shoulder.

"You get yourself back here in one piece. If you're not here in an hour, I'm coming for you."

"Understood."

A breath hissed through the sergeant's teeth. "Go get him."

Bernie nodded sharply before he jogged into the thick of the woods without a backward glance.

Chapter Twenty-Seven

Hanna didn't return to the barracks last night.

Margot lay on her back in the bunk, filling the space Hanna and Ilse would have taken up. Her face was still swollen and bruised, the cuts healing slowly without proper medicine. Her mind was racked with questions about where Hanna was. Had she been taken away to her death? Did she get caught up in another group and placed in separate barracks? Was she standing in a crowded block somewhere, awaiting her execution?

Temples throbbing, she rolled over on the bunk, curling her arm around her head to support herself. Her nose had grown accustomed to the stench thickening in the air. Her ears no longer searching for any and every sound drifting on the air from the other bunks. Her heart was a deep void, dark shadows circling in her chest until she couldn't breathe. When she closed her eyes, she saw Ilse die. When she opened them Hanna still wasn't there.

A rough hand grabbed her shoulder, giving her a soft shake. Margot sat up slowly, watching Franz's form take a step back from the bunk. The other women sharing the bunk with her turned away, pretending to be asleep.

"Come with me," he ordered.

Margot hesitated, her anger over being so commanded by the brother she no longer knew raising bile in her throat. But she still found herself lowering her feet to the floor and standing slowly from her bunk. She followed him out of the barracks and into the early rays of dawn. They marched in silence, neither looking at each other until the moment she realized they were walking toward the expansion where she and Hanna had killed the guard.

"What are we doing, Franz?" she asked softly.

He didn't respond, simply kept walking toward the fence. Reaching back, he took hold of her, giving her a shove in front of him so she faced the fence. His opposite hand rested on his holster and Margot gasped. Slapping his hand from her shoulder she spun to face him.

"If you intend to kill me, *mein bruder*," she hissed, glaring. "Then you will look me in the eye as you do it!"

Franz's lip twisted, is eyes glossy. "Do you truly think I would murder my own flesh and blood?"

"You murdered Ilse," Margot replied. "She was as much a sister to you as I am. Do you deny it?"

"*Nein*, I deny nothing. But you are wrong about me, Margot." He lifted his head higher, blinking until the glisten of tears left his eyes. "I did not bring you here to kill you."

"Why are we here, then?"

Franz inhaled, his chest swelling. "The fence has been shut off."

Margot's eyes went wide. "What?"

"They can only stay off for a few minutes, Margot, so you have to hurry."

"Franz, what are you talking about? What's going on?"

A rough sigh of frustration passed his lips, and he took a step closer to the fence. He pointed to the lower wire, brows lifting. She looked down, her heart beating faster when she saw some had been cut away, leaving enough space for someone to crawl through on their belly. If she went now, she might be able to run across the meadow and into the cover of the woods before the morning gong. She might be able to slip away before anyone else noticed.

Escape? He is offering me an escape?

"Why?" Margot asked, raising her gaze to his once more. "Why are you helping me now?"

"Because it's only a matter of time before Mengele comes for you again, and next time I won't be able to stop him." Franz grabbed her arm, yanking her toward the fence. "Go, Margot!"

"*Nein!*" She pulled out of his grasp. "You may so easily be able to abandon and kill your friends, but I will not! If I go, Horst and Hanna go too."

"There is no time, Margot."

"I said—"

"Margot, who do you think helped me plan this?"

Words instantly died on her tongue. Franz took off his hat, raking a hand through his hair.

"Horst knows he will only slow you down. Hanna believes she has survived this long and can continue to. Hanna was helping me all night with this, that is why she never returned to the barracks."

Margot shook her head, her eyes welling. "I do not understand."

"Margot ... what happened with Ilse ..." Franz grimaced with pain, pausing briefly before he continued, "She asked me to do it."

Margot stared at him, unblinking. "You're lying."

"She was sick, Margot! And getting sicker. She knew and I knew it was only a matter of time before they came to take her away to die a horrible death in the infirmary." Franz's eyes glittered now with fresh tears. "She asked me to allow her a quick death while she had some dignity left. She *begged* me, Margot. So I gave her one."

Margot thought she was going to float away. Her head spun, her heart racing out of control.

Promise me you will not be angry with Franz. Ilse's voice whispered in her ear. *He is still the großer bruder you remember.*

Now, it all made sense. The peaceful smile on her face just before her death—why Franz let her stand instead of forcing her to kneel. Why his finger had hesitated for a split second before he pulled the trigger.

"Oh, Franz," Margot sobbed, gasping for breath. "She could have had a chance!"

He shook his head. "Not in this place, *meine schwester.*"

She rubbed the tears from her face, taking a calming breath. Looking through the barbed wire, she watched the fiery rays of sunrise lifting over the top of the trees. Watching how the light made the thin layer of snow coating the meadow glisten like a thousand white jewels. Then she looked back at the camp. Staring at the crude buildings, the watchtowers rising above the rooftops, the billowing smoke from the crematoriums in the distance.

"I cannot leave here without Hanna," Margot whispered. "Or Horst."

"*Ja*, you can." Franz's eyes softened, a strand of his hair falling across his forehead, reminding her of when they were younger. "Hanna has been here for a long time now, Margot, you have not. She does not have the strength to survive the sort of journey you will have to take. You are stronger. And Horst will be all right. Like you said, he is clever. He will not risk slowing you down."

"But—"

"Listen to me, *meine liebe.*" Franz came closer, his hands trembling when he rested them on her arms, letting his palms slide up over her elbows then back down to grip her fingers.

Suddenly, she noticed the new lines in his face. The definition around his eyes and mouth—the silver beginning to shine through the blond at his temples. The shadows clouding his crystal blue eyes.

"You have to live," he murmured. "If you do not go now, Mengele will come for you. I cannot let that happen. Neither can Hanna."

He pressed something rough into her palm, followed by the crinkle of paper as he folded her fingers over it.

"Franz—"

"Ah." He placed a finger over her lips to silence her.

Margot stared at her brother, fresh tears sliding warmly down her cheeks. Franz closed the distance, gently taking her face between his palms. A smile trembled across his lips, the hint of the boy he used to be shining for a fleeting moment in his eyes.

"All our lives, our father tried to raise us to be exceptional. Hans and I did our best. We followed in his footsteps—we lived by his example. We blended in. We survived. We were a silent exception to a public rule. But you, Margot," he paused, bending to rest his forehead against hers. "You always have been and always will be … extraordinary."

A cry burst from her throat. She grabbed his arms, her fingers curling around the thick material of his coat. She shook her head fiercely.

"I am not!"

"*Ja,* you are. You have to go, Margot. You must survive and tell the world what happened here." He caressed her cheeks with his thumbs, swiping the tears away with every stroke.

"Come with me!" Margot gripped him tighter. "We can go together!"

Franz sighed, his nose rubbing hers when he shook his head. "I dug my grave here long ago, *schätzchen*."

"*Nein!*" Margot sobbed.

"Horst and Hanna will be safe. No one will ever know they helped me."

"I-I cannot!"

"You can." Franz gripped her shoulders, pulling her down to her knees with him. He tapped her hand where she still gripped the paper he'd given her. "Open that when you are well away."

"But … but where will I go?"

"Trust me." He pressed his lips to her ear. "Run as fast as you can. You will not be alone."

Placing his hand on her head he pushed her to the ground, forcing her flat on her belly. Margot whimpered, the icy mud soaking through the thin material of her dress as she struggled beneath the wires. The center of her stomach burned, her hunger turning into a fiery pit of fear as she made it through to the other side of the fence. Gasping, she spun back around, reaching through to grab her brother's hand.

"Franz …" The tears began to stiffen on her cheeks in the frozen breeze.

Her big brother smiled at her the way he used to, the gentle hope in his eyes warming her heart.

"It's all right, Margot," he whispered.

Margot twisted their fingers together, clinging to him for one moment more.

"I was wrong," she said hoarsely. "Papa would forgive you … and he would understand."

Franz bowed his head, hand tightening so hard on hers his knuckles paled. Then he smiled at her.

"*Danke, mein schatz.* Now go. Go!"

He shoved her hand away shuffling back and onto his feet. Margot stared at him for a moment longer, his words echoing in her head.

"Go," he breathed again. "It's all right, *meine schwester*. Run."

Forcing herself off the ground, she turned away, lifting her feet high as she ran through the snow toward the border of the forest. Every step she took she saw their faces.

Commandant Höss sneering at her as he announced her mother was dead.

Geisler snarling orders.

Hanna, crying in their bunk.

Franz staring stonily at her.

Ilse's peaceful smile right before …

Margot's foot caught on a rock beneath the snow. She tripped, hurtling to the ground. Her cry cut short from a mouthful of snow. Trembling and gasping she pushed back to her feet, a gust of wind freezing her straight through. Behind her, the morning gong sounded, sending a different rush of cold wafting over her.

Struggling through, she pushed every image—every sound—out of her mind. Keeping her eyes on the line of trees up ahead. Her chest ached, legs straining as she forced herself faster. Never in her life had she felt so weak as her feet grew heavier, arms flailing at her sides and every breath straining painfully through her lungs. She reached out as she came closer to the trees, watching them grow bigger with every few feet.

A low, rough gasp of relief burst from her throat when she crossed the border of the woods, her palm scraping the bark on the nearest tree.

Pop!

Margot's back stiffened as the single gunshot echoed through the air across the meadow. She waited. Waited to feel the sting of the bullet somewhere in her body. Waited to hear another shot sound as they began to pursue her. Instead, silence stretched as the sound of the shot faded in the wind.

Slowly, she turned around, a well of tears blurring the view of the camp in the distance. Blinking, she cleared her vision, staring at the heap of a body on the other side of the camp fence. Staring at the rising sun catching in his golden hair—the metal gleam of the luger gripped in his own hand. No other guards or prisoners in sight. Only his body, lying limp on the wet ground.

Margot shoved her hand against her mouth, her teeth sinking into her skin when she screamed into her palm.

I dug my grave here long ago ... Horst and Hanna will be safe ... No one will ever know they helped me.

She fell to her knees as she stared at his body, his guilty plea practically screaming in the air where he lay beside the purposely broken wire. They would not torture the truth from him. They would not publicly execute him.

And they will blame no one but him for my escape. He has seen to that. Margot squeezed her eyes closed, bending until her forehead brushed the snow.

Run as fast as you can, he whispered in her ear. *You will not be alone.*

Far away shouts brought her head back up, eyes stinging when she saw the first figure appear around the nearest building. Margot's throat nearly closed. She turned, stumbling between the trees before they noticed her tracks through the meadow. Before they realized the reason behind what her brother had done.

Run. Margot gasped, her breaths clouding on the frozen air. *Keep running, Margot. Just ... keep ... running.*

Chapter Twenty-Eight

THE ARDENNES FOREST

Bernie spun, his feet slipping out from beneath him. With a grunt, he slammed back into the tree, a throbbing pain shooting down his neck from the crown of his head. Swinging back around, he raised his rifle in the direction he'd heard the sound. A gasp caught in his throat when he saw Graham a couple trees down, crouched low to the ground.

"What're you doing here?" Bernie hissed, lowering his weapon.

Graham jogged toward him, knees half bent to the ground and head down before he stopped behind a closer tree.

"You and Bru came back for me," he replied. "So here I am."

"Me too."

Jensen came sliding between them, rolling onto his belly beside Bernie. He glared at the two of them.

"Woodley's gonna wring my neck if we get back," Bernie hissed.

"Key word there, Berns." Graham winked at him. "*If* we get back."

Bernie craned his neck to look around the tree trunk, staring into the dense fog shrouding the woods.

"Any of this familiar, Graham?" he asked.

His friend arched a brow before swinging his head back and forth. Then he shrugged. "Bernie, trees look alike. Or didn't you notice?"

Bernie rolled his eyes before moving on, listening to the soft crunch of their boots in the snow following him. A fresh layer of powder coated the ground, covering any footprints Graham and Ellis might've left on their way back from patrol.

Including a blood trail from Bruno. Bernie swallowed.

Ellis mentioned there was blood, but not how much. A few drops? A puddle? Enough to know he might be looking for Bruno's corpse? Half of him wanted to know, the other half was glad he hadn't asked.

"Bernie," Jensen murmured suddenly, brushing a hand on Bernie's shoulder before hurrying ahead of him.

He followed, hearing Graham pick up the pace as well behind him. Jensen went to one knee in the snow, brushing his hand on a stone. Turning, he held up his hand—fingertips stained red.

"I think he was here."

Bernie nodded, gripping his rifle tighter before they moved deeper into the forest.

"Bruno!" he called, his voice low and hoarse as he restrained shouting. He could feel Jensen and Graham tense to either side of him every time he opened his mouth.

The enemy could be anywhere waiting to pounce. One wrong step, they could fall into an enemy foxhole. One snap of a twig, they could be pelted to death with bullets. One word, spoken too loud, and it could all be over.

Bernie raised his scope, looking through it into the distance. The trees seemed closer together here—not a clearing in sight. The snow and thick moisture in the air attempting to enclose his lungs with ice. He shivered, searching first the ground then the area around for any abnormalities.

"Bernie!" Graham poked him with the end of his rifle. "Look!"

Bernie turned, his eyes going wide when he caught in his scope what Graham had spotted. A foot, from ankle down, sticking out from behind one of the larger trunks. This foot ... covered in an army-issued boot.

Bernie took off, the thunder of the boys on his heels filling his ears before he slid to the ground on his knees.

Bruno snapped a curse, raising his bayonet in his fist before he took in Bernie's face, relief instantly easing the crease of tension in his brow.

"Berns!" he gasped roughly, the knife trembling in his fist.

"You hurt, Bru?" Bernie gently took the bayonet away from him before observing.

He'd lost his helmet and rifle, a small puddle of blood soaking into the snow beneath his right ankle.

"Stupid flesh wound," Bruno panted, snarling at his ankle. "You shouldn't have come, Bernie."

"I wasn't gonna leave you out here." Bernie looked over his shoulder. "Graham, you got a bandage left in your kit?"

"I got one," Jensen offered before Graham could, digging in his pocket before producing the bandage.

"Thanks, kid," Bruno mumbled as Bernie began to wrap his ankle. He clenched his teeth, hissing softly when Bernie yanked on the bandage. "Hurts like h—"

His voice was swallowed by a distant blast shaking the ground. They all ducked slightly, heads turning in all directions. Two seconds later, another explosion split the air—closer now.

"We better move, Bernie," Graham said.

"Agreed."

Bernie swung Bruno's arm around his shoulders, pulling him with a groan to his feet. Bruno hopped, holding his wounded ankle a few inches above the ground as they started moving back in the tracks they'd left. Jensen and Graham were gaining ground ahead as Bernie struggled.

To the left, a tree burst into a fiery shatter of bark and splinters, spattering their heads and shoulders. Bruno groaned, his fingers digging into a fistful of Bernie's shoulder as they kept moving—half running, half hopping toward their goal. The burst of another shell shaking the woods echoed in his ears, making him stumble.

Bruno cried out when his bad ankle slammed into the ground. They both tumbled, falling in a mix of slush and snow.

Boom! Boom! Boom! Bernie curled up, throwing his arms over his head as the series of explosions thundered through the woods. As suddenly as the blasting started, it ended, leaving the trees vibrating. Slowly, he lowered his arms, chest pumping with rapid breaths as he looked around.

"Graham!" he shouted. "Jensen!"

"We're good!" Graham's voice replied up ahead.

Bernie pushed onto his hands and knees, letting his head drop forward while he tried to catch his breath.

"You should go, Bernie," Bruno panted, rolling onto his back.

Bernie shook the snow from his hair, brushing the mix of flakes and wood chips off his shoulders. He grabbed his helmet from where it had fallen, leaning back to sit on his heels. Then he looked at his friend, breathing a little easier.

"Not a chance." He pulled Bruno up into a sitting position and checked the bandage around his ankle.

"Bernie, I mean it." Bruno clasped eyes with him, making Bernie go still.

The sorrow and pain shining back at him ripped through his body to his soul. Bruno took hold of his hand, squeezing his knuckles tight.

"Leave me," Bruno whispered. "It's okay, Bernie."

Another explosive tore through the ground—the distant sound of men shouting between blasts reaching them. Bernie barely heard any of it as his brow puckered, mouth firming in anger.

"No." He gripped Bruno's shoulders. "We survive, remember? We are the ones who survive. I'll drag you if I have to, but you're coming with me or neither of us leaves these woods."

He dropped his helmet on Bruno's head, clasping the strap beneath his chin. Then Bernie yanked him to his feet, grabbing him firmly around the waist for support.

"Let's go, brother."

Bruno groaned with every hop-step they took. Bernie quickened their pace, huffing every breath as he kept his focus on Graham and Jensen ahead of them. Bruno's hand tightened on his shoulder, fingers digging deep.

"Berns," he grunted. "Berns, wait. Stop!"

"What?" Bernie growled.

"Listen!"

Bernie went still, noticing Graham and Jensen had both stopped up ahead, crouching low to the ground. The forest had gone deathly quiet. Only the whistle of the December breeze rippling over them filled his ears followed swiftly by the sound of his own roaring heart.

No more shelling. No gunfire. No shouts.

Bernie closed his eyes, slowing his breath as he focused on simply listening. The rustle of the tree branches, the whispering wind ... the crunch of snow beneath a multitude of boots.

"Everybody down!" Bernie hissed.

Graham and Jensen scrambled, all of them hurrying behind a tree. Bernie dragged Bruno with him, falling hard on his backside. He pulled his friend's back against his chest, crossing his arms over Bruno's torso to hold him tight behind the limited cover the trunk offered them. Turning his head slowly, he squinted in the dense air of the forest.

They took shape slowly, big shoulders slouched and weapons ready as they marched in a slow line between the trees. Despite the cold, a drop of sweat rolled down Bernie's temple. He looked at Jensen a few feet away, watching the boy's hands tighten on his rifle, eyes big. The boy looked his way, lifting his weapon slightly. Bernie shook his head, tapping a finger to his lips. Jensen shuddered, squeezing his eyes shut and letting his forehead fall against the barrel of the rifle.

They sat as still as possible, listening to the heavy footfalls of the Nazi soldiers passing behind them.

Chapter Twenty-Nine

AUSCHWITZ, POLAND

Margot could go on no longer. Yet how long had she been running? Five, perhaps ten minutes? Her lungs burned, her legs shook uncontrollably, her heart was thumping so hard she thought it might careen to a halt at any moment. Wheezing, she fell against the nearest tree, wrapping her arms around the trunk and her cheek scraping on the rough bark. Her finger brushed against the purposely carved dent in the side of the tree, tears rushing to her eyes.

She'd noticed the markings the first time she'd fallen. At first, she thought perhaps she was seeing what she wanted to. But the further she'd gone, the more she saw the pattern. The small X carved into every three or four trees, guiding her deeper and deeper into the forest away from the camp.

You will not be alone. Franz's words repeated over and over in her head.

Steadying herself once more she started running again. The snow turning to slush in her boots, freezing her toes. The merciless wind clawing at her clothes until she thought she'd turn to ice herself. Then the ground went out beneath her.

Margot shrieked, landing hard on her side before somersaulting down the incline. Snow blinded her, rocks scraped her as she tumbled end over end down the hill before landing with a splash, half of her body crashing into freezing water. The fist still clutching the paper her brother gave her trembled as she held it high, protecting it from the creek water.

Sobbing, she pushed herself up on her elbow, dragging her limp, frozen body out of the creek and onto the icy heap of snow along the edge. She curled up, pressed her knees against her chest and shivered. Her stomach sucked in toward her spine—hunger gnawing at her from within in an accompanying song to the cold. The water her scarf had soaked in dripped along the side of her neck, leaving a numbing trail down the curve of her throat to her shoulder.

Run as fast as you can. Her brother's voice urged.

Margot forced herself onto her hands and knees, crawling back up the incline to the last tree she'd seen with a marking. Bark scratched her wrist when she leaned on one of the trees, getting her feet back under her. Her toes were stiff, shooting pains rushing over her feet and up her ankles. She kept moving, the forest tilting with every dizzying step she took.

In the distance, she was sure she could hear them shouting. Could hear the sounds of them preparing to pursue her—the rumble of their feet racing across the meadow, pounding the snow into the ground. She was sure every rustle in the snow, every flutter of a bird's wings, was an SS guard preparing to run her down. She quickened her pace, her fingertips brushing another marking.

A stab of warmth shot through her arm, her mind hastily recognizing the feel of fingers sinking into her flesh. Margot opened her mouth, her scream muffled by a large palm over her lips. She was drawn back into the heat of a broad chest, nearly swallowed in the folds of a thick, soft coat.

"Margot," a familiar voice breathed against her ear. "It's me. You're safe."

His hand slipped away from her lips and she turned. "Ludwig?"

He rubbed her arms, sending shocks of heat into her skin before he started pulling off his coat.

"W-What are y-y-you d-doing h-here?" Margot said, every word slipping between the clatter of her teeth.

Ludwig wrapped his coat across her shoulders, and she groaned, clutching the warmth of the material tighter around her body.

"I'm getting you out of here," he replied, glancing nervously over his shoulder.

He put his arm around her, tucking her against the side of his waist as he guided her through the woods.

"F-Franz—"

"I know." Ludwig pressed his lips firmly against her temple. "I am sorry."

Margot shuddered. "H-He is ... d-d-d ..."

"Don't," Ludwig whispered, his arm around her waist practically lifting her off the ground to carry her. "Do not speak, Margot. He did what he meant to do. He got you out."

Margot skidded to a halt, nearly causing Ludwig to lose his balance. The trees were beginning to thin here. Up ahead the glimmer of a truck waiting for them on the road appeared in her sight. But instead of quickening toward the vehicle, she turned away, looking up into the sad eyes of a boy she remembered in the deepest recesses of her mind. Ludwig had been one of the many school friends of her twin she barely took notice of. He had made little impression on her and never in all her life would she have dreamed they would meet again this way.

But now, looking up into his worried, uncertain eyes, her heart filled with a mix of anger and anguish for a boy who claimed to be her friend.

"What ..." she paused, steadying her voice and clenching her teeth to keep them from chattering. "What did you mean when you said you knew?"

"We do not have time—"

"Make time!"

Ludwig growled in frustration, taking her by the arm to propel her forward. Too weak to fight back, Margot let him lead her toward the edge of the road.

"I meant," he said quietly. "I knew Franz had no intention of surviving to the end of this war. Whether he was prepared to be killed by the Soviets or Americans ... or even by his own hand ... I did not know or ask. But he told me once, long ago, he'd—"

"Dug his grave in Auschwitz," she finished for him.

Ludwig cringed. "*Ja.*"

They stepped cautiously out of the forest onto the road, Ludwig yanking the door of the truck open and reaching in.

"And you?" Margot asked. "Do you not also feel so deeply the guilt *mein bruder* did?"

Ludwig turned back, a few articles of folded clothing between his palms.

"I promised your *bruder* I would get you out of Poland alive. So *ja*, I can live with what I've done if it means I've helped you survive."

He shoved the clothes into her hands.

"Now get changed. We do not have any more time to waste."

Margot climbed into the back of the truck, clutching the trousers, linen shirt and thick cotton coat to her chest. The wind breathing through the thin canvas over the top of the bed of the truck swept over her as she peeled her damp dress off, letting it drop with a *splat* near her feet. She would've given anything to wash before tugging on the clean clothes. Shivering, she pulled the scarf off her head, dropping it on top of the soaking wet work dress.

Her palm scraped against the short hairs on her head as she ran her hand back and forth across her scalp. Her eyes focused on the cap in her hand, seeing Ludwig's plan clearly now. Two young *men*, driving in a farm truck down the road. Margot sniffled, shaking off the sudden rush of fear as she tugged the cap onto her head. Her toes were stiff and red when she pulled them out of the old boots. She bounced slightly to keep her balance as she wrapped her feet in a pair of thick, dry socks before putting on the sturdy pair of boots Ludwig had left for her. The heavy coat shot a thousand needles into her skin when she climbed back out of the truck. Ludwig looked her over once, nodded, then took her old dress and boots away from her.

"Get in the front," he ordered.

Margot hesitated, clamping her bottom lip between her teeth. "Shouldn't I ... hide?"

Ludwig shook his head. "Do as I say, Margot. Everything will be all right, I promise."

She stared at him, her heart pounding faster as she reached back to grasp the door handle on the truck. The rusty hinges groaned in protest as she opened it, finally turning away from Ludwig to climb into the front seat. She scooted over away from the wheel, scrunching herself into the corner against the passenger door. He disappeared briefly into the woods, returning a few seconds later empty-handed.

Margot clenched her fingers tighter around the paper Franz had given her, wanting more than anything to read its contents. But fear clutched at her tighter than her fingers wrapped around the note. Were they his words, or Hanna's? Perhaps Horst's? As Ludwig climbed in beside her, her heart screamed for the last words of one of the people she loved most. The engine rumbled to life, preparing to carry her far away from the fate that awaited her within the gates of Auschwitz.

Margot sank lower on the seat, trying to keep herself as far away from the window as possible. The wheels began to roll over the uneven ground, Ludwig's pace slow enough as to not draw too much attention should they be spotted moving down the road. Gently, she unfurled her fingers, staring at the crumpled piece of paper trembling in her palm.

She glanced at Ludwig, his big shoulders tensed forward, cap pulled low and brow furrowed. His jaw creaked when he ground his teeth, his own nerves thickening in the stuffy air within the truck.

Margot swiped her sleeve on her nose, her remaining bruises burning the delicate flesh of her cheek. Shuddering, she unfolded the note, staring down at the hastily scribbled words. Her eyes welled, nearly overflowing as the Polish words sprung from the page into her mind.

> Margot, you said God was never here. You are wrong. He came with you the moment you stepped off the train. He came when you stabbed the guard trying to hurt me. He came when you held me in our bunk as I told you about my son. He came when you eased the suffering of two innocent, murdered children. He came when you fought back the moment Ilse died. I have never felt, from the moment I arrived here, the kind of hope you brought with you.
>
> God was here, my friend. In you.
>
> Thank you. Be safe. Live.
>
> Love, Hanna

Margot pressed the letter to her heart, bent until her forehead touched her knees, and wept.

★★★

When Margot opened her eyes, waking from a dreamless sleep, night had fallen outside. The truck lumbered on, Ludwig keeping his silence as they continued their journey away from the camp. Her fingers and toes were cramped tight from the lingering bite of winter—every breath sending shocks of pain through her chest. She curled up tight, still clutching Hanna's note to her heart and pressing her knees into her ribs attempting to salvage what little warmth the interior of the truck offered.

They seemed to have picked up some speed, the stars flashing by outside her window in bright, white streaks overhead. The woods had been left behind now, replaced with rolling hills covered in frost. In the distance, she thought she caught sight of the glistening golden lights of a town.

How far have we come? Margot shuddered.

She'd slept away the many hours between sunrise and sunset only to awaken as cold, frightened, and hungry as she'd been when Ludwig ordered her into the truck. Her thoughts instantly turned to Franz—the image of his body sprawled behind the fence flashing through her mind the moment she closed her eyes again.

Hans ... Mama ... Gretl ... Ilse ... Hanna ... Horst ... Franz ...

Their names pounded in her head like a drumbeat. Every member of her family—every person she loved. Gone. Even if Hanna and Horst still drew breath, in her heart she knew she would never see them again. How much longer could they survive? Hanna grew weaker every day, and Horst ...

Margot trembled, turning sharply from the window so she faced Ludwig. He glanced her way, worry pinching his brow. Then he removed one hand from the wheel to dig in his coat pocket.

"I was going to give you this earlier," he said. "But you fell asleep so quickly."

A tiny gasp slipped between her lips when his hand reappeared holding a crust of bread. She snatched it, stuffing the dry, cold morsel into her mouth. Her stomach rumbled with the desire for more as the clump of bread went down her throat in a painful swallow. Margot coughed, wrapping her arms over her middle.

"We are almost there," Ludwig reassured her.

"Where?" Margot whispered.

He shrugged slightly. "A safe place. There will be more food and dry clothes. We cannot stay long, but you will have a chance to bathe and rest."

Margot shook her head slowly. "How did you do all of this? How long did you and Franz plan to get me out?"

Ludwig narrowed his eyes and shifted awkwardly. His silence did nothing to ease the rising tension between them—her curiosity peaking with every second that ticked by without an answer to her question. Wrapping her arms tight across her shins, Margot pressed her bony knees into her chest. Her eyelids began to droop, the much-needed sleep she hadn't gotten over the past weeks attempting to snag her in its web.

Only when the truck came to a quivering halt did she realize she'd fallen asleep again. She blinked rapidly, trying to adjust to the darkness as the engine stuttered into silence. Ludwig removed the keys before peeking out the window. Margot leaned forward, rubbing the sleep from her eyes as she adjusted to the darkness. The glow of moonlight illuminated the farmyard—a little house taking form in the shadows.

Margot bit her lip, watching as the front door opened, allowing a large, rather round figure to lumber out. Ludwig looked back at her, a reassuring smile touching his lips.

"Wait here," he whispered.

Trusting him was about as easy for her as swallowing a stone. But she nodded anyway, clutching her hands tight in her lap. She watched in silence as he climbed out of the truck, jogging across the snowy front yard toward the man who'd emerged from the house. Margot scooted closer to the wheel, squinting in the dark and wishing she could hear what they were saying to each other.

Ludwig knows him, that much is clear. A deep, roaring grumble rose in her belly, filling the silence inside the truck. She rubbed her middle, feeling every ridge of her ribs beneath her fingertips.

The clothes Ludwig had provided hung on her slight body, practically swallowing her whole, the belt pulled as tight as it could go to keep the trousers from falling off her bony hips. Margot curled up on the seat, staring at their figures. Watching Ludwig's hands wave as he spoke and the stranger shake his head over and over again.

She sat up when Ludwig turned back for the truck, closing the distance with a few quick steps. He yanked open the door, leaning in to speak to her.

"Come, Margot. It is safe, I promise." He held out his hand, the breath steaming from between his parted lips onto the cold night air.

Margot grasped his fingers, allowing him to help her down out of the truck. He kept a supportive arm around her waist, guiding her through the snow to the front door of the farmhouse.

Heat struck her hard in the face, a harsh gasp tightening her throat when her skin burned with the shock of it. The door closed quietly behind them as she was pulled through the dimly lit room, her feet vaguely registering a soft rug beneath her boots before they clunked quietly on wood floors. Then she was dropped into a chair, the crackle of a fire filling her body with a rush of warmth.

She looked around the shadowy room, noting a kitchen table, black iron stove, and a sink with freshly washed dishes sitting beside it. To her right, an arch opened to the parlor decorated simply with a worn settee, round woven rug, and a rocking chair. Margot shivered, her body leaning of its own accord toward the heat of the stove.

"*Cześć*," a soft, feminine voice murmured.

Margot raised her gaze, watching the grey-haired woman step in front of her. She placed the candle she carried on the table, glistening rays of golden light flooding the room. Margot's throat nearly closed as the woman crouched down in front of her, softly taking her hands before looking up at her with dark, gentle eyes.

"You have nothing to fear here," the woman whispered. "You are safe now. No harm will come to you in this house."

A strangled cry convulsed in her throat before she could stop it. Margot fell into the woman's arms, burying her face in the warmth of her shoulder. And for a single moment, every one of her fears slipped out of her heart as easily as the tears coursing down her cheeks.

Chapter Thirty

THE ARDENNES FOREST

Bernie grimaced with each step they took, the sharp *crunch* of twigs and ice as loud as the thunder of the shelling from moments ago. Bruno leaned heavily into his side, grumbling every time his bad foot scraped the ground. Night had fallen like a dark blanket over the sky—the moon and the stars their only guiding light back the way they'd come.

After waiting for an unbearable period of time for the enemy to pass by behind them, they'd finally gotten started back to their camp. Only to be stopped moments later by another round of shelling, forcing them flat to the ground, praying they would escape being blown to bits or crushed by falling trees.

Bernie clasped his arm tighter around Bruno's waist, the extra weight making his back blaze. The dark silhouettes of Jensen and Graham ambled along in front of him, weaving around every tree cautiously. A gust of wind brought another gentle snowfall, blanketing the ground in a fresh layer of powder.

He stopped, falling hard against one of the trees to catch his breath. Bruno bounced to the side, lifting his weight off Bernie. He whistled softly, signaling Graham and Jensen that they'd stopped before turning back to Bernie. His big shoulders shuddered with the cold.

"Thought you said Ellis was going to come looking for us," he commented.

Bernie eyed him, his breath coming too hard and his face too cold to respond.

"We're lost, aren't we Berns?" Bruno mumbled.

Bernie rubbed his eyes, bringing his thumb and finger together to pinch the bridge of his nose.

"Probably," he answered.

Bruno limped across the uneven ground, leaning back against the tree trunk shoulder to shoulder with Bernie. He sighed heavily, resting the crown of his head back against the rough, icy bark.

"So, is this it?" he muttered. "Almost four years being shot at only to freeze to death under a tree?"

"Would seem so," Bernie replied, his chest deflating with a painful breath. "How's the ankle?"

Bruno shrugged. "Swollen as big as this tree. Can't really feel it anymore."

Jensen came stumbling to a stop in front of them, breathing hard. The whites of his eyes glowed in the starlight, so round they seemed ready to pop right out of his head.

"Fire!" he gasped.

Bernie jerked away from the tree. "What?"

"Campfire! Over there!" Jensen pointed behind him. "Graham's checking it out now."

Bernie shoved his rifle into Bruno's hands, swinging the kraut rifle off his back into his palms.

"Jensen, stay here with Bru."

"Where are you going, Bernie?" Bruno asked.

"To see what Graham is seeing."

Bernie hurried away before Bruno could protest, moving in the direction Jensen had come from. He strode half-bent over around the trees, the distant spit and crackle of sticks burning reaching his ears.

Falling to the ground the louder the sound became, he crawled on his elbows up alongside Graham behind a fallen log. His friend merely glanced at him before they both lifted up slightly to peek over the top. Bernie held his breath, staring at the three huddled figures around the fire. Perhaps they thought if they sat close enough around it, they could hide the orange glow lifting all around them.

"They're bold," Graham grumbled. "Wish I was that bold."

"Best to try to go around them," Bernie replied.

"Think they're as lost as we are?"

Bernie swallowed a snort. "Wouldn't be surprised. Let's get moving."

He started to turn, moving as quietly as possible away from the log in the hopes the sound of the flames snapping at the twigs would muffle any shuffle their feet made in the snow. A sudden stream of light glared off the snow when one of the soldiers shifted away from the fire, causing Bernie to freeze. The shimmering gold wristband peeking from the edge of his thick sleeve held Bernie's gaze like a vice.

No. It can't be. Bernie's breath came faster, his eyes moving up the big arm from the watch to the rifle strapped across a curved back. He'd raised the collar of his coat and the low slope of his helmet hid the back of his neck entirely.

But the figure remained the same. The familiar way he moved—but the rifle told him all he needed to know. Almost identical to the enemy gun he carried in his own hands. The same weapon he'd been carrying for months, refusing to ever give it up. Then the man turned, shadows and light dancing across his features. Defining the lines around his mouth, the sharpness of his cheekbones, a long, pointed nose and round eyes. The man had haunted his dreams nearly every night, appearing to him in many different ways. Bernie had never expected him to appear so ... normal.

"Bernie!" Graham hissed, tugging on his sleeve. "What's wrong?"

Bernie fell away from the log, his hand numb where it sunk into the snow.

Seems like you won't have to worry about finding him. Starting to feel like he's looking for you. Bruno's voice uttered in his ear.

He followed Graham away from the campsite, his head spinning with all the reasons he needed to get back with his friends. All the reasons stopping now to pursue some vengeful satisfaction was foolish. And only one reason why he had to stay behind.

Joey.

Bruno's bent-over silhouette appeared up ahead, his shadow and Jensen's blending in the darkness as they approached. Both he and Graham pushed to their feet, jogging the last few feet to their sides.

"I think we can go around without alerting them. They're too busy trying to keep warm to notice us," Graham said, rubbing his hands together.

"Move quickly and quietly," Bernie murmured, staring at Bruno. "Graham you be sure to get Bruno back in one piece and right to an aid station."

"Why're you talking like you're not coming with us?" Jensen asked.

Bernie took a breath. "He's here."

Bruno didn't blink, the darkness dancing across his face and shadowing his eyes so Bernie couldn't read him.

"Who?" Graham wondered, brow arching.

"Let's not do this again, Bernie," Bruno growled. "I don't know who you think you saw, but the chances ... it's just ... it's not possible, okay?"

"Bru I have to stay. I know what I saw back there. It's him, Bruno, I know it is."

"Fine, let's say I believe you. Guess what? I don't care!" Bruno grabbed him by the shoulders, squeezing. "You're going to walk away you hear me?"

"I can't."

"Why not? You tell me why you can't just turn your back on this guy and come back with us!"

Bernie shook his head. "I can't explain it, Bruno. All I know is this is something I have to do … alone."

Bruno's mouth tightened and he shook his head furiously. "No, you—"

"Yes, I do." Bernie pushed his friend's hands away, reaching inside his jacket. His hand returned a moment later, clutching Margot's diary along with the packet of photographs and letters.

Her pretty face smiled up at him and after a moment's thought, he tucked her picture back inside his jacket.

"I need you to protect these with your life, Bru," Bernie whispered, shoving the diary and packet into Bruno's pocket before his friend could respond. "They're important. If I don't come back, show them to Woodley. I think he'll understand."

"Don't do this, Bernie."

Bernie looked away. "Jensen, Graham, get him back safely. Don't stop for anything. You run through from here on out, you understand?"

"I'll stay with you," Jensen said. "Maybe I can help."

"No. Graham is going to need you to watch his back while he helps Bruno keep a good pace."

"Bernie …" Graham breathed, shaking his head slowly.

"Do as I say." Bernie grabbed Bruno, yanking him close in a rough hug. "You're my best friend. Thanks for watching my back this far."

"Don't do this," Bruno repeated hoarsely.

Bernie spun away on his heels. "Get him out of here."

"Berns." Graham grabbed his arm as he started to pass. "We split up now we might not be able to come back for you. You get that right?"

The corner of Bernie's mouth tilted slightly. He gave Graham a light slap on the shoulder. "Good luck. God speed."

He shuffled away, picking up the pace when he heard Bruno call his name in a low hiss. Bernie kept going, jogging quietly through the snow back to the log. He crouched down behind it, peeking over again to watch the campfire. There were only three of them now, making Bernie's heart stop for a moment until he caught the glint of the watch.

Bernie squinted, observing the two other soldiers. One was short and bulky, most of his back facing him and the other was directly opposite him on the other side of the fire. The glow of the flames outlined the smooth, youthfulness of his face. He couldn't be more than eighteen, the bulky coat he wore barely hiding his thin physique.

He didn't care about them. He only needed to get them to scatter—separate. Bernie scooted away, putting a little more distance between them before getting his feet under him and spinning with his back to one of the trees. He propped the rifle beside him before tugging his colt from its holster. Closing his eyes, he waited a few counts then spun, raising the sidearm high before squeezing the trigger.

Branches split apart over the heads of the enemy, sending snow and twigs over their campsite. Every round blasted in his ears like a gong, followed by their panicked shouts as they all dropped to their bellies. Bernie stopped, turning away again and holding his breath. They were shouting furiously at each other, the steady *stomp stomp stomp* of one of them putting out the fire with their boot filling the air. Bernie turned his head, glancing back when a gruff voice raised the hair on the back of his neck.

The sniper was pointing into the woods, giving the younger boy a shove in one direction and the bulky one a push in the other. Then he picked up his rifle, tugging sharply on the bolt. Bernie closed his eyes, sliding his colt back into place before taking his rifle in both hands again. He listened to the crunch of snow between the other two men's feet, waiting for the sounds to get further and further away as they went looking for him.

Then another set of feet joined theirs, this one walking toward him instead of away. Bernie swallowed, his fingers groaning around the barrel of the rifle when he tightened his grip. A heavy footfall right beside the tree made him spin. One quick jerk, he clipped the sniper in the face with the butt of the rifle, sending him stumbling backward.

"Remember me?" Bernie spat, moving in.

The sniper roared, lunging at him. Bernie grunted when they slammed into each other, the rifle toppling out of his hands. They landed hard on the ground, rolling in the snow. Bernie shoved him away, whirling around on all fours. His eyes went wide, watching the Nazi rise slowly from the ground, a bayonet glistening in his hand. The rifle had slid away on the slick ground, far out of reach.

Before he could reach for his sidearm, the sniper pounced, slashing Bernie across the chest. He ducked low, grabbing him around the waist to take him back to the ground. He pressed the hand with the bayonet down flat on the ground, slamming his knee hard into the sniper's ribs. His head flew back, blood spurting from his mouth from the unexpected punch. The knife caught him—the warmth of blood streaming down his thigh. Bernie scrambled away, ignoring the fiery burn in his chest and the metallic taste flooding his mouth.

The Nazi grinned at him, the blood pouring from his nose dripping down his lips and over his teeth when he muttered. He waved the bloodied knife back and forth, still speaking in his language as they paced opposite each other. Bernie leaped back when he thrust the knife, trying to inch himself in the direction of the rifle. He jumped again, hissing between clenched teeth when he felt the swipe of the bayonet barely miss his side.

A sudden rush of gunfire and shouting in the distance claimed the attention of the sniper. The bayonet lowered slightly in his fist, giving Bernie an opening. He lunged, his hands curling around the rifle before he spun on the flats of his feet with weapon raised.

His enemy stared at him, the glisten of the gold watch around his wrist seeming to shine brighter in the moonlight and glaring off the flat of the blade in his hand. They stood for a moment in silence, both breathing hard. Bernie with rifle ready and the sniper with his knife raised.

"You should've died that day," Bernie growled. "You put another boy behind your gun. My bullet was for you, not him."

The Nazi spat into the snow. Then he threw back his arm, the blade glinting.

Bernie pulled the trigger as the man's arm swung forward. The sniper's neck flung backward, the bullet blasting a hole straight through the front of his helmet followed by a steady spray of blood. He watched the sniper flop to the ground, landing face down in the snow. Slowly, he lowered the rifle, staring at the pool of blood soaking into the white blanket beneath his feet.

Bending over, his fingers trembled as he removed the watch from the dead man's wrist, his thumb leaving a smear of blood across the glass face.

"I got him, Joey," he whispered. Then he dropped heavily to his knees.

Bernie turned his head. His chin brushed his collarbone when he looked down at the bayonet lodged in his left shoulder. Grunting, he took hold of the handle, squeezing his eyes tight as he slid the blade out of his flesh, the pressure building as with each tug blood poured down his chest and side. He gasped, a rush of frozen air sweeping over him when the bayonet finally came loose.

The weapon slipped between his fingers, falling with a light thump beside his knee. Bernie shuddered, the forest spinning as his heart thundered out of control. Slowly, his weight shifted and he rolled onto his back, staring up through the tree branches at the night sky. He blinked slowly, the blood soaking into his clothes and seeping from the wound in his leg onto the ground. Reaching inside his jacket, he closed his hand around Margot's picture.

"I'm sorry I won't make it to you," he whispered, a drop of moisture escaping from the corner of his eye. "I'm ... sorry ..."

Bernie's eyelids grew heavy, the sting of his wounds crawling over the entire surface of his body as a black haze began to settle over his vision. A figure suddenly bent over him, big hands reaching out to grab him the moment his eyes closed.

Chapter Thirty-One

Margot's neck craned back on the edge of the copper tub. The hot water encompassed her, soothing her sore muscles. She raised her hand, watching the water trickle down her forearm to drip from her elbow in a steady *glip, glip, glip*. Her remaining cuts stung when she splashed handfuls of water into her face, guiding the moisture up over the top of her head to soak her slowly growing hair.

The couple who owned the farm, Alina and Jan Górski, had said very little to her. But words seemed unnecessary as they cared for her. Alina had served her a light broth to soothe the hunger burning her belly and Jan had been certain to keep the house warm while her bath was prepared. Ludwig hadn't left her side until the moment Alina poured the last bucket of steaming water into the tub, leaving Margot to cast off the clothing Ludwig had provided.

Turning her head, she stared at the chair beside the door. A neatly folded gray dress with thick wool stockings, sturdy black boots, and a dark blue bandanna lay on the seat of the chair waiting for her. She rolled her hand across the surface of the water, listening to the soft ripple of the warm liquid. Putting on such normal, clean clothes would seem strange now after wearing the same dress week after week for the past two months.

Wincing, she pulled herself up into a sitting position, reaching for the dish on the floor with the bar of soap Alina had left. She started to scrub, the sweetly scented soap stinging her skin as she rubbed the layer of filth off her body. Her arms and legs were raw by the time she finished, clumps of soap beneath her fingernails from how tightly she'd squeezed the bar.

Holding her breath and pinching her nose, she slid beneath the surface of the water to rinse the soap away. Rising a few seconds later she gasped, rubbing the water from her eyes before setting the soap back in its dish, half the size it was when she started washing. Her arms shook when she gripped the sides of the tub, pushing herself unsteadily to her feet. The water splashed and spilled over the sides as she stepped out.

Hastily drying herself with a rough towel she slipped into the undergarments Alina provided, pausing when she caught her reflection in the mirror. Margot took a hesitant step toward the glass, warily watching the girl staring back at her. Eyes sunken, cheeks thin and well-defined—half her face bruised a sickly yellowish-green. Her thin fingers shook as she moved them across her flat belly, over her ribs where they stuck out against her skin to the bottom edge of the brassiere.

Her golden-brown hair had grown more than she realized, spiking at least an inch up from her scalp. But even as her hair had grown and her eyes still shone their same color, she didn't recognize herself. How could she have lost so much weight and not realized? How was she even standing?

Why am I alive? Margot's knees trembled, knocking together violently to nearly send her to the ground.

She dragged her feet across the wood floor to the chair, trying to keep her balance as she tugged the wool stockings on her legs before raising the dress over her head. The soft garment was too big for her but covered her decently and warmly. Sitting down on the chair, she wiggled her feet into the boots, tying the laces as tight as she could.

She'd just finished wrapping the bandanna across the top of her head when a knock sounded on the door.

"Margot?" Ludwig's muffled voice called on the other side. "We have to go."

She opened the door, staring up at him. His gaze drifted over her slowly, a smile touching his full lips when his eyes stopped on her boots.

"You look fine," he said.

Margot pulled on her left sleeve, cringing when she caught a glimpse of the black row of numbers marring her inner forearm.

"I am too thin. My hair is not long enough yet. How will we explain if we are stopped?" Her eyes burned.

"Then we must not be stopped." Ludwig reached around her, tugging a coat across her shoulders.

Margot thrust her arms into the sleeves, folding the heavy garment across her front to hold in the warmth her body had soaked in from the comfort of this quiet little house. Ludwig put his arm around her shoulders, leading her out of the room and down the hall to the kitchen.

Alina turned from the stove, her affectionate smile reminding Margot of her own mother. She broke away from Ludwig to circle her arms around the woman.

"*Danke*," Margot whispered. "I will never forget you."

Alina patted her back in silent acknowledgment of her thanks. Margot stepped away without looking back, hugging herself across the ribs as she walked outside into the frigid air. The moon was still high in the sky, surrounded by dozens of twinkling stars and not a cloud in sight. She stomped in the snow over to the truck where Jan was waiting, holding the door open. Margot nodded at him slightly when she passed, reaching to grasp the wheel of the truck to pull herself onto the seat. Ludwig's hand pressed into the small of her back, giving her some added support before she landed with a thud on the hard seat and scooted over quickly to make room.

Ludwig shook Jan's hand, mumbling something under his breath before he joined her. Bending forward, Margot lifted her hand in a wave when Alina's silhouette appeared in the doorway right before the truck rolled away from the yard. She sat back with a sigh, the cold tickling her nose.

"There is a bag at your feet," Ludwig announced. "Alina packed some bread and cheese. There is a canister of milk as well from Jan."

Margot reached down, tugging the sack from the floor of the truck and onto the seat beside her. A sloshing from inside warned her to keep the bag upright so the milk wouldn't leak—the temptation to rip open the sack and eat every morsel, drink every drop, nearly overwhelming her.

"The food should last until our next stop," Ludwig continued.

"Where will that be?" Margot wondered, twisting a loose string on the sack around her finger.

"Far away from here."

A vein in her temple pulsed—his vague answer setting her nerves on edge. Unable to resist any longer she reached inside the sack, tearing a small piece of bread from the loaf to nibble.

"I scrubbed nearly until I bled," she whispered. "Still I do not feel clean."

Ludwig rolled his shoulders, his neck popping softly when he bent his head side to side. "I know what you mean."

Margot closed her eyes, licking the crumbs from her lips as she finished the bite of bread. The heaviness of sleep began to settle over her once again. After sleeping a day and half a night away, she didn't think she'd still be so tired. But even now she could feel herself drifting, her hands falling limp in her lap as she let her entire body droop.

The wheels to the truck came to a screeching halt. Margot's eyes fluttered, squinting in the early rays of dawn. Ludwig sat stiffly behind the wheel, staring wide-eyed at the road ahead. Margot moaned, turning away to look out the windshield. Her heart stopped, staring at the line of Nazi trucks blocking the road. The uniformed soldiers marching toward them, helmets shadowing their faces and stern mouths pressed into straight lines.

"What do we do?" Margot gasped. "Ludwig, what do we do?"

He didn't answer, simply sat their frozen like a statue. Margot grabbed him by the sleeve, shaking him hard.

"Ludwig! *Bitte*!"

Still, he didn't move, only stared unblinking at the soldiers approaching the truck. Margot scrambled away, deciding to make a run for the forest before it was too late. The door to the truck swung open and Margot shrieked, leaping back when the stony-faced soldier appeared.

"*Nein*," Margot rasped when he reached inside, grabbing her by the arm. "*Nein!*"

Her voice rose to a piercing shriek as he dragged her out of the truck, the heels of her boots digging into the hard dirt of the road as she resisted him. She twisted her neck but couldn't get a glimpse of Ludwig as she writhed in the grip of the soldier. He threw her to the ground, her hands scraping in the mix of snow and dirt and her knees throbbing.

Margot stayed on all fours, her shoulders rising and falling rapidly with every breath, every exhale steaming and rushing back into her face.

This cannot happen. Mein bruder did not die saving me so my life could end like this! Margot squeezed her eyes closed.

The leisure, heavy footfalls approaching directly in front of her made her freeze. With every step he took, she knew who he was. With every rough breath he breathed, she sensed his eyes, chilling her straight to the bone.

Slowly, Margot raised her head. Glaring up into the eyes of Josef Mengele, she wished her heart would stop now. She wished death would come quickly, claiming her as swiftly as it had claimed her father what felt like so long ago now. Margot leaned back, a heavy fog swirling all around them as she sat back on her heels. He bent on one knee in front of her, gripping her chin tight in his hand.

In his other hand, the glimmer of a knife started to rise toward her eye.

"Hmm," he purred. "You see, little German girl? You cannot escape me."

"*Nein!*"

★★★

Margot woke screaming, clawing at the air as the truck swerved violently on the road.

"Margot!" Ludwig grabbed her arm while using his opposite hand to keep control of the vehicle. "Margot wake up! It is a dream!"

She jerked away from him, her head bumping into the window when she lost her balance. Bile burned the back of her throat, rising swiftly up. Margot grabbed the door handle.

"Pull over," she gasped. "Pull over, Ludwig!"

He did as she asked, bringing the truck to an abrupt halt on the side of the road. Margot stumbled out of the truck, landing on her knees before she crawled away and emptied her stomach. Tears poured from her eyes, every heave stabbing her stomach and scorching her throat.

Ludwig's heavy hand landed on her back, soothingly rubbing as she gasped desperately for air between her sobs. She fell back against his chest, letting him wrap her up in a warm embrace. She clung to his arm, turning until her face was buried in his shoulder.

"Here," Ludwig whispered as the soft slosh of water sounded near her ear. "Drink."

Margot turned her head, keeping her swollen eyes closed as he pressed the canteen against her lips. The water was cold, soothing her throat as it streamed down into her now empty belly.

"*Danke*," Margot murmured, pushing the canteen away. "I am sorry."

Ludwig shook his head. "Do not ever be sorry, Margot."

He tucked her close, cupping his hand on the back of her head to cradle her against his chest. Margot closed her eyes, trying to rest in the comfort of his arms and the steady beat of his heart beside her ear.

"I have to tell you something," Ludwig said.

Margot bent her head back, keeping her cheek on his shoulder while she stared up at him. He didn't meet her eyes, looking instead into the woods before them.

"This was not meant to be your escape. It was meant to be mine."

Margot lifted herself away from him, her hand pressing the center of his chest for support as she sat up.

"I planned the route. I arranged where I would stop for rest and supplies. I was meant to disappear from Auschwitz without a trace. Without the risk of—"

"Of taking a prisoner with you?" Margot swallowed the lump in her throat.

Ludwig grimaced. "Franz discovered my plan and asked me to take the risk."

Margot tilted her head. "Why did you?"

"Because Hans was my friend," Ludwig replied. "And you should never have been sent to that place."

"No one should have been sent there, Ludwig."

He nodded, covering her hand with his over his chest. "*Ja*, I know."

He raised the canteen to her lips again so she could take another sip. Margot placed her hand on his wrist, tilting the canteen further so the fresh, clean water flowed more steadily into her mouth. Every swallow was painful, but she took as much as she could get before he took it away.

"I promised your *bruder* I would get you to safety." Ludwig stepped away from her, rising from the ground. He held out his hand, the golden rays of sunrise glistening in his chestnut-colored hair. "You can trust me, Margot. I will keep my word."

Margot slid her hand into his, gripping tight and leaning her weight into him when she steadied herself back on her feet. He clutched her limp fingers in his palm so hard she thought her bones might snap. The glitter of hope shining in his eyes tempted her to respond. To reassure him she had complete faith in him. To tell him that considering how he'd helped her in the camp and how far they'd already come, she trusted him above anyone else in the world. But the truth was wrapping quickly around her throat like an invisible hand, cutting off her words.

Because the truth was simple—she *had* to trust him. There was no other choice. She only knew if Rolf or Gerhard were to appear suddenly before her, she would leave Ludwig behind in an instant. She would run as far away from him as she could get, leaving behind every horrid memory his presence provoked. If there was another choice, she would not choose to place her trust in Ludwig Volk.

But there is no other choice. Margot sucked in a long draw of air.

"We should go," she rasped.

Ludwig bowed his head and Margot turned away, shuffling back across the road to climb into the truck.

Chapter Thirty-Two

Time had no meaning.

After the first few days, Margot stopped counting the minutes, the hours, that ticked by as they drove from place to place. Stopping briefly to rest with quiet strangers and accept the gift of some food and drink before moving on. They switched trucks once, the new vehicle smaller and less conspicuous as they continued their journey across the wintery countryside. With every exhausting mile, Margot's heart sank a little lower. The thought of everything and everyone she was leaving behind bore down on her like a hefty wind.

Margot rolled over onto her left side away from the window. Ludwig stole a quick glance at her, bouncing slightly in his seat as they hit a bump in the road. She reached into the sack between them, her hand curling around an apple. The piece of fruit seemed to sparkle at her, her mouth watering at the mere sight of it. Their last stop had provided at least half a dozen apples from their cellar as well as a fresh canister of milk.

She raised the fruit to her nose, inhaling the sweet scent deeply. Relishing the smell as she resisted taking a bite. They'd both already eaten more than enough for today and her companion was not very forthcoming about when their next stop would be. Cupping it in both hands, Margot tucked her knuckles beneath her chin, rubbing the smooth skin of the apple around on her palms.

"Tell me about Hans," she said, her voice loud in the quiet.

Ludwig cleared his throat. "What do you wish to know?"

"About your friendship. About the adventures you went on as little boys. I do not remember you well, but I do remember Hans spending time with you after school." Margot's nose wrinkled. "He often excluded me when we were thirteen."

"We did what many mischievous boys did, Margot. It would be of no interest to you now."

Her brow furrowed. "I have lost my whole family, Ludwig. Right now, I am trying to think of anything but *mein großer bruder* lying dead on the ground. I have not spoken of my twin for so long. *Bitte*, I do not care how dull the story, tell me one."

Ludwig's lips parted, a small, stuttering sound escaping before he cleared his throat. Lips moved but no sound emerged. Margot sighed, prepared to give up and resign herself to the silence between them. Then his shoulders rose and fell, a softness touching the stress lines around his eyes.

"I remember one time," he murmured. "Hans and I skipped school to go to the Grunewald Forest. Hans wanted to hunt. Instead we fought over who would set the trap and hold your father's knife. We ended up falling down the hill and in a puddle of mud."

Margot smiled. "I think I remember that day. Hans came home filthy!"

"I was with him. Your housekeeper, Gretl, let us in through the back door to the kitchen." Ludwig turned his head, taking his eyes briefly off the road to look at her. "You spent ten minutes scolding your *bruder* for being so childish."

"And Franz stood in the doorway laughing!" Margot added, a small giggle bubbling in her throat.

She could see the scene as clearly as if it were happening all over again. Gretl fussing over the tracks of mud the boys left on her kitchen floor. Margot pacing back and forth with her arms crossed tight, glaring at her twin. Hans with mud smeared on his face and hands, his usually immaculate golden hair mussed and in need of a good wash.

Those blue eyes she loved and missed so much, glaring back at her in annoyance. She could almost hear him mumbling that she was not his *mutter*. Could almost smell the scent of sweat and dirt lifting off him when she sat down in front of him to harshly rub the crusted mud from his cheeks.

Oh, how I miss him! She sniffled, wiping her sleeve across her nose and mouth.

"You wiped my face with a warm, wet cloth." Ludwig's voice lowered to a deep purr.

"I did?" Margot's head tilted.

"*Ja*," he paused, his Adams apple bobbing when he swallowed. "You were wearing a green dress with a brown belt. You were barefoot because we returned as you'd been preparing for bed, and you came down to see what the commotion was about. Your hair was down too—long, past your shoulders."

Her smile began to fade, her mind digging deeply for a memory of him that day. She'd been so angry at Hans for not telling her his plan to skip school. So focused on scolding her twin for coming home nearly in the middle of the night covered in mud and nearly worrying their *mutter* half to death. Those were the things she remembered about that night.

But washing Ludwig's face for him? Caring for him the way she had her own *bruder*?

I cannot remember him, but he remembers me from that night so clearly. A shiver skittered over her body.

Desperate to change the subject, she said, "Tell me about your family. I ... I cannot remember ... do you have siblings?"

"*Ja, meine kleine schwester* left a few years ago to study in France. I have not heard from her in nearly a year."

"I am sorry."

"*Nein*, do not be. I worry for her sometimes, but she is strong. She will be all right." Ludwig's jaw clenched. "*Mein kleiner bruder* is still living at home. He is only fourteen and moved to our country home with our *mutter* three years ago."

"You are the oldest?"

"*Ja.*"

Margot rested her head back, letting her hands drop back to her lap still cradling the apple. "You did not come to our house often, did you?"

Ludwig shook his head. "*Nein*, I lived most of the year with my *großeltern* in the country, helping them on the farm since my *großvater* could no longer do the work himself as he grew older."

"Is that where your *mutter* and *bruder* moved? To be with your *großeltern* until the war is over?"

"*Ja*. They are my *mutter's* parents, so it is a comfort to her to be close to them while I am away."

"And your *vater*?"

Ludwig's shoulders tightened at the mention of his father. Her own heart flip-flopped in her chest, recognizing the pain now pinching her companion's face. The same expression she was sure tightened her own features whenever someone mentioned her dear Papa.

"He passed away nearly four years ago."

Margot reached across the space between them without thought, resting her hand on his arm warmly.

"You loved him very much," she said.

Ludwig cleared his throat, staring straight ahead at the road. But even though he refused to look at her, he could not hide the sheen in his eyes. Margot's hand slipped away from his forearm, returning to her side.

"How far do you think we've come today?" she wondered.

He bent forward over the wheel, squinting out the windshield at the cloudy sky overhead.

"Nearly far enough, I think. We should start looking for a place to stop for the night."

Margot shuddered. These were the nights she despised the most on this journey. The nights they had no choice but to pull off the road a mile or two and hope the darkness covered them in enough shadow as to not be noticed while they slept. Looking at the dark circles beneath Ludwig's eyes, she wondered how much sleep he actually got on the nights they rested in the truck. Every time she stirred from her sleep, he was already awake and driving.

Margot shrieked when a bump bounced her off the seat into the air. Ludwig chuckled and she glared at him, rubbing her backside as he pulled off the road, driving across a meadow. The truck rumbled to a halt, the engine sputtering into silence when he twisted the key and turned off the headlights. Margot bit her lip, a sticky layer of nervous sweat coating the back of her neck despite the cold.

Whenever darkness encircled her along with the eerie silence of twilight, her fears rose like fire in her throat. She coughed into her sleeve, trying to shake away the feeling and remember how to breathe. Ludwig slid closer to her, reaching his arm across the back of the seat. Margot sat back, startled.

"What are you doing?" she asked.

"Keeping you warm." Ludwig's eyebrow curved. "Unless you want to freeze in your sleep."

"I haven't needed you to keep me warm before."

"*Ja*, you did. You just didn't know before."

Margot narrowed her eyes, her upper lip twisting with irritation. She supposed, with how deeply she'd been sleeping, it was possible she would not have woken when Ludwig put his arms around her. She also had to admit there had been some mornings she'd woken up from a sudden rush of cold, as if a blanket had been quickly pulled off her body.

Or the loss of another's body heat. Hesitantly, she rested her body against his side, curling her knees to her ribs as he circled his arm around her shoulders.

"Go to sleep now, *mein freund*," he said.

Margot closed her eyes, anxious to obey. She turned her head to bury her face in his coat, her muscles beginning to relax as she sunk deeply on the curve of his side. The whistle of the wind, along with the rhythmic beat of his heart, lulled her quickly to sleep.

As she nearly slipped away into oblivion, she felt his other arm come around her, holding her tighter to his chest. Then his whisper breathed into her ear.

"I'm going to keep you safe, Margot. No matter where we end up, I'll keep you safe. I promise."

Chapter Thirty-Three

In sleep, the strong arms wrapped around her belonged to Bernie Russell. His warmth seeped into her, banishing the frigid air. His lips brushed her temple as she drifted in and out of a restless slumber. His hands held her tight, pressing her securely against the beat of his heart.

But when she opened her eyes, Ludwig was pulling away, slipping his arm out from beneath the pressure of her back to start the truck again. Dawn attempted to peek through the dark clouds covering the sky—a steady, thick snowfall beginning to flutter from the sky as the truck struggled through the thick layer of frost on the ground and back onto the road.

Margot said nothing, keeping perfectly still so he would think she was still sleeping even as she watched him through the veil of her eyelashes. His eyes were bloodshot, making her wonder if he'd slept at all. Even with the roar of the engine, she could hear his stomach grumbling furiously, yet he didn't reach for the sack of food. His fingers were curled tight around the wheel, his knuckles pale either from his grip or the cold, she couldn't be sure.

Sighing, she sat up, stretching her stiff neck from side to side before shivering when another rush of cold swept her body like a breeze. Her own fingers were red, having been crushed inside the pockets of her coat as she slept, a thousand needles stabbing her as she massaged them to bring life back into her flesh.

Bending at the waist she tugged the sack back up from where it had fallen off the seat, her hand vanishing inside briefly before returning wrapped around an apple. Closing her eyes, she took a bite, the sweet juices squirting onto her tongue and down her dry throat. Then she held it out to Ludwig.

"You need to eat," she said.

"I'm fine," he replied.

Margot rolled her eyes. "You are driving. I would rather you not faint from hunger. Take a bite."

She raised the fruit to his lips. Mumbling, Ludwig turned his head, sinking his teeth into the apple for a big bite. Margot giggled when some of the juices dribbled down his chin, swiping the drops away with her thumb. She leaned back, finishing the apple before tossing the core out the window. Her stomach was slowly adjusting to more solid food with each passing day, but still sometimes her innards swirled. She still had moments of needing to leap out of the truck to be sick.

It will get better. Margot closed her eyes.

The truck began to slow, causing her eyes to flutter open. Every muscle in her body stiffened when she saw the trucks up ahead—the soldiers climbing in and out, some milling about in the middle of the road smoking. Ludwig brought the truck to a complete stop, his own breath coming harder as they waited to see if they'd been spotted.

"There is another way," Ludwig whispered. He reached over, covering her hand where it was fisted tight on the seat. "Relax, Margot. We're going to simply back away slowly."

She nodded vigorously, trying to keep herself calm as he started to do just that. The truck rolled backward, every soft *crunch* of the tires on the snow, every sputter of the engine, making her heart shudder. He twisted the wheel, turning them around to go back the way they'd come. Margot watched in the mirrors, her fingernails digging into her leg when she saw one of the soldiers' heads come up.

"They've seen us," she gasped. "Ludwig, they've seen us!"

"Stay calm, *schätzchen.*"

Margot whimpered, wiggling on the seat as Ludwig began to pick up speed. One of the soldiers pointed at them and she squeezed her eyes closed, forcing herself to keep still. She could feel the truck gaining speed in every vibration of the vehicle—could hear his breaths slowing to a calm, steady rhythm. But her own body and mind felt no such peace, even when she opened her eyes to see they weren't being followed.

"Are you all right?" Ludwig asked, glancing at her.

"*Nein!*" Margot sobbed, slamming her fist on the seat. "I have never been so frightened in all my life! So *nein*, I am not all right! I left behind people I loved to die horrible deaths in a Nazi camp while I run away to freedom! All I can think about is how I cannot ever go back there!"

She covered her face with her hands, tears seeping between her fingers. "I should have died there. I am a terrible person."

"You are not. Your *bruder* wanted you to live, Margot. You cannot blame yourself for escaping when others did not."

"I should have sent Hanna to you. I should have stayed behind and sent her to you in the woods that day."

Ludwig squeezed her shoulder. "There was no time for that, Margot. Franz's plan was for you from the start. It was always about you."

"Well," Margot paused, sniffling and wiping the tears from her cheeks with her sleeves. "It shouldn't have been. He should've gotten Hanna and Horst out."

Ludwig let his hand fall away from her shoulder, returning it to the wheel. He didn't respond, keeping his focus on the road as the silence threatened to swallow her up. Then he took a breath, his voice barely audible when he spoke.

"One day, you will be able to forgive yourself for living, Margot. It will take time, but someday you will be glad you survived."

Margot turned her back on him, burying her face in her hands to cry.

★★★

"Bernie!" Margot woke with a gasp, the dream disappearing like a puff of smoke from her memory.

Rolling over off her shoulder to her back, she knew only that she'd been dreaming about him again. Her beacon in the darkness. The man who'd inspired hope in her heart after she'd thought she'd lost it forever. Margot massaged the sudden pressure in the center of her chest, her body bouncing with the movement of the truck.

"You were dreaming again," Ludwig said.

Margot's head fell to the side so she could look at him, her cheek brushing her shoulder.

"*Ja*, I know."

"Who's Bernie?" he wondered. "You have said his name before in your sleep."

"Have I?" Margot bowed her head, sliding her hands into the warmth of her coat pockets. "Bernie is ... well he's ..."

She squeezed her eyes closed, trying to find words to explain who Bernie was. To say he meant everything to her—to say he was all she had left in the world, would make little sense to the man sitting beside her. How could she explain that with two letters Bernie Russell had saved her life? And how could she say such a thing to the man who believed he was saving her life right now?

"Bernie is complicated," she finally said on a heavy sigh. "I do not know how to explain."

Ludwig turned the wheel, taking them off the main road and onto a path over the hill. Margot frowned, peeking out the window in the shadows of the night. They moved over the hill, the truck swaying from side to side on the rough terrain. She rubbed her arms, wishing there was something else to do besides sleep and dream. Every day seemed longer than the last as she began to recover and grow stronger.

The headlights illuminated the road, the dark silhouette of a house taking shape up ahead as they drove back down the other side of the hill. Margot wiggled anxiously on the seat.

"Is this our next stop?" she asked.

Ludwig nodded mutely.

Margot smiled, the thought of sleeping inside four walls with a warm stove nearby and the possibility of another bath filling her belly with flutters of excitement. They came to a stop in front of the barn and Ludwig turned to her.

"Wait here a moment."

Margot frowned. He hadn't asked her to wait since the first night of their escape, since then letting her come with him instead of sitting frightened in the truck.

"Why?"

"The house is dark. I want to make sure it's safe." He pressed the key to the truck in her palm. "If anything happens, you start driving and don't look back."

Margot nodded, enclosing the cold metal key in her fist. Ludwig hopped down from the truck, striding across the yard toward the back door of the house. She held her breath, watching him knock softly before pushing the door open and stepping out of sight. The seconds ticked by, her lungs beginning to throb before the air left them in one heavy exhale. Every breath was a wheeze as she tried to relax, telling herself Ludwig was just fine. That if something was wrong there would've been a commotion.

Then the back door opened and Ludwig reappeared, the silhouette of another man at his shoulder. He beckoned her with one wide wave of his arm. Margot slid down out of the truck, her boots sinking in slush when she landed on the ground. She scurried across the yard, dropping the key into her pocket when she approached the door, Ludwig's strong arm circling her waist to hurry her the last few feet across the threshold.

Margot smiled when she found herself standing in the middle of a small kitchen, the heat of the stove to her right seeping quickly into her cool skin. A young woman appeared, holding open a swinging door to give Margot a peek into an equally small living room. She stared at Margot with wide brown eyes, her matching hair falling in a tightly wound braid over her shoulder. The man who'd been standing in the doorway stepped around Margot, coming to the woman's side.

"*Cześć*," Margot greeted.

The couple exchanged a glance before looking at her again curiously. Ludwig gripped her elbow from behind.

"Come, Margot." He gave her a small push forward.

The couple moved away from the door as Ludwig pulled her out of the kitchen. Margot looked back over her shoulder at them, brow pinching.

"Is everything all right, Ludwig?" she asked.

"*Ja*, it's just—"

"You're alive."

Margot went still, the familiar voice falling over her like a bucket of ice water. Slowly, she turned, a gasp followed by the well of tears in her eyes nearly brought her to her knees at the sight of him. He seemed not to have changed at all these many months. Still the same tousled brown hair, the same glowing hazel eyes, and the same mud-stained clothes.

Gerhard.

He closed the distance between them in two strides, yanking her right off her feet in his arms. Margot wrapped hers around his neck, feeling the moisture of his tears when he pressed his face into the curve of her shoulder. His large hands sunk against her back and waist, holding her flush against him with her toes barely touching the floor.

"Ilse?" he asked, voice muffled in her shoulder.

Margot trembled. "Gone."

Gerhard's arms tightened on her, his shoulders quaking violently before he set her steadily back on her feet. He raised his head, looking down at her with glossy eyes.

"How?"

Margot rubbed his arms in an attempt to comfort him. "She was accused of stabbing one of the guards at the camp and was shot by ..."

Her words stopped—throat closing. Swallowing hard she closed her eyes, giving his arms a gentle squeeze.

"By one of the SS officers," she finished on a rough whisper.

Gerhard nodded slowly, averting his gaze. Gently, she stroked his face, the moisture of his tears rubbing off on her fingertips.

"When did you return to Poland?" she wondered.

Gerhard's brow furrowed deeply. "What?"

"How long have you been back? I thought when you returned to Berlin you would not come back here but ..." her voice faded when he looked into her eyes again.

The depth of confusion staring back at her rocked her to her core. Then he raised his gaze over her head to glare at Ludwig.

"You haven't told her?" he hissed.

"Told me what?" Margot turned halfway around, her eyes rounding so wide they began to ache. She took a small step toward Ludwig, releasing Gerhard as she did so. "Ludwig ... we are still in Poland aren't we?"

He wouldn't look at her, his hands stuffed deeply in his pockets and his feet shuffling nervously. Margot moved even closer, the striped wallpaper covering the walls of the parlor beginning to spin behind Ludwig's head.

"If we are not in Poland then we are in Czechoslovakia, aren't we? We are going *around* Germany toward France, aren't we?" she asked, barely above a whisper.

"Margot, *bitte*, try to understand ..."

"Ludwig," Margot gasped, breathless. "Are we in Germany?"

"I—"

"Did you bring me back to Germany?" her voice rose to a piercing shriek, hot tears falling unchecked down her cheeks.

"*Bitte*," Ludwig murmured, wringing his hands. "I had to try to see my family, Margot! I need them to know I am alive before I leave Germany forever. Can't you understand that? Can you tell me if it was your family—?"

"My family is dead!" Margot screamed, launching herself at him.

Gerhard grabbed her from behind, grasping her wrists in his fists to hold them tight across her middle.

"And if you try to see them, yours will be too!" she spat.

Gerhard dragged her out the front door, his arm wrapped firmly around her waist as he picked her up, swinging her over the threshold before dropping her back to her feet.

Margot yanked herself out of his grasp, walking a few feet into the yard. She covered her mouth and nose with her hands, her hot breath rushing back into her face.

Looking out over the countryside, she could hardly believe she was looking at German land. That she was standing on German soil twisted a new knot in her stomach. Everything her *bruder* had done to save her—every risk he and Hanna and Horst had taken to get her out of the camp— would be for nothing if she was caught now.

"I will talk to him," Gerhard said, drawing her back from her thoughts. "If he does not see sense, I will take you the rest of the way myself."

Margot closed her eyes, nodding silently.

"Did ... did she suffer?"

A subtle groan rose in her throat—one of the many questions she'd been dreading answering echoing like thunder in her ears.

"Do not do this to yourself, Gerhard," she whispered. "*Bitte ...*"

"I want to know how bad it was for her. Tell me."

Margot turned around, forcing herself to face him when she spoke. "For many weeks, Ilse and I were kept separated. I did not know—and still do not know—exactly what she was put through. But when she found me, she was very ill."

He cringed, his mouth twisting in pain.

"We hid her illness as best we could for as long as we could. Then ..." She bowed her head, her feet shuffling beneath her. "Then it was ... over. She was killed for a crime she did not commit."

Gerhard placed his hand over his eyes, his shoulders trembling with a muffled groan as he resisted tears. Margot lifted her arms, taking his face between her palms and forcing him to uncover his eyes. They stood in silence, her thumbs moving in gentle circles over the rough stubble on his cheeks and his reddened eyes staring glossily into hers. Then he placed his hands on her waist, gently moving her away.

"I will go talk to Ludwig now," he mumbled.

Her heart sunk when he shuffled toward the door, the snow rolling over his boots as he dragged them across the ground. Margot stumbled forward a step.

"Gerhard?"

He stopped at the door, looking back at her.

"You will come with us, won't you? Out of Germany?" her voice broke. "You will not leave me, will you?"

A shadow crossed his eyes, the corners of his mouth turning down grimly. "I do not know, Margot. First, let me discuss your course with Ludwig."

He hurried inside before she could respond. Margot hugged herself, turning her back on the house once again. A harsh wind rippled her skirt, sending icy stabs straight through the stockings covering her legs. She gritted her teeth and stood still, refusing to shield herself from the cold. This winter seemed endless, December having faded into January so quickly her head spun. The amount of days since she'd left Auschwitz blurred together in her mind.

A low rumble on the air made her frown. Margot strained to see in the darkness, taking a few more steps down the path away from the house. Then the soft glow of headlights came glittering over the top of the hill, setting her heart on fire.

Tripping in her rush, she burst back inside, frantically pointing behind her.

"Trucks!" she panted.

Gerhard grabbed her arm, giving her a shove toward Ludwig before he and the young owner of the farm went to peek out the window. Ludwig placed his hand on her shoulder, and she sidestepped away, shrugging him off. The roar of the trucks was coming closer, the sound freezing the blood in her veins.

The young woman she'd seen suddenly appeared at her shoulder, circling around her with a pistol in each hand. She passed one off to the man Margot assumed was her husband before she slipped out of sight into a room off the parlor.

"One of their men must have followed me from the village and gone back to report our location," Gerhard muttered.

He strode away from the window, coming to a stop beside her. Margot looked up at him for a few breathless moments, their eyes locked in an unblinking stare. His hand trembled when he brushed his fingertips on her cheek, the sadness in his face tightening around her heart like a fist. He took her arm, gesturing for Ludwig to follow as he guided her through the kitchen and out the back door.

"My truck is over that hill," Gerhard announced, pointing to the ridge beyond the house. He tossed Ludwig a pair of keys. "Take it and go."

"Gerhard, *nein!*" Margot grabbed him by the sleeves. "You cannot leave me!"

He pulled her close, hugging her until she thought her ribs would crack.

"I am nothing without her, Margot." He gripped her shoulders, stepping away before bending to peck the tip of her nose. "Now go. Ilse would want you to go."

"She would want you to come with me!"

"Gerhard!" a voice hissed from within the house. "They are coming!"

He shoved his hand in his pocket, the stark white of two pieces of paper appearing between his fingers. He held them in front of her face.

"These people will help you. They will provide you with shelter for as long as you need." Gerhard forced the paper into her coat pocket. "I told Ludwig about them, he knows where to go. But if anything should happen to him, you must do everything you can to find them. Promise me, *mein freund*."

Margot bobbed her head. "I promise."

Gerhard kissed her nose once more before giving her a hard shove away. "Go, Margot, hurry!"

Her feet planted heavily on the ground, her head spinning with the familiarity of it all. How could this be happening again?

I cannot lose another person.

Ludwig snatched her hand, giving her such a hard tug that she fell over in the snow. Then she was up again, her feet stumbling over each other as she ran alongside him over the hill. Gunfire exploded behind them and she nearly fell to her knees, her instinct to drop to the ground overwhelming her. But Ludwig kept her moving forward, cresting the hill within moments.

Below, they could see the gleam of Gerhard's truck beneath the stars. The faint scent of smoke suddenly reached her nose and she spun, eyes widening when she saw the billows rising in the sky accompanied by a faint orange glow.

"They're burning the house," she rasped.

Ludwig kept silent, forcing her back to his side with a firm pull on her hand. They moved faster down the other side of the hill, Gerhard's truck becoming larger and larger until they finally reached it. Margot slammed into the door, the cramp in her side burning and stealing her breath.

"I am sorry, Margot," Ludwig said. He was bent at the waist, hands on his knees as he tried to catch his breath.

"You should be," she replied.

She snatched the keys from him with one hand and pulled Gerhard's instructions from her pocket with the other.

"From now on," she growled. "I drive."

Margot waited for him to argue—waited to see a glow of stubbornness or anger in his eyes. Instead, Ludwig climbed into the truck with her in silence and did not speak for the rest of the night.

Chapter Thirty-Four

Give my other note to Frau Leitz and tell her I sent you.
She will take care of you.

Your Friend,

Gerhard

Margot looked up from the last line of the note, staring up at the house. She had driven two days and nights stopping only to refuel, barely able to keep her eyes open anymore. She'd used the last can of petrol Gerhard had left in the back of the truck last night and prayed the rest of the way they wouldn't break down. But she'd been determined to follow the path Gerhard had drawn on the map he'd given to Ludwig. Now they stood beside each other in front of the little house, lamplight shining dimly on the other side of the closed curtains in the windows.

They'd left the truck near the edge of the woods, coming the rest of the way on foot to the house overlooking a small village. To the right, chickens clucked in their coop, and to the left she heard the soft moaning of a cow in the barn. Margot took a deep breath before marching up the stone path, Ludwig lumbering along behind her.

She knocked twice, the rap of her knuckles on the wood door piercing her ears. Margot held her breath while they waited, listening to the soft padding of feet on the other side of the door. The gentle murmur of voices and then the turn of a lock right before the door opened.

A woman stood there, her silver hair twisted in a bun at the nap of her neck and a lavender silk robe tied tight around her thick waist. Her head tilted when she saw them, soft wrinkles defining her cheeks and eyes.

"*Ja*? Can I help you?" she asked, her voice warm and smooth.

"Frau Leitz?" Margot replied.

"*Ja*, I am."

Margot reached into her pocket, removing the second note Gerhard had given her. The woman took it hesitantly, her fingertips pinching the edges of the paper as if afraid to touch it.

"Gerhard Engel sent me," Margot announced. The woman's brow rose. "He said we would be safe here with you."

Frau Leitz opened the note, the paper crinkling in her hands as she quickly skimmed the contents before folding it again. She gestured them inside hurriedly.

"Come, come," she said.

Margot crossed the threshold, glancing back to find Ludwig close on her heels as they stepped into the front hall. Frau Leitz turned out the lamp before Margot could get a good look around, her calloused hand cupping Margot's elbow to guide her toward the stairs.

"Gerhard told you the truth," Frau Leitz murmured as they started up the narrow staircase. "You will be safe in my home. I live here with my granddaughter, but you needn't worry about her. She will say nothing of your arrival and will know only you are guests. I have known Gerhard since he was a child—his *mutter* was a friend of mine."

"*Danke*," Margot whispered.

They reached the top of the stairs, walking down the hallway to a door at the end. It opened to another set of stairs, Frau Leitz hastily lighting a candle on the little table beside the door to light their way up. Margot hesitated a moment, staring up at the small space leading into what she assumed would be an attic. Feeling more and more like she was entering a prison instead of a place of safety.

What choice do I have? Margot reminded herself to breathe before following the woman through the doorway.

"We will discuss the reason you are here in the morning in case you should be seen by one of my neighbors. Eventually, perhaps, you will be able to visit the village with me."

"I do not think we will be here that long," Margot replied, cautiously.

Frau Leitz eyed her over her shoulder. "Traveling is ill-advised. Word reached us only yesterday the Allies are pushing through the Nazi lines. The people are becoming frightened—restless. Especially those soldiers still here in Germany. This is the safest place for you to be if you are in trouble. We are a small, unimportant village. The Nazis do not bother with us very often."

They came to the top of the stairs, opening to a practically empty, square room with shuttered windows. The bareness made the attic seem larger than it was, two cots set up on either side of the room, made up with sheets, blankets, and pillows. Nothing else occupied the room, only the beds.

Frau Leitz placed the candle on the floor between the cots before turning to them, a tense smile curving her mouth. "Get some sleep now. We will talk again in the morning."

She swept passed them before either of them could reply, closing the door behind her. Margot waited a few heartbeats, her own tension beginning to ease when she didn't hear a lock *click* in the door after the woman. Ignoring Ludwig, she went to the cot on the right side of the room, sitting herself on the edge of the thin mattress to kick off her boots and unbutton her coat.

Ludwig seated himself cautiously on the other cot, his eyes boring into her. Margot tried to ignore him as she removed her coat and reached beneath her skirt, not caring if he was watching as she removed her stockings. When she started to pull down the covers, he finally spoke.

"Do you think you could ever forgive me?" he wondered.

Margot froze, her hand clasped around a handful of the blanket.

"I didn't mean to deceive you, Margot," he continued. "I only wanted to see my family one more time. Once I leave Germany with you ... I know I will never return, no matter the outcome of the war. Who I was for the SS ... what I did for them ... I can never go home and be Ludwig Volk again."

"I can understand why you did it, Ludwig," she answered. "But to put me at risk! To risk everything *mein bruder* wanted for me ..." Margot yanked the bandanna from her head, tossing it on top of her coat on the end of the cot.

"I know you're angry." Ludwig leaned forward, interlocking his fingers and resting his elbows on his knees. "At least tell me there's a chance you might be able to forgive me one day."

Margot sighed. She crawled beneath the blanket, tucking herself warmly within the sheets as she curled near the edge of the mattress.

"Of course, I will forgive you one day," she said groggily.

The moment her head touched the small pillow, she began to drift. The exhaustion of the past two days catching up with her in moments. Ludwig snuffed out the candle, plunging them into total darkness.

"Perhaps it will take a while, but ... but I could never ... stay ... mad ... forever ..." She slipped away before he could respond, falling deeply into restful oblivion.

When the sun began to peek through the cracks in the shutters on the windows, Margot stirred. Opening her eyes, she found the cot across from her had not been slept in, nothing but one of Gerhard's notes resting on the middle of the cot. Margot threw back the blanket, sliding her bare feet to the rough wood floor. She reached across the small space, grabbing the note and spotting a few new lines scrawled on the blank side of Gerhard's note.

> I tried, Margot, but I cannot do it. I must see my family. You trusted Gerhard, and he said you would be safe here. If I survive, I will come back to see you safely out of Germany.
>
> I am sorry.
>
> Ludwig

Margot crumpled the paper in her fist and curled up on the cot again as the truth hit her, sending her head into a whirlwind.

I am truly alone now.

Chapter Thirty-Five

Dear Bernard,

Yesterday, our neighbor Mrs. Ramsey received a telegram. Her son was killed. I have been thinking about you ever since. The last time we saw each other, I said things I do regret. Then your mother became ill and I said nothing. I wish I could change the past, but I cannot. These past three years, I have kept stubbornly silent, I know. But I have thought of you every day since I heard you were being sent overseas. Every day I see your picture, especially since your mother passed, I have regretted how we parted ways.

I want you to know I did everything in my power to save your mother. But her cancer had spread rapidly and no matter what procedures I may have performed, they would have only caused her even more pain. She did not want to pursue further treatment if it meant she would be bedridden for what remained of her life. You know me, son. I fought with her for weeks about her decision. But in the end, it was *her* decision.

I am sorry I did not tell you sooner. I am sorry I did not contact you so you could come to say goodbye to her. I can do nothing now but say how sorry I am and pray to God you forgive me. Since you've been gone, it has hit me even harder that you are all I have left. When I realized yesterday how easily a telegram could arrive at my door, I knew I could wait no longer to contact you. Waiting for you to return to America would not do, because I realized you may never return.

I know how you feel about me. I understand what I have put you through. I do not expect you to forgive me. I only ask that you try. For both our sakes.

I love you, son.

Dad

★★★

"I really shouldn't be doing this."

Bernie raised his head, the soreness in his shoulder deepening to a steady pounding. He lay stretched out on the backseat of the jeep, his feet hanging off the side as they bounced down the road toward the front. They'd left the hospital behind nearly an hour ago, the young soldier he'd roped into helping him in his escape muttering his anxieties ever since.

Readjusting the sling cradling his left arm, Bernie laid flat again, staring up at the puffy white clouds whizzing by overhead. After receiving more stitches than he could count, plasma and morphine, he'd finally found his strength coming back. The doctors said the loss of blood had been the greatest concern when he was first brought in, but by some miracle no arteries had been nicked, and he'd been spared infection.

Despite the wounds still feeling raw, he couldn't lie there anymore watching others with far worse injuries roll in. He also wasn't going to risk being assigned elsewhere when he heard his division was going to be moving out soon, possibly leaving him behind.

Digging in his pocket, his finger brushed the letter he'd received from his father in the hospital, along with the sharper edge of Margot's photograph. Bypassing the letter, he took out her picture, eyes tightening when he saw the smear of his blood now marring her image. Lying in the snow that night, he'd been sure he was going to die. So sure he'd never get back to Germany to find her.

Now I have a second chance. Can't pass it up. Bernie's chest swelled and he put her photograph back inside his jacket.

The jeep came to a halt. Bernie grunted when he pulled himself up, his driver leaping down out of the jeep and reaching back for the sack he'd come to deliver. Bernie followed him, the fresh layer of snow smashing beneath his boots when he landed. The sharp wind chilled his face, filling his senses with leftover smoke and freshly torn tree bark from a recent shelling.

He strode away from the jeep, ready to start his search for some familiar faces.

"Look who's come back from the dead."

Bernie grinned, turning back to watch Ellis jog forward. Graham was close behind, shaking his head slowly at the sight of him. He clasped hands with Ellis, grasping his stiffly cold fingers hard.

"Good to see you, Sarge."

"You sure you're okay to be here?" Graham wondered, nodding subtly to the sling.

Bernie shrugged his good shoulder. "Doesn't really hurt that much."

"How's the leg?" Ellis asked as they started walking back toward the line.

"Don't even feel it." Bernie patted his thigh. "Docs said my shoulder got the worst of it. The rest were quick fixes."

"Russell!" Woodley's stern voice boomed among the trees.

Bernie looked over his shoulder, watching the captain march across the space toward him. He gestured for the guys to move on without him, turning back on his heels to walk calmly over to his commanding officer.

"You go AWOL from the hospital, soldier?" Woodley asked, coming to a halt a few feet in front of him.

Bernie nodded. "Yes, sir. I did."

A smirk lifted the corner of Woodley's mouth, his gaze settling on the sling holding Bernie's arm.

"Am I going to have to order you back?"

"I truly hope not, sir."

"What good is a one-armed sniper to me?"

Bernie hesitated, then started to raise his left arm. He kept his face placid even as his shoulder began to burn. In one slow motion he raised the sling from around his neck, removing it completely before lowering his arm to his side.

"I'd like to get back to work, Cap. I'm fine, I swear."

Woodley eyed him a few seconds longer before nodding. "Okay, private. I'll take care of it."

"Thank you, sir."

"By the way." Woodley paused, reaching inside his coat. "We didn't think you were gonna make it when Jensen and Ellis brought you in. Agnelli gave me these."

He held out Margot's diary, thicker now with the photographs and letters stuffed inside. Bernie snatched them instinctively, his hand trembling with the desire to tuck them away out of sight.

"Did you read the letters?" he asked, quietly.

Woodley tilted his head. "You know, if I did, I'm having trouble remembering exactly what they said."

Bernie's throat tightened, a small smile playing across his lips.

"Oh, but I did pass on some of the photographs to my higher ups. That, at least, is out of our hands now."

"I understand. Thank you, sir." Bernie started to walk away, relief settling the heaviness in his chest as he put the diary out of sight. Then Woodley cleared his throat, drawing Bernie's gaze back over his shoulder.

"Oh, and Russell?"

"Yeah, Cap?"

"Welcome back."

Bernie grinned, nodding mutely in response. He moved deeper into the woods, passing a few foxholes as he went. Some of the men murmured greetings as he went by, Bernie acknowledging a few familiar faces before he moved on.

Then one soldier crawled out of the foxhole nearest the tree line, recognition in his movements alone causing Bernie to stop. His back was to him, helmet securely on his head and shoulders rolling in a stretch as he stood near the edge of the trench. Then he turned around, coming stiffly to a halt when he spotted Bernie.

Bruno didn't move, dark circles beneath his eyes and a fresh growth of stubble darkening his face. Bernie looked him over carefully, saw no evidence he'd ever been wounded. The doctors said once they'd gotten the swelling down and the bullet out from beneath his skin, Bruno's recovery had been quick. A few days off his feet and he was ready to go back, returned to the frontlines long before Bernie was ready.

"Hey," Bruno said, breaking the silence.

"Hey," Bernie replied.

His friend moved toward him slowly, as if afraid to come too close. Bruno stopped a foot in front of him, glancing down at the sling still clutched in Bernie's fist. The flat of his palm landed heavily on Bernie's right shoulder, giving him a few reassuring slaps.

"Good to have you back," Bruno said hoarsely.

Bernie grinned. "Good to be back."

Bruno gave him a light slap on the side of his helmet before pulling him forward, both jumping down into the foxhole together. Bernie leaned back against the solid soil, tilting his head far back to gaze at the ceiling of tree branches sheltering them. He watched his breath cloud on the cool air, the clearness in the sky settling an odd sense of peace washing over him.

"Yah know, Bru," he murmured, crossing his arms as he settled back and closed his eyes. "I think we might actually make it to the end of this thing."

Chapter Thirty-Six

GERMAN COUNTRYSIDE
LATE-FEBRUARY, 1945

"What do you think of this, *Fräulein*?"

Margot twisted away from the sink, elbow deep in soapsuds. She smiled at the little girl sitting in the center of the kitchen, a pencil in one hand and a large sheet of paper flat on the surface of the table in front of her. Shaking the soap and water off her hands, Margot snatched a towel from the counter and took two steps over to the table. She smiled, staring down at the attempted portrait of Frau Leitz, her eye catching every imperfection from the lopsided eyes to the circular mouth.

"Very *gut*, Gisela," she said, bending over to lightly blow on the pencil dust left on the page. She stroked the soft hair of her hostess's granddaughter. "It is a shame you do not have color pencils or paint."

"I think it looks very much like *meine großmutter*." Gisela nodded sharply in approval.

"As do I." Margot bent over, lightly kissing the girl's forehead before returning to the dishes.

After the first week, Frau Leitz had allowed her to begin some light housework. By week three, she was cleaning, cooking, and helping with the farm animals. Then, for the first time since Ludwig left her here, she walked down to the village with Frau Leitz and Gisela. No one stared or whispered—the people barely even seemed to notice her as she helped do the shopping and strolled the sidewalks holding Gisela's hand. For the first time in a long time, Margot had felt normal again.

"Margot, *meine liebste*," Frau Leitz said on a sigh as she entered the kitchen, sorting through some envelopes. "Do you think you could go down to the village for me today? There are a few things I need and these old bones of mine are aching horribly today."

Margot's eyes rounded. "By myself?"

"Certainly." Frau Leitz smiled gently, defining the wrinkles around her eyes. "The people know you as my *nichte* and if someone hasn't recognized you as Margot Raskopf by now, I doubt anyone ever will. You will be fine."

A pit briefly dropped in her stomach, her instinct to be afraid of walking the streets of the village alone nearly overwhelming her before she let it go. Frau Leitz walked out of the kitchen, her focus returned to her letters.

"I will give you a list!" she called over her shoulder before disappearing down the hall.

Margot stood still for a moment, clutching the towel tight in both fists. The scratch of Gisela's pencil on the paper tingled her spine. She returned to the sink to finish up the dishes from their afternoon meal, focusing on work instead of on the short walk she would take all by herself later.

"Why are you afraid to go down to the village alone, *Fräulein*?" ten-year-old Gisela asked. "*Großmutter* did not tell me why you came to stay."

Margot didn't answer, uncertain what to say to the child. She finished the dishes and dried her hands before adjusting the bandanna on her head. Her hair had grown another inch, thickening atop her head and surprisingly soft when she ran her hand over it. Not long enough for her to be comfortable without the bandanna, but with every new inch it grew, she began to feel more like herself.

A knock on the front door, followed by the low murmur of voices set her heart to racing. Frau Leitz did not often receive visitors, and even after nearly a month with her and Gisela, Margot was still frightened when a stranger came to the door. She tiptoed quietly toward the door of the kitchen, biting her bottom lip worriedly.

"Gisela," she said. "Why don't you go play in the garden now?"

The little girl sighed, but bounced off her seat anyway, skipping out the back door of the kitchen at the same moment her *großmutter* reappeared in the kitchen. Frau Leitz's brow was raised, surprise alight in her eyes. Then she whispered,

"Ludwig is back."

Margot didn't blink. The last thing she'd ever expected Frau Leitz to say had just slipped passed her lips. The last man she'd expected to walk back through that front door had apparently done just that.

He came back. Inhaling deeply, she steadied her nerves and walked toward the older woman.

"Where is he?" she asked.

"I left him by the stairs," Frau Leitz answered. She reached out, softly massaging Margot's arm. "You do not have to speak to him if you do not want to, *meine liebste*. I will send him away if you want me to."

"*Nein.*" Margot shook her head. "*Nein*, I will speak with him."

Frau Leitz narrowed her eyes, searching Margot's face briefly before she released a heavy breath. "All right. I will be right here if you need me."

"*Danke.*" Margot kissed her cheek before stepping around her quickly.

The Good German Girl

She forced one foot in front of the other down the hall, stopping when she reached the banister. Ludwig was sitting on the bottom step, his head bent deeply forward and his elbows on his knees. He didn't look up when she came in front of him, turning to settle herself silently on the step beside him. She tugged her skirt down over her knees before interlocking her fingers around them, staring at him.

His hair was longer, curling at the nape of his neck and he wore an old brown coat with holes in the elbows and matching trousers. His boots were scuffed and muddy, but they looked sturdy enough for the journey he'd taken.

"Did you see your family?" she asked softly.

Ludwig's eyes fluttered open as he nodded, keeping his head bowed. Margot's fingers trembled when she reached back, placing her hand lightly on the nape of his neck. He turned his head, the glisten of tears in his eyes when he looked into hers.

"I ... I am ..."

"I know." Margot gently squeezed the back of his neck. "I know you are sorry. I am not angry at you anymore, Ludwig."

"I did not want to leave you." He looked away, rubbing the moisture from his eyes. "I know I should not have left you, but ..."

"Hush." Margot slid a little closer to his side. "You do not need to explain, Ludwig. If my family was out there, I would try to see them too. You have come back now, and that is what I'd like to talk about. Why?"

He let his hand drop from his face, looking at her from the corner of his eye. Margot tilted her head.

"Why did you risk coming all the way back here?" she wondered.

Ludwig took her hand off his neck, twining their fingers together in a firm grip. He traced her knuckles with his fingertips, sending tickles up her arm.

"I always liked you, Margot," he said, voice rough. "Even when we were children you were unlike anyone I'd ever known. Deep down, I knew you never really saw me but I always hoped …"

Ludwig paused, taking another breath. "Now you are all I have, and I think I am all you have too."

Margot curled her fingers over his knuckles, her heart squeezing in her chest.

"I thought if you could forgive me then perhaps … one day …" His thick brow rose when he looked up at her, the unspoken words hanging between them.

She covered his knuckles with her other hand, sandwiching his between her palms. Her throat ached with the breath she took, what she knew she had to say hurting more than she would have first expected.

"I am so grateful to you, Ludwig, for all you have done." Margot hesitated, pressing his hand tighter until her knuckles whitened. "If you choose to take me the rest of the way out of Germany now, I would be so thankful for the rest of my life. I can forgive you for all the mistakes you have made, for all the danger you have put me in … but to tell you we might be anything more than friends one day would be a lie."

Ludwig closed his eyes, beginning to draw his hand away. At the feel of his resistance, she held on tighter, not allowing him to pull away from her.

"Perhaps, one day, you will meet someone who never has to know who you were during this horrible time. Who never has to know what you were made to do in service of the *Führer*. But I cannot look at you without seeing the gates of Auschwitz." Margot sniffled, blinking her tears away quickly. "You are right that we are all we have now. Please do not run away from me again."

Ludwig nodded, no longer trying to resist the hold she had on his hand.

"May I ask you something?"

"Of course." Margot dipped her head.

"Does that man have anything to do with your decision?" He looked into her eyes again, his so sad her heart burned. "The one whose name you say in your sleep. Bernie?"

Margot's breath caught at the sound of his name, a fresh rush of tears flooding her eyes.

"*Ja*, some." She placed her temple on his shoulder, closing her eyes and releasing a tear down her cheek. "I've never known anyone like him, yet we've never even met in person. But his courage and the hope he inspired in me was unlike anything I've ever felt and I cannot forget him."

Ludwig pulled his hand out of hers to wrap his arm around her shoulders. His cheek pressed down on the top of her head while they sat in silence. Margot placed her palm over the center of his chest, feeling the throb of his heart against her wrist.

"Will you stay this time?" she asked. "Will you get me out of Germany?"

Ludwig's mouth brushed her temple. "I promised your *bruder*, didn't I?"

Margot smiled, lifting her head from his shoulder.

"I will drive you down to the village today. We will purchase some provisions and leave tomorrow morning."

"*Danke*, Ludwig." Margot put her arms around his neck, hugging him tight. "*Danke*."

***

Driving with Ludwig again felt strange. The truck rolled unevenly along the rough dirt road, taking them down the hill from Frau Leitz's house to the village below. Telling the woman who'd been taking care of her for weeks that she would be leaving the next morning was the hardest thing she'd ever done. It felt like poor thanks to simply invade a person's home and then abruptly leave with so little warning. But Frau Leitz had drawn her into a warm, soft hug, kissed her cheek and made her promise to write as soon as they reached a place of safety.

The truck began to slow as they reached the edge of the village, Ludwig frowning as he leaned forward over the steering wheel.

"Uniforms," he said.

The truck came to a jerking halt and Margot gasped, her hand thrusting forward to grip the dashboard, keeping herself steady. They sat quietly, staring at the two soldiers walking down the street among the villagers. Up ahead, she could see a line of trucks moving through the town along with a whole division of men.

"I do not understand," Margot whispered. "I have been here nearly a month and have not seen one Nazi."

She squinted, looking harder. Then her brow winged.

"Ludwig!" She pulled on his sleeve. "Americans! They are Americans! They made it!"

Before he could respond, she jumped out of the truck, running the rest of the way down the road into the village.

"Excuse me!" she called, the English words stuttering across her tongue. "Excuse me, sir!"

One of the soldiers turned, his dark eyes widening in surprise as she approached. His face was shadowed in dark stubble, of average height with slightly curled black hair poking out from his helmet over his ears. Margot came to a skidding halt, gasping for breath. She pressed a hand to her stomach, taking a moment to compose herself.

"Are you all right miss?" the soldier asked.

"*Ja*." Margot swallowed hard. "When ... when did you get here?"

His eyes grew bigger, probably shocked to hear her speaking English. Then he cleared his throat, shifting his rifle from one shoulder to the other.

"Last night," he replied. "We'll be moving on in a couple hours."

"Have many of you crossed into occupied territory?" she asked. "Have ... have any of your armies reached Poland yet?"

"I'm sorry, miss, I'm not sure. I don't think so." He hesitantly brushed his hand on her arm. "Are you sure you're all right?"

"I ... I was just wondering ..." Margot stopped, the words halting on her tongue.

"What, miss?" he encouraged gently.

"I was wondering ... have any of your men found the extermination camps yet?"

Chapter Thirty-Seven

Bernie let his legs dangle off the end of the truck. In the month since he'd run away from the hospital they'd managed to press through, getting themselves out of the Ardennes and back into Germany. Now they were making slow progress across the German countryside, and according to Woodley, their next stop would be Czechoslovakia. Breathing in the cool February air, he watched the little village go by—the German citizens observing them warily as they passed through.

He pulled out the letter from his father, reading through it for the second time that day. He hadn't responded—the words simply refusing to come whenever he tried to put pencil to paper. The truck came to a stop in the middle of the village, pulling off to the side to let another go by in the opposite direction. Bernie looked up briefly, his eye catching a couple inside the truck as they rolled by.

"Reading that letter again?" Jensen nudged him with his elbow. "He's your father. Is it really that hard to answer?"

Bernie shrugged. "Complicated."

Bruno suddenly appeared at the corner of the truck, shaking his head as he watched the other one make slow progress down the street.

"Everything okay, Bru?" Bernie wondered, folding the letter back into his pocket.

"Yeah, just some crazy girl." Bruno leaped onto the truck, Jensen scrambling out of his way.

"What happened?"

Ellis climbed up next. "Some German girl who spoke English wanted to know if any of our guys found extermination camps."

Bernie froze. "What?"

"Yeah," Bruno snorted. "Asked me and Ellis if any of our forces reached Poland yet and found these prison camps. Said the Nazis are murdering thousands of people in them."

"Where is she?" Bernie asked, jumping down from the truck. "Where'd she go?"

The boys shared glances before looking down at him as if he were crazy too. Bernie's blood thundered in his veins, their words repeating in his ears like a heartbeat. What were the odds? A German girl who spoke English asking their men about extermination camps?

Not a coincidence. Can't be. Bernie's breath came faster.

"Some guy hurried her into a truck." Bruno pointed behind Bernie at the vehicle that passed by moments ago. "They just took off into the village after that."

Bernie spun, ignoring Ellis when he shouted his name. He pushed through the people walking down the sidewalks, trying to catch a glimpse of the truck again. Then, his voice rose above the hustle and bustle of the village.

"Margot!"

***

"What were you thinking, Margot?" Ludwig yelled, glaring at her.

Margot rested her elbow on the edge of the truck window, leaning her forehead into her palm. The soldiers hadn't had a chance to answer her before Ludwig had appeared at her side, taking her by the arm and quickly apologizing to them before pushing her back into the truck. The men had looked so confused by her question, snuffing her hope they'd found the camps like one would a candle.

"I had to ask, Ludwig."

"Why would you draw such attention to yourself? We are not out of Germany yet!"

"But the Americans are here! We are safe."

Ludwig slowed the truck, the engine puttering softly as they continued their journey of stop and go down the street.

"Nowhere is safe."

She closed her eyes turning toward the window. He honked the horn, turning the wheel this way and that as he avoided the mix of civilians and soldiers crossing the street.

"Margot!" a distant call reached her ears. "Margot Raskopf!"

The voice was distinctly American, deep and rough as he shouted her name through the village. Her heart bolted like lightning in her chest.

"Ludwig stop the truck!"

"What?"

"Stop the truck! *Schnell*!" Margot grabbed the door handle, shoving it open as he came to a complete stop.

She rose, placing her arm over the roof of the car for support to look over the heads of the people on the street behind them. An American soldier was making his way through the crowd, a few blocks back from where they'd been.

"Margot!" he shouted.

Her heart flipped. Jumping from the truck, she pushed her way around the people filling the sidewalks.

"Bernie!" she yelled back. "Bernie Russell!"

Sweat trickled down her neck, cooled instantly by the breeze that rustled the bandanna on her head. She pushed another person aside, stumbling to a halt on the sidewalk.

He stood a mere three feet away from her, dark hair mussed from his helmet and eyes as brown as chocolates. At least a foot taller than she, broad, muscular shoulders, and big, rough-looking hands hanging at his sides. There was a layer of stubble on his face, giving him an unkempt look, and his full mouth was parted, breaths puffing rapidly through his lips. He was shorter and thinner than she thought he'd be. Absolutely nothing like she'd pictured him. But she didn't care.

"B-Bernie Russell?" she whispered hoarsely, eyes flooding.

He nodded slowly, his own eyes red.

Margot flung her arms around his neck as she burst into tears. His big hands moved over the curves of her waist, traveling all the way around until she was completely wrapped in his arms.

How many times she'd thought of him! How many times she'd fantasized about being in Bernie Russell's embrace. This moment encompassed everything she'd wanted from the moment she read his first letter.

Only, this was not her fantasy.

This ... was better.

Chapter Thirty-Eight

Lord, please don't let this be a dream. Bernie buried his face in the soft curve of her neck, pressing gentle kisses to her skin. Her little body shuddered against him, tiny gasps jolting her chest as she cried. He raised his head, cheek rubbing the bandanna around hers before his lips brushed her ear.

"Shh," he soothed. "I've got you. I told you we were coming, didn't I?"

Margot sobbed harder, his words provoking more tears instead of easing them. Her arms loosened around his neck, hands sliding to the surface of his shoulders as she lowered herself onto her heels. She sniffled, her little nose red and cheeks flushed bright, gleaming with her tears. Bernie stroked his thumbs across the delicate curves of her eyebrows, down her nose and over her lips. The face he'd memorized for over six months was now staring up at him and he could barely breathe.

She was thinner than her picture, cheekbones sharper in her face and he was certain he felt every ridge of her ribcage when she pressed herself against him. But there was no doubt it was her. Those big, beautiful eyes—not quite brown, not quite blue—stared up at him the same way they did in the photograph. The same full, soft lips smiled at him now and light hair peeked from beneath the edge of the bandanna, surprisingly short.

"Wait here," she said, each word passing her lips slowly as if she had to think about them before she spoke.

He nodded, the cold air hitting him hard when she pulled the warmth of her body away. Bernie stayed right where he was, watching her run back over to the truck to say something to the driver quickly. Then she turned back, returning to his side. Margot grabbed his hands, squeezing his fingers.

"There is so much I want to say to you," she murmured. "So much I want to tell."

"I only have a couple of hours," Bernie said hoarsely.

Her face fell, the realization he couldn't stay with her striking her as if he'd slapped her in the face. Then she turned, keeping their hands tightly linked.

"Come with me."

He followed without question as she led him down the street, around the people milling about. Ignoring the curious stares of some of the other soldiers passing by, she brought him away from the shops toward some of the homes. Bernie's curiosity grew when she led him between two houses, opening a white picket fence at the end.

They walked into a simple little garden, the bushes bare as winter was only just beginning to recede. Margot smiled, facing him as she backed into the little space.

"The woman who lives here is a friend of the people I'm staying with," she announced. "This is the time she does her shopping, and I don't think she'd mind if we sit here for a little while."

She brushed some leftover snow off the bench in the middle of the garden before seating herself, drawing him down beside her. Bernie settled, sliding his hand inside his coat.

"I received your diary," he said, pulling the book out. "I couldn't read most of it, but I thought you might want it back."

Margot stared at the diary, her fingers trembling when she reached to take it away. She pressed it to her heart, closing her eyes.

"*Danke*," she murmured. Then she blinked quickly. "Oh, I mean, thank you."

Bernie chuckled. "Yes, I know."

She shifted awkwardly on the seat beside him, massaging the diary between her palms as they both searched for something to say. Then Bernie leaned forward.

"I do have a question I've been wanting to ask you."

"Yes?" Margot tilted her head curiously.

"How do you understand English?"

Her mouth stretched in a wide grin, showing rows of clean, white teeth. "My Papa taught me. When I was twelve, Papa decided we would take a trip, first to England then to America. He was determined his children would be able to understand and communicate with the citizens of those countries."

"Did you make it there?" he asked.

Margot shook her head. "No, it was not to be."

Bernie played with the corner of the bandanna on her head, brow furrowing.

"What happened to your hair?"

The moment the question slipped out he regretted it. Her eyes darkened, overflowing with fresh tears and her lower lip trembled. Bernie slid closer to her on the bench and she sniffled. Then, she started to speak and every word chilled Bernie to the core.

★★★

From the moment she burned his letters to the moment she saw him on the street of the village, Margot's story poured from her lips. She held nothing back, telling him about Ilse and Franz, Hanna and Horst, Ludwig and Gerhard. Reliving every moment of horror from her arrest in Berlin to her alighting from the train in Auschwitz and everything that came after.

Bernie listened in comforting silence, wiping her tears away with his fingers and stroking her arms when she began to tremble. When she finally finished, the silence was deafening. They sat together simply staring at each other, her story now standing between them like a wall.

Then, he reached for her bandanna. Margot sat completely still as he pulled the cloth from her head, dragging it down the back of her neck and over her shoulder. He raised his other hand, sliding his palm over her cheek until his fingers sank into her short hair. Margot turned her head deeply against his hand, resting her fingers on his wrist and pressing her lips into his palm.

"If I could take it all away," he rasped, drawing her gaze back to his. "I would. I would wipe your life of those horrors so you could start again."

"And if you did," she replied, breathless. "Then I would not be sitting here now. With you."

His large hand curled against the back of her neck, pulling her until his lips pressed hard on the center of her forehead. Margot fell forward, resting her cheek on his shoulder as he stroked her hair soothingly.

"I have something else to show you," he said.

She lifted her head, watching him hesitate for a moment before reaching inside his coat again. A light gasp slipped between her lips when she saw the worn photograph, her eye catching her handwriting on the back. Bernie placed it in her hand, releasing her picture reluctantly. There was a stripe of red across her image, making her heart beat faster.

"I have carried it with me since the day we landed on Omaha beach," he murmured. "Until we reached the Ardennes, I kept it unmarked."

"Were you wounded?" she asked, unable to take her gaze off the picture.

"Yes, but I'm fine now."

Margot's head lightened, staring at the photograph she'd handed to her twin the last day she'd ever seen him. Seeing Hans's face flash across her eyes—his warm, loving smile and bright blue eyes and messy blond hair all came together in her mind to create her twin brother as if he stood beside her now.

"I want you to know," Bernie said, distracting her from the memory of her brother. "His last words were for you. He said …" Bernie paused, eyes narrowing in thought before he struggled to get the words out. "*Meine schwester.* A friend of mine told me that means *my sister.*"

Margot nodded, rolling her lips to hold back tears.

"You should know too, that I looked at your picture every day. Every hour. Every time I had a chance, I pulled out your picture and looked at you. You kept me going."

Margot raised his hand to her lips, kissing his knuckles firmly. Then she smiled at him, returning her photograph into his possession.

"Then you must keep it," she whispered. "Keep it and keep going until this war ends."

"Thank you."

His eyes locked on hers, holding her still. Then his gaze lowered to her lips and her breath whooshed out of her. Anticipation rose like a flame in her chest when he started to lean forward, the warmth of his breath skimming her cheek when he hesitated. The way he leaned slightly back, as if waiting for her consent. Then, the moment she started to bend toward him, a shout rent the air.

"Bernie! Hey, Berns!"

Bernie groaned and Margot giggled, wiping the remaining tears from her cheeks. He took her hand, helping her back onto her feet. They strolled leisurely out of the garden, both reluctant to leave. He held the gate for her, allowing her to step ahead of him toward the street.

Margot's hand slipped back into Bernie's, twining their fingers together tightly as she walked him back to the street where they first met. His fellow soldiers were moving out, marching down the street toward the edge of the village. Her eyes burned as she thought of him moving on toward Czechoslovakia while she traveled for Austria. Going in opposite directions after finally meeting was unbearable.

She closed her eyes when they stopped on the sidewalk. Margot felt him turn to face her and she fell forward, placing her forehead on the center of his chest. He stroked her head, replacing the bandanna over her short hair.

"Are you going to be all right?" he asked, his warm breath tickling her ear.

Margot nodded softly. She looked up at him, forcing a smile.

"Will you be?" she wondered.

"Of course, I will," he replied, smoothing his hands up and down her arms. "I found you once. I'm determined to find you again."

Margot brushed a tear from the corner of her eye before it had a chance to fall.

"Do you mean that? When this is over, will you come looking for me?"

Bernie brushed his fingertips down her cheek. "Nothing could stop me."

Margot clasped his hand between both of hers, squeezing tight. Then, he sighed, backing away from her.

"Write to me," she said.

"You bet I will."

"Once I am settled, I will send a message through the Red Cross so you will know where to reach me."

He nodded, then murmured, "*Auf wiedersehen.*"

Margot rolled her lips, swallowing her laugh over his terrible accent. She clutched his fingers tighter.

"Goodbye," she answered.

Bernie continued to back away until his hand slipped out of hers and he turned, striding into the street. Margot watched him walking away, her heart racing faster and faster the further he went. Her blood rushing—whole body beginning to shake.

"Bernie!" she called.

He twisted back around, brow raised in question as she leaped into the street, running to him. As he opened his mouth, probably to ask her what was wrong, she threw her arms around his neck. Margot raised herself on her tiptoes and softly pressed her mouth to his. She felt his surprise in the way he stiffened, his lips hard for a moment against hers before they softened, melting into the kiss.

Bernie wrapped his arms around her waist, pressing her deeply against his body as he kissed her back, tilting his lips on hers. She sighed, savoring the feel of his mouth, the taste of his kiss. Memorizing how his hair felt between her fingers and the gentle way he held her.

Then she broke away, her nose bumping his as she caught her breath.

"Stay alive," she whimpered, no longer trying to stop her tears. "Come back to me. I cannot lose you too."

"You won't," he said, his lips grazing hers. "I promise, Margot. As soon as this war is over, I'll find you."

Margot whimpered, clinging to him as hard as she could even as he pulled away. Then he spun, striding away faster than before as if afraid he would stay if he didn't.

She watched him go, a new, trembling smile beginning to spread across her face again.

Because even as he disappeared around the corner, she could feel him. His strength, his affection. The warmth of his lips, the comfort of his arms. He was all around her, surrounding her with the same hope he'd given her in his letters. Margot rushed forward, racing around the corner in time to see him jump up onto the end of one of the trucks.

He turned, as if sensing her eyes on him. Bernie raised his hand to her, a huge grin brightening his handsome face. Margot waved back vigorously, bouncing on her toes. She waved until the truck left the village—stood there until he was nothing but a speck on the horizon. Because even as he vanished in the distance, she knew in her heart this wasn't goodbye.

She would see Bernie Russell again.

And when she did, their forever would begin.

Chapter Thirty-Nine

FOUR MONTHS LATER
VIENNA, AUSTRIA

> Last week, we came across a camp. Some of our men
> had already arrived and opened the gates, providing the
> survivors with proper clothing, water, and food. I have
> never seen anything like it and never want to see anything
> like it ever again. Knowing you were in a place as bad,
> or worse, sickens me.

Margot looked up from the letter she'd received from
Bernie last month. Once she and Ludwig had made it out of
Germany, they could see where the war was headed. They'd
stopped in Austria, choosing to take the chance the Allies
would break through. When Vienna was liberated a few
weeks later, she'd known they made the right decision.

Making contact with the American Red Cross had been
more difficult than she anticipated, but eventually she was
able to get a message out to Bernie. Three weeks later, she'd
received his reply. Their correspondence was slow, but she
took comfort in the knowledge that, for now, he was safe
from being shot at. With the unconditional surrender of Nazi
Germany, the war in Europe had finally come to an end.

Knowing Bernie had to wait to see if he would be sent
across another ocean to help the fighting in the Pacific come

to an end was torture for them both. But his letters kept coming, keeping her hope alive. Margot folded the paper neatly, tucking it into the small purse Frau Leitz had given her. The line was beginning to move again and she swayed along with the other people around her.

This was the fourth facility she'd been to and—if she truly intended to keep her promise to Ludwig—her last.

You only hurt yourself going to those places, Margot. Their names have not been on the lists so far, and every time you leave you're tortured all over again with memories. His words from the night before whispered in her ear.

So, she'd promised him faithfully this would be the last time. If they weren't on this list, then she would stop. She would not keep looking—she would not try to find them anymore. She would let them go, as she'd been forced to let her family go.

This particular facility was a hospital, converted into living spaces for those refugees liberated from the camps. People milled about all around, some sitting on the steps of the building, others watching the people in the line— hoping to spot a relative or friend before they even had a chance to reach the front of the line to make an inquiry. Three times before, Margot had stood on a line like this, and three times, she'd been sent away brokenhearted.

The line moved another foot, a light summer breeze tugging at the hem of her dress. The three decent dresses she possessed had been provided by Frau Leitz. Ludwig had managed to get work, providing them with some decent living quarters now they were on their own. She could feel the world settling around her, some normalcy returning to the order of her life. For the first time in a long time, she was once again in control of how she lived.

The person in front of her stepped away from the desk, leaving the space free. Margot approached, biting her lip nervously.

"Yes?" the woman wearing a Red Cross uniform said without looking up. "Do you have a name?"

"*Ja*," Margot croaked. She cleared her dry throat. "Hanna Krakowski?"

The woman flipped through her ledger, a tired sigh puffing through her thin lips. Margot forced herself to stand still, twining a strand of her hair around her finger. Her tresses had grown nearly to the tops of her shoulders, falling in soft waves past her ears and down the length of her neck.

"No, I'm sorry," the woman said bluntly, looking up at Margot for the first time. Her gray eyes seemed to stare straight through her, and Margot wondered how many people she'd been forced to turn away. "I do not have a Hanna Krakowski on my list."

Margot nodded, her heart dipping into her stomach. "C-Can you check o-one more for me?"

The woman's gaze softened slightly. "Certainly."

"Horst Stück."

The pages hissed again with every turn, the woman finally stopping on one and running her finger down the line. Then her brow rose, finger halting over halfway down the paper.

"Oh," she exclaimed. "Yes! Yes, I have a Horst Stück on this list."

The ground tilted beneath her feet. Margot nearly stumbled, placing her palm on the desk for support.

"You do?" she whispered, hoarsely.

"Yes!" The woman laughed, the blandness leaving her eyes and replaced with an excited sparkle. "I do. He's here."

"Is he all right? Is he …?"

Her voice faded when she caught a movement in the corner of her eye. She stepped to the side of the desk, staring at the steps leading up to the hospital doors. He was leaning heavily on a small cane, taking one trembling step at a time down the stone stairs. He hadn't seen her yet, focused instead on not falling as he depended entirely on the cane to keep him from toppling. Margot could barely breathe, her legs shaking when she approached the stairs, stopping a few feet away.

Horst finally looked up, his clouded gaze settling on her. Disbelief sparked in his eyes, followed quickly by a sheen of tears. Margot could stand no longer, buckling to the ground. Horst limped down the last three steps, the cane clicking loudly on the cobblestone courtyard as he crossed over to her. Margot's shoulders began to shake, short gasps slipping out as her tears fell freely.

He stopped in front of her, searching her eyes. They both opened their lips, but no sound came out. Both trying to speak but unable to. Then Margot bent forward, resting her forehead on his shoulder. Horst dropped the cane, wrapping his arms around her and cupping the back of her head in his palm.

Margot smiled, breathing in the crisp scent of his clean clothes, feeling the strength in his arms. He was still horribly thin—his limp was even worse than when they were in the camp, and his arms trembled with leftover weakness, even as his grip on her tightened. But his heart was beating stronger than ever.

He is alive. We are alive.

Horst's chest swelled with a deep inhale, his small hands moving across the back of her neck until he cupped her cheeks. Gently, he tilted her head back so she was forced to look at him. A soft smile touched his lips as he whispered,

"Oh, *mein schatz* ... look what God has done."

Tears leaked unchecked from her eyes, soaking the delicate skin of her cheeks. Margot burrowed against his slight chest, burying her face in the coarse material of the coat he'd been given. Hope swirled around them like a warm breeze, banishing the last of her fears. As she knelt there, clinging to a person from the past she thought she wanted to forget, Margot felt her new future beginning. A life without looking over her shoulder for the enemy. A life she could live without the pain of the past.

A future filled with the promise of peace.

Epilogue

A cardinal landed on her windowsill.

Margot smiled, pausing in her scrubbing of the morning dishes to watch the songbird. His brilliantly red pointed head tilted from side to side before he let out a sharp *chirp* and flapped his wings, soaring away. Nearly forty years living in this house, and the little visits of the songbirds at her open window still surprised her.

One year after the war came to an end, Bernie Russell asked her to marry him. Two months later, he carried her over the threshold of this beautiful two-story home sitting on twenty acres of ranchland. And one month after their first child was born, Bernie finally invited his father to come visit them. Their lives had woven back together with ease, the forgiveness Bernie found in his heart for a man who had hurt him so deeply making her love him all the more.

The first few years of their marriage, they both would wake in the middle of the night with their own nightmares. One night he would wake, and she would hold him until he found peace again. Another, she would wake and find comfort in his embrace. Even now, after thirty-nine years of marriage and four children together, the dreams still came to haunt them. But as time went on, they had faded—not nearly as frequent as in those first years.

As she stood in the solitude of her kitchen, rubbing the sponge in gentle circles around and around the dish in her hand, her thoughts turned to those last days she'd spent in Austria. The memory of saying goodbye to Ludwig when she'd finally received her papers allowing her to go to America. How tightly he'd held her in those last moments! She'd heard from him only once after that—one quick letter telling her he'd left Austria, found a home in Switzerland, and a brief mention of a young woman Margot prayed he'd built a future with.

After two years of hoping and praying, Bernie had finally been able to bring Horst over to live with them. She could still remember the moment he'd stepped across their threshold, his silvering hair shining in the sun and a gleam of contentment in his eyes. Bernie's friend, Bruno, had driven Horst out to the house upon his arrival in the country, using the trip as an excuse to stay a day or two himself so he could spoil their toddler son.

Not that either of us minded. Margot smiled, remembering.

The hiss of tires coming up their pebbled drive distracted her from her memories. She leaned over, her belly digging into the edge of the sink as she tried to catch a peek at the car. Her brow rose when she realized it was Bernie's sedan, coming to a stop a few feet away from the front porch.

Wiping her hands on her apron, she padded across the kitchen floor in her bare feet. She swung her braid from her shoulder, pausing by the mirror near the front door to check not too many hairs were loose. The silver streaking her golden locks seemed to catch in the dim lighting of the hall, the lines in her face seemed more defined every time she looked in the mirror. There'd been a time in her life when a single day felt like a lifetime. Then one day, thirty years had gone by and she was no longer twenty-four.

Margot stepped out onto the porch, a smile brightening her face.

"Stephen!" she exclaimed, skipping down the steps.

She held out her arms to her oldest son as he climbed out of the sedan, jogging to close the space between them. He wrapped her up in a tight hug.

"Hey, Mama," he said, kissing her cheek.

"Did you bring my grandbabies?" Margot stepped back, trying to peek in the backseat of the car.

"No, sweetheart," Bernie said, coming around the front of the car. "Not today."

She went to him for a quick kiss, wrapping her arm around his waist. Even with the gray at his temples and wrinkles around his eyes, he was still as handsome as the first day she'd seen him. Bernie stroked her back soothingly, the tension seeping out of him in waves. Margot's eyes darted between her husband and son, trepidation building in her chest.

"Is everything all right, *meine lieben*?"

Stephen cleared his throat, stuffing his hands in his jeans pockets. "Mama, I have something to tell you."

"Stephen is everything all right? Louisa and the children—?"

"Oh, no, Mama. They're fine. Everything is fine at home."

Margot breathed a sigh of relief, leaning more heavily into Bernie's side. "Then what is wrong?"

Stephen looked at his father, shaking his head slowly.

"I don't think I can do it, Pop."

Margot's brows drew together, pinching the bridge of her nose. She looked up at her husband, finding his eyes had softened with understanding, his hand tightening on her shoulder.

"That's okay, son." Bernie turned her around to face him, sliding his hands up and down her arms. "We have some news, Margot."

She tilted her head, a loose strand of her hair falling across her temple.

"You know Stephen has some friends in high places. For months now, we have been trying to find … a certain person." Bernie swallowed hard, his voice catching. Beads of sweat gathered on his forehead, his nerves unsettling her. "We wanted you to know, before the information was released to the press."

"Know what, Bernie?" Margot gripped his wrists tight, stroking her thumbs along the ridges of his knuckles.

"You still wake up from nightmares. I wanted you to have some closure, my love." Bernie swept his lips across her temple. Then he took a deep breath, speaking on his exhale. "Josef Mengele's body was found."

Margot gasped, clapping a hand over her mouth. Bernie moved her quickly to the porch, settling her down on the steps as her knees began to knock. Her heart was racing out of control as Bernie sat down beside her, putting a strong arm around her shoulders.

"They exhumed the body from a grave on the outskirts of São Paulo," Stephen said softly. "They are still conducting forensic testing, but my friend is positive. It's him, Mama. They finally found him."

"Dead," Margot whispered. "He's dead."

"Yes, honey." Bernie drew her nearer. "He's dead. You don't have to look over your shoulder anymore. He's not out there. He can't hurt you."

Margot collapsed on his chest and released a torrent of tears.

***

"I know I never asked you how you survived the camp. It never seemed important. What mattered was you did survive. You survived the camp, you survived *him*, and you somehow made it out to safety. Then when you passed away, I wished I had asked you. I wished I'd known what you did to escape the death *he* had in store for you."

Margot paused for breath, staring at the intricately carved name in the gravestone.

Horst Stück
January 5, 1898-December 3, 1975
Beloved Friend
For his strength, love, and courage
we are forever grateful

She dabbed the moisture from the corners of her eyes with her handkerchief. Tilting her head back, she shifted where she knelt on the moist ground. They had buried him beneath a beautiful oak tree on their land, overlooking the most peaceful hillside view she'd ever seen. He had loved the spot, and she knew he would've been pleased she laid him to rest here.

"I wish you had lived for the day we didn't have to look over our shoulders," she continued. "I wish you could know what it has been like, this one day alone, to live knowing he is not out there somewhere."

Looking over her shoulder, she saw her family. Her daughter, Hope, standing with her new baby in her arms and her husband by her side. After ten years of trying, they'd finally had the child they'd been praying for. Ecstatic and nervous, her gentle son-in-law hadn't left Hope's side since the baby was born.

Her three sons stood solemnly beside their father. Her youngest boy, Alec, with hands clasped behind his back. Middle son, Matthew, resting a hand on his father's shoulder, and Stephen off to the side, his arms crossed and head bowed. They each had a little bit of Bernie in them—even Hope. But most of all, especially in Stephen, she saw her brothers. Alec had Franz's stern brow, Matthew had Hans's nose, and Stephen ... well, Stephen had a little bit of both of them.

Then there was Bernie. Her strong, brave Bernie, who would do anything to see her sleep through one night in peace. The same Bernie who'd found a way to write a letter to a German girl in the middle of a war with Germany had now reached even higher to bring her peace in the gentlest of ways, instead of letting her find out in a newspaper or on the radio.

Turning back to the grave, Margot dried the remainder of her tears.

"I suppose," she said. "You did not need this sort of peace, though, did you? You made your own, as we all did these many years since the war. Now, you are truly at peace, aren't you?"

The soft whistle of the wind was her only answer. Margot raised her hand, softly kissing her fingertips before pressing them lightly to the cool stone.

"I miss you every day. I love you, *mein freund*."

Margot rose from the ground, her knees aching from having been kneeling so long. She started slowly back toward her family, Bernie holding her gaze all the way. When she reached him, he placed his hands on her waist, drawing her close.

"Are you all right?" he whispered.

Margot smiled. "*Ja*, I am fine."

She stroked his face, savoring the smooth feel of his freshly shaven cheeks beneath her fingertips. Breathing in his spicy aftershave and the clean, crisp scent of his clothes. No one had ever meant more to her than this wonderful man who'd saved her life and captured her heart in every way.

Wrapping her arms around his waist, she lifted herself on the tips of her toes to whisper against his lips.

"Let's go home."

THE END

AUTHOR'S NOTE

Dear Readers,

Thank you for reading *The Good German Girl*! I hope you loved Margot and Bernie's story as much as I loved writing it. While the events in this novel echoed with historical truth, this was not based on a true story and most of my characters themselves were fictional. During my research of Omaha Beach, Aachen, Auschwitz II - Birkenau, and the Battle of the Bulge, I came across so many stories I had never heard before. I uncovered horrific tales told by survivors of the camps and small historical facts surrounding the journey of American forces across Europe that may have been forgotten. For this reason, this novel is extremely precious to me.

Let me tell you, it takes an army to raise a book baby. When I first announced my intention to write a World War II story, I was told at several turns that getting Historical Fiction published was going to be extremely difficult. There are so many authors out there who write Historical Fiction and in order to get your work noticed, it has to be unique. You have to stand out from the crowd. You need to give it all you've got in order to make a publisher sit up and take notice. You need an army to fight for your story. Being a one-woman army won't do it.

I had nearly given up on *The Good German Girl* seeing the light of day and was three seconds away from indie publishing when bam! I got a contract. But the work wasn't done. The contract was only the beginning, the hard parts came after. Now, I'd like to talk about my commanding officers.

I'd like to take a moment to acknowledge my deep gratitude for Deb Haggerty, my publisher, who reached out to me and told me I didn't need an agent to submit a manuscript to her—who reminded me I was already part of a publishing family, and who saw value in my work during a time when I was feeling really down about my writing.

My editor, Cristel Phelps, who I absolutely love working with! Cristel, I love how you love my stories. I love how you call me and tell me when you cried over or screamed at your computer screen and encourage me with your passion for this craft. You're the best and I look forward to working with you again soon!

Derinda Babcock, who created the absolute perfect cover for this novel! Derinda, you have so much patience with me and my vague ideas of what I want for my covers. But you always manage to give me exactly what I didn't know I wanted! The cover for *The Good German Girl* speaks with so much power, beauty, and tragedy. The essence of the book is on the cover. You nailed it!

Now, of course, my army! The soldiers who stand by me, encourage me, and love me through this whole process.

My beautiful family! My parents who love me no matter what and support me faithfully through every writing journey I take. Mom, who loves everything I write and pushes me to be my best self. Dad, who gave me a deep love for history since I was very little. My sister, Denise, and my brother-in-law, James, who I miss like crazy but who always listen with love and encouragement when I tell them about my latest project! And all my aunts, uncles, cousins, and MeMa—you're all so far away, but you support me more than you realize. I love you all dearly!

Becky, Janelle, Kayleigh, Jasmin & AnnCamille, who listen to me go on, on, and on some more about my books. They listen patiently to my writing troubles every single day in the office and encourage me to make my goals and let me know they're proud of me. *The Good German Girl* would not have been possible without you!

My amazing endorsers: Janine Rosche, Darlene Oakley, Ann Brodeur, A.F. Lamonte, Mikaela Miller, & Lianne Kay. Thank you so much for reading and endorsing *The Good German Girl*. Your beautiful words touched my heart deeply and helped this book move forward toward success!

And finally, to my Heavenly Father. My faith has been tested, my hope shattered and restored, my strength diminished and repaired, over and over again these many years of my life. But you were always constant in my heart. I may have doubted this world and the people who crossed my path, but your love has always been there, even in the darkest moments. Living every day in faith can be hard sometimes, but I always come back to you. Thank you for your unconditional love and thank you for reminding me every day what unconditional love truly looks like.

Glossary

GERMAN

Bitte—Please

Bitte schön—You are welcome

Danke—Thanks/Thank you

Ja—Yes

Nein—No

Heil—Hail

Gut—Good

Mein freund—My friend

Mein schatz—My sweetheart

Mein schwester—My sister

Mein bruder—My brother

Mein kleiner bruder—My little brother

Meine kleine schwester—My little sister

Meine liebste—My dearest

Meine lieben—My loves

Schätzchen—Sweetie

Tochter—Daughter

Mutter—Mother

Vater—Father

Großvater—Grandfather

Großmutter—Grandmother

Großeltern—Grandparents
Nichte—Niece

POLISH

Cześć—Hello
Tak—Yes

ITALIAN

Ragazzo—Boy

About the Author

From as far back as she can remember, Erica Marie Hogan loved to write. When she was a little girl she adored make believe, but gradually her imagination became too big to restrict it to playtime and so, she wrote.

Erica was born and raised for nine years on Orient Point, Long Island, New York. After that she moved with her family to Virginia and, finally, to Texas where she now lives. She was homeschooled, is an avid reader, and is a member of American Christian Fiction Writers. She lives to plot new stories, enjoys a good tear-jerker, and chocolate is her cure for any ailment.

Erica's wish is to continue to write stories that not only drop her readers into the middle of historical time periods, but also show the ability to rise up out of adversity and tragedy in hope, faith, love, and strength. When it comes to genrew, she has no limits.

Erica's World War I standalone novel, *The Lost Generation*, along with *The Winter Queen Series* is available through Amazon, your local bookstore, or from Elk Lake Publishing, Inc.